# THE
# WANDERING
# GHOST

# THE
# WANDERING
# GHOST

**A NOVEL**

# MARTIN LIMÓN

Published by
Soho Press, Inc.
853 Broadway
New York, NY 10003

Library of Congress Cataloging-in-Publication Data


Limón, Martin, 1948–
The wandering ghost: a novel / Martin Limón.
p. cm.
ISBN 978-1-56947-481-5 (hardcover)
1. Sueño, George (Fictitious character)—Fiction. 2. Bascom, Ernie
(Fictitious character)—Fiction. 3. United States. Army Criminal
Investigation Command—Fiction. 4. Missing persons—Fiction. 5.
Americans—Korea—Fiction. 6. Soldiers—Fiction. 7. Korea (South)—
History—1960–1988—Fiction. I. Title.

PS3562.I465W36 2007
813'.54—dc22


10  9  8  7  6  5  4  3  2  1

This book is dedicated to my wonderful daughters,
Maria and Michelle.

Zilu asked how to serve the spirits.

The Master replied, "Not yet being able to serve men, how can you serve the spirits?"

Zilu asked about death.

The Master replied, "Not yet understanding life, how can you understand death?"

THE ANALECTS OF CONFUCIUS (11.12)

# 1

Stray flakes of snow swirled around the fur-lined edges of the MP's parka. He kept his M-16 rifle clutched close to his chest, glaring at us, and snatched the clipboard out of Ernie's hands.

"Emergency dispatch," Ernie said. "Good for anywhere Eighth Army operates, at any time of day or night."

"This ain't Eighth Army," the MP answered.

He was right. We were twenty miles north of Seoul sitting in a jeep at a checkpoint on the MSR, the Main Supply Route. Naked poplars lined the road, quivering in the cold wind of February. Five miles farther north stood Tongduchon, the city that straddles the front gate of Camp Casey, the headquarters of the United States Army's 2nd Infantry Division.

"You're a subordinate unit," Ernie said.

The MP tossed the clipboard back to Ernie and said, "We ain't subordinate to nobody."

Ernie studied the MP and the armed *hon-byong*, Korean Army military policeman, standing only a few feet away. Then he glanced at another American crouched behind an M-60 machine gun, muzzle pointed our way, safely ensconced behind sandbags in a reinforced concrete gun emplacement. Apparently, Ernie decided against raising hell. Instead, he grinned at the MP, shrugged, and handed the clipboard to me. Then he shoved the jeep in gear. Slowly, we zigzagged our way through rows of crosshatched metal stanchions strewn across the roadway like jacks discarded by a careless giant.

"Welcome to the Second Infantry Division," I said.

Ernie grunted.

Wind-borne cones of snow swirled across the ice-slick blacktop. Ernie maneuvered the jeep smoothly from first to second gear and then shoved it into third and finally fourth. The road was lined on either side with frozen rice paddies, fallow now during the long Korean winter. In the distance, narrow chimneys above straw-thatched roofs spewed wisps of gray smoke toward the abodes of revered ancestors.

My name is George Sueño. My partner, Ernie Bascom, and I are agents for the 8th United States Army Criminal Investigation Division in Seoul, Republic of Korea. A congressional inquiry, a demand for information from an elected member of the United States House of Representatives, had dispatched us up here to the DMZ, the northernmost area near the Korean Demilitarized Zone. Why? An American female MP assigned to the headquarters of the 2nd Infantry Division was missing. Disappeared. Evaporated. The entire manpower of the 2nd Infantry Division had searched but had been unable to find her.

Nor her body.

The missing woman's name was Corporal Jill Q. Matthewson, but she wasn't just any missing female soldier. She was the first woman MP ever assigned to the 2nd Division Military Police. Female soldiers had only recently, within the last year, been allowed in the Division area. Prior to that they were prohibited.

A peace treaty had never been officially signed between the United States and North Korea. A ceasefire, and a ceasefire only, was agreed to in June of 1953. Now in the early seventies, more than twenty years later, the 2nd Infantry Division area of operations was still considered to be a combat zone. As if to prove it, about a dozen firefights per year flared up across the 150-mile Korean DMZ. With 700,000 heavily armed North Korean communist soldiers on one side of the Military Demarcation Line and almost half a million South Korean troops on the other, this was to be expected. Despite the danger, Congress decided to allow women to serve in the 2nd Division, smack dab in the middle of mayhem.

Back at 8th Army, the bulk of the speculation about Corporal Jill Matthewson's disappearance centered around rape. Namely, that someone had sexually assaulted her, murdered her, and then disposed of her body. That was certainly possible. But there was another school of thought that postulated Matthewson might have been killed due to professional jealousy. Wielding the baton of a military policeman in the midst of 20,000 barely civilized combat soldiers, most GIs thought, was not a job for a woman. If she had been doing her job, and doing it well, male egos would have been bruised. Not a comfortable position for a woman alone. Besides Corporal Jill Matthewson, only three dozen other women soldiers—none of them MPs—were assigned to the Division area of operations out of nearly 20,000 American troops.

We wound around a curve in the road and passed beneath a massive concrete overhang: two hundred tons of cement riddled with plastic explosives. A tank trap. Ready to be blown up by retreating Republic of Korea soldiers if the heavily armored North Korean Army tries to bull its way south again. Running perpendicular to the road, as far as the eye could see, were double rows of closely packed concrete megaliths. Dragon's teeth, GIs call them. Another obstacle designed to slow down any future communist juggernaut.

Since Jill Matthewson disappeared almost three weeks ago, the 2nd Infantry Division Military Police Investigators had yet to locate any clue as to her whereabouts. For some reason, 8th Army Criminal Investigation thought that a couple of outsiders, like Ernie and me, could do what the Division MPI couldn't. Maybe it was because I spoke the language and Ernie knew the back alleys and brothels of Korea better than any CID agent in country. Or maybe it was because our bosses wanted to send us as far away from the flagpole as possible. That is, away from 8th Army headquarters in Seoul.

Ernie and I had acquired the nasty habit of following an investigation wherever it led, even into the carpeted and mahogany-paneled war rooms of the honchos of 8th Imperial Army. Whatever the reason, the 8th Army provost marshal had chosen the two of us for the assignment and now it was our duty to find Corporal Jill Matthewson.

And find her we would.

Ernie didn't talk about it but I knew his determination was total. He'd spent two tours in Vietnam, seeing fellow GIs and Vietnamese civilians being wasted for no reason. He'd become fed up and now, day to day, he tried to do the best he could to protect people. If you asked him, he'd deny it. He'd claim that he was just doing his job, keeping a low profile, trying to put in his twenty. But he knew and I knew and even the honchos at 8th Army knew, that Ernie and I worked for the little guy. We worked for the private or the sergeant or the Korean civilian who'd been stepped on by criminals or by the system. And a female corporal who'd disappeared from a military environment where everyone and everything is accounted for daily—and then accounted for again—definitely fell into that category.

As we continued north, the landscape became more barren and the wind became colder and every few feet seemed to harbor a new military compound or gun emplacement.

"Cozy," Ernie said. "Just like 'Nam."

"But colder."

"A tad. 'Nam on ice."

I pulled Corporal Jill Matthewson's photograph out of my inside jacket pocket. Ernie gave me a sidelong glance.

"You still mooning over that photo?"

"Not mooning," I answered. "Investigating."

I turned my attention to the photo and studied it once again, for the umpteenth time. Full-length, black-and-white, taken directly from Corporal Jill Matthewson's military personnel records. She was tall, five-seven-and-a-half according to her recruitment physical, husky-appearing in her uniform but not fat. She had long hair, light I guessed from the photo, tied back tightly behind her head. She wore the mandatory army dress green uniform sporting a corporal's stripes on her sleeves and, on her collar, the crossed-pistols brass of the United States Army Military Police Corps. She was smiling, just slightly, just enough to show that she was confident in who she was and what she was doing. Her face was dusted across the nose with a smattering of freckles, the cheeks broad, the nose rounded at the end. Not a beauty but an attractive woman nevertheless. The type of woman who seemed full of life. The type of woman most healthy young GIs would like to get to know better.

Maybe Ernie was right. Maybe I was mooning over her a little. But what was wrong with that? Until we found her, she'd be the object of all my affection.

Ernie swerved past an ox-drawn cart laden with frozen hay. I shoved the photo back into the folder and pulled out a copy of the letter attached to the congressional inquiry cover sheet. It was from Jill Matthewson's mother, to her congressman in the district that includes Terre Haute, Indiana. The handwriting was childish. The ink was smeared and some of the letters were difficult to read. Still, it was legible. Jill had grown up in a trailer park, her mother wrote, and her mother had struggled to get by, working nights in a convenience store. Jill's father never paid his child support and never, not once, came to visit Jill. In fact, the only thing he'd ever done for his daughter was send her a birthday card on her fifth birthday. Jill treasured it. Kept it wrapped in plastic and took the card with her when, at the age of eighteen, she enlisted in the army and shipped out to boot camp. Her mother asked that we check for the card amongst Jill's personal effects. If it was gone, if Jill had taken it, then her mother would know that she was still alive. If, on the other hand, the card was still there, her mother would know she was dead.

Maybe. As a cop, I couldn't assume any such thing. Still, I'd search for the card. Immediately.

The letter also explained why Jill had joined the army. To buy her mother a car. After years of interminable waits at bus stops—lugging torn bags of groceries home from the supermarket and baskets of damp clothing back from the Laundromat—Jill had sworn, even as a little girl, that someday she'd buy her mother a car. After six months in the army, Jill kept her promise and managed to buy her mom a used Toyota Corolla. It didn't run anymore, according to Jill's mom, but she was grateful for the months that she'd been able to drive it. And then the letter trailed off in smeared ink as Jill's mother said that Jill was her only child and she pleaded with the congressman to find her daughter and send her home. The congressman, as far as I could tell from the paperwork enclosed in the congressional inquiry packet, hadn't answered. Yet.

I would. As soon as I had more information. You could bet on it.

A convoy of ROK Army two-and-a-half-ton trucks passed us rolling south. Attached to the front bumpers were white placards splashed with red lettering in *hangul,* the indigenous Korean script: *UIHOM! POKPAL MUL.* Danger! High Explosives.


A twenty-foot-high statue of a military policeman stood in front of the 2nd Infantry Division Provost Marshal's Office. The huge MP wore a black helmet emblazoned with the letters MP and was clad in a dark green fatigue uniform and black boots laced with fake white strings. One hand rested on his hip, just above a holstered .45. His face was bright pink and his eyes a glassy blue, with an expression about as mindless as some flesh-and-blood MPs that I knew.

The PMO building was, like most buildings here on Camp Casey, a series of Quonset huts connected by mazes of corridors made of plywood and glass, topped with corrugated tin. The entire edifice was then spray painted in a camouflage pattern of various shades of puke green.

GI elegance.

We pushed through the front door at the end of the main Quonset hut into a reception area lined with wooden benches. At a high counter in front, a mustachioed black sergeant glowered at us. His shoulders were bulky—hunched—as if expecting the worse. The embroidered name tag on his fatigue blouse said OTIS. Five black stripes were pinned to his lapel: sergeant first class.

When we approached him, he said, "Why you dressed like that?"

He was referring to our civilian coats and ties.

Ernie didn't bother to answer. Instead, he brushed melting flakes of snow off his shoulders and then pulled out his identification. With a flourish, he flipped open the leather case. The desk sergeant peered at the Criminal Investigation badge and then aimed his red-rimmed eyes at me. I performed the same ritual.

"You here about Druwood."

It wasn't a question, it was a statement of fact. Ernie didn't correct him; he just waited. Sergeant First Class Otis shook his head slowly. "Shame. Young trooper like him."

Lost in thought for a moment, Otis seemed to realize that we were still waiting. He looked up at us and as he did so he understood, probably from the blank expressions on our faces, that we'd never heard about anybody named Druwood. He sat up straight, thrust back his shoulders, and cleared his throat. This time his voice was even gruffer than before.

"Who you want to see?"

"Bufford," Ernie replied.

"MPI?"

Ernie nodded.

"Then it's 'Mister' Bufford to you," the desk sergeant said. "You in Division now. You call a warrant officer by his proper title."

Ernie squinted at the desk sergeant, unable to fathom whether or not he was serious. Kowtowing to a wobbly-one military police investigator? At 8th Army headquarters in Seoul, there's so much brass wandering the hallways that warrant officers empty the trash. Sergeant Otis grabbed the black phone in front of him and started dialing. I took the opportunity to pull Ernie aside.

"Remember," I told him. "We're in Division now."

Ernie mumbled something obscene.

Cradling the phone against his beefy shoulder, Otis scribbled in his logbook and told us to spell our names. Then someone apparently picked up on the other end of the line; the desk sergeant whispered discreetly into the receiver and, after listening for a few seconds, hung up.

"Room 137," he said, pointing to his right. "Down the hall, take a left at the water cooler, then follow the signs."

As our highly spit-shined footgear clattered down the hallway, MPs and clerical staff in fatigues stopped what they were doing and stared at us from their cramped cubicles. The suits gave us away. They knew we had to be from Seoul and they knew we had to be from the Criminal

Investigation Division. It all has to do with the way the military mind works. The honchos at 8th Army are smart enough to realize that for criminal investigators to be effective they have to blend in with the general populace. To do that, they have to wear civilian clothes. However, being military men, they didn't want us to gain an advantage over them by not having to wear a military uniform during duty hours. Therefore, they dictated that, while on duty, the civilian clothes we were required to wear would be white shirts, ties, and jackets. But this is the seventies! Nobody wears a coat and tie unless they're getting married, attending a funeral, or having an audience with the Pope. So the whole purpose of allowing us to wear civilian clothes—to blend in with the general populace—was defeated. Whenever anyone—Korean or American—saw a young American male with a short haircut wearing a coat and tie, they automatically assumed that he was an agent for the Criminal Investigation Division.

So much for sneaking up on the bad guys.

Mumbles followed us down the hallway: "REMFs." The acronym for Rear Echelon Mother Fuckers.

If the coddled staff at 8th Army headquarters looked down their snooty noses at the 2nd Infantry Division, the combat soldiers up here at Division returned the animosity tenfold. Anybody stationed in Seoul, they believed, lived in the lap of luxury and would be no more useful in a firefight than a hand grenade with a soldered pin.

"So far," Ernie said, "we're receiving a warm reception."

In addition to the epithets, I also heard the name *Druwood* spoken a few times, in hushed tones. At the water cooler we hung a left, wandered down the meandering hallway until we spotted the signs, and this time turned right. Finally, after two more turns, we stood in front of a placard that read: ROOM 137, MILITARY POLICE INVESTIGATION.

We strode through the open doorway.

The office was plastered from floor to ceiling with enlarged black-and-white photos of blood, guts, and gore. An overhead fluorescent light buzzed. At a small gray desk, a lanky GI seemed to rise from his chair in sections. The name tag on his faded fatigues said BUFFORD and the rank insignia on his collar was the black-striped rectangle of a warrant officer one.

I expected Mr. Bufford to hold out his hand but, instead, bony fingers clenched hip bones. His face was narrow and his black crew cut contrasted with the paleness of his flesh. His waist was thin and his chest so emaciated that I'd seen more robust rib cages on porcelain platters at Thanksgiving. It was his eyes that held you. Black and deep set. The pupils shining like tiny eight balls, above a nose that pointed forward like a bayonet on the end of an M-16. He sniffled as he studied us and both nostrils clung to inner flesh. Then he snorted and the moist flesh released with a pop.

The room smelled of cigarettes and burnt coffee. Bufford didn't say anything. Neither did Ernie. I broke the ice.

"Mr. Bufford?" I asked. Inanely, because his name and his rank were sewn onto his uniform.

He stared at me with no sign of response. Puffy dun-colored bags sat beneath eyes so dark they were almost purple. I glanced from his odd, ravaged face to the celluloid carnage that surrounded us. Brutality, rape, murder, assault. All of it was here. Frozen in time and plastered on the walls of this Quonset hut as if to preserve it for posterity. As if someone here, probably Bufford, hated to let it go.

Finally, Warrant Officer Bufford's voice emerged as a nasal whine.

"I stand by my report," he said. "It's all in there. That's *it*." He slashed a bony finger in the air. "And if you talk to the provost marshal, he'll tell you the same thing."

"Whoa," Ernie said, holding up both hands. "Whatever happened to 'Hello'? 'How you doing?' 'What's new in Seoul?' and all that shit?"

Bufford looked puzzled, as if he'd never heard of anything as mundane as social amenities.

"It's in my report," he repeated.

"'Hello' is in your report?"

Bufford was growing more confused by the minute.

Ernie eyed him, still trying to figure out what we'd stumbled into. I sat on a gray steel chair beneath a photograph of a dead GI slumped over a steering wheel. I cleared my throat and spoke.

"Mr. Bufford," I said. "Where is Corporal Jill Matthewson?"

For once, he couldn't say it was in his report. Bufford's pasty flesh was no longer white but almost aflame now and his sunken cheeks didn't quite quiver but seemed to suck in, like a bellows drawing breath.

"It ain't going to work," he said.

"What ain't going to work?" Ernie asked.

"You're CID. Eighth Army. You're not going to make us look bad."

"We're not here to make anybody look bad," I told him. "We're here to find Corporal Jill Matthewson."

His skull swiveled away for a moment, as if he were in pain, and then he turned back to look at me. "You got no rights. You're REMFs. From Eighth Army. This is Division." Then he started to scream. "This is Division!"

Ernie leaned across the desk. Bufford backed up, ready to leap away from Ernie's grasp but as he did so the door to the small office squeaked open and a stranger entered the room. He was a short man, about five and a half feet tall, wearing green fatigues. Sandy brown hair was slicked across his round head and, through a pair of square-lensed glasses, he smiled, all of which gave him the air of a deacon attending Sunday services at a Southern Baptist church. As a military man, what my eyes latched onto first was his name tag, which said ALCOTT, and then his rank insignia—a silver maple leaf—indicating that he was a lieutenant colonel. I already knew that LTC Stanley X. Alcott was the Provost Marshal of the 2nd United States Infantry Division.

Bufford composed himself long enough to thrust back his shoulders and holler, "Attention!"

Lieutenant Colonel Alcott smiled and waved his soft palm. "At ease," he said. "At ease. Everybody take a seat."

I pulled two metal chairs from the stack leaning against the wall, unfolded them, and the three of us—the provost marshal, me, and Ernie—sat in a semi-circle in front of WO1 Bufford's desk.

Most 8th Army GIs, stationed comfortably in Seoul, would consider being sent north to Division as the equivalent of a temporary duty assignment in hell. Now, after only the first few minutes of our sojourn at the 2nd ID, I was starting to understand why.

"I'm so glad you two gentlemen took the time to travel all the way up from Seoul to help us," Colonel Alcott said. He was smiling even more broadly than he had been when he entered the room. He motioned again with his open palm. "Mr. Bufford has been working around the clock trying to locate Corporal Matthewson. It's a tragedy that she disappeared. Believe me, it's touched all of us here deeply. And since it's been over two weeks that she's been gone, we thought it would be a good idea to bring in a pair of fresh eyes to review the evidence."

I glanced sharply at Ernie, warning him not to laugh. The reality of the situation was that Ernie and I had been crammed down Colonel Alcott's throat. He knew it and we knew it. 8th Army didn't want any more letters from irate congressmen accusing the 2nd Infantry Division of not being able to keep track of its own female soldiers.

"And I know," Colonel Alcott continued, "that Mr. Bufford will bring you up to speed on the case right away."

As if the joints in his neck had been suddenly lubricated, Bufford nodded his head vigorously.

Colonel Alcott glanced at me and then at Ernie. "You've read the report. What are your thoughts so far?"

Actually, Ernie hadn't read the SIR, the serious incident report. Too boring. He left that sort of thing to me. I spoke up.

"Must've been something personal, sir," I said. "No indication that Corporal Matthewson was having trouble in her work. No black marketing indicated by her ration control records. No history of mental disorder."

Alcott nodded sadly. "True. True enough. So what's your plan of investigation?"

"Shoe leather," I said. "Talk to everyone who knew her. Reconstruct her every move up to the moment of her disappearance."

"We've already done that," Bufford said. "It wasn't personal. I'm telling you, we've already covered that ground. Had to be random. She was attacked by someone she didn't know, probably a Korean after a rich American. He robbed her, killed her, got rid of the body. We just haven't found it yet."

Ernie's green eyes flashed behind his round-lensed glasses. Here it comes, I thought.

"Robbed her?" Ernie asked, his voice a growl. "Murdered her?"

Buford leaned back reflexively, as if to protect himself from Ernie. "Yes," he said.

"And how many times," Ernie asked, "in the more than twenty years since Camp Casey was established, has an American GI been robbed and murdered by a Korean?"

Bufford, confused, glanced at Colonel Alcott for support. Before either could reply, Ernie was back on the attack.

"I'll tell you how many times," he said. "Never! Koreans don't do that. They might slicky money from a GI or cheat him on a business deal or con him out of a few dollars, but they don't hit and they definitely don't murder!"

Ernie was right. Korea is a tightly controlled society with a former general for a dictator and the Korean National Police patrolling every street corner. But more importantly, they're Confucian. They give unquestioning allegiance to their superiors and anyone who so much as threatens physical violence loses face and is forced to slink away in shame. Sure, Koreans become emotional. Often. They're not called the Irish of the Orient for nothing. And sometimes they punch out one another on the street for everyone, including their neighbors and their ancestors in heaven, to see. But those are personal disputes. And as loud and as prolonged as they sometimes are, no one gets hurt. Violent crime is rare in Korea. And against Americans, it's unheard of.

"First time for everything," Bufford said.

"What evidence do you have?" Ernie asked.

Bufford's face flamed but his thin lips remained taut.

Colonel Alcott jumped in. "She was a woman."

"That's evidence?"

"A woman on the street," Alcott persisted. "An American woman. Tall. Blonde. A much more tempting target than a Korean would have seen before."

"So you think her creamy white flesh drove some Korean mad with lust," Ernie said.

Colonel Alcott nodded vigorously. "And why not?"

Before Ernie could answer, I jumped in.

"There's always more evidence to be found," I told Colonel

Alcott. "Ernie and I will go over the same ground again, although I'm sure it's been covered thoroughly by Mister Bufford. Like you said, sir, 'a pair of fresh eyes.' Maybe, just maybe, we might find something new in her personal life."

"Not possible." Bufford crossed his arms so tightly that his skinny elbows stuck out like spikes.

Ernie's face was turning red. He'd heard enough.

"What do you mean, not possible?" he said. "If my partner wants to talk to her acquaintances, he'll talk to her acquaintances. Until he's blue in the face if he wants to."

"Waste of time," Bufford said.

I was about to say something when Colonel Alcott, once again, raised his open palm.

"Personal," he said. "I agree. A good place to start. You never know what secrets lurk in someone's background. You never know what nugget might be turned up that was missed the first time around. Don't you agree, Mr. Bufford?"

Bufford unfolded his arms and placed his palms flat on his desk, leaning forward. The look on his face was so reverential that, for a moment, I thought he was going to bow. "Absolutely, sir," he said. "Starting with her personal acquaintances makes sense. That'd be the way to go."

I glanced back and forth between the two men. The complete 180-degree revolution of opinion that Bufford had just performed was being ignored by both of them. They've done this before, I realized. Warrant Officer Bufford floats his ideas, Colonel Alcott floats his, and immediately they agree to do it the colonel's way.

I glanced at Ernie. He rolled his eyes. His opinion was clear. Colonel Stanley X. Alcott and Warrant Officer Fred Bufford were both nuts.

"Regarding Private Druwood," I said. "Has the body been examined yet?"

Colonel Alcott swiveled in his chair and studied me head on. Warrant Officer Bufford sat up straighter and re-wrapped his skinny arms around his chest.

"Why, yes," Colonel Alcott said. "By local staff. The body will be shipped down to the coroner in Seoul later this morning."

"Suicide?" I asked.

Colonel Alcott grimaced. "Oh, no. Accident. Strictly an accident. But how did you know? The report hasn't been sent to Seoul yet."

Ernie's eyes were as wide as the headlights on his jeep, wondering how I knew all this. I ignored Colonel Alcott's question and asked one of my own.

"Did Private Druwood know Corporal Jill Matthewson?"

"Know her?" Colonel Alcott glanced toward Bufford but received only a blank stare. "I suppose so," Alcott replied. "They were both MPs. But there's no relationship. None at all. Druwood was simply a highly motivated young soldier who hadn't done well on the obstacle course and he wanted badly to improve his skills. He climbed to the top of the tower in the middle of the night, to practice and gain more confidence we imagine. Unfortunately, he must've lost his balance. A tragedy. Head first. Cracked his skull on cement."

"He was alone?" Ernie asked. "And he climbed to the top of the obstacle course tower in the middle of the night?"

"That's what the evidence indicates," Alcott replied.

"Was he a boozer or a druggie? Had he received a Dear John letter?"

"If what you're implying," Alcott replied, "is that Private Druwood committed suicide, you're dead wrong. He was a highly motivated soldier. Dedicated to his mission. Besides," Alcott added, "there was no note."

"Alone in the middle of the night," Ernie said. "Sounds like suicide to me."

Alcott's face turned red. He'd had enough. Suicide is one of the problems that the army hates to talk about, but every year in every duty station in the United States and around the world, young GIs take their own lives. What are the reasons? Loneliness. Mental illness. Depression from drugs or alcohol. Harassment from other soldiers. The day-to-day pressures of military life. You name it. But whatever the reasons, the honchos hate to classify any GI death as a suicide. Every commander looks bad when his suicide statistics go up and if there's an excuse to classify a suicide as an accident, they'll take it.

Colonel Alcott spread his stubby fingers. A gold wedding band twinkled on his left ring finger. "I think," he said, slapping his knees, "this concludes our interview."

As he rose to his feet, the three of us rose also. Then Alcott waggled his forefinger at my nose. "Stay away from Druwood," he told me. "Corporal Matthewson will keep you busy enough."

The provost marshal of the 2nd Infantry Division swiveled and left the office.


We were outside of the Provost Marshal's Office, back in the cold crisp air of the 2nd Division morning, walking across blacktop beneath the shadow of the twenty-foot-tall MP, heading for our jeep. The snow had stopped. Only a few clumps still clung to slumping pine boughs and to the corrugated iron roofs of Quonset huts. Now, in late February, the question everyone kept asking was: Will winter ever end?

Ernie cleared his throat and spit on ice. "How in the hell did you know all that stuff about Druwood?"

"Most of it I guessed," I said.

"How?"

"Well, Druwood was clearly on everyone's mind in the Provost Marshal's Office. Sergeant Otis figured that's why we'd come up here from Seoul, and the other folks were whispering his name as we walked down the hallway. So something must've happened and happened recently. If it was a routine sort of incident—theft, AWOL, a fight in the ville—there wouldn't be such a consensus of concern. So it must've been serious. Death. Not a vehicular accident, Sergeant Otis never would've expected Eighth Army CID to come north to investigate that. So it had to be murder. Or at the very least, suicide. The way everybody seemed sympathetic and concerned led me to believe that Druwood must've been the victim and not the perpetrator. Therefore, Druwood was dead."

"But you called him 'Private Druwood' right off. How'd you know his rank?"

"If he was an officer, Otis or somebody in the Provost Marshal's

Office would've mentioned his rank. The death of an officer is rare in Division and would've been remarked upon. So he had to be enlisted. Otis said that Druwood was young."

"He did?"

"Yeah. You weren't listening. Young means low rank. Corporal, PFC, private. If he somehow got himself killed maybe he was inexperienced. So I guessed the lowest rank: private. Just lucky on that one."

Ernie studied me as we walked. "Too bad you didn't finish high school, Sueño. You might've developed some brains."

When we reached our jeep, Ernie jumped into the driver's seat and started the engine. Using a stenciled map attached to the serious incident report, I guided him through the maze of Camp Casey, the headquarters compound of the 2nd Infantry Division.

We spent the morning visiting the chow halls and the administrative buildings and the barracks that had been home sweet home to the missing Corporal Jill Matthewson. After inventorying her personal effects, we realized that one complete set of fatigues had disappeared from her room, along with Jill's MP helmet and her combat boots and her army-issue pistol and her web gear.

Why had Jill packed her full MP regalia? Most GIs, when they go AWOL, don't take their uniforms. After all, the whole point of bugging out is to flee all things military.

We interviewed the "house girl." Actually, she was a middle-aged Korean woman allowed on post to clean and do laundry for the female soldiers billeted on Camp Casey. She told us that Jill had also packed a tote bag full of clothes, a hair brush, and other things a woman needs. But not much. Only one pair of soft-soled shoes was missing and a couple of blouses and a pair of blue jeans and a skirt. The rest of Jill's civilian clothes and uniforms were lined up and pressed, hanging neatly inside her open wall locker.

What we did not find, no matter how hard we looked, was the birthday card Jill's father had sent her when she was five years old.

In ten more days, when Corporal Jill Matthewson had been gone a total of thirty days, she would cease being merely AWOL, absent without leave; she would be dropped from the 2nd Division roles as a deserter. She wouldn't be facing local punishment anymore; she'd be facing a court-martial. Time in a federal penitentiary would not only be likely but almost a sure thing.

Could Jill have jumped on an airplane and returned to the States? Not possible. South Korea is a tightly controlled society. Jill's name and service number—along with the names and service numbers of every AWOL American GI in country—was on a list at the single international airport in Korea: Kimpo, outside of Seoul. The Korean authorities check such lists carefully. Nobody enters or leaves the Republic without the Koreans being damn sure that the person is who they say they are—and that they're not on any watch list. Another way out of the country is by sea from Pusan, but that embarkation point is watched just as closely as the airport at Kimpo. After that, the only way out of South Korea is across the Demilitarized Zone. Trying to cross the DMZ would be suicide. You'd either be blown up by a landmine or shot by a North Korean soldier.

Jill Matthewson was still in Korea, of that we could be sure. Maybe dead, maybe alive. But still here.

# 2

**F**ootsteps echoed off distant walls.

The 2nd Infantry Division Central Issue Facility was an open warehouse as big as an aircraft hangar. Far overhead, above gnarled wooden rafters, rays of sunlight fought their way through soot-smeared skylights. The entire facility reeked of damp canvas and decayed mothballs. A cement-floored walkway was lined by square plywood bins, each bin filled to overflowing with steel pots, web gear, helmet liners, wool field trousers, fur-lined parkas, ear-flapped winter headgear, rubber boots, inflatable cold-weather footgear, ammo pouches, and everything the well-dressed combat soldier needs to operate in the country once known as Frozen Chosun.

Ernie and I had decided to interview Jill Matthewson's roommate, a supply clerk who worked here at the CIF. From what people told us about her, she'd be worth talking to. The opposite, they said, of Jill Matthewson.

The facility was quiet. No troops were lined up to receive their initial issue of combat gear. Off to our left, stuffed into wooden shelving twenty or thirty feet high, was more army-issue equipment. This time, an enormous pile of metal canteen cups. In a back office, we heard voices. Ernie and I strode toward a buzzing fluorescent bulb.

Sitting at a desk, shoulder-length blonde hair hanging limply, sat a woman in wrinkled fatigues. Although she was young, her face seemed to sag. Her eyes were blank and her mouth open. I almost expected to see spittle roll across her pink lips.

"Korvachek?" Ernie asked.

Slowly, she looked up. The embroidered name tag on her fatigue shirt confirmed that Ernie was right. The insignia pinned to her collar was PFC.

A. Korvachek. Private First Class. Corporal Jill Matthewson's roommate.

Korvachek gazed at Ernie, but the expression on her face didn't change.

Ernie reached down, cupping her narrow chin in the palm of his hand, and tilted her head back. Blue eyes continued to stare up at him. Lifeless.

Ernie let her chin go and stepped away. He turned to three men standing at the far end of a counter. They'd stopped working now and were looking at us. The ranking man wore the insignia of a buck sergeant.

"You let her come to work like this?" Ernie asked.

The buck sergeant shrugged. "It's her life."

I read his name tag: HOLLINGS.

"She should be in a program," Ernie said.

"Been in one. Fell off the wagon a week ago."

Ernie looked back at Specialist Korvachek. The MP report said her first name was Anne. Ernie walked over to the water cooler in the corner of the office, grabbed a paper cup from the dispenser, and filled it with water. Then he walked across the office to Korvachek's desk and tossed the cold water directly into her face.

She sat up sputtering.

I expected her to start cursing but she was too surprised. Ernie stepped around the desk, grabbed her by the arm and hoisted her to her feet, walking her toward the open door.

I followed, closing the door as we left the office, warning off the three men inside with my eyes. Soon, the three of us were in the center of the warehouse. Piles of folded canvas and green wool blankets towered above us like pungent cliffs of cloth.

"Matthewson," Ernie said, grabbing Korvachek by her narrow shoulders. "Talk."

The young woman's head swiveled and her eyes rolled. "You're cops."

"Good guess, Miss Marple. What happened to Jill Matthewson?"

"I don't know. She's gone."

"Gone where?"

"There." She pointed vaguely toward the main gate and beyond to the city of Tongduchon.

"She went to the ville?" Ernie said.

"Yeah."

"How do you know that?"

"She always went to the ville. She worked there and when she was off duty she went there, too."

"Why?"

"Why?" Korvachek seemed surprised by the question. She waved her hand again. "To get away from this shit."

"To get away from the army?"

"Yeah. And all the jerks who are trying to pinch your butt and call you names."

"Some of the other MPs were giving her a hard time?"

"Of course. I told that other guy that. The one with the big nose. What's his name?"

"Bufford?" Ernie asked.

"Yeah, that's right. Mr. Bufford."

"So this GI who was giving Jill a hard time, what was his name?"

"Not *a* GI," Korvacheck said. "Any GI. They're always making comments about your body, or what they want to do with you, or rubbing their crotch and leering. You know, things like that. That's why Jill wanted to get away."

None of this had been in Bufford's report. Not surprising. Not only would he not want to embarrass the Division but in the United States Army such behavior is so routine that it's not worth mentioning.

A door opened and slammed, the same door Ernie and I had

used to enter the Central Issue Facility. I motioned to Ernie and we ushered Anne Korvachek deeper into the bowels of the CIF warehouse. Once in a position where we hoped nobody could hear us, we stopped. Above us now, instead of mothballed army blankets, a jagged mountain of entrenching tools—short-handled shovels— loomed. Ernie resumed his questioning.

"When Jill went to the ville," he asked, "where did she go?"

"I don't know exactly," Korvachek answered. "We weren't that close. She didn't tell me."

She pouted as she crossed her arms. Ernie let go of her and stepped back, giving her a chance to breathe. After a moment of silence, I said, "It's important, Anne. I know you didn't want to tell those other investigators. But we're not from Division, we're from Eighth Army."

She snorted. "Same difference."

"No. There is a difference. We don't want to embarrass Jill or harm her in any way. Her privacy is her privacy and if she doesn't want to be in the army anymore . . ." I waved my hand in a broad circle. "If she doesn't want to put up with all this, that's her decision. We'll honor it. We'll tell her what to do and who to talk to and how to go about requesting a discharge. It may not be easy and she might be punished for going AWOL, but we'll tell her straight. And the only reason we're up here and the only reason we're looking for her is because she hasn't contacted her mother. Her mother wrote to her congressman about Jill's disappearance and started this investigation rolling. At least Eighth Army's part in it."

"Her mother?" Korvacheck asked.

"Yes. Jill hasn't contacted her. No letter, no phone call, no nothing."

Anne's brow furrowed and she started to chew on the nail of her thumb.

"You promised you wouldn't tell," I said. "Didn't you?"

When she didn't answer, I took her silence for consent. "But it's beyond that now," I continued. "Jill Matthewson could be in danger. She could be hurt. She could be praying that someone finds her."

Anne Korvachek let out a deep sigh. "I didn't want to tell that other guy. What's his name?"

"Bufford," Ernie said again.

Korvachek nodded. "Yeah, Bufford. He acted like Jill had done something wrong."

She had, actually. In the military, not reporting for duty is a crime but I didn't say that. Instead, I said, "We don't think she's a criminal. We think she needs help."

She studied Ernie and me again and made her decision. "I don't know much. While she was on patrol, out in the ville with the other MPs, she came to know some of the girls who work there. Korean girls. You know, strippers and stuff like that. She said they weren't so bad and some of them were friendly and started talking to her. One of them helped her find a hooch. A cheap place, somewhere in the ville, away from the bar district. I don't know exactly where 'cos she never invited me to go with her. But it's quiet, she told me, and there was a nice old mama-san who taught her how to do things. You know, how to get water out of the well, where to hang her laundry, how to change the charcoal, things like that. It was the only place where Jill could get away from all the GIs leering at her and making comments and trying to talk her into taking off her pants."

"This friend of hers," I asked, "this stripper who helped her find the hooch, do you know her name?"

"No."

"Which club does she work at?"

"I don't know. More than one, I think. And I don't know what she looks like. Jill and I weren't close."

Neither Ernie nor I asked why. Instead, we stared at her. When she could no longer bear the silence, Anne Korvacheck said, "Me and Jill, we're into different things, you know?"

We knew. According to everyone we'd talked to, Corporal Jill Matthewson didn't smoke or drink or do drugs and, until she disappeared, the Division chaplain claimed that she'd attended church services every Sunday. Something told me that Anne Korvachek hadn't attended church services in quite a while. I wanted to hug her and tell her to forget all this military stuff and go home to her family. Instead, I remembered she was a soldier. And I remembered that she might have information important to our investigation.

"Druwood," I said.

"The dead guy?"

"Yes. Do you know what happened to him?"

"Jumped off the tower at the obstacle course. That's what everyone says."

"Do you believe it?"

"In this hellhole? Why wouldn't I?"

"So you think he killed himself."

Anne Korvachek shrugged. "How would I know?"

"Did you know him?" Ernie asked.

"No. But Jill did. He was an MP."

"Did she know him well?"

"Too well. He was always hanging around the barracks, asking about her."

Ernie and I froze. This could be the connection we were looking for, the type of connection that broke a case. I didn't want to ask a question that would lead Anne Korvacheck down a preconceived path, so I used an old technique. I simply repeated the last thing she had said.

"Asking about her?"

"Yeah. You know. Trying to get a date. Hoping she'd start liking him. Jill didn't dislike him but she didn't like him either. She avoided him."

Ernie glanced around, listening. I heard it, too. Squeaks. Shoe leather? No, more like mice. Pest control should've been a high priority in a huge warehouse like this. Apparently not so. I turned my attention back to Anne Korvachek.

"Was he stalking her?"

"No. Nothing like that. He was just a big dumb puppy dog. Sick with love."

"Love for Jill Matthewson?"

"Not 'love' love. A crush, like."

I was about to ask Anne Korvachek another question when something hard thumped against wood. Anne and I glanced toward the sound but Ernie looked up. And then he leaped at us. Screaming.

For a moment I thought my partner, Ernie Bascom, had gone mad. He shoved me with his right hand and shoved Anne Korvachek with his left and knocked us both against the open wood frame foundation of the holding bin. I clunked my skull against a two-by-four but Ernie kept pushing until I dropped to a sitting position and kicked myself backwards beneath the safety of the wood-slat platform. Anne Korvachek did the same.

The Central Issue Facility rained shovels.

About two tons of them. They clattered to the cement floor with an enormous din, sometimes slamming down hard on their flat metal edges, sometimes gouging sharp corners into the cement, leaving half-inch-thick, arrow-shaped dents. Ernie kept shoving Anne and me until our arms and legs and other vulnerable body parts were protected beneath the wooden platform from the landslide of entrenching tools.

Finally, the shovels stopped falling.

Ernie and I clawed our way out of the avalanche. He ran behind the platform that had only recently held the entrenching tools. I followed. When we found no one there, we ran toward the door that had opened and slammed.

No one there either. Not inside. Not outside.

Wheel marks in gravel. Nothing we could trace. Apparently a getaway vehicle had been waiting. Whoever had slipped into the warehouse and toppled the enormous pile of entrenching tools had planned his escape well.

Ernie and I dusted ourselves off.

Sergeant Hollings and his crew were still cowering, afraid to come out of the back office. When we frightened them into talking, they claimed they hadn't seen anyone enter or leave the warehouse, and they had no idea who'd tried to shove two tons of entrenching tools atop Ernie, me, and Anne Korvachek.

I believed them. But only because they appeared to be genuinely scared. But why were they so scared? What was happening on Camp Casey that was creating a climate of fear? When I asked that question I received only shrugs and grunts and finally I gave up. I figured there was no way—short of torture—I was going to extract any information from them.

In a corner of the warehouse, Anne Korvachek sat alone on a stool. Crying. I tried to comfort her but it didn't work. Instead, when she wouldn't stop sobbing, I told her to get herself back into the rehab program. She said she didn't want to and anyway it was none of my business.

I thanked her for her cooperation and we left.

Coincidences, of course, are something cops are taught never to believe in. The fact that another young MP, Private Druwood, had been involved in a serious incident—an incident that led to his death—only a few days after Corporal Jill Matthewson's disappearance was a coincidence in and of itself. But when you added the fact that Private Druwood—at least according to Anne Korvachek—had harbored an unrequited crush on the selfsame Corporal Jill Matthewson and he'd actually been following her around, then the coincidence was too great for Ernie and me to ignore.

Late in the morning, Ernie and I stopped at Camp Casey's 13th Field Dispensary. As usual, four or five Quonset huts of various sizes were hooked together by short walkways. I wanted to take a look at Private Druwood's body. Maybe it would tell me something that would give me a clue as to Jill Matthewson's disappearance. More likely, it wouldn't. But if the corpse was still here on Camp Casey, I wanted to see what I could. In any investigation, more information is always better than less.

We entered through the back, via a loading dock where Division ambulances pulled up and delivered soldiers who'd been injured in field training. Field training is the lifeblood of any infantry division. A way for young soldiers to stay in combat trim. As such, it was constantly being conducted somewhere in the Division area.

We pushed through double swinging doors. A young man, stripped to the waist, sat on a metal table staring at his bleeding arm. A jagged shard of purple bone stuck through the flesh. A tall man with swept-back brown hair ministered to him, blood spattering his white coat. He jabbed the young soldier's biceps with a syringe and told him to lie back and try to relax, the MEDEVAC to transport him to Seoul would arrive in a few minutes. The young man seemed unsure but then, apparently, the drugs kicked in. His eyeballs rolled back in his head and he leaned to his side and the tall man in the white coat eased him down onto the metal table.

When the young soldier was arranged neatly, the tall man turned to face us.

"What are you doing here?"

His name tag said WEHRY. His rank was specialist six. Not a doctor, a medic.

"Druwood," I said, flashing my identification. "The body still here?"

The man's eyes narrowed. "Yes. We're going to send it down to Seoul on the same chopper transporting this young man."

"We want to look at it," Ernie said.

Wehry straightened his spine, thrusting back his shoulders. "Absolutely not. The body is encased and prepared for transport and no one is going to look at it until it reaches the medical examiner in Seoul."

Ernie and I glanced at one another. We had developed a routine for this type of contingency. In a bureaucracy as cumbersome as the United States Army, we're forced to perform it often.

Ernie approached Wehry, his face twisted into a sneer, his body relaxed, hands on hips, doing everything he could to convey to Spec 6 Wehry that Ernie was totally disgusted with his response.

"Do you *realize* what you're doing, Wehry?" Ernie asked. "Obstructing justice? Do you have any idea who sent us here?"

"I don't care," Wehry replied. "We have procedures. No one can traipse in here and start examining bodies."

Ernie stepped to his left, opening his jacket, letting Wehry see the hilt of his .45 in its shoulder holster, making him worry that Ernie was about to pull it. I moved to the right. The injured soldier moaned as I did so, and then Ernie raised his voice and started gesticulating wildly. Wehry crossed his arms and was having none of it, shaking his head resolutely. I stepped to the far side of the room and pushed through a single swinging door.

It wasn't hard to spot the corpse. A body bag, full of something long and lumpy, lay on a metal cart. I stepped quickly toward the bag and examined the red tag on the bottom. DRUWOOD, MARVIN Z., PRIVATE (E-2). I reached to the top of the bag, grabbed the zipper, and pulled.

I don't think anyone ever gets completely used to the odor of death. I know I haven't. It slapped me like a clammy hand enveloping my face, suffused with the raw, gamy scent of meat.

Holding my breath, I examined the body as best I could. Feet, legs, genitals, hips, abdomen, chest: all body parts were intact but none of them looked normal. Everything, especially the arms, was scraped red and raw. The elbows and fingers had virtually no flesh left on them whatsoever. The nails, without exception, were torn, bent back. Had the body been dragged behind a jeep? That was the first thing that leaped into my mind. But then some part, like maybe the lower legs and feet, would've been spared the shredding. But nothing on Druwood's body had been spared. It was as if he had been dragged, face down, along cement. The neck was bruised and slightly askew; it had probably snapped. The face looked surprised, mouth open. I closed the eyes. But the biggest attention-getter on the body of the late Private Marvin Z. Druwood was the front top quadrant of his skull. Smashed in. Red and pulpy with shards of bone sticking out. That impact is what had killed him, and probably snapped his neck at the same time. I leaned down to look more closely at the gaping wound and saw gravel. Flecks of it. I carefully removed one of the larger pieces and held it up to the overhead light. I rubbed it between my fingers. It was jagged. Applying only a very light pressure, the tiny chunk crumbled into powder.

Cement.

He'd fallen from a great height and cracked his skull on something made of cement. Pretty much what the provost marshal and Warrant Officer Bufford contended. Still, there were things here that didn't add up. Had the body been scraped in the fall? Or after it?

The door squeaked behind me. I turned. Red-faced, Spec 6 Wehry stood in the open doorway.

"What in the *hell* do you think you're doing?"

I didn't bother to answer. Instead, I zipped up the bag, rubbed my hands on the side of my coat, and walked past him. In the back room of the dispensary, I passed Ernie and the injured soldier still laying on his gurney. I kept going, onto the loading dock. Then I hopped down onto the gravel-topped parking lot. At the far edge, I stood for a while, staring across a vast expanse of lawn at the helicopter landing zone on the far side of the Camp Casey parade ground. Hands on my hips, I took deep breaths. The cold Korean winter filled my lungs.

I felt it now. The old remorse. The old anticipation of something horrible that was about to happen that I couldn't do anything about.

My mother was still young. Still healthy, still beautiful, and yet she was dying. I was her only child. The women stood around her, their heads covered with black shawls, candles flickering in brass holders. They mumbled prayers in Spanish, kissed the tips of their fingers, and then caressed the silver crucifixes hanging at their necks.

I wanted it to stop. I wanted things to return to normal. I wanted my mother to laugh and shout and pinch me and chase me around the backyard of the little hovel in East L.A. in which we lived. But she was so pale and her breathing was labored and she didn't move. And then later—I'm not sure how much later—the priest told me that she was gone. My father had already fled, run off to Mexico like the coward that he was. I moved in with foster parents, first one set and then another, the entire program compliments of the Board of Supervisors of the County of Los Angeles. Living like a fugitive, I started to become alert to people's moods, the flickering of their eyes, the inflections in their voices, the double meanings in the words they spoke. I dealt with the jealousy of the other kids in the families, the hatred of the fathers when they watched me shovel beans into my mouth, the impatience of the mothers when I dirtied one pair of blue jeans too many.

But through it all, I remembered what my mother had told me before she died: Be strong. Don't lie to people. Don't be like your father.

I promised her I wouldn't.

At the pedestrian exit from Camp Casey, Ernie and I flashed our identification at a frowning MP. Then we walked past a line of waiting kimchee cabs, across the MSR, and entered the bar district of the fabled city known as Tongduchon.

*HUANYONG!* a sign said, in the indigenous Korean *hangul* script. Welcome!

It was followed by three Chinese characters: *tong* for east, *du* for bean, and *chon* for river. Tongduchon. East Bean River. Welcome to Tongduchon. Or TDC as the GIs loved to call it.

For a young American GI, the bar district in Tongduchon is the French Riviera, Las Vegas, and Disneyland all rolled into one. It's brightly lit and there's bar after bar and nightclub after nightclub and hundreds of young women parading around in various stages of undress. A bottle of Oriental Brewery Beer costs 200 *won*, about forty cents, and a shot of black-market bourbon costs 250 *won*. An "overnight," an evening with a beauteous lady, costs anywhere from ten to twenty-five dollars, depending on a few variables: her pulchritude, your willingness to spend, and how close it is to the end-of-month military payday.

Night had fallen. Therefore, Ernie and I had changed out of our coats and ties and were now wearing our "running-the-ville" outfits: nylon jackets with fire-breathing dragons embroidered on the back, blue jeans, sneakers, and broad, mindless grins on our smoothly shaven faces. We may have looked like a couple of idiots wasting our money in a GI village that's designed to do nothing else but separate a GI from his pay, but actually we were conserving the twelve bucks a day in travel per diem 8th Army authorized. We were tailing an armed military police patrol.

The patrol was composed of three men: a U.S. Army military policeman; a *bonbyong*, an ROK Army military policeman; and a KNP, an officer of the Korean National Police. The reason for its odd composition was that the mayor of Tongduchon and the commander of the 2nd Infantry Division wanted to ensure that all jurisdictions were covered. Whether any given miscreant was an American GI, a Korean soldier, or a Korean civilian, one of the triumvirate of law enforcement officers would have the authority to arrest him. Or her.

The patrol wound through a vast labyrinth of narrow alleys filled with flashing neon and jostling crowds and rock music blaring from vibrating speakers. They entered bar after bar, checking out the American GIs and shoving through small seas of scantily clad Korean business girls. Usually, they were greeted and bowed to by an elderly female hostess. More often than not, she wore a brightly colored *chima-chogori*, the traditional Korean skirt and blouse. These women were the *mama-sans*, the older sisters to the business girls, the moms to the American GIs, the managers of all operations in the nightclubs for the absentee bar owners. These women wore their black hair formally, knotted high atop their heads and held together with jade pins, and often they wore earplugs, so they wouldn't go deaf listening to the obnoxious American rock music pulsating out of enormous stereo speakers.

The ville patrol paraded into each nightclub like a pack of young kings. They searched not only the environs of the nightclub but also the areas behind the bar and the back storerooms and particularly the bathrooms, both women's and men's. If everything seemed to be in order—there were no fights, no drugs being dealt, nobody passed out—they departed and marched to the next bar. Ville patrol was the job Jill Matthewson had done. For years—probably since the Korean War ended in 1953—the ville patrol had consisted of three policemen. Adding Jill was an innovation. She became the fourth member of the team. Since American women had first been assigned up here to Division, a few of them complained about Korean cops barging into ladies' rooms and checking the stalls, with them in it! So the Division provost marshal assigned Jill Matthewson to the ville patrol with the understanding that it was her duty to check the female latrines.

Now that she was gone, and with no female replacement in sight, the ville patrol was back to the same old intrusive routine.

So far, Ernie and I had been discreet. The ville patrol hadn't noticed that we were following. Unprofessional of them but who can blame them? They were bored. They did this every night, and it figured that in the history of the 2nd Infantry Division the ville patrol had probably never been followed before. Not once. We wanted to see how they operated before questioning them. When it became clear that nothing untoward was going on and they were conducting themselves in a professional manner, Ernie and I stopped them outside the Montana Club.

The American MP's name was Staff Sergeant Weatherwax, Rufus Q., a thin black man with an aquiline nose and eyelids that seemed to be having trouble staying open, like a jazz musician maintaining his cool. We flashed him our CID badges and asked about Jill Matthewson. He knew her but had worked with her only a few nights due to the fact that the ville patrol was a rotating duty.

"But Matthewson didn't rotate," I said. "She was on full time."

"Right. Because she was the only female MP."

"We heard she was friendly with some of the Korean women," Ernie said. "Can you give us a hint on that?"

"Can't be sure."

"There must be something."

Then Weatherwax started conversing with the Korean cop and the ROK Army MP. I helped the conversation along by speaking Korean.

They remembered. Down the road, through a narrow passageway known as "the crack," an area of Tongduchon frequented mostly by black American soldiers, in a joint called the Black Cat Club, Jill had smiled and hugged the female bartender. And once or twice they'd seen her there, in civilian clothes, when she was off duty.

I asked Weatherwax another one: "Did Corporal Matthewson have a boyfriend?"

"Not that I know of."

"Why not?" Ernie asked.

Weatherwax thought about it for a while. "I'm not sure exactly but it seemed she didn't like GIs much."

"But a lot of them were hitting on her."

"*All* of them were hitting on her."

"Including you?"

He grinned. "Hey, I gave it a try once." As he studied our faces, his grin turned to a frown. "When she didn't go for it, I left it alone."

"That makes you a minority of one."

Weatherwax didn't respond.

Ernie inhaled sharply and took a step toward Weatherwax. "I remember you now," Ernie said. "As soon as you smiled. You were in the hallway this morning. At the Provost Marshal's Office."

Weatherwax stared at Ernie blankly.

Ernie waved his forefinger at the hooked tip of Weatherwax's nose.

"Having a good time with your pals, eh Sarge? Hooting and howling about Eighth Army REMFs."

Weatherwax groaned and rotated his head as if his neck hurt. "If you can't handle the heat up here in Division," he said, "then run on back to the rear echelon."

I stepped between the two men. "Come on, Ernie. We have work to do."

Ernie allowed me to shove him backwards a few steps but he kept staring at Weatherwax. "We'll talk, Sarge. Again."

Staff Sergeant Weatherwax placed his palm atop the hilt of his holstered .45. "Anytime," he said. Then he turned and the other two cops fell in behind him and the ville patrol continued their rounds.


"Ain't no bag, man," the bartender explained.

She was Korean but wore dark makeup and her jet black hair was frizzed into a towering Afro. Her face was round and her lips full and the smooth features of her soft flesh were nicely accentuated by the hoop earrings she wore. Her body was something to write home about. Plenty of curves and, as she moved about, her red silk blouse caressed each and every contour.

"Ain't no bag," had been her response when Ernie asked her if there were ever any problems when white GIs entered the Black Cat Club. She went on to explain that not many "T-shirts" entered here but when they did it was "ain't no bag," as long as they treated the brothers with respect.

Maybe she was right but I had my doubts. We were only a week away from end-of-month payday, but the Black Cat Club was still about half full. Mostly with Korean business girls, many of them doing their best to look like "sisters." A soft red glow illuminated the smoke-filled room. The rest of the customers were black GIs, some of them wearing brightly colored outfits they'd designed themselves in the local Korean tailor shops. Almost to a man, they glanced at us warily. I was happy that we were here early, before the place became crowded and before any of the brothers were fully toked up.

The bartender's name was Brandy.

Probably not a name that her Confucian ancestors would've approved of but a name that worked well in the Black Cat Club. Marvin Gaye wailed as Ernie leaned across the bar and shouted his questions into Brandy's ear.

She knew Jill Matthewson and she liked her. They'd become friendly one night after there'd been a fight in the Black Cat Club. One of the business girls had been injured in the melee and when the ville patrol arrived, Jill provided first aid for the teenage prostitute. Brandy assisted by bringing towels and water and Corporal Jill Matthewson made sure that the young Korean woman was treated for free at the 2nd Division emergency room rather than being left to her own devices as some of the male MPs wanted to do.

"Jill good people," Brandy said.

Ever since then, Brandy couldn't do enough for her.

I asked Brandy if she knew what had happened to Jill Matthewson.

"I don't know. I go to KNPs, tell them everything I know, but they say they no can find."

"*You* went to the Korean National Police?" Ernie asked.

"Yes."

"They didn't come to you?"

She shook her head negatively and her hoop earrings jingled.

"And no GIs came and asked you about Jill Matthewson?"

She shook her head again.

Apparently, the 2nd Division investigation hadn't been as thorough as we'd been led to believe.

Then we asked more about Jill, trying to encourage Brandy to open up. Between bouts of pouring drinks, she did. She said that after the night of the fight, Jill stopped in a few times, off duty, just to talk. She ordered orange Fanta, a soft drink, and when GIs approached and tried to talk to her, she told them she was here to talk to Brandy. When Jill told Brandy that the female barracks on Camp Casey were too noisy and filled with drunken GIs chasing women at all hours of the night, Brandy suggested Jill rent her own hooch.

"She afraid at first," Brandy told us. "You know, not used to Korea. But I fix up."

Brandy referred Jill Matthewson to a *bokdok-bang*, a local real estate office, and within a week, Jill had picked out a hooch on the other side of town. In my open notebook, using *hangul* script, I jotted down the address as Brandy recited it to me.

After that, Jill hadn't stopped in the Black Cat Club often, only once or twice a month to bring gifts from the PX. American-made hand lotion for Brandy and chocolate for the business girls.

We asked about a boyfriend. Again, Brandy said that, as far as she knew, Jill didn't have one. We asked her why not.

"She waiting," Brandy said. "She no like stinko GI."

"Stinko" as in drunk.

Once again, I asked the big question. "Where is Jill Matthewson now, Brandy?"

She shook her head sadly. She didn't know. But she promised if she heard anything, she'd come and find us. She also promised that she'd use her contacts, and ask around town. But she wasn't optimistic. If Jill Matthewson was still in Tongduchon, Brandy said, she'd know it.

Maybe we'd had a few too many drinks. Maybe I just couldn't get over the coincidence of Private Marvin Z. Druwood, a military policeman, dying an accidental death—supposedly—only a few days after a fellow MP, Corporal Jill Matthewson, disappeared. Nothing in the Division serious incident report indicated that there'd been any connection between the two of them. Yet Ernie and I had discovered their connection on the first day.

From the ville, Ernie and I walked back to Camp Casey. A huge arch straddled the main gate. Lit up by a row of bare bulbs, it said: 2ND INFANTRY DIVISION, SECOND TO NONE! Above the guard shack, a smaller sign, written in both English and *hangul*, said: INFORMATION ON NORTH KOREAN INTRUDERS WELCOMED AT THIS GATE.

A stern-faced MP examined our identification carefully. Too carefully. The MPs all knew who we were and what we were here for. Finally, he snorted, tossed the identification back, and waved us through. After a half mile of walking, Ernie and I had just about reached the room we'd been issued at transient billeting. That's when I suggested we continue on to the obstacle course.

"Are you nuts?" Ernie asked. "The obstacle course in the middle of the night?"

"We'll drive," I said.

Ernie's jeep was parked near the transient billets. He protested for a while, but I told him we might need it for the investigation. He didn't see how but finally he relented. We jumped in the jeep.

Many of the main buildings of Camp Casey—like the Provost Marshal's Office and the PX and the Indianhead Snack Bar—were clustered near the front gate. But "the flagpole," the line of wooden buildings that composes the Division headquarters complex, was three-quarters of a mile in. We drove beyond the main parade ground that stretched dark and empty in the moonlight and beyond the three flagpoles that during the day held the flags of the United Nations, the United States, and the Republic of Korea. Another mile on, we reached the turnoff for the firing ranges and the physical training grounds. Camp Casey is huge. And this in a country that, although lush with fertile river valleys, is also hilly and mountainous. As a result, farmland is precious. Every parcel is measured by the *pyong*, a unit of measure not much larger than two meters square.

A wooden sign announced the obstacle course: 2ND INFANTRY DIVISION CONFIDENCE COURSE. The military loves euphemisms. Ernie parked the jeep in a gravel parking area. Then he crossed his arms.

"I'll wait here."

"Okay."

He was morose and drunk and pissed off at having to sit out here in the cold night air; there was no point in arguing with him. I pulled out my pocket flashlight and started traipsing through sand. A log stretched across the "confidence course" starting line. Beyond that a well-trodden pathway led through quivering elms. I glanced back at Ernie. He still sat there alone, comfy in the jeep. I shivered in the cold. The snow from this morning clung in small scattered clumps on bushes and grass. The lights of Camp Casey proper flickered far off in the distance. On the hills surrounding us, moonlight illuminated ten-foot-high wooden posts linked by thick strands of barbed wire. The perimeter was patrolled by Korean security guards armed with Korean War vintage M-1 rifles. At the moment I couldn't see any of them. Would they notice my little flashlight? Probably. Would I be reported? Who knew? I started walking the course.

First there were wooden balance beams to run on and sandbag-lined moats to leap across and wooden walls to climb over. I walked around them. I passed long tubes to crawl through and metal poles to swing from and rubber tires to bounce against. Again I circled the obstacles. I was heading for the tower. The spot where, according to Division PMO, Private Marvin Z. Druwood had voluntarily leapt to his death.

Finally, I reached the tower and looked up. It was about as high as a three-story building. Made of wood. Four long beams on the corners, square wooden platforms placed about ten feet apart until the top one. Like an air-filled layer cake. No ladders. No handholds. Just smooth, slippery wood.

To me, the tower had always been the most frightening part of any obstacle course. Standing here in the moonlight, staring up at the sleek structure, I discovered nothing to disabuse me of that opinion. And just last night, Private Druwood had climbed this tower, stood on the top—who knows for how long—and then leaped off, head first, to his death.

I stuck my flashlight in my pocket, marched to the base of the tower, and started to climb. Resolutely, I stared at the silver moon. Praying to it. Making it my own personal goddess. Trying not to look down. Maybe it was my imagination but the higher I climbed, the more fiercely the wind howled.

# 3

I remember the day I hit five feet.

I was eleven years old and proud after I measured myself because I was taller than most of the kids in my elementary school. I was proud because now I had a chance to protect myself. And protect the kids who I lived with while being shuffled around to various foster homes.

Some kids were more vulnerable than others. When they were shoved or spanked or shouted at, they took it to heart. They identified with the criticism and little by little the life in their eyes began to fade, and that's when they began to die. I remember Fausto. He was a cute kid always ready to smile, but the foster father who was raising us wouldn't stop badgering helpless little Fausto. This foster father saw the entire world as conspiring to keep him down and he not only resented the food and space that Fausto took up, he also resented Fausto's cheerful attitude. So from the day Fausto arrived in our home, the guy started in on him. Day by day, I saw the life dying in Fausto's eyes. I tried to stop it and as a reward for my efforts, I was slapped myself. But I was older than Fausto. And three years had passed since I'd hit five feet. I was fourteen now, and five foot ten. The football coach measured me in the high school gym and I was surprised that I'd sprouted up so much. There was something about the magic number. Five-ten. I felt like an adult. Like a man.

One day I arrived home from school and my foster father was already slapping Fausto—enraged because he'd been caught stealing a slice of bread from the cupboard. But it wasn't stealing. Fausto was hungry because he'd been forced to skip breakfast and then lunch. It was the foster father who was stealing, from the money provided to him by the County of Los Angeles. He slapped Fausto one more time.

I dropped my books, strode into the kitchen, and slammed a straight left into my foster father's nose. Blood flowed and from the way he squealed you would've thought I was the worst killer since Attila the Hun. And, of course, he refused to fight back. Instead, his wife called the social workers and two days later I was escorted from the home.

Fausto stayed. I remember the look in his eye as I left. Later, Dante taught me the words for it: "Abandon all hope, ye who enter here."

In the next three years I grew six more inches—to six foot four—and at the age of seventeen nobody wanted me around. I cramped too many people's style. After a brief stint in an orphanage, I dropped out of high school and joined the army. An army that included *obstacle* courses.


I was halfway up the 2nd Division tower. Perspiration poured from my forehead. My arms were straight out, clinging to the flat, smooth surface of the middle platform. These towers were designed by diabolical minds. No protrusions, no handholds, not so much as the head of a bolt sticking out of the smooth wooden surface. Still, you had to hold on somehow, by the pressure of your limbs on flat surfaces and the occasional grip of an edge. The trick was to shinny up from one smooth platform to the next.

Finally, I stood at the top of the tower.

Below sat the jeep. It was too dark to see if Ernie was still in it. Farther to the west stretched the dark Quonset huts and sporadic firelights of Camp Casey. At the far edge of the compound the twenty-foot-tall MP stood as we'd left him. Silent. Staring mindlessly toward the main gate. Beyond the gate, across the MSR, Tongduchon blazed. Blinking lights, flashing neon, rotating yin and yang symbols promising an endless nirvana of entertainment. Even from this distance I could hear taxi horns and the low murmur of rock music and the occasional shout from a drunken GI. Then, in counterpoint, the startled shriek of a Korean business girl.

A cold wind from the north picked up and chilled the perspiration that swathed my body. I hugged myself, staring down at the obstacle course below. The square platform I stood on was about fifteen feet across. If I stood with my back to one edge and ran full tilt to the other I could probably leap about twenty-five or thirty feet out. Just far enough to reach an obstacle on either side of me. One was a row of elevated logs, the other a sandbagged tunnel. No cement. And yet there'd been cement in Private Druwood's head wound. I'd touched it myself, felt the dried cement crumble in my hand.

I pulled out my flashlight, knelt down, and studied the platform. Smooth as a baby's complexion. Designed that way and kept that way by the constant rubbing of GIs in fatigues lying up here, face down, hugging the platform. Resting. Grateful to have made it safely to the top but wondering how in the hell they were going to survive the climb back down.

I clicked off the flashlight and stood. But I wasn't seeing Camp Casey or Tongduchon or feeling the cold Manchurian wind. I was seeing the pale face of Private Marvin Z. Druwood. His corpse. And then his eyes popped open, staring at me, but although I'd never met the man I knew those eyes didn't belong to Druwood. I'd seen them before. But where? The wind whipped up and slashed cold fingers across my face. And then I knew. Fausto. The little kid I'd left alone. The little kid I'd abandoned to his fate. Those were *his* eyes in that corpse.

A shot blasted and something tiny and evil whizzed past me, not ten feet away. I dropped to the platform and flattened myself. Unmoving. Hoping that by stillness I would become just a shadow and not a target. I waited ten minutes. Nothing more happened.

Quickly, I climbed down the tower.

When I reached the jeep there was just enough moonlight for me to see that Ernie was dozing. I shook him awake.

"Did you hear that shot?"

"What shot?" he asked.

"When I was on top of the tower, someone took a potshot at me."

"Who?"

"I don't know."

Ernie started the jeep. "How much did you drink out in the ville, Sueño?"

"Not much."

Ernie snorted. "I'm going to have to get you into rehab."

I didn't answer. I was wondering who had shot at me and where the shot had come from and why they'd shot at me. From the sound of the bullet as it whizzed past, the shooter must've been a few hundred yards away. Rifle, almost certainly. He could've been firing from the shrubbery surrounding the obstacle course, or from a vehicle back on the main road, or even from one of the guard posts on the hills surrounding Camp Casey's perimeter. If he was trying to kill me, why hadn't he fired again? Once he'd gotten the range, the second shot would've been more accurate.

Our reception here at Division, so far, had been miserable. First, the atmosphere of hostility at the PMO. Then an avalanche of entrenching tools. And now this. Had the same person been behind both incidents? And if so, what was he trying to tell us?

Ernie admitted that he'd actually heard the shot but hadn't thought anything of it. Just a late-night combat-training exercise, he presumed. Maybe he was right. Maybe that's what it was. A bullet gone astray.

But also, maybe not.

The next morning, using the address Brandy had provided, Ernie and I located Jill Matthewson's hooch in a back alley on the west side of East Bean River. Children ran through narrow lanes and street vendors pushed rickety wooden carts, chanting out the nature of their wares. The area teemed with life, primarily because the economy of

TDC was booming. Not only was there a steady flow of U.S. dollars from the local GI village, but also agriculture in the surrounding valleys was more productive than ever. President Pak Chung-hee's *Sei Maul Undong*, the New Village Movement, was paying off. Government investment in small family farms had improved life throughout the country. Straw-thatched roofs were disappearing, being replaced by weather-resistant tile. TV antennae were springing up. After two decades of drudgery following the devastation of the Korean War, life was improving in Frozen Chosun. Slowly.

The woman who owned the property was surprised to see two GIs duck through her front gate and enter her courtyard. She'd been squatting in front of a tub of laundry but as we approached she stood, holding her lower back. At first, she was startled when I spoke Korean to her. A lot of Koreans are. They don't expect it from a GI. My Korean is far from perfect but I can communicate and, as long as they keep it simple, I can read and write the language. The U.S. Army makes it easy to learn. Free classes are offered on base and a free textbook is provided, along with a personable young Korean woman to do the teaching. However, on a compound of five thousand GIs only two other guys showed up regularly. Still, I enjoyed studying. Deciphering a sentence was like solving a puzzle, and I've always loved puzzles.

Once I told the woman what we were there for, she didn't hesitate. She led us along the raised porch surrounding the courtyard and pulled open one of the oil-papered doors. This, she told me, was the hooch that Jill Matthewson had lived in. Other GIs had been here before, along with the Korean National Police, examining the place and questioning her renters.

It was a tiny single room. Like most of the hooches in Korea, its dimensions were only about twelve feet by twelve feet. It did, however, have an overhead fluorescent light, a vinyl-covered *ondol* floor—heated by charcoal gas running through ducts in the stone foundation—and a beat up wooden armoire. There were five hooches in the horseshoe-shaped compound. Two of them empty: Jill's and the one next door. I asked what had become of Jill's personal effects.

The landlady told me that all Jill had kept here were civilian clothes. That jibed with the MP report and what Ernie and I had observed in the barracks. In order to be ready for emergency deployment, all 2nd Infantry Division GIs were required to keep their uniforms and combat gear in the barracks, even if they maintained an unauthorized hooch out in the village. Other than civilian clothing, the woman told us, Jill had kept only toiletries and a few books and magazines here. About three weeks ago, without saying anything, Jill had packed up her few belongings and left. As the landlady told the Korean police, she had no idea where Jill had gone. She'd left without warning. Was she friendly with anyone here or in the neighborhood? No. After learning how to change the charcoal that heated her hooch and how to pump water from the well and where the *byonso* was located, she'd kept to herself. By mimicking the other renters, Jill Matthewson had learned to remove her shoes before stepping up on the wooden porch and then she'd mastered the most tedious Korean housekeeping chore of all: using a moist rag to keep the warm vinyl floor of her hooch scrubbed and free of soil.

"She very clean," the landlady told us, "for an American."

On the way back to the bar district, Ernie and I stopped at the real estate office Brandy had tipped us to. Having already been questioned by the Korean police, the Korean agent was very cooperative, providing all the particulars about Jill's rental. Then I put the question I'd really come to ask: Why did Jill Matthewson's landlady have two vacancies?

The real estate agent seemed surprised and thumbed through his records. Jill's hooch had remained unoccupied because the Korean police told the owner not to rent it out until they gave her permission. They had already examined it, finding nothing, but it was still, theoretically, a crime scene. Until the case was closed they didn't want anyone moving in. The other hooch had also been recently vacated.

The real estate agent handed me a five-by-seven card and I studied the *hangul* script. Kim Yong-ai had been the tenant of the hooch next to Jill's. A woman's name. I jotted it down, along with her Korean national identification number. She'd moved out three weeks ago, the same day Jill Matthewson disappeared.

Why hadn't the landlady told us that?

The real estate agent had no idea.

I asked about Kim Yong-ai's occupation.

Entertainer, he said.

What type of entertainer?

Apparently, there was no Korean word for it. Instead, he mimicked dancing and removing articles of apparel.

"Stripper," Ernie said in English.

The real estate agent nodded his head vigorously.

At our request, the Korean National Police arrested Jill Matthewson's landlady.

At the Tongduchon Police Station, she was more voluble. Yes, Kim Yong-ai was a stripper and, yes, she worked the GI bar district of Tongduchon. Yes, she had become good friends with Jill Matthewson and, during the day when they were both off duty, they talked for hours. The MP and the stripper. Both worked the night shift and they'd become fast friends. When Jill Matthewson left, she'd left with Kim Yong-ai.

Why hadn't the landlady told us this? Jill and Miss Kim made her promise not to say anything. They knew the MPs would try to follow them and, she believed, there might be someone else following Kim Yong-ai also.

Who? She didn't know. But she had the impression that Kim Yong-ai owed a lot of money. Paying her rent had been a struggle for the young stripper and sometimes she'd been so broke that she'd gone hungry. So hungry that the landlady had fed her from time to time.

Where had the two women gone? This was the question that the KNPs, with no regard for the landlady's civil liberties, pounded home hour after hour. Finally, we realized that the landlady was telling the truth. She really didn't know.

The stripper, Kim Yong-ai, and the military policewoman, Jill Matthewson, had disappeared together and they purposely had not told anyone where they were going.

Why? That was the question.

* * *

"At least she's alive," Ernie said.

It was early evening now; the sun had just gone down. We sat at the bar in a joint called the Silver Dragon Club, drinking cold draft OB, Oriental Brewery lager. It had taken a few hours to elicit the cooperation of the KNPs, and then a few more hours for them to conduct the interrogation. They'd taken their time. Watching the landlady cry hadn't been easy, but sometimes a cop has to frighten people to pry information out of them. The Korean cops are experts at it.

"Maybe," I said.

"What do you mean 'maybe.' Of course she's all right. Jill Matthewson was healthy and strong when she packed up and left TDC, and she had a Korean friend by her side to help watch out for her."

"A friend who owed money. And if this Miss Kim Yong-ai was so frightened that she had to disappear, who do you think she owed money to?"

*"Kampei,"* Ernie said. Gangsters.

"Exactly. So maybe Jill Matthewson isn't so safe after all."

A business girl wearing hot pants and a halter top came up and threw her arms around Ernie's neck. Then the rock band started and more GIs flooded into the club. They'd just gotten off duty. I knew the routine. After work they hot-footed it over to the mess hall, wolfed down chow and then, after a quick shower, threw on their blue jeans and their sneakers and their nylon jackets. Finally, assuming their pass hadn't been pulled, they flooded toward the main gate and out into the ville. Freedom.

The jackets they wore were made of black or dark blue nylon with a layer of cheap cotton for insulation. They were easily available at the stalls throughout Tongduchon and it seemed virtually mandatory for every GI to own one. On the back, the jackets were hand embroidered with one of three things: a flame-breathing dragon, a map of Korea, or a scantily clad Asian siren. Sometimes they crammed all three onto one jacket. Usually there was a motto beneath. Maybe the designation of their unit, like the "502nd Military Intelligence Battalion." Or the dates of their tour, "June 1972–July 1973." Or some stupid saying like, "When I die I know I'm going to heaven because I've already served my time in hell."

To blend in, Ernie and I wore similar jackets. His featured a naked Asian woman being embraced by a fire-breathing dragon. The dates beneath touted his two tours in Vietnam. My jacket featured a map of Korea and the start and end dates of my first tour here. When we'd had them made, Ernie asked me why I didn't buy something with a little more flare. I'm not sure why I didn't. A time and a place seemed good enough to me.

OB draft is what the Silver Dragon served; it came from a venerable brewery in Korea that had supposedly been established by Germans just after the turn of the century. The business girl hanging off Ernie's neck was named Ok-hi. She was tall and buxom and besides the hot pants and halter top wore black leather boots that enveloped her thick calves all the way to the knee. She had a girlfriend and a few minutes later I was introduced to Ji-yon, who called herself Jeannie. Jeannie was slender, willowy compared to full-figured Ok-hi, and her personality was polite and reserved. She told me she was from the southern province of Cholla-namdo. Ernie and I continued to drink the draft Oriental Brewery lager and we bought the girls drinks. They seemed fascinated by us. We were from Seoul, not "Cheap Charlies" like the Division GIs. Ernie winked and said, "Wait until they get to know me better."

Even amidst the mad swirl of women and booze and rock and roll, I continued to think about the case. I wanted to explain to Ernie that I thought the death of Private Druwood hadn't happened the way Colonel Alcott and Mr. Bufford said. And I wanted to speculate with him about the various reasons that Jill Matthewson might've decided to go AWOL. If we could figure out her motive, maybe that would help us break a lead. But Ernie was too busy with Ok-hi. Instead, I asked Jeannie who booked entertainment in Tongduchon. She was helpful and when the band took a break, Jeannie introduced me to their leader, a young Korean man with straight black hair hanging over his ears. He was surprised that I could speak Korean and after a little hesitation, he gave me the name and address of his booking agent.

Ernie and I put away about a six pack each. Ok-hi suggested that the four of us adjourn to a chop house and have something to eat. Drinking on an empty stomach, the Koreans believe, is bad for the health. Ernie and I hadn't eaten since breakfast, so we readily agreed. The girls asked us what type of food we wanted. Neither Ernie nor I could tolerate the *Miguk*-style chicken houses or hamburger joints that infested the bar district. The chow in those joints was routinely horrible and sometimes caused dysentery. We told them we wanted Korean food. The girls left and returned wearing warm coats and the four of us paraded onto the main drag of Tongduchon.

The Division GIs were drunk now. Raucous crowds of them shoved their way from bar to bar: the Oasis Club, the 007 Club, the Players Club, the Kimchee Club. Rock and roll erupted from open double doors and young Korean women stood outside, trying to coax GIs into their establishments.

The narrow walkways were jammed with pedestrians: American GIs, Korean business girls, old ladies in shawls pushing wooden carts laden with bean curd soup, even the occasional uniformed student humping a backpack, trying to make her way home without being molested. Ernie breathed deeply, savoring the aroma of diesel and garlic and stale beer. A smile crossed his chops and I knew what he was thinking. The ville! Life! A beautiful woman clinging to his arm. How could it be better than this?

As we walked, Ok-hi chattered happily, using the combination of broken English and Korean that passes as the lingua franca in every GI village in Korea.

"Ok-hi *taaksan ipo. Kujiyo?*" Ok-hi's very pretty. Isn't she?

"So-so." Ernie replied.

Ok-hi pinched him. "You number ten GI."

Number ten: the worst. As opposed to number one: the best.

"*Kuenchana,*" Ernie replied. It doesn't matter.

But after we'd passed a few bars, Ernie was no longer listening to Ok-hi. Instead, his eyes began to dart from side to side. Whenever he swerved in the flow of the pedestrian traffic, he glanced back. Surreptitiously. Jeannie walked casually next to me, not noticing what I was noticing. Ernie had spotted someone—or something—behind us. I didn't swivel my head to look. That would've tipped whoever was following us that we were on to him. Instead, I watched Ernie. Over the months we'd worked together, we'd developed hand signals for simple instructions like "danger" or "let's go" or "you first." They'd helped in tight situations, but Ernie wasn't flashing me any signals. And he wasn't happy. As we wound through the crowded alleys of Tongduchon, Ernie seemed to become more agitated. I checked beneath my armpit, making sure my .45 was snug in its holster. It was.

All I could do now was watch Ernie, pretend nothing was amiss, and be prepared to act.


When American GIs first arrive in Korea, they receive something commonly referred to as their "Kimchee Orientation." It is a series of briefings given by NCOs and officers appointed by the 8th Army commander. The orientation room features a huge wooden map of Korea. The jagged line of the Demilitarized Zone slashes across the waist of the country and a falling line of circular targets indicates the locations of the major cities: Seoul, Taejon, Taegu, and Pusan. Unit patches the size of dinner plates—the 8th Army red-and-white cloverleaf, the 2nd Division Indianhead patch—are used to graphically demonstrate to young soldiers that 8th Army covers Seoul and the rear areas, while the 2nd Infantry Division is stationed right up along the edge of the DMZ. After the geography lesson, a medic is brought in and the young GIs are treated to a series of films showing men suffering from advanced stages of venereal disease. Most of the young GIs are frightened so badly that they vow never to venture off base into the ville. This vow usually lasts about twenty-four hours. Then a representative from the Judge Advocate General's Office takes the stage to inform the GIs that their Constitutionally guaranteed rights have been totally abrogated by the U.S. ROK Status of Forces Agreement. The only reaction this usually engenders is the occasional yawn. Finally, the post chaplain takes over and leads the men in a nondenominational prayer. After the amen, the men are eligible to be issued a pass to leave the compound and mingle in Korean society. After two nights in the ville, they will consider themselves experts on Korean culture. This despite the fact that Korean culture is over 4,000 years old and is based on Confucian and Buddhist traditions that are, in many cases, diametrically opposed to Western traditions.

Once the GIs hit the ville, all hell breaks loose. These barely educated teenage Americans feel they can lord it over the Koreans. And with their abundant spending money, for the most part, they can. Until they go too far. Then the Koreans fight back, and that's when the Korean National Police and the American MPs step in.

When I first arrived in Korea, I assumed that 8th Army had somebody monitoring the clash of cultures that occurs when obnoxious American teenagers are thrust willy-nilly into an ancient society. The more time I spent here, the more I realized that 8th Army and the American government were not only *not* concerned with this phenomenon, they were unaware that it even existed. In fact, when I occasionally mentioned this clash of cultures back at 8th Army headquarters, I was looked at as if I were mad. As long as the troops returned to the compound every day, still able to perform their duties, that's all the U.S. Army cared about.

It was left for those of us in law enforcement to pick up the pieces. And it was left to those of us of a more reflective nature to marvel at the endless cornucopia of heartbreak and joy that was being churned out nightly on the streets of the GI village of Tongduchon.

Ok-hi still clung to Ernie's arm and I was still watching him. We'd passed two dozen nightclubs when, suddenly, Ernie turned and charged back through the crowd.

Ten yards behind us, a black GI came to a sudden halt and pretended to be interested in the statuettes displayed in the front window of a brassware emporium. Ernie ran right at him. As he closed, the GI glanced at Ernie nervously, flexed his knees as if to flee, but before he could move, Ernie plowed into him with such force that the man reeled backwards, slamming into a cement-block wall.

I let go of Jeannie and ran.

Stunned, the GI staggered to his feet, cursing, and as he started to raise his hands to counterattack, Ernie punched him with a hard right cross. The man's nose burst. He reached for his face but blood squirted through his splayed fingers.

Somehow, the man launched a low kick to Ernie's groin. Ernie dodged it but at the same time the man's right hand snaked out and grabbed the lapel of Ernie's dragon-embroidered jacket. Using the leverage of his crouching position, the injured man managed to jerk Ernie off balance and pull him closer in until they both crashed to the ground. Even in the split second I had to think about it, I admired the move. Whoever this guy was, he was trained in hand-to-hand combat.

Ernie and the other man rolled and punched and grunted. Blood kept pumping from the man's nose and now it was spread across Ernie's hands and face and shirt. Shoving my way through the crowd, I reached Ernie and pulled him away. The black man sprang to his feet, waving his fists in the air. I stepped in front of him.

"Keep your damn hands off me," he said, the voice muffled.

That's when I realized who he was. Weatherwax. Staff Sergeant Rufus Q. The same MP we'd questioned last night while he worked on the ville patrol. He was not in uniform now; he was wearing civilian clothes: slacks, a sports shirt, and a waist-length leather jacket. All of it glistening with blood.

Ernie pushed past me. "You've been following us," he said. "Picked us up after we left the Silver Dragon."

"Bull," Weatherwax said.

"Just enjoying the weather then?"

Weatherwax launched himself at Ernie. The left jab was ineffectual. Ernie dodged it easily and I grabbed Weatherwax and held him.

"Calm down, Sarge," I said.

"*You* calm the hell down," he replied. Then he grabbed his nose again, trying to stanch the bleeding.

I let go of him but kept myself between the two men. A crowd of jerks had gathered. I knew the type. When a fight erupts they're always there. It happened when I was a kid in school. They'd gather around like a pack of baboons, hopping and hooting. This type of behavior knows no ethnic boundaries. I'd seen it in blacks, in Anglos and, I'm not proud to say, in Chicanos. But this type of man, when challenged personally, finds a way to deflect the insult or, better yet, pretend it didn't happen. Now, gathered safely around the glow of a fight, their faces gleamed. A few of them even hopped on the balls of their feet, pretending that they wanted to fight, too, searching for approval from their fellow gawkers.

How I despised them. If I could've, I would've pulled my .45 and shot as many of them as I could until the rest scattered like the cowards they were. Instead, I kept my mind on business.

With his left hand, Weatherwax fumbled in his jacket for a handkerchief and held it across his nose. Gradually, the flow of blood subsided.

"MPs don't run the bars," I told him. "Too dangerous. GIs you've busted get juiced up and want to come after you. And I don't really believe you're interested in any of this brassware."

Inside the display window, a brass index finger pointed toward the sky.

"So what?" Weatherwax said. "I'm off duty. I can go where I please."

"Where you please," Ernie said, "is where Warrant Office Bufford tells you to go."

"He got nothing to do with it."

"Then why are you following us?" I asked.

Weatherwax looked away, as if he were very tired, still holding the handkerchief to his nose. I could see it coming. I believed Ernie saw it, too. Weatherwax was still enraged and he was about to try something.

Men in the crowd hooted. One of them bounced too close and Ernie shoved him so hard the skinny guy reeled backwards, slammed into his buddies, and fell backward on his butt. More angry voices erupted.

Ok-hi and Jeannie stood behind the growing crowd, huddled beneath a plastic awning, looking worried.

That's when Weatherwax tried it. I'm not sure where it came from. There must have been a stone or a brick lying on the ground and suddenly it was in his hand, then winging through the air, heading straight for Ernie's head. Ernie flinched. The missile sliced his ear, barely making contact, veered to the right, and hit one of the GIs in the crowd.

It was as if a hyena had been thrown into a gaggle of chimps. The howling started. Ernie was trying to punch Weatherwax and Weatherwax was trying to punch Ernie and, as I strained to hold them apart, the same guy who'd been knocked backward onto his ass sneaked out of the pack of gawkers and slammed his puny fist into

Ernie's kidney. I lunged for him but he retreated into the crowd and then Ernie and Weatherwax were going at one another again. Brutally.

"MPs!" someone shouted and over their heads I could see, heading our way, bobbing black helmets.

I grabbed Ernie, ripped him away from Weatherwax. The front of his jacket was slathered in blood. Weatherwax wheeled drunkenly, unable to follow. I shoved through the gawking crowd. It wasn't difficult because most of them were starting to back off now that the MPs were on the way. Ok-hi and Jeannie stood at the mouth of an alley about half a block farther down the narrow road. They waved us on. Together, the four of us—me supporting Ernie, Ok-hi and Jeannie leading—entered the darkness, Ernie still howling about how he was going to kick some MP ass.

The alley narrowed, the darkness grew, and the hooting voices behind us faded.

We spent the night with Ok-hi and Jeannie in a *yoguan*, a Korean inn. Sitting on the warm *ondol* floor Ok-hi did her best to nurse Ernie's wounds, but Jeannie had to do most of the practical work: bringing in a pan of hot water; washing out the scratches and bruises; asking the middle-aged woman who owned the *yoguan* to loan her some antiseptic ointment. Ok-hi mainly cooed and rubbed Ernie's shoulders and nibbled on the edge of his damaged ear.

"He was clumsy," Ernie told me. "I spotted him before we entered the Silver Dragon Club and then, when we came out, he was standing down the street, staring our way. Don't they teach MPs up here how to conduct a proper tail?"

"I don't think Division needs to tail people too often."

I'd bought four cold liters of OB at a local shop and while the girls ministered to Ernie, I popped the bottles open and poured the frothing beer into porcelain drinking glasses, the type usually used for serving barley tea. Ok-hi downed hers almost as fast as Ernie. Jeannie left her beer for me.

"Bufford and Colonel Alcott put him up to it," Ernie said. "You can bet on it."

"Probably," I agreed.

"Sure they did. They want to keep tabs on what we're up to. The Division chief of staff is probably breathing down their necks."

I'd heard stories about the Division chief of staff: Brigadier General H. K. Pacquet, a decorated veteran of combat in Vietnam. "Hong Kong" Packet is what they called him. Had something to do with a special type of antipersonnel explosive he'd devised while working with the Special Forces. Pacquet had been wounded in Vietnam. Wounded so badly that his face was hideously deformed but he was otherwise healthy, which is why the army decided to keep him on active duty. He's a hard charger and a bad ass and everyone in Division is terrified of him. Even the honchos at 8th Army back off when "Hong Kong" Packet catches a case of the ass.

"So they send Weatherwax out to watch us," I said. "And you beat the crap out of him for his troubles. That's certainly going to help our position back at Division PMO."

"Screw Division," Ernie said. "They're interfering with an official investigation."

"All they were doing, Ernie, was watching."

"Same difference."

I wished Ernie would've talked to me before he punched out Weatherwax. Maybe there's something we could've done to mislead him. Make him—and the Division honchos—believe we were doing one thing while we were actually doing another. Too late now. By punching out Weatherwax, Ernie'd given Division PMO ammunition to use when they approached 8th Army and asked—as I believed they would—that we be removed from the Jill Matthewson case. They'd wanted us gone from day one. Outside law enforcement nosing around in their territory would never sit well with the Division honchos. I didn't bother to mention all this to Ernie. Bureaucratic infighting meant nothing to him.

Ok-hi ordered chop from the woman who owned the *yoguan*, and twenty minutes later a Korean boy of about twelve years of age brought in a square metal box that he set in the middle of the floor. As he shuffled into the room, the boy kept his eyes down. Respectful in the Confucian tradition, but it also gave me the impression that he was ashamed to look at us. Two debauched American GIs and two even farther-fallen Korean women. It was as if this delivery boy didn't want to be contaminated by evil. Without speaking, the boy slid open a side panel on the metal box and pulled out steaming bowls of *pibim-bap*, fried rice; *meiun-tang*, hot mackerel soup; and a plate of *yaki-mandu*, fried pork dumplings. Then he closed the box, bowed, and backed out of the room. All performed without once having actually looked at us.

Jeannie broke open my wooden chopsticks, unfolded a paper napkin, placed it on my knee, and motioned with her open palm. "*Dub-seiyo,*" she said. Please partake. It wasn't quite as polite as "*chapsu-seiyo,*" which means the same thing but is spoken to one's superior rather than to one's equal. I was pleased to be equal with this Korean business girl named Jeanie, so I dug in.

After chop, Ernie and Ok-hi retired to their own room. Jeannie cleaned up, setting the empty dishes outside in the vinyl-floored hallway. Then she slid shut the oil-papered door and rolled out two down-filled sleeping mats. I was tired, but not tired enough to ignore her.

In the morning, Ernie and I were up just after dawn. We said our goodbyes to Ok-hi and Jeannie who lingered in the *yoguan* since both rooms were paid for until noon.

The narrow alleys of Tongduchon were quiet and cold in the early morning hours. All the shops and nightclubs and bars were padlocked and shuttered with heavy iron gratings. A low mist spread along cobbled lanes. As we walked, Ernie stuck his hands deep into his pockets and breathed deeply of the frigid air, pungent with the odor of fermented cabbage and stagnating beer and *ondol* charcoal gas floating from the hotels and *yoguans* that dotted the bar district.

Most of the GIs had already left. A mandatory PT formation was held at 0630 and it was now almost 0700 hours. In the distance, on the other side of the main gate of Camp Casey, we could hear huge groups of GIs doing jumping jacks while they shouted martial cadences.

The narrow walkway we were following bled onto the main drag of the bar district and soon Ernie and I were walking past the shuttered facades of the Oasis Club, the Montana Club, and finally the Silver

Dragon Club. Then we crossed the railroad tracks, went through another narrow alley, and came out on the four-lane wide Main Supply Route. Down the road about a half mile we could see the illuminated arch of the 2nd Division main gate. Beyond that, the twenty-foot-high MP, still standing at the ready, still observing everything. When I thought of what we would face at the PMO today, after the Weatherwax incident last night, I groaned inwardly.

Ernie seemed completely unconcerned.

A unit of GIs emerged from the main gate. All of them wore sneakers, gray training pants, gray sweatshirts, and red woolen caps pulled down low over their ears. All fifty or so men ran in unison, a senior sergeant shouting out the cadence. One man ran in front of the formation holding the unit flag. The guide-on, he's called. We could tell by the colors they wore, and by the unit designation on the flag, that they were combat engineers.

"Where are the MPs?" Ernie asked.

"Don't be so anxious to see them," I replied.

We trotted across the MSR until we reached the southwestern corner of Camp Casey. A ten-foot-high cement-block wall on our right, topped with concertina wire, stretched along the sidewalk all the way to the main gate. Ernie and I walked it quietly, both lost in our own thoughts.

Me, I was thinking about Jeannie. She was a slender woman, and tall for a Korean, but sweet and gentle and considerate. I'd had some good times since I'd been in country but last night had been one of the best.

Ernie heard it first.

"What the hell's that?" he asked.

It was the typical shouted cadence of a military unit doing its morning physical-training run. The sergeant shouted something out and the men answered as if in one voice, almost like singing. But this sound was close and loud and garbled. Ernie and I glanced around, unable to figure where the noise was coming from.

It couldn't be the combat engineer unit. They'd run off in the other direction.

And then I understood. It came from the narrow alleyway we'd just walked out of. It had been barely wide enough for Ernie and me to walk abreast, certainly not big enough for a company formation four-squads wide. But that's where the sound was coming from, and that's why Ernie and I were having trouble locating it. The narrow alley concentrated the sound, causing it to reverberate between its brick walls. And then the sound erupted onto the MSR and spread out every which way.

"Why in hell did they go down there?" Ernie asked.

"They came out of the main gate," I said. "We know that. Then they must've entered the village and taken a left down the road running along the railroad tracks."

"So close to the ville?"

Ernie meant that there'd be a lot of civilians woken up by their shouting and the pounding of their feet. In the States, that's never allowed. Even in Seoul, it's frowned upon.

Now it was my turn to shrug. "This is Division."

"But why turn up that narrow alleyway?" Ernie asked. "They've hardly run a half mile."

I didn't know. But the question was answered almost as soon as it was out of Ernie's mouth. The guide-on of the unit, holding the unit flag at port arms, emerged from the mouth of the alley. He wore a green cap pulled down low over his ears, the same gray sweat pants, same gray sweat shirt, same cheap sneakers. But the realization of the meaning of the designation on the flag fluttering in the breeze smacked Ernie and me at the same time. Right across the chops.

Crossed pistols.

The unit emerging out of the narrow alley—the men stumbling into one another, packed like sardines, and now redeploying on the wide expanse of the MSR—was none other than Headquarters Company of the 2nd Infantry Division Military Police.

"They've been hunting us," Ernie said.

I didn't want to believe it. "Don't be ridiculous," I said. "They're doing their morning exercise."

But even as I spoke, I realized Ernie was right. They had to be hunting us. Why else would they squeeze through the ville, run down dangerous railroad tracks, and then turn up an alley too narrow to hold them?

The MP company emerged from the gap in the dark red wall, all wearing bright green caps pulled down low over their ears, looking like a giant reptile slithering out of a cave. And then, without anyone barking orders, they re-formed into four columns behind the guide-on. The sergeant was shouting out the cadence now and the unit started its relentless trot, heading down the MSR toward the main gate. Heading directly toward us.

"Just keep walking," Ernie said. "We're not going to run."

He shoved his fists into the pockets of his jacket, hunched his shoulders, and continued to march resolutely down the sidewalk. We had more than a quarter of a mile to go. The arch of the main gate of Camp Casey loomed in front of us. Above us, the glassy-eyed MP statue stared impassively at our dilemma. We'd never make it. The MP formation was already bearing down on us. The sergeant leading the formation had spotted us and he was shouting a new song:

"On your right!"

"On your right!" the MPs repeated.

"*On* your right!"

As if to get our attention.

"Sick call!"

There's nothing lower than a GI who shirks his duty by riding the sick list.

"Sick call!" the MPs repeated. And repeated again. "Sick call! *Sick* call!"

The sound was thunderous and getting louder. Still, neither Ernie nor I looked back. Here it comes, I thought.

Feet trod on cold cement. Big feet. Dozens of them, breaking away from the formation, cantering toward us.

# 4

Before I dropped out of high school to join the army, I played some football. Being as big as I am made me an anomaly among the Chicanos of Lincoln High School in East L.A. The coach wasn't sure what to do with me so, of course, he put me on the line. Right tackle, but then he moved me to guard. Although I was too tall to play guard—in the usual way these things are looked at—the coach saw that I could pull off the line quickly. As soon as the ball was snapped, I moved to my right or my left, behind my other teammates on the line who were lunging forward. My job was to hit some defender, when he was least expecting it, and knock open a hole for the ball carrier to plunge through. That was the theory.

The fact of the matter was that our coach wasn't the greatest tactician who ever paced the edge of the gridiron, and most of the other guys on the team—almost all Chicanos like me—were barely big enough to support their shoulder pads. We lost every game. Except for the one brawl we had with Roosevelt High—but that's another story.

Still, our coach was right about one thing. I could move off the line quickly, without tipping the defenders as to which way I was going to move. It was a skill that I reverted to when I heard those MP footsteps closing on us.

I swiveled and crouched and launched myself at them, body parallel to the ground, in a flying block that I hoped would throw them off stride. It did. My shoulder hit one guy in the stomach, my rump hit another in the knees, and the third guy got whacked on the shins by my flying feet. All three went down. I rolled atop them, hoping to cause as much damage as possible and, as soon as I was able, popped back to my feet. Then I slugged another guy coming in, and another. It worked for a few seconds, but finally I was enveloped by a sea of sweaty gray. I crouched, winging punches to my right and my left. Fists rained down on my back. I covered my head as best as I could, bulled forward and would've fallen flat on my face but there were so many bodies around me that I was held upright. Punch after punch landed on the back of my head and my spine and flailed against my aching ribs.

Someone shouted. "Back in formation, dammit! Form your ranks. What is this? A freaking mob?"

The sergeant leading the formation, the same voice who'd been calling out the cadence. God bless him. The men around me started to back off but one or two of them winged in another *chingaso*, a sneak punch.

When the MPs moved away, I turned unsteadily on my feet and saw the face of my benefactor: Sergeant First Class Otis, the desk sergeant who'd first greeted me and Ernie when we arrived at Division PMO. He was dressed in the same gray sweats and green pull-down cap as his troops. I felt like embracing him for saving me but instead he shoved me back.

"I should've let them *kill* you," he said. Then he shoved me again, his fist in my chest. Hard. "*That's* for Weatherwax."

A blast filled the air.

Ernie. He had fired his .45 into the air, above the MP formation. Some of the men fell to the ground, a few of them crouched. Most held their ground. He stood behind me, jacket ripped off his right shoulder, face bruised, but holding the .45 steady, smoke pouring from its barrel, aimed right between the eyes of Sergeant Otis.

"Move 'em out, Sarge," Ernie growled. "Smartly."

Otis glared at him for a moment, as if trying to decide if he should cross the five yards between them and slap the automatic pistol out of Ernie's hand. But he decided against it. Instead, he turned back to the grumbling formation, started shouting at them to fall into ranks and, within seconds, the Headquarters Company of the 2nd Infantry Division Military Police was trotting down the road. Silent now. No one calling cadence. The pounding of their feet faded into the distance. Ernie reholstered the .45.

"You look like shit," he said.

"Thanks. So do you."

Ernie fingered some of the new bruises on his face. "Touchy, aren't they?"

"Apparently."

I straightened myself out as best I could and ran my fingers through my hair and Ernie and I marched to the main gate. This time, when we entered the guard shack, the lone MP didn't give us any shit. Maybe it was the look in our eyes.


At the transient billets, Ernie and I washed up and changed into coats and ties. It was the duty day now and we wanted to look sharp so as not to give the 2nd Division honchos anything extra to criticize us for. On the way back to the main gate we stopped at the Indianhead Snack Bar, dragged a couple of trays through the chow line, and took a table next to the window near the entrance. Ernie shoveled pulverized scrambled eggs into his trap. I sipped coffee. Gingerly. Between bruised lips.

"We should go to the dispensary," I said.

"Screw that," Ernie replied. "So Spec Six Wehry can laugh at us?"

"Not everybody in Division is against us, Ernie."

"They could've fooled me."

Ernie was right. So far we hadn't made many allies. Everywhere we turned people were worried that we'd embarrass the Division. Cause them grief. And were outraged if we so much as laid a finger on one of their comrades. Where did this loyalty come from? Was it a healthy thing in a combat unit? Or was there something deeper?

Something everybody was afraid of? I reminded myself to fight off paranoia. An occupational hazard for a cop.

And I reminded myself that we had, in fact, found three allies. Brandy, the "soul sister" bartender at the Black Cat Club, and Ok-hi and Jeannie, the business girls who'd helped me cadge a lead from the band leader at the Silver Dragon. All of them were Korean women. That didn't bother me. I liked Korean women.

"How's your paperwork coming?" Ernie asked.

"What paperwork?"

Ernie smirked. "Your marriage paperwork."

He was referring to the fact that for an American GI to marry a Korean woman, a whole series of certifications and permissions must be requested, both from the U.S. military and from the Korean government. He was also referring to the fact that a few weeks ago I'd submitted such paperwork.

"Pulled it," I said.

"I thought you and Miss Ryu were doing well together."

Miss Ryu had been my Korean language teacher. She was a graduate student at Ewha University and almost exactly my age. Her job on the U.S. Army compound was helping to finance her master's degree. At first, I'd been her best student. Then we'd started seeing one another at coffee shops and afterwards taking long strolls through parks and museums and ancient palaces. Our interests were similar, our personalities in tune. And, although she wore thick-lensed glasses and most GIs thought she looked bookish, to me she was beautiful.

"We *were* doing well," I said.

Ernie leaned back in his chair. "Okay," he said, "you can tell Uncle Ernie. What went wrong?"

I didn't answer right away. Instead, I stared at two GIs jostling one another for the right to drop a quarter into the snack bar's jukebox. Finally, one of them relented and clanging rock music emerged from the speakers.

Once our marriage paperwork was submitted, Miss Ryu knew she had to tell her parents about our romance. But she also knew that the thought of her marrying someone other than a Korean—and worse yet an American GI—would be a crippling blow to them. The loss of face amongst their family and friends and her father's colleagues at work would be enormous. It's not racism exactly. *Ethnocentrism* describes it better. Koreans have lived together as one tribe on this narrow Asian peninsula for so long that the thought of a well-brought-up woman marrying a long-nosed foreigner is difficult to bear. We're just too different. Culturally, physically, psychologically. She thought about it and thought about it. Finally, Miss Ryu lacked the courage to speak of such a thing to her parents. She told me to pull the paperwork.

"My father's sick," she explained. "His heart." She tapped herself on the chest. "And I'm their only daughter."

Her parent's only daughter, lost to a foreigner. What would their ancestors think?

I took the news with what I hoped was stoicism. And I tried to reassure her that I understood. Actually, I supposed I did. Her parents were everything to her. If I had parents, I'd probably feel the same way. Still, that didn't mean that her decision didn't hurt. Since then, I hadn't been to class and we hadn't met socially. The temporary assignment to the 2nd Division area had, in fact, come as a relief. A chance to be by myself. A chance to think.

"All that?" Ernie said, responding to my silence.

"Yeah." I sipped on my coffee. "All that."

I didn't feel guilty about having spent the night with Jeannie. Miss Ryu and I were no longer an item. I was a free man. Free as a pigeon flying over the DMZ. With GIs taking potshots from below.


The man who booked the entertainment in the Tongduchon area worked days only. It was already half past nine in the morning but in the cold winter air, the morning fog that blanketed the alleys of Tongduchon had not yet burned off. We turned down one narrow walkway and then another until finally I found it: 21 *bonji*, 36 *ho*. The sign above the door said KIMCHEE ENTERTAINMENT in English. *KUKCHEI UMAK*, in Korean: International Music. That's not unusual for Korean companies. They'll have one name that sounds good in English and another that sounds good in Korean. The two don't necessarily have to match.

The door was open and we walked in.

His name was Pak Tong-i. He was a wrinkled Korean man who wore a French beret atop his round head and as we spoke, he continued to puff on a Turtle Boat brand cigarette through an ivory holder. Yes, he knew all about Kim Yong-ai.

"One of my best strippers," he said. The English was accented but understandable. "GI love her too much. You know, big *geegee*." He cupped his hands in front of his chest.

"So who did she owe money to?" Ernie asked.

"Stripper always owe money," he said. "That's why they get into business. Maybe their mom owe money, maybe their daddy owe money, maybe they have younger brother who want to go to school. Very expensive, how you say, *hakbi*?"

"Tuition," I told him.

While Pak Tong-i shook his head, thinking about the high cost of tuition, I asked another question.

"So when Kim Yong-ai ran away, somebody must've been very angry that she ran away without paying what she owed."

Pak's eyes widened. "Nobody angry."

"Why not?"

"When she run away, she don't owe money."

"Wait a minute," Ernie said. "I thought you just told us that she owed a lot of money."

"She did. But before she left, same day, she pay all."

Now it was our turn to be stupefied.

"She come in here," Pak continued, "that morning. With big American woman. They have big pile of GI money. They pay all."

"How much?"

"*Miguk* money?" Pak asked himself. American money? He puffed on his cigarette while he thought about it. Finally he said, "*Peik man won*. Maybe two thousand dollar."

Ernie whistled.

I showed Pak the photograph of Jill Matthewson.

"That her," he said. "She make great stripper."

"Where did this Miss Kim find the money to pay you off?"

"I don't know," he said. "I no ask."

"Did they tell you they were leaving Tongduchon?"

"Yes. Miss Kim say she no workey for me no more."

"Where'd they go?"

"I don't know," Pak answered. "I no ask."

We pressured him for a while but finally gave up. If he knew where they'd gone, he wasn't talking.

Later that morning, I reviewed Corporal Jill Matthewson's bank records. Eighth Army can do these things. The banks that do business on base camps in Korea are chartered under military regulation and sign away most of their stateside rights. Anyway, that's the way it was explained to me. True or not, the Office of the Judge Advocate General says it's legal. But of course JAG says it's legal mainly because the 8th Army commander says it's legal. I perused the records carefully. No major withdrawals before she disappeared. Mainly because there was nothing to withdraw. Her balance was less than ten dollars. Most of Jill Matthewson's military paycheck had been forwarded by allotment to her mother in Terre Haute, Indiana. The rest was what you'd expect for a young woman to spend on herself, for clothes and other personal items. About a hundred dollars a month. Jill had only been in country a little over five months. In that amount of time, she certainly hadn't saved two thousand clams by being thrifty.

Theoretically, Jill could've raised the two thousand dollars to pay off Kim Yong-ai's debts from black-marketing. U.S.-manufactured goods are shipped by the boatful from the States to the military PXs in Korea—all at U.S. taxpayers' expense. No customs duties are paid so the goods are cheap. For example, a GI can buy a portable tape recorder in the PX for say, forty bucks and turn around and sell it out in the ville for 40,000 *won*, the equivalent of eighty dollars. In other words, double his money. Of course, black-marketing is strictly illegal and GIs are prosecuted for it all the time. Still, it's widespread, the temptation being too much for ordinary mortals. But Jill Matthewson's ration control record was clean. She'd purchased very little out of the PX, only what she needed for what the army likes to call "personal health and welfare."

So where had the two thousand dollars come from?

Certainly, Miss Kim, a poor Korean stripper, couldn't come up with that much money. *"Peik man won,"* Mr. Pak had told us. Literally,

"One hundred ten thousand *won*." By our way of counting, a million *won*. By today's exchange rate, equivalent to roughly two thousand dollars U.S. *Taaksan tone*, in the GI parlance. A lot of dough. How in the world had either Corporal Jill Matthewson or the stripper Kim Yong-ai come up with it? I set the question aside for now. Instead, I concentrated on the other tip that the owner of Kimchee Entertainment had provided.

"Corporal Jill very famous in Tongduchon," he told us.

"Famous? Why?"

"She help Chon family." I stared at him blankly. "You *arra*." You know. "Chon family daughter run over by GI truck."

Then I understood. The case had made news even down in Seoul. Two GIs, driving a two-and-a-half-ton truck near Camp Casey, had struck a young Korean girl. The accident happened early in the morning while she was on her way to middle school. The girl, they say, bounced twenty yards and, according to the eyewitness reports, died just minutes after impact. There had been demonstrations calling for the GIs to be punished, but a 2nd Division court-martial determined that the death was accidental. The two GIs were transferred back to the States. More demonstrations ensued. 8th Army's attitude was that the Koreans were being ungrateful. After all, we are here defending their country and accidents do happen.

The price of freedom you might call it.

According to the booking agent, Pak Tong-i, Corporal Jill Matthewson had been the first MP on the scene. She'd provided first aid—futile, as it turned out—and later she'd done everything she could to help the family of the deceased girl. As far as the citizens of Tongduchon were concerned, Jill was the only American who had tried to do the right thing. The rest of the American reaction—trying the GIs in a secret tribunal on Camp Casey, not calling all relevant witnesses, and finally acquitting the GIs and sending them back to the States—had been totally unacceptable. Demonstrations outside the main gate of Camp Casey were the result. And if it hadn't been for the brutal intervention of the Korean National Police, those demonstrations might've turned into anti-American riots.

The missing woman's connection to the Chon matter was news to us. Why hadn't the 2nd Division mentioned Jill Matthewson's involvement in this case in their report of her disappearance? Did they consider it to be irrelevant? Maybe it was. Still, I needed to know for sure. It just seemed like a heck of a big thing to leave out.

After checking Jill's account at the bank, Ernie and I drove over to the Division motor pool.

"*Anyong-bashi*-motor-pool," Ernie said as we drove in.

*Anyongbashimnka* is the Korean formal greeting, like "hello." Literally, it means "Are you at peace?" with an honorific verb ending added on to sweeten it a bit. GI slang has morphed this long greeting into something more pronounceable: *Anyong-bashi*-motor-pool. Don't ask me why. It makes no sense. But it sounds funny.

A red placard above a side door to a Quonset hut read: TRAFFIC SAFETY OFFICE, SECOND INFANTRY DIVISION, SECOND TO NONE!

Ernie parked the jeep and we walked in. It was a tiny office with a diesel space heater, a gray desk, and a few beat-up old metal file cabinets. Nobody home. Ernie and I walked back outside and as we did so, a small man with a bright red mustache hustled up to us.

"Had an accident?" he asked.

"Not yet," Ernie replied. "You the Safety NCO?"

"That's me." He thrust a thumb into his chest. "Oscar L. Bernewright. What can I do for you?"

He was a short man, oddly proportioned, almost like a dwarf. He wore grease-stained fatigues and the insignia of a sergeant first class pinned to his collar at a slightly twisted angle. Green eyes shone brightly over his red mustache and he gazed at us intently from beneath his fur-lined cap.

"Chon Un-suk," I said.

His wrinkled features fell. "The dead girl," he said. His voice came out raspy.

"Yes."

His green eyes moistened and for a minute I thought he was going to cry. Then he recovered and studied our civilian attire and our grim demeanor. "You're those CID agents I been hearing about. From Eighth Army."

Our fame had spread.

"That's us," I said.

"I been waiting for you," Sergeant Bernewright said.

Ernie and I glanced at one another. Waiting for us?

"Come on." Bernewright waved with his left hand. "We'll talk. Not in my office, it's too small. There's a fresh pot of coffee brewing in the toolshed."

We followed him across a vast expanse of blacktop. Engines roared. Two-and-a-half ton trucks swirled in slow circles like skaters on a field of ice. Sergeant Bernewright hustled rapidly across the lot on his short legs.

"If he's been waiting for us," Ernie told me, "maybe we should go in guns blazing."

"This isn't an ambush," I replied. "Relax."

The inside of the toolshed reeked of oil, diesel fumes, and coffee. After serving ourselves a hot cup of joe and finding seats on wooden benches, Sergeant Bernewright described the accident involving the now famous middle-school girl, Chon Un-suk.

"Two GIs in a deuce-and-a-half driving through Tongduchon early in the morning. Poor driving conditions. Fog. Narrow road. No sidewalk. Middle-school kids lining the muddy edge of the road waiting for their bus."

"Were the GIs speeding?" Ernie asked.

"Of course they were speeding," Bernewright answered. "They're GIs, aren't they? Nothing more than teenagers. The guy in the passenger seat has a little more rank than the other one, but do you think he's going to ask his buddy to slow down? No way. They're having fun. The speed limit there is thirty klicks, about twenty miles per hour. After measuring the skid and the other evidence at the scene, I figure those two bozos were doing at least forty. Maybe more."

"Why weren't they pulled over?"

Bernewright winced. "Korean traffic patrols never stop GIs," he explained. "Not up here at Division anyway. That would be interfering with military operations. Not a chance. Not when the president of the country is a former general and the whole damn government is run as if it were a military operation. Which it is. Or might as well be. And on our side, we don't have enough MPs to patrol the roads anywhere but on Camp Casey itself. So young American GI drivers are given a huge vehicle, a tank full of diesel, and they're set loose on an unsuspecting Korean populace."

"Sounds like you get a lot of this."

"Over a hundred accidents a year. That's the ones that are reported. Ten percent of them result in injury or death."

"Chon Un-suk was standing in front of the other students." I remembered this from Korean newspaper reports. "She was the safety monitor."

"Right. She had a whistle, white gloves, a sash across her chest that said 'safety first' in Korean. The works. They tell me that she was blowing her whistle and holding up her hand, palm out, ordering the deuce-and-a-half to slow down when it slid sideways in the mud and smacked her head-on at full speed."

Ernie grimaced.

"A mess," Bernewright continued. "Little girls screaming, parents frantically running through the crowd searching for their children, an enraged pack of Korean men kicking the crap out of the GI who'd been driving the truck and his passenger. And then Jill Matthewson and her partner pull up in their MP jeep, siren blaring.

"Her partner jumps out waving his billy club. Jill approaches the accident victim, Chon Un-suk, trying to force the crowd back to let the girl have a chance to breathe. So far, no one's attending to the girl so Jill kneels down and does what she can. Clears the air passage, checks for bleeding, loosens the girl's clothing and elevates her feet. Then she takes off her own fatigue blouse and wraps the girl to keep her warm, hopefully delay the onset of shock. Meanwhile, a Korean ambulance arrives but at the same time the girl's father erupts on the scene. He shoves Jill out of the way, sees his daughter on the ground and then, realizing she's still breathing—barely—he lifts her up and starts to carry her home. The Korean paramedics stand by and do nothing. Jill's shocked. She's sure the girl's suffering from internal bleeding, and she knows enough about first aid to know that in order to save her life the girl has to be taken to an emergency room immediately, if not sooner.

"When nobody acts, she does. Jill grabs the father and holds him, screaming and pointing to the ambulance. The father won't hear of it. Why, no one knows."

I did. Or at least I thought I did. I explained it to Sergeant Bernewright. And to Ernie. In Korean tradition, it is believed that if someone dies away from home their spirit, when it rises and leaves the body, will become disoriented. It will become lost and then, being away from home, away from the shrine set up by its family, the spirit will become a wandering ghost. Without the proper ceremonies, without offerings of incense and food, without the prayers of the people who loved the spirit in life, it will never be able to make the transition from wandering ghost to revered ancestor. So Chon Un-suk's father's reaction was rational from his point of view. He didn't want his daughter to be hauled away by strangers to die alone in some emergency room. He wanted to take care of her. He wanted to make sure she died at home, not on the street where she'd be lost and would wander alone for eternity—with no one to burn incense at her shrine, no one to pray at her gravesite, and no one to make offerings of food and drink to ease her sojourn through the underworld.

A hungry ghost, the Koreans call such a creature. A spirit whom no one remembers. A spirit who can't find its way home.

Ernie stirred more sugar into his coffee. "When did this shit start?" he asked.

"What?" I asked. "Wandering ghosts?"

"Yeah."

"In ancient times."

"How come I never heard of it?"

"How many Koreans have you been around that died away from home?"

He thought about this. I knew the answer. None.

"Besides," I said, "ensuring that a loved one dies at home is not a modern custom. Most Koreans trust Western medicine nowadays and most of them die in hospitals. Alone."

"Progress," Bernewright said.

"When Jill couldn't stop the father," I asked, "what did she do?"

"She wrestled with the old man," Bernewright told us. "He wrestled back. And then a horrible thing happened. Chon Un-suk fell to the ground. 'With a big thud,' Jill told me. Everyone was shocked and for a moment—Jill said it seemed like hours—there was a deathly silence. Then, like one person, the Korean crowd inhaled and when they exhaled it was in a solid rush and they fell upon Jill like a pack of demons."

"So the father took Chon Un-suk home?" Ernie asked.

"Yes. The best we can tell, she was dead before she arrived."

"So maybe her ghost is still wandering."

"Maybe," Bernewright said. "Luckily, three MP jeeps arrived about the same time Jill went down. They waded into the crowd, busting heads, and pulled her to safety. She kept screaming for them to leave her alone, and one buck sergeant told me that she cracked him a good one in the chops."

"Bold," Ernie said.

"Yeah," Bernewright agreed. "But he was just trying to help. When Jill pushed through the crowd searching for Chon Un-suk, the Korean mob attacked her again. The MPs pulled her out once more and this time they handcuffed her, threw her in the back seat of a jeep, and drove her to the dispensary on Camp Casey."

"She was hurt badly?" I asked.

"Not exactly. But she was hysterical, she wanted to go back, save the girl. One of the medics told me they had to strap her down on the gurney and shoot her up with a sedative. Even then, it took ten minutes to calm her down."

Ernie's eyes were glassy by this time; he'd stopped stirring his coffee. The faraway look in his eye told me that, for once, Ernie Bascom had found a woman he could respect.


Later, at the Indianhead Snack Bar, I placed a call to Seoul. Sergeant Riley, the CID Detachment Admin NCO, was anxious to talk to me.

"What kind of hell are you two raising up there?" he asked. "The Division honchos have been messaging Eighth Army asking us to recall you because you're looking into all sorts of things that have nothing to do with the disappearance of Jill Matthewson."

"What things?"

"They didn't specify. But they also said you've been running the ville, drinking all your travel pay, and punching out MPs."

"He was tailing us," I told Riley.

"Who?"

"An off-duty MP."

"What did you expect? You're in *Division*."

I was getting tired of people telling me that, as if I hadn't figured it out for myself.

"Are we withdrawn?" I asked.

"Not yet. But the Eighth Army provost marshal is taking it under advisement."

I asked Riley to use his influence at the 8th Army Data Processing Center and pull a few ration control records for me. I heard paper rustling and ballpoint pen being popped.

"Shoot," Riley said.

I gave him three names.

"You must be kidding," Riley said.

"No kidding involved," I replied. "Get me the information, Riley. I need it."

Before he could protest further, I hung up.

The Chon family home sat on a hill gazing down on the western edge of Tonguduchon. Brick and cement apartment buildings, none over three stories tall, were interspersed between ancient-looking wooden huts that must've once been part of a traditional farming village. At the edge of the line of homes, fallow rice paddies stretched toward a two-lane highway that ran west from Camp Casey. About twenty miles farther on, across a range of hills, the road reached the city of Munsan in the Western Corridor.

Flagstone steps led up to the Chon residence. As I gazed at the cool, mist-shrouded morning, it was easy to see that this homestead, with its commanding view of the valley, had once been the ancestral home of the local *yangban* family, the educated Confucian elite who had ruled Korea during the Yi Dynasty.

How long had the Yi Dynasty lasted? From the fourteenth century right up to modern times, when the Japanese Imperial Army annexed Korea as a colony in 1910.

Carved wooden poles on either side of the pathway represented *Chonha Daejangkun*, the General of the Upper World, and *Jiha Yojangkun*, the Goddess of the Underworld. The walls of the Chon compound were made of lumber slats faded to a deep amber. The buildings behind were topped with tile roofs upturned at the edges.

Clay beasts perched along the ridges, protecting the family from evil spirits.

Ancient shamanistic traditions still exist in Korea. Everywhere.

The big wooden entrance gate stood wide open. From within floated the muffled snicker of girlish laughter. Ernie and I stepped through the gate. The courtyard was well kept. Gravel raked, naked rose bushes knotted with strips of white cloth, tiny cement pagodas flanking blue ponds shimmering with golden koi.

An open area in the center of the courtyard held a shrine: A stone foundation with wooden stanchions supporting a tile roof that was a replica of the tile roof that covered the entire home. Bolted into the stanchions was a framed photograph, bordered with black silk, of a young Korean girl. Her face was unsmiling. She stared straight ahead, almost as if she were cross-eyed, trying to focus. Her jet black hair was pulled back and braided into two plaits and she wore the immaculately pressed white blouse of a middle-school student. Directly in front of the photograph was another stone stand, this one holding an ornate bronze urn. From the urn, three sticks of incense smoldered. Pungent puffs of smoke rose past the photograph, wafting their way to the gray-skied heavens above.

Two teenage girls, wearing the white blouses and long black skirts of middle-school students, knelt in front of the shrine. Nervously, they kept trying to light additional sticks of incense but as one of the girls fumbled with the match, the other berated her for her clumsiness. They both worked hard at stifling their giggles.

Ernie and I stopped and stared at the photograph for a moment. Quietly. Waiting for the two girls to finish their homage. They did. They stood and bowed. When they saw us, their eyes widened in surprise. Both smooth faces flushed red, the girls snatched up their school bags, nodded to us as they passed and, holding hands, they hustled out the main gate and down the pathway heading back toward Tongduchon.

"Cute kids," Ernie said. "Must've been friends of the dead girl."

"Maybe," I answered. "Or just schoolmates. Koreans are very reverential of the dead. There's an old saying my language teacher taught us."

"Here we go."

I pressed on. "'A man needs three wives,' the Koreans say. 'A Chinese wife for his kitchen, a Japanese wife for his bed, and a Korean wife to tend his grave.'"

Ernie stared at me, amused. "I like the Japanese part."

"You would. Come on."

We walked across the courtyard to the front of the Chon residence. The home featured a traditional elevated wood-slat floor, varnished and sparkling with cleanliness. Ernie and I slipped off our shoes and, in our stocking feet, stepped up onto the slick surface. I knocked on the edge of the oil-papered door. We waited. No answer. I knocked again and then again. Finally, I shouted, *"Yoboseiyo!"*

When there was still no answer, I looked at Ernie. He shrugged and I leaned forward and slid back the sliding, latticework door. Together, we entered the Chon family living quarters.

The *ondol* floor was covered with padded vinyl instead of a rug. Against the wall, mother-of-pearl tables, varnished chairs, cabinets. Artwork everywhere. Traditional Yi Dynasty paintings, both framed and embedded into standing silk screens.

*"Yoboseiyo,"* I said again. Still no answer.

Something was burning.

We followed the smell down a long a hallway: jasmine. More latticework sliding doors lined either side. Finally, we entered a wood-floored hall. Candles flickered, more incense burned, and a bronze Buddha held his left hand upright, thumb to forefinger, pinkie sticking straight out. Indicating, by this simple sign, that the universe is one.

A middle-aged Korean woman sat cross-legged on the floor. Her black hair hung down in greasy strings and she wore loose pantaloons and a blouse made of sackcloth, the traditional Korean garb of mourning. In front of her sat a short-legged serving table bearing a photograph of Chon Un-suk, the same picture as outside but smaller. A pair of chopsticks, a spoon, and a metal bowl of rice gruel had been carefully placed in front of the photograph, as if in offering. Breakfast for a spirit. In the guttering candlelight I could see that the woman's skin was cracked and tight. Her features looked similar to the girl in the photograph. Chon Un-suk's mother, without a doubt. Calmly, she stared at us, a look of perplexity on her face.

I knelt on the floor. So did Ernie.

"*Anyonghashimnika*," I said. The formal greeting. Are you at peace?

She stared at me a long time. Confused. Finally she said, "*Nugu?*" Who?

"*Nanun Mipalkun*," I said. I'm from 8th Army. Then I launched into my standard explanation of being an investigator, giving my name and Ernie's name and then briefly flashing my badge.

The woman seemed totally uninterested.

I told her I was sorry about her daughter's untimely death.

"Sorry?" she said in English. "You sorry?"

"Yes," I replied.

She turned her head and barked a sardonic laugh. "You Americans kill her, then you sorry?"

She barked the laugh again.

Ernie started to say something but I waved him off.

"Jill Matthewson," I said. "The woman MP at the accident. She tried to help. She tried to save your daughter."

Madame Chon gazed into the darkness of the incense-filled hall. Before answering, she grabbed the bowl of rice gruel, pushing it forward slightly, mumbling something indecipherable as if speaking to a presence sitting across the table from her. Satisfied, she turned her attention back to me.

"Yes," she said. "Jill try. She no understand. She no understand we want to bring Un-suk-i back home. We want Un-suk-i die here. So she no lose." She gazed at me with a quizzical expression, realizing that her English was faltering. "How you say?"

"So Un-suk-i wouldn't get lost."

"Yes. That right. So she no get lost."

Ernie coughed, shuffling uncomfortably, not used to kneeling on a hard wooden floor.

"Is that why you're continuing these ceremonies?" I asked. "Because Un-suk-i is lost?"

"Yes. If Jill not stop my husband, he bring Un-suk-i back here, we perform . . . how you say?"

She placed her palms together and bowed rapidly.

"You'd perform ceremonies," I said.

"Yes. Ceremony for people pretty soon going to die. And then Un-suk-i's spirit happy. Un-suk-i spirit know she at home. Know mama and daddy take care of her. No have to wander around, looking for food, looking for smell."

She cupped her right hand and waved it toward her nose, indicating the smoke from the incense.

"Un-suk-i no have to wander," she continued, "all over place looking for someone to pray for her. She come home, mom and dad help her, and she go to heaven."

Madame Chon pointed toward the roof and then dropped her hand and bowed her head. She sat silent for a long time. Then, softly, she spoke.

"I know. Jill feel bad. That's why she go *demo*."

*Demo*. The Korean word for a political demonstration.

Ernie sat up straight. Electrified.

I leaned forward and spoke English as clearly as I could. "You mean, *ajjima*, that Jill Matthewson went to the demonstrations that happened after Un-suk-i died?"

She looked up at me and her eyes widened slightly. "You don't know?"

"No. Nobody told me."

"Jill feel bad. She come here, bow to me, bow to Un-suk-i's daddy, she say she sorry many times. She no understand Korean custom. But now GI get . . . how you say?"

She pounded her fist into her palm as if banging a gavel.

"Court-martial," I said.

"Yes. GI get court-martial. Jill angry, she no can speak at court-martial. Jill angry because GI drive truck too fast but GI no get punishment. Just go back to States. Jill very angry. She go *demo*. Many Korean people there, only one American. Jill. How you say her last name?"

"Matthewson."

"Yes. Jill Matthewson."

I allowed the silence to stretch and then I asked the question I'd come to ask.

"Madame Chon, where is Jill Matthewson now?"

"Where? I don't know. Many times I look, I no find."

"*You* searched for Jill Matthewson?"

"Yes."

"But why?"

Un-suk's mother, Madame Chon, stared at me as if it were the most obvious thing in the world.

"Because I want her to help find Un-suk-i. Show Un-suk-i how to get home."

Ernie and I glanced at one another.

"You mean," I said, "pray to Un-suk and help guide her spirit home to you?"

"Yes."

"What makes you think Jill Matthewson can do that?"

Again, she stared at me and then Ernie as if we were both a little dense.

"*Mudang* say."

*Mudang*. A Korean sorceress. A female shaman.

Madame Chon continued. "*Mudang* say Jill last person Un-suk-i saw, then Jill can find Un-suk-i. Bring her home. *Mudang* dance, sing, drink *mokkolli*." Rice beer. "Help Jill find Un-suk-i. No problem. *Mudang* show Jill how to do."

It took me a moment to puzzle out exactly what she was saying. Then it became clear. The sorceress would teach Corporal Jill Matthewson how to travel to the land of the dead, commune there with spirits, find Chon Un-suk, and convince the wandering ghost of Chon Un-suk to return with her to the home of her parents.

"Sort of like TDY," Ernie whispered. The military acronym for traveling on temporary duty away from your home compound.

Excited now by the idea, Madame Chon brushed her hair back and scooted across the lacquered wooden floor until she sat cross-legged directly in front of me. Then she reached out and grabbed both my hands in her cold grip.

"You find Jill," she said. "You find, bring back here."

She wouldn't let go of my hands until I promised to bring Jill Matthewson back for an interview with the *mudang*. Then Madame Chon slid across the floor to her left, grabbed Ernie's hands, and made him promise the same thing.

After we'd both promised, she told me what she could about the demonstrations held outside the Camp Casey main gate. About how many people had participated. About the anger directed at the 2nd Infantry Division. And, more gruesomely, what the Korean National

Police had done to break up the demonstration. And what they'd done to the demonstrators they'd managed to catch. It wasn't a pretty picture. But Madame Chon recited it all as if she were revealing her family recipe for winter *kimchee*.

So far, Ernie and I'd managed to gather more information about Corporal Jill Matthewson than the 2nd ID had during their entire investigation. Why? Maybe they'd been sloppy. Or maybe they hadn't actually wanted to gather information on her disappearance. Maybe. But my theory was that they were unable—or unwilling—to gather information from Koreans. There's an arrogance that infects Americans in Korea and it often transcends their common sense. They begin to believe that only people who speak English can be trusted, that any American who believes otherwise is simply naïve. Why exactly they believe this is beyond me, but they do. Also, it's laziness. They conduct their investigations amongst Americans, usually on compound, and that's it.

I didn't have much time to figure out why 2nd ID had conducted such a miserable investigation. Something more pressing was occupying my mind: finding Jill Matthewson. And learning what, if anything, the death of Private Marvin Z. Druwood had to do with Jill's disappearance. What I could be sure of was that someone working for the Division PMO, or the Division provost marshal himself, had lied. I'd seen the evidence with my own eyes. Druwood's corpse revealed that he'd cracked his skull on cement, but there was no cement near the obstacle course tower.

And now I had another burden. Not only was it my duty to find Jill Matthewson—and report back to her mother in Terre Haute, Indiana—but I also had to worry about the spirit of Chon Un-suk wandering through eternity as a hungry ghost.

I didn't believe in hungry ghosts; Ernie didn't believe in hungry ghosts. But Chon Un-suk's mother *did* believe in hungry ghosts. And I'd promised to find Jill Matthewson so she could convince a hungry ghost to stop its wandering.

An odd promise, I'll admit. But like any promise I'd ever made, I was determined to keep it.

# 5

After leaving the Chon residence, Ernie and I wandered aimlessly through the narrow pedestrian lanes of the western edge of Tongduchon. Men on bicycles piled high with layered shelves of *dubu*—Korean tofu—jangled their bells and shouted for people to make way. Old women pushed carts laden with glimmering green cabbages through crowds of pedestrians; young women carried infants strapped to their backs; toddlers wearing heavy sweaters but no pants gazed up at us and peed innocently by the edge of the road.

After a few minutes, Ernie and I reached a twenty-foot-wide cement bridge that stretched across the East Bean River. A narrow trickle of water ran below down the center of a broad, muddy riverbed. The backs of homes and apartment buildings lined either bank of the Tongdu River: kimchee jars on balconies; laundry hanging from wire lines fluttering in the morning breeze; an occasional housewife leaning out a window to toss the contents of a porcelain pee pot onto the muddy banks below. A few dozen yards beyond the bridge, back in the city proper, a large wooden archway announced the entrance to *TONGDUCHON SICHANG*. The East Bean River City Market.

Ernie and I entered. A canvas roof held in place by twenty-foot-high bamboo poles sheltered acres of produce stands. Behind the piled vegetables, women in white bandannas waved their arms and shouted at customers. Housewives with plastic baskets hooked over their elbows browsed along the lanes, seemingly ignoring the chanting vendors. Warm air reeking of green onions and garlic and Napa cabbage freshly plucked from verdant earth suffused the entire market.

Ernie breathed deeply and a broad grin spread across his face. We both felt it. The tactile caress of human life, unsullied by advertising and corporate greed. This is what our lives had once been on this planet. What they should be now. Everywhere.

We wound our way past the produce until we reached walls of shimmering glass tanks holding wriggling mackerel, eels, and octopi. Beyond the tanks a cloud of dust advertised the poultry, flapping smelly wings and cackling, within handmade wooden crates. Finally, like an oasis of calm, the dry goods. Hand-embroidered silk comforters, leather gloves, umbrellas, plump cotton-covered cushions, and then the porcelain: china dolls; effigies of Kumbokju, the chubby god of abundance; pee pots; tea cups with no handles; and tiny drinking glasses made for jolting back shots of *soju*, the fierce Korean rice liquor.

At last, our search was rewarded. We found what we were looking for. Noodle stands. Billowing steam announced their environs and Ernie and I found a tall, round, rickety table made of splintered wood and shouted our order to an elderly proprietress: *"Ramyon, tugei"*. Spicy noodles, two.

The other customers were all Koreans and they studiously ignored the two *Miguks* in their midst. They inhaled noodles or chatted with their neighbors in rapid sentences or gazed intently at books, studying for the exam that always seemed to be looming on the Confucian horizon.

A pig-tailed teenage girl with a solid physique and a blank expression brought us chopsticks and spoons and two cups of barley tea. She must've been about the same age that Chon Un-suk would've been except her parents weren't rich. Not fortunate enough to attend middle school, she was forced to work. Ernie started to say something to her—probably something flirtatious—but then thought better of it. What was the point? He wasn't going to be able to change her fate. Ever. As the quiet girl plodded away I thought she probably had a rough life ahead of her. But at least, unlike Chon Un-suk, she had life. Breath. Feeling.

When the noodles came, Ernie lifted a clump with his chopsticks and slurped them into his mouth. Still chewing, he started to talk.

"So far," he said, "we don't know shit."

"That's not true," I replied. "We're making progress."

Ernie snorted. "Yeah. Like a snail. What we gotta do is beat the crap out of somebody."

"Anybody in particular?"

Ernie shrugged. *"Kuen-chana."* It doesn't matter.

"Why should we beat somebody up?" I asked. "To gather information? Or just for the hell of it?"

"For both. I wouldn't want to beat somebody up *just* for the hell of it."

Instead of continuing down this road, I recapped what we knew so far, starting with motive.

According to PFC Anne Korvachek, Jill Matthewson's roommate, Jill had been fed up with the stereo sexual harassment that women at the 2nd Division live with day in and day out, hour by hour. It came from men of low rank and men of high rank. All-pervasive. Complaining about it was about as useful as complaining about the weather. Still, when you don't like the weather in the place you live, you move.

That's what Jill Matthewson had done.

But there were other motives. Her friend, the Korean stripper Kim Yong-ai, owed a ton of money. To pay it off she and/or Jill had raised the Korean *won* equivalent of two thousand dollars. Exactly how they'd done that, we didn't know. What could either one of them do to earn that kind of money? Crime, of course, came to mind. Had Jill ripped somebody off—or assisted in the ripping-off—and then fled Tongduchon?

Maybe.

The next possible motive was her disgust with the court-martial of the two GIs who'd run down Chon Un-suk. The fact that they'd been tried by American military judges—and not a Korean judge—had enraged the Korean public. But what had enraged Jill most was that, as the first MP on the scene, she'd never been called as a witness and that the two perps had been let off so easily.

Ernie and I resolved to check into the trial more thoroughly.

The final motive was that, according to Madame Chon, Jill had actively participated in the demonstrations held outside the main gate of Camp Casey. That, in itself, was a violation of 8th Army regulations and—I wasn't sure—might even be a court-martial offense. Had Corporal Jill Matthewson's politics become so radicalized that she'd decided she'd had enough of the U.S. Army?

By the time I laid all this out for Ernie, he'd finished his noodles, drank down the remaining broth directly from the bowl, and ordered another cup of barley tea from the poker-faced teenage waitress.

"So we have a lot of possible motives for going AWOL," Ernie said. "All of them might be true; none of them might be true. We don't know. But what we do know is that if Jill Matthewson is still alive, somebody had to facilitate her escape."

I whistled softly.

"What?" Ernie asked.

"'Facilitate?'"

Ernie grabbed his crotch. "Here. Facilitate *this*."

"Okay. I'm just impressed by your vocabulary. Go ahead."

"Where was I?" Ernie gulped down the last of his barley tea and slammed the bottom of the cup on the rickety wooden table. "Oh yeah. So if somebody *facilitated* Corporal Matthewson's unofficial resignation from the Second Infantry Division, they would have had to help her find a place to stay, a source of income, and maybe even a way to avoid the scrutiny of the Korean National Police."

"That's a lot to provide," I said. "A tall, good-looking, Caucasian woman in Korea would be sort of conspicuous."

"'Conspicuous?'"

"Okay, Ernie. Can it. So what you're saying is instead of fretting about motives, what we should be working on is who helped her leave, who's providing her income, who is offering her a safe place to hide."

"By Jove, I think he's got it."

I finished the last of my noodles and the waitress came by and poured us both more barley tea from a large brass urn.

"If I were an American female MP," I said, "and I wanted to leave the Division, and I knew I needed Korean help, who would I talk to?"

"The people you'd *been* talking to," Ernie replied. "Your friends."

"In this case, the stripper Kim Yong-ai. But she didn't have much in the way of money."

"No," Ernie said, "but she knew how to make it."

I looked up at Ernie. "You think Jill could be working the Korean nightclub scene?"

"Or something like it," Ernie said. "An American chick as good-looking as her could make a fortune from Korean businessmen. We need to talk to that Kimchee Entertainment guy again."

"Pak Tong-i," I said.

"Right. Maybe he was lying to us. Maybe he knew where they were going. But even if he didn't lie, he has contacts in the entertainment world. He can provide leads."

Pulling out wrinkled Korean *won* notes, I paid the old woman behind the stand for our noodles. Thinking I wasn't looking, Ernie pulled a couple of dollars worth of MPC, military payment certificates, out of his pocket and palmed them to the young, poker-faced girl who'd waited on us.

I'm not sure but I think she cracked a smile.


The front door to Kimchee Entertainment was padlocked from the outside. Ernie pounded on the door anyway just to make sure, but there was no answer.

"Show-business people don't keep regular hours," I said. "We'll try back later."

We returned to the spot where we'd left the jeep. Ernie unlocked the chain wrapped around the steering wheel, fired up the engine, and drove us back to Camp Casey. After a thorough identification check at the main gate—and the usual inspection of the back of the vehicle for contraband—we were allowed to pass. Immediately after we rolled away, the MP headed back to the guard shack and switched on his two-way radio.

"They're keeping tabs on us," Ernie said.

"Night and day," I replied.

We cruised through Camp Casey. GIs everywhere. Some marching in military formation, some walking together in small groups. Tanks and self-propelled guns and two-and-a-half-ton trucks and resupply vehicles of all descriptions rumbled past us, everyone moving on compound at a safe, sane fifteen miles per hour. MP jeeps lurked behind hedges, making sure everyone kept within the posted speed limit.

"No little girls are going to be run over here," Ernie said.

"Yeah," I agreed. "Except there are no little girls here."

The 2nd Infantry Division JAG Office was located deep inside the environs of Camp Casey, facing the enormous quadrangle of the Division parade ground. On the opposite side of the field, the three flags of the United States, the Republic of Korea, and the United Nations loomed above the Division Headquarters building. A lifer NCO had once advised me, "Keep a low profile and stay away from the flagpole." Ernie and I weren't following either dictum. Not because we wanted to, but because we had no choice.

Second ID JAG was the usual cluster of single-story Quonset huts painted puke green. Instead of a huge statue of an MP outside, they sported a simple whitewashed wooden sign with black stenciling: OFFICE OF THE 2ND INFANTRY DIVISION JUDGE ADVOCATE GENERAL.

Ernie and I walked inside. Our shoes sunk into plush carpet. Behind a low mahogany counter, an attractive Korean secretary smiled up at us.

"Can I help you?" she asked, in expertly pronounced English.

We showed our badges and I explained that I wanted to talk to the legal officer who had worked on the recent case involving the death of Chon Un-suk. The young woman's smile flickered. It wasn't much, just a cloud fleeing across the sky on a sunny day, but it told me much. Koreans knew about the case. All Koreans.

Motioning with her open palm, she said, "Please have a seat."

Then she hustled off into the quiet back corridors of the connected Quonset huts.

Ernie and I sat on cushiony leather. A painting hung from the wall. Traditional Yi Dynasty silk screen: Siberian tiger rampant. But more than rampant. Somehow the artist managed to make the tiger's eyes look not only human, but crazed.

"Nice digs," Ernie said.

"You should've gone to college," I told him, "then law school. You wouldn't have to be traipsing around the ville all day."

Ernie smiled. "I'd have a good-looking secretary like that one."

"Yeah."

"And an air-conditioned office, heated in the winter, cooled in the summer."

"Of course."

Ernie thought about it. Finally, he seemed to come to a decision. "Nah. Wouldn't work."

"Why not?"

"I'd get my secretary pregnant and punch the presiding judge on the Chon Un-suk court-martial right in the nose."

"You probably would." I shook my head. "All that schooling gone to waste."

"Exactly."

A few minutes later the secretary returned and beckoned for us to follow. She ushered us down the long corridor, past well-appointed offices with military officers behind teak desks and their Korean civilian assistants in dark suits and ties. We turned right and then left and at the end of the hallway, we were ushered into the office of Lieutenant Colonel Wilbur M. Proffert. The secretary hurried out of the office as Ernie and I saluted the man.

His face was narrow and his glasses were polished so brightly that they shone like cheap jewelry. After chewing us out for a while about arriving without an appointment, Colonel Proffert checked our identification thoroughly and jotted down each of our names and badge numbers. He cleaned his glasses and told us to be seated. Then he shoved across his desk a copy of the trial transcript of the court-martial involving the death of Chon Un-suk. He told us that beyond what was included there, the 2nd Infantry JAG Office had no further comment.

Ernie thumbed through the transcript, snorted, and handed it to me. "Were they speeding, sir?" he asked.

"What?"

"The two GIs driving the deuce-and-a-half. Were they exceeding the speed limit just prior to plowing into Chon Un-suk?"

Colonel Proffert rose from behind his desk and placed his hands on narrow hips. He was a jogger, that was for sure. Officers have to stay thin in today's army if they expect to be competitive for promotion. Especially staff officers.

He wagged his forefinger at Ernie's nose.

"Whether those two young men were speeding or not," Colonel Proffert said, "has no bearing on this case."

It was my turn to be surprised. "No bearing?"

"None," Colonel Proffert repeated. "Driving conditions in Korea are atrocious. The roads are narrow, jammed with pedestrians, choked with bicycles and pushcarts and Korean drivers who don't know even the rudiments of safe motoring. On top of that the weather is treacherous, there's little de-icing equipment or anything as fancy as snow plows and despite all this we expect young soldiers to go out in the middle of night, in the middle of howling storms, and perform their duty and drive where and when their military missions require them to. Under these stresses, can we punish them for driving ten or fifteen miles over the speed limit?"

He waited for our answer. I gave him one.

"When there's thirty school girls standing on the side of the road, yes."

He shook his head vehemently.

"You're missing the big picture." Dramatically, he pointed toward the north. "We have seven hundred thousand bloodthirsty communist soldiers less than twenty miles north of here. Every one of them just waiting for a chance to push south past the Second United States Infantry Division and invade Korea. What do you think would happen to those middle-school girls then? Rape. Pillage. Murder. That's the big picture we're looking at, and we can't have GIs driving out into ungodly dangerous road conditions while at the same time having to look back over their shoulders, wondering if Division JAG is going to nail them for violating some petty traffic regulations. We can't do it. Our job, first and foremost, is to protect freedom here in Korea." He wagged his forefinger once again, more forcefully this time. "And don't you ever forget it."

I tossed the trial transcript onto his desk.

"Thanks for your time, sir."

I grabbed Ernie by the elbow but he wouldn't budge. He kept staring at Colonel Proffert.

"So the facts of the case don't matter?" Ernie asked.

I tugged on his arm. Ernie shrugged me off.

"I didn't say that," Proffert answered mildly.

"The hell you didn't. That's exactly what you said."

Colonel Proffert's face started to turn red. "Don't you come in here and lecture me, young man. Eighth Army CID or not."

"No point in lecturing you," Ernie replied. "Because you *know* what you did."

Colonel Proffert's voice lowered. "And what exactly," he said, "was that?"

"You let two GIs get away with murder."

Colonel Proffert sputtered but before he could reply, Ernie plowed on.

"And what's more important, you sent a message to every GI in Division that no matter how recklessly they drive, no matter who they kill or maim, the Division will protect them from having to take responsibility for their actions."

"*Out!*" Colonel Proffert roared. "Get out of my office!"

I practically lifted Ernie off of his feet and dragged him out of the office and down the hallway. JAG officers in their neatly pressed fatigues were standing in front of their cubicles now, watching Ernie and me struggle down the corridor, listening to Colonel Proffert cursing behind us.

As she held the front door open for us, the cute Korean secretary stared at the floor. Very modest. Very Confucian. I dragged a struggling Ernie Bascom out of the JAG Office and onto the gravel-covered parking lot. We stood by the jeep until Ernie's breathing became regular once more.

This time I took the wheel. As we drove away, Ernie sat in the back seat of the jeep, arms crossed, fuming.

* * *

Late that afternoon, when Ernie pounded on the door to Kimchee Entertainment, we knew it was futile because the hasp was still padlocked from the outside. He did it out of frustration and to attract attention. A ploy that worked. Within seconds another resident of the two-story brick building emerged from her lair and began sweeping the blacktop in front of the building with a short-handled broom.

I greeted her in Korean and asked her if she knew where Mr. Pak Tong-i, the owner of Kimchee Entertainment, had gone.

"*Moolah*," she told me. I don't know. "*Haru cheingil anwasso*." He hasn't been in all day.

I asked her if he did this often and she told me that he's in show business and therefore very unreliable and she never knows when he's going to show up and start making noise. I asked her what kind of noise and she told me that he often plays the radio too loud or has some musician banging away on drums or other foreign instruments. When she couldn't give us his home phone number or his address, we thanked her and went on our way.

About a half block down the road, Ernie asked me, "Did you see him?"

"See who?"

"The chubby guy. Korean. Bald head. He bought a newspaper at the stand next door and stood around pretending to read all through your conversation."

"He wasn't Pak Tong-i, was he?"

"No. Too husky for that little twerp. Just a big guy in pajamas."

Koreans, especially middle-aged men, think nothing of parading around their neighborhoods in pajama bottoms and slippers.

"What makes you think he was paying attention to us?"

"Maybe he wasn't. I just wondered if you noticed."

"I didn't. Where did he go?"

"Back to the alleyway on the far side of Kimchee Entertainment."

"Probably just a local resident."

"Probably."

The purple Korean night started its slow descent upon the city of Tongduchon. Bulbs burst into brightness; neon flickered to life. Clumps of uniformed students pushed past us, toting backpacks bursting with books. Farmers rolled empty carts back toward the countryside. Without really planning to, Ernie and I wandered closer to the bar district.

"We've talked to just about everyone who knew Jill Matthewson," Ernie said. "So now it's time to stop talking and *do* something."

I thought about that for a minute. A girl in a dirt-floored *mokkolli* house, an establishment that sells warm rice beer to cab drivers and construction workers, gazed out at us in mute awe. Despite all the American movies and television programs they see, most Koreans still think of Americans as being odd. Almost nonhuman. In all her life, she'd probably never spoken to a foreigner. For a moment, I was tempted to go in and talk to her. Let her know that although we looked strange, Ernie and I were still human. Sort of.

And then I thought of Corporal Jill Matthewson on her first night of ville patrol. How strange the ville must've seemed. How awful. Wailing rock music, drunken GIs, desperate business girls, persistent old farm women selling packages of warm chestnuts to overly made-up cocktail waitresses. She wasn't in Terre Haute anymore. But she must've seen humanity too. People who were fundamentally the same as her. That's why she'd become friends—or at least we thought she'd become friends—with the stripper, Kim Yong-ai. That's why, together, they'd disappeared.

But had she become friends with anyone else?

That's when it hit me. Brandy. The bartender in the Black Cat Club. Of course. There must be more she knew, more facts that we could pull out of that sharp brain beneath that bouffant Afro hairdo.

I told Ernie. He liked it. Any nightclub in a storm. Besides we had an entire evening to kill until the midnight to four a.m. curfew, which was when I wanted to try something else I'd been planning.

Had I proposed the plan to Ernie yet? No need. It was crazy and bold and reckless, and that's why I had no doubt he'd love it.


Brandy wasn't in. We checked with the old mama-san behind the bar and she said Brandy wasn't feeling well. I asked for her address but the woman claimed she didn't know it. How then, did she know that Brandy was sick? A boy arrived with a note, she claimed. I pressed but the old woman wasn't budging. Can't say that I blamed her. In a joint like the Black Cat Club a woman's privacy is important. A drunken GI would be likely to barge in on her at any hour of the night or day if they gave out her address to anyone who asked.

I considered flashing my badge and threatening the old woman with calling in the Korean National Police if she didn't cooperate. But that wouldn't ingratiate me to Brandy and it was her goodwill and cooperation that I needed. Besides, a few of the soul brothers were beginning to mumble amongst themselves, upset that a couple of "T-shirts" were monopolizing the women at the bar.

Ernie grinned at them and flashed the thumbs-up sign. He could either defuse a situation with his charm or punch somebody and end up causing a riot, depending upon his mood. Rather than wait for that decision, I thanked the old woman and asked her to please tell Brandy that we'd been in.

She agreed and Ernie and I strolled out of the Black Cat Club.

Outside, I told Ernie what I wanted to do tonight. Ernie not only agreed but he laughed and rubbed his hands in glee. We decided to bypass the neon lights of TDC and return to Camp Casey. There were three reasons. One, we wanted to have some *Miguk* chow: meat and potatoes. Two, we needed to stay relatively sober. And three, we wanted to change out of these suits and ties and into clothing more appropriate for the task I had in mind.

Ernie kept running ideas and scenarios by me, thrilled to have something to do other than just walk around interviewing people. His enjoyment was further enhanced by the fact that what we planned to do tonight after the midnight curfew was, and still is, completely illegal.

On Camp Casey, we stopped at the Gateway Club, less than a hundred yards in from the main gate, eighty yards past the Provost Marshal's Office and the twenty-foot-tall statue of the MP. The Gateway was theoretically an all-ranks club but mostly young enlisted men used it. The officers had restaurant/bar establishments of their own, as did the Senior NCOs. Ernie and I sat at the bar, sipping on beers, studying the Gateway Club menu in the dim glow of an overhead blue light. Behind us, a Korean go-go girl gyrated wildly on a raised stage. GIs cheered. Rock music blared from a jukebox. Both Ernie and I felt completely at home.

The plastic-coated menu bore the Indianhead 2nd Division patch on the front. The numbered list inside featured the usual adventurous fare one found in military dining facilities: hamburgers, cheeseburgers, fries, sirloin steak, fried chicken, and a couple of exotic foreign dishes like onion rings and coleslaw.

The dining room was operating, the cocktail lounge was operating, but the main ballroom of the Gateway Club was still closed. Later this evening a rock band would start and the ballroom would be packed with young GIs—and the twenty to thirty business girls whom the club manager was authorized to escort on post. Right now, the big room was dark and empty except for one man sitting alone at a table on the far edge, hunched over a plate of food. I recognized him. Sergeant First Class Otis, who'd greeted us upon our arrival in 2nd Division and the NCO who'd been leading the physical training formation this morning, the formation that had been so anxious to express their feelings—in a knuckle sandwich kind of way—toward Ernie and me.

I told Ernie I'd be back, rose from my barstool, and sauntered toward Sergeant First Class Otis.

"I don't want no trouble," was the first thing he said to me when he looked up. He was eating fried chicken with rice and gravy. A glass of iced tea stood next to his plate.

"No trouble." I pulled a chair out from the table and sat down across from him. "Thanks for saving our butts during the run this morning."

He shook his head and shoveled a spoonful of rice into his mouth. "I ain't your friend," he said.

I let that sit for a while. Then I said, "So why'd you stop your MPs from beating the crap out of us?"

"Nothing to do with you," he said. "When I'm in charge of a formation, it don't turn into a mob."

I appreciated that. Whatever those MPs did, right or wrong,

would reflect on his ability to lead. His ability to control men in formation. NCOs, most of them, take their leadership role seriously. Obviously, Sergeant Otis did.

"Weatherwax had it coming," I said. Ernie had punched him for following us through the ville.

Otis shrugged. "You say."

A middle-aged Korean waitress approached and poured more iced tea into Otis's glass from a plastic pitcher. He knew her, they seemed relaxed with one another, and Otis probably tipped well to convince her to serve him dinner some twenty yards from the boisterous young GIs in the well-lit dining room. I figured Otis was working the desk tonight. That's why he was wearing a freshly pressed set of fatigues and why he was having chow at the Gateway Club, the eating establishment nearest to the Provost Marshal's Office. The waitress gazed at me quizzically, feeling the tension between me and Otis. When she asked if I wanted anything I told her no. She left. I waited for her footsteps to fade.

"You know more than you're telling me," I said.

Otis didn't even look up from his plate. "Of course I know more than I'm telling you. What the hell you think?"

"Why aren't you telling me?"

"First, you didn't ask. Second, you a rear echelon motherfucker just up here to make Division look bad."

I paused again, letting the silence grow. It wasn't *silence* exactly. We could still hear the rock music from the cocktail lounge and the clang and buzz of people talking and eating and laughing in the dining room. But for Camp Casey, a place where men and heavy equipment were always on the go, it came as close to silence as we were going to get.

"Druwood," I said. "You know what they're saying about him isn't right."

Otis picked up a drumstick and chomped into it, chewing resolutely.

"Private Druwood didn't die out at the obstacle course," I continued. "Crumbled cement was still lodged in his skull. I saw it. No way he could've jumped from that tower. No cement around there. Somebody dumped him at the obstacle course. Said he jumped from the tower. Said it was an accident."

Otis stopped chewing.

"He was an MP," I continued. "White. Young. Not black and old and wise like you. But he was your responsibility, Sergeant Otis. Your soldier. You were supposed to look out for him."

Otis swallowed the last of the chicken, as if it were something dryer than sand. He stared at his plate, at the half-eaten remains of the bird and the gravy smeared through glutinous Korean rice. Slowly, he looked up at me.

"He wasn't in my platoon."

"Doesn't matter," I said.

Otis stared so steadily that for a minute I thought he was going to come across the table at me. I wouldn't use my pistol, I knew that, but I might pick up a chair to hold him off. Although I was taller, and probably heavier, he was a strong man, the thick muscles of his shoulders bulging through the material of his green fatigues. I held his gaze. If we had to fight, I'd fight.

Instead, his lips started to move.

"Bufford," he said. It was almost a rasp, as if his vocal chords had suddenly been stricken by laryngitis.

"What?"

"Bufford," he repeated. "Maybe he drove Druwood on compound, maybe he didn't. But he was behind it. Arranged it so it would look like a training accident."

"Druwood was killed off base?" I asked.

"Maybe not killed. Maybe he killed himself."

"But you're not sure?"

"No. But the excuse to bring him on base was that the Division suicide rate is too high. Had to make it look like an accident."

"Bufford didn't want Division to look bad."

"Not him," Otis said. "Somebody higher."

"How high?"

"I don't know. I don't want to know."

"How do you know all this?"

"I listen," he said. "And I think."

"So they don't confide in you?"

"I don't know which 'they' you're talking about but no, they don't."

"Where was Druwood killed?"

"You don't know that he was killed."

"Okay. Where was his body found?"

"In the ville, that's what I heard. Where the black-market hon-chos operate. An off-limits area."

"Which one?" In Seoul there are numerous areas designated as off-limits to United States Forces personnel. Sometimes they're placed off-limits for health reasons because of poor sanitation or disease. Sometimes because there'd been altercations between GIs and the local populace and 8th Army didn't want a repeat. I assumed the same was true in Tongduchon, that there were many off limits areas. I was wrong.

"There's only one off limits area," Sergeant Otis said. "The Turkey Farm."

I'd heard of it. Almost as if it were a footnote in history. The Turkey Farm was an old brothel district that during and after the Korean War had been infamous. Infamous for the number of desperate business girls the area housed, for the amount of venereal disease that was spread, and for something neither the U.S. military nor the Korean government liked to talk about: child prostitution.

"Where is it?" I asked.

"There's a map at the PMO. In the MP briefing room. Every nightclub and bar and chophouse is listed."

"How do you know that it was Bufford who had Private Druwood's body driven back on post?"

"I don't. Not for sure. But he does everything else."

"Everything else? Like what?"

A group of MPs stormed into the Gateway Club. A couple of them glanced our way.

"You ruined my dinner," Otis told me. "It's time for you to leave."

I knew he meant it. Still, I had one more question for him. "Matthewson. Where is she?"

"Don't know."

"Why'd she leave?"

"You would too if you had to put up with the shit she put up with."

"Like what?"

"What do you think?"

I waited, my arms crossed, knowing that he was becoming increasingly uncomfortable with an 8th Army CID agent sitting across from him at his table. He sipped on his iced tea and then set the glass down, hard.

"She was white pussy," he told me. "Everybody was after her, from the top honchos to the bottom maggot E-1 privates. And then she gets involved in that traffic case, the one where the middle school girl was run over."

"Chon Un-suk."

"Yeah. That one. Matthewson couldn't handle the pressure. She left."

"What pressure?"

Otis shrugged. "The usual pressure."

"The pressure not to make Division look bad."

He shrugged again.

"You know this for a fact?" I asked.

"I don't know *nothing* for a fact. You want testimony under oath, you ain't getting it from me."

"Why not?"

Sergeant First Class Otis lay down his fork and stared at me as if I were the biggest idiot in the world.

"For one thing," he said, "because I finish my twenty in less than two years. And for another, I've slept out in the snow and the rain on field maneuvers and put up with white officers and drunken GIs and their slut girlfriends for so many years that I'm not going to jeopardize my retirement check just so Eighth Army can feel good about itself for five minutes. An Eighth Army that been ignoring Division for all the three tours I spent up here. An Eighth Army that let the Division commander run his area of operations as if he were the king of the world and all the rest of us be slaves, and nobody get out of line because if they do they be subject to humiliation and the loss of everything they been working for."

Otis's right hand clutched his butter knife; his knuckles were pale brown, heading to white. Also, his language was losing its precise military cadence, returning to the rhythms of the streets.

"Now get the hell outta here," he told me. "Build your own case and leave me the hell alone."

I figured that was enough. For the moment. If Ernie and I ever broke this case wide open—if it turned out as bad as I was afraid it might—we'd corner Otis, read him his rights, and force him to make a formal statement under oath. But I wasn't ready for that yet.

I rose to my feet, snapped Sergeant First Class Otis a two-fingered salute, and left.

The more Ernie and I talked about it, the angrier we became.

Sure, we knew Division PMO was dragging their feet. We'd been expecting that since we came up here. But Mr. Fred Bufford—with the probable collusion of his boss, Lieutenant Colonel Stanley Alcott—had withheld information that bordered on being a criminal obstruction of justice. To wit, the involvement of Corporal Jill Matthewson in the case of the accidental death of Chon Un-suk and the true nature of the facts concerning the death of Private Marvin Druwood.

When we walked through PMO's reception area, the swing-shift desk sergeant looked surprised. We veered to the right, before he could say anything, and entered the MP briefing room. Behind us a phone jingled and a dial turned. The MP briefing room was a small auditorium with a narrow stage in front. Overhead lights shone down on rows of metal chairs, providing dim light. The map Sergeant Otis had told me about hung from the back wall, next to posters warning of the danger of venereal disease. An overhead bulb shone directly on the map. Bright colors formed an intricate mosaic that seemed to pulsate.

It was an ingenious design. Right away, just by the style, I guessed that a Korean graphic artist had created it. It looked Asian. That is, not precisely realistic, not precisely to scale. Not scientific. Everything about it was slightly off kilter. But in many ways it conveyed the confusion and teeming life of Tongduchon better than any machine-manufactured topographical map could.

The background was a polished cherrywood panel of about four feet by four feet, hanging from thick brass hooks. Etched onto the right side of the panel was the main gate of Camp Casey fronted by the north-south running Main Supply Route. On the left was the

East Bean River with various of the vehicle and pedestrian bridges depicted, some of which Ernie and I had already walked over. Beyond that, farmland. In the center, between the main gate of Camp Casey and the sinuous flow of the East Bean River, stood the bar district of Tongduchon.

The streets were drawn with black lines while the buildings of Tongduchon were moveable, held by thumbtacks, and depicted by various colored symbols. Gold stars for nightclubs, red hearts for brothels, circular targets for suspected black-market operations. The stores, factories, living establishments, and markets were just various covered rectangles with Chinese symbols painted onto them. The MPs couldn't understand those symbols of course, but they did understand where the bars and the brothels and the black-market operations were. That's where the GIs hung out and that's all the MPs really needed to know. Ernie stepped back to better study the huge mosaic.

"It's breathing," he said.

"I'll say."

The teeming jumble of life in Tongduchon was somehow conveyed in the glowing map. We pointed out details to one another: the Tongduchon City Market; the street where Pak Tong-i's office could be found; the location of the Chon family residence; the bar district; the Black Cat Club; the Silver Dragon Nightclub; the *yoguan* where we'd spent the night with Ok-hi and Jeannie. And finally, surrounded by red dashes, the off-limits area known as the Turkey Farm.

"It's right in the middle of the ville," Ernie said.

He was right. Although we hadn't seen it in all our sojourns through TDC, the Turkey Farm sat behind the main row of bars, the row that held the Oasis Club and the Montana Club and the Silver Dragon Club—but while we walked those streets we hadn't even realized it was there. Why? Because you couldn't see it from the main drag and who would walk down those dark alleys to look? To the east of the Turkey Farm sat the Black Cat Club. Then I spotted something that surprised me. According to the map, right in the center of the off-limits area, the artist had deftly inserted a black inverted swastika. I pointed it out to Ernie.

"What the hell's that?" Ernie asked. "A Nazi meeting hall?"

"No. That's not a swastika but something more ancient. The symbol for a Buddhist temple."

"A Buddhist temple in the center of the Turkey Farm?"

"Yeah. Go figure."

Ernie searched the legend below the map. "That symbol's not here."

"That's why the artist must be Korean. There are a few other symbols on this map that American MPs probably wouldn't recognize. Look here."

I pointed at the symbol for *myo*, a Confucian shrine. I'd remembered it from my Korean language class because it looked like two capital Ls turned upside down with their bases pointed outwards. Then, about two-thirds of the way up the spines of the Ls, a horizontal line slashed across them. The symbol looked to me like one of those tall horsehair hats Chinese priests wear when conducting Confucian ceremonies. And that's why I could remember it.

Ernie stared at me quizzically. "A Confucian shrine," he said, "in the center of the Turkey Farm? Not too far from a Buddhist temple?"

"Apparently," I told him, "there's more to this Turkey Farm place than GIs have been saying."

The double door of the briefing room swung open with a crash.

"Freeze!" someone shouted.

Tall, gawky Warrant Officer One Fred Bufford stood in the doorway, his knees flexed, both arms held straight out in front of his body. Clasped firmly in his white-knuckled fists, he held an army-issue .45 automatic pistol. The dark pit of the barrel was pointing right at us.

Ernie started to laugh.

# 6

Warrant Office One Fred Bufford's forearms quivered with tension. The barrel of the .45 bounced up and down and side to side, variously aimed at Ernie and then me. Ernie kept laughing and I wished he'd shut up.

"Hands on your heads," Bufford shouted.

I put my hands on my head.

Ernie placed his hands on his hips and, finally, stopped laughing.

"Who do you think you're going to shoot with that thing, Bufford?" Ernie asked. "What's our crime? Entering the Provost Marshal's Office without a permit? Studying a map of Tongduchon without proper authorization?" Ernie barked another laugh.

"No," Bufford shouted. "Assaulting a fellow MP out in the ville, for no apparent reason."

Ernie groaned in disgust. "I bopped Weatherwax in the nose," Ernie told him, "for a damn good reason. You ordered him to follow us. To keep tabs on us. To find out what we were doing." Ernie pointed his finger at Bufford's nose and took a step closer. "And that's interfering with an official investigation."

I dropped my hands from the top of my head and grabbed Ernie's elbow, keeping him from walking into that loaded .45.

"You don't know that," Bufford said.

"I don't know that you sent him," Ernie said, his voice taking on a mocking tone. "And maybe Weatherwax likes to spend his spare time following CID agents around because it makes for interesting entries in his diary. Give me a break, Bufford. You're so damn transparent. Go ahead. Shoot! Do with our bodies the same thing you did with Private Druwood's body. Pretend we jumped off the obstacle course tower and killed ourselves."

By now, a few MPs had gathered in the reception area. They were elbowing one another, pointing, mumbling amongst themselves. Bufford lowered his gun and looked back at them and shouted at them to be at ease.

That's all Ernie needed.

Before I could tighten my grip, he launched himself across the wood-slat floor at Warrant Officer Fred Bufford. Bufford heard the footsteps pounding, turned, and started to raise the .45 but Ernie leaped at him. The two men crashed backward into the crowd of MPs.

All hell broke loose. Men were shouting and cursing and a few of them tried to pull Ernie off Bufford but failed. Ernie continued to pound away at him unmercifully. One of the MPs, thankfully, had the presence of mind to grab Bufford's .45. Kneeling on Bufford's skinny forearm, he yanked the weapon out of Bufford's grip. I ran forward, wrapped my arms around Ernie's waist, and pulled with all my might. For a moment, Ernie held onto Bufford's neck but then he let go and we tumbled backward onto our butts. Just as I was rising to my feet, someone shouted "Attention!"

Suddenly, all the MPs stood ramrod straight, their arms held tightly at their sides. Except for Fred Bufford who still lay on the floor, clutching his throat, trying to breathe. Apparently, Ernie's headbutt had knocked the air out of him. I helped Ernie up. Colonel Stanley X. Alcott, in a civilian coat and open-collared shirt, strode into our midst.

"What the hell? Bufford, are you okay?"

Without being told, two MPs knelt and helped Fred Bufford sit upright. One of them yanked upwards on Bufford's armpits to give his lungs maximum inhaling capacity. After a few seconds, he started to breath normally. He pointed at Ernie.

"He came at me," he told Colonel Alcott.

"After your man here," I said, pointing at Bufford, "pulled his .45. For nothing more than standing inside the briefing room and reading this map."

Alcott glanced back at Bufford.

"No, sir. I was arresting him for the assault on Staff Sergeant Weatherwax."

Alcott glanced back at me. "That wasn't good."

"Weatherwax was following us," I said. "Interfering with an official investigation. He had it coming."

"That's not what I heard,"" Alcott said. "I heard you two were drinking beer and chasing women."

So Weatherwax *had*, in fact, been reporting his observations up the chain of command.

"It doesn't matter what we were doing," I replied. "Weatherwax shouldn't have been following us. Besides, your man here," I pointed at the still-seated Bufford, "failed to put in his serious incident report that Corporal Jill Matthewson had been involved in the Chon Un-suk traffic fatality."

"That has nothing to do with her disappearance!" Bufford shouted.

"How the hell do you know that?" Ernie roared out the question so loudly that everyone, including the armed MPs, took a half a step backwards. "You been cherry-picking information ever since you arrived in Division, Bufford. Whatever, in your opinion, might have a chance of making the Division look bad, you exclude from your reports. Don't you understand? That's dangerous! Lives can be lost. For all we know Corporal Matthewson has been kidnapped and is being raped and tortured as we speak. And you want to dick around and tell me that something as big as the Chon Un-suk death has nothing whatever to do with her disappearance? Maybe some enraged Korean decided to take revenge for Chon Un-suk's death and right now Jill Matthewson is paying the price."

That was a long speech coming from Ernie and it was a measure of how much Division had pissed him off. I don't think Ernie really believed that Jill Mathewson had been kidnapped, but it was a possibility and every possibility had to be taken into consideration. A few of the MPs started to mumble. Ernie was right about the danger of excluding information and they knew it.

"And now," Ernie continued, "you pull a gun on me just because me and my partner are in here doing our jobs." Ernie took a step closer to Bufford. "Well, I'll tell you something, Mr. Fred Bufford. Me and my partner are going to do our jobs and I don't give a shit if you or the provost marshal or the entire goddam Division tries to stop us. Whether you like it or not, Corporal Jill Matthewson was a soldier and an MP and we're going to find her. We all have to stick together, or we'll all go down together because there's a lot of assholes out there and if we don't stop them nobody else will!"

The MPs were mumbling louder now, in total agreement with my partner, Ernie Bascom.

Colonel Alcott must've known that he was losing control of the situation so he gestured for silence. As he did so, Bufford piped up.

"They were tired," Bufford said.

"Who was tired, Bufford?" Ernie asked.

"Privates Elliot and Korman. They were ferrying cargo back from the Western Corridor. They'd been driving in the dark and under poor road conditions. When they approached those girls on the side of the road, they weren't expecting such a big crowd. The truck slid, one of the girls was killed. It was an accident."

Most of the MPs murmured in assent.

This was news to me. I'd assumed that at seven thirty in the morning, the truck had been *leaving* Camp Casey. Instead, they'd been returning to Camp Casey, with cargo no less. What sort of cargo would you pick up in the middle of the night? I needed to confirm what I'd just heard.

"The two drivers," I said, "Elliot and Korman, left Camp Casey in the middle of the night, drove to the Western Corridor, and then were back in Tongduchon by zero-seven-thirty?"

Alcott shot Bufford a look, but the taller man was too busy talking to notice.

"Yes. They were exhausted. They were good MPs, but exhausted. You can't blame them."

And they were also MPs. Why hadn't that been in the safety report? Or if it had, I'd missed it. Attention to detail, what the army always harps on. I cursed myself for not being more alert. But the more I thought about it, the more certain I was it hadn't been mentioned anywhere in the safety report. It must've been in the court-martial transcripts but I had yet to read those.

Colonel Alcott found his voice. "At ease, goddam it. At ease!"

Everyone shut up.

"Bufford, you apologize to these two men for pulling a gun on them. Bascom, you're going to see the desk sergeant and fill out a complete report on what happened between you and Weatherwax last night. Whether or not charges will be brought is still an open question. You'll be informed later. Sueño, you make sure that Bascom here completes the report, answers all follow-up questions, and then and only then will you two be free to go. Is that understood?

"Understood, sir," I replied.

"That's it then. Bufford?"

An MP handed Warrant Officer Fred Bufford his .45, butt first. Bufford grabbed it by the handle and, as he rose to his feet, slipped it into the leather holster hanging off his bony hip.

"Okay," Bufford said. "I overreacted. But you make that statement," he told Ernie, "and sign it and answer all our questions. You got that?"

Ernie crossed his arms and shrugged.

Before anyone could object to the deal, Colonel Alcott shouted, "Back to your duties! Everybody. Move it!"


While Ernie was making his statement, Colonel Alcott called me out into the hallway. When we were alone, he came so close I had to retreat a step. He was clean shaven and smelled of cologne and his civilian clothes were neatly pressed. My guess was that he'd encountered us as he'd taken a last turn through the Provost Marshal's Office before heading off to the Indianhead Officers' Club. Socializing is a big part of an officer's life, if he's ambitious.

In a low voice, Alcott said, "You will not make any further false accusations about the Druwood case. That was a training accident and *only* a training accident. Do you understand?"

"Yes, sir." I understood only too well. These guys were not going to let two low-level 8th Army CID agents rock their cozy little boat.

"If you persist in these accusations," Alcott continued, "you will be guilty of spreading false rumor concerning the integrity of the chain of command, a crime that is prohibited under the Uniform Code of Military Justice. And, I might add, a crime that is taken extremely seriously up here at Division. Do you understand?"

"I understand, sir." Colonel Alcott was right about the UCMJ. One of its provisions specifically states that it is a criminal offense to spread rumors that can be shown to have a deleterious effect on the morale of a military unit. But one man's rumor is another man's fact.

Two armed MPs marched down the narrow hallway. Colonel Alcott stepped away from me and acknowledged their greeting. After they'd passed, he closed in on me again.

"I suggest, Agent Sueño," he told me, "that you and your partner wrap up your investigation and wrap it up soon."

"We haven't found Corporal Matthewson, sir."

"Maybe she doesn't want to be found. Did that ever occur to you?"

"It did, sir."

"So maybe you'd better cut your losses and head back to Seoul before one of these peripheral issues you've been nosing into explodes in your face." Colonel Alcott paused and stared at me. "Now I'm not going to ask again if you understand me because, let's cut the shit, I know you understand me. I'm telling you, for the last time, wrap up your report and get the hell out of Tongduchon."

With that, he swiveled smartly and marched his little body down the hallway.


Ok-hi led the way, the heels of her black leather boots clicking down a flight of stone steps that led toward the East Bean River. About twenty yards below us, lining the muddy banks, were row upon row of wooden shanties. Candles glowed from within, as did an occasional cooking fire; some of the homes were lit by electric bulbs. The river moved sluggishly beneath the weight of moonlight, and the odor from the almost stagnant flow was what you'd expect from any waste dump. Rancid. Laundry fluttered from lines; water sloshed from buckets; old men barked; children shouted.

"The Turkey Farm," Ok-hi said. "No more bad thing here. KNPs say no can do."

So the brothels had been replaced by poor families. Families that had probably traveled from all over the Korean countryside, looking for work in Tongduchon, a city that, because of its proximity to Camp Casey, had become an economic boomtown.

A three-quarters moon hovered above the hills on the far side of the valley, its red glow shining on the Confucian shrine, a pagoda-like structure made of stone. The back of the pagoda was to the river but its face frowned out onto a small plaza. The entrance to the shrine was guarded by stone *heitei*, mythical lionlike creatures that guard all religious sites in Korea.

"There," Ok-hi said, pointing with her open palm. "Old king die."

"Sorry to hear that," Ernie said. "How old was he?"

"No." Ok-hi shook her head vehemently. "Not old. King young but he die long time ago."

"How long ago?"

"Long time." Her cute nose crinkled. "How long? How you say?" She looked at me. "*Menggu.*"

"Mongols," I said.

"Yeah. King die when Mongol come."

Ernie whistled. "That had to be before I got drafted."

About seven hundred years ago, to be exact.

Surrounding the plaza were shops and teahouses and what looked like chophouses and bars. None of the buildings were very big. The largest, an ancient wooden edifice some three stories tall, stood directly opposite the shrine. The people milling about appeared, from this distance, to be Koreans. I didn't see any GIs. I did notice, however, that a paved, two-lane road ran north from the shrine. Large enough for a KNP patrol car or an American jeep or even, with a good driver, a two-and-a-half-ton truck.

So here it was. The Turkey Farm that I'd heard so much about. An eyesore that had caused so much embarrassment for both Korean and U.S. authorities that they'd finally mustered the will to clean it up. What stories this village must hold. Of young girls sold into indentured servitude, forced into prostitution. Of GIs during the Korean War, and in the years after, rolling their vehicles down muddy roads, pulling up along the banks of the river, paying for sex with a bar of soap or a pack of cigarettes. The girls from the impoverished countryside being brought in younger and younger, being used, worn out, and tossed aside to make room for more. Whole seas of young women ruined, lost, ravaged by disease. And GIs, their biological lust never sated, experiencing all this, experiencing the unbridled satisfaction of all their desires and then returning home to Dubuque, Iowa or Little Rock, Arkansas, or Pasadena, California, trying to forget what they'd seen. Putting it out of their minds. Getting on with their lives. But never, by no stretch of the imagination, being the same again.

"Sueño!"

It was Ernie's voice. Angry.

"You just going to stand there all night or are we going to get some work done?"

"Work," I said. "Right."

I stepped gingerly down the steep stone steps.

Ok-hi looked at me quizzically, unable to figure me out. Then she shrugged her shoulders, turned, and resumed tip-toeing sideways down the narrow steps. Wading through moonlight.


I'd seen hookers in L.A. Some just high school girls, working to pay for their drug habit. But how did their drug habit start? When they fell in with gang members and pimps. Gang members and pimps who brought the curious young girls along until they were hooked, under their power, and then, and only then, would they put them out on the street.

Even when I was still in junior high school I saw this and marveled at how young girls could fall for it. One of my classmates, Vivian Matatoros, started hanging out with gang members. Everything about her changed. The glasses she wore disappeared, the brown hair pulled back into a pony tail became a frizzed-out mess, and she slid down from the classes that held the top students to the lowest rung of academic hell. So I seldom saw her or had a chance to talk with her or laugh with her. I spotted her only occasionally in the hallways, swaggering with girlfriends who chomped on as much gum and wore as much makeup as their jaw capacity and facial measurements would allow.

One morning, in the passageway behind the girl's gym, I cornered her. I stood in front of her so she couldn't ignore me and she couldn't walk past me. When she realized that she was trapped, she gazed up at me, ready to fight.

"What's happened to you, Vivian?" I asked.

"Get away from me."

I wouldn't let her go. I forced her to talk.

"I was bored," she told me finally. "No one was paying attention to me."

I knew the feeling. I told her I often felt the same way. I offered to talk to her, to meet her after school. She looked at me with contempt.

"Where were you when I needed you?" she asked.

I had no answer.

She shoved past me roughly and marched away. Soon she dropped out of school. Weeks later some of the guys told me that she was working a corner off Whittier Boulevard. They wanted me to go look—and laugh and shout names at her—but I couldn't do it. I remembered the Vivian who used to help me with my algebra. The girl who'd shared a sandwich with me when I had no lunch. That Vivian was the only Vivian I wanted to remember. The only Vivian I could bear to remember.


A huge slab of polished marble stood at the front of the shrine, flanked by the snarling stone *heitei*. By flickering candlelight I read as much as I could. Some of the *hangul* script and the Chinese characters were too complicated for me but I managed to understand the gist of the story.

His name was Yu Byol-seing and he wasn't a king, as Ok-hi had assumed, but merely a general. As a young man he started his career as a common soldier but by his intelligence and daring rose through the ranks rapidly. The Koreans were desperately trying to hold off the invading Mongol hordes and the carnage was such that there were plenty of promotion opportunities. Kublai Khan, the grandson of Genghis Khan had already conquered most of northern China. He expected that conquering Korea would be like pulling ripe fruit off a plum tree. Instead, much to the Mongols' surprise, they met fierce resistance.

By the time the Mongols had crossed the Yalu River into Korea and conquered the north, there was only one small army left, led by General Yu. This battered force was all that stood between them and Kaesong, the ancient capital city. The Mongol cavalry, of course, was the best in the world. After all the defeats the Koreans had suffered, General Yu had no cavalry left, only foot soldiers. For foot soldiers to face Mongol horsemen on flat land was suicide. Yet making a stand in rocky mountain retreats might slow them down but would do no good in the long run. The Mongols had shown that they were perfectly willing to ride past Korean soldiers holed up on rocky ridges, and continue south to rape and pillage. General Yu had no choice. He had to face the Mongol army.

He chose the environs of East Bean River for his stand. Many small streams intersected in this open valley. None of the rivers were broad enough to totally stop a cavalry advance, horses could wade across them and climb the muddy banks, but the damp geography slowed them down. And the narrow rivers ran in jagged patterns, slicing the valley like a complex jigsaw puzzle. General Yu took advantage of this terrain. First, he arrayed his army in full view of the advancing Mongols. When their cavalry flanked him and charged, he let loose with his archers and pulled his foot soldiers back, retreating across a muddy stream. On the far bank the men turned and made their stand, emplacing iron pikes and holding their ground as the mounted Mongols struggled up and out of the mud. Before the horsemen could find any room to maneuver, the Koreans attacked. The battle was fierce and General Yu moved his soldiers around the chessboard of the East Bean valley with consummate skill, befuddling the Mongol cavalry at every turn. The Mongol losses grew and the Koreans became bolder but Kublai Kahn and his generals hadn't conquered the world by being timid. With lightning speed, a horseman raced to the rear requesting reinforcements. By the next morning, they arrived. Over ten thousand strong, according to the stone slab, all of them arrayed on the hills surrounding

Tongduchon. Wounded but still willing to fight, the Koreans were defiant. By now, the Mongols had a better idea of how to maneuver in the tricky terrain of East Bean River. They placed various units of cavalry in different sectors so they wouldn't have to cross rivers so often. By the end of the second day, General Yu and his entire force were destroyed. According to the stone tablet, not one soldier surrendered.

The Korean king in Seoul retreated to Kanghua Island and sued the Mongols for peace. They gave it to him, but in return for maintaining his life and his throne, he turned Chosun, the Land of the Morning Calm, over to Kublai Khan.

When I was finished reading, I glanced around at the little village that surrounded the shrine. From glory to degradation and some day, I hoped, back to glory.

Ernie trudged up the steps of the shrine, Ok-hi by his side.

"While you been reading, Ok-hi and I were out asking questions. Everybody in that chophouse over there saw it." He pointed at a noodle shop with a wooden sign that said, *TONGDU NEING-MYON.* East Bean Cold Noodles.

"They all saw it? What do you mean?"

"I mean they all heard the thud and when they ran outside they found a dead body. A GI with his skull crushed in."

"Where?"

"Right there."

Ernie pointed to the *heitei* nearest the three-story building. I walked over, shining my small flashlight on the snarling beast. His left ear was shattered. I touched the wound. Tiny bits of gravel broke off on my finger, the same type of gravel I'd plucked from Private Druwood's skull.

Across from the shrine, the woodwork of a three-story building creaked in the gentle breeze. It was an old and venerable construction, almost like a Victorian mansion except there was no intricate gingerbread trim. A lone electric bulb burned inside a window on the third floor. The sign on the lower level said *TONGDU SSAL-GUANG.* East Bean Rice Storage.

At the top of the roof, moonbeams glinted off a ledge. From there it would be an easy leap to the stone *heitei.* Skulls would meet.

Bone would crunch. Blood would flow, but only for a moment. Then the man's heart would stop and the flowing blood would cease and people would rush out of East Bean Cold Noodles and the KNPs would be called and the 2nd Division Military Police would be notified and someone would come out with a jeep or an ambulance and transport the dead GI back to Camp Casey.

But no one would dump the body at the obstacle course, if normal procedure was being followed.

I turned to Ok-hi. "Did you ask about black-market honchos?"

"Yes," she replied. "Everybody say there, in *ssal changgo.*" She pointed to the rice warehouse. "Old mama-san work there, do black market all the time. Everybody say she called *Chilmyon-jok Ajjima.*" The Turkey Lady.

Actually, nobody knows for sure why GIs christened this old brothel area the Turkey Farm. Some say because it was full of young chicks. Whatever the reason, the name had caught on not only with the GIs but also with the Koreans. To call the black-market honcho, *Chilmyon-jok Ajjima,* the Turkey Lady, implied that she'd been here a long time.

Ernie turned to Ok-hi. "You wait here."

"No way," she answered. "I go, too."

Ernie shrugged. It was a free country. Sort of.


The front door of the warehouse was locked from the outside. We walked around back and found a wooden loading platform. The metal shuttered entranceway from the platform was padlocked, also from the outside. A side door, however, was open. We walked in.

I shone my flashlight around a large space. The first floor was about a third full of what you'd expect a granary to be full of. Large hemp sacks on wooden pallets. They were slashed with Chinese characters and apparently contained rice, barley, and millet, whatever in the hell millet was used for. Feeding livestock, I supposed. The floor of this main warehouse wasn't completely flat. Elevated platforms raised some pallets above others. And then I realized why. There had been a stage against the far wall and a bar to our right.

The ground level, before it had been turned into a grain warehouse, had served as a nightclub.

How long ago? During the Korean War, once the frontlines stabilized? Maybe. How many GIs just in from the field, wearing muddy boots and reeking of two weeks worth of stink, had traipsed in here? How many frightened young girls just in from the countryside had been dragged through these doors by procurers? Girls who'd never seen a building this big nor heard a live band nor even gazed eye-to-eye with a Westerner.

Ernie elbowed me, bringing me back to the present. Sometimes he became exasperated by my moods. At a time like this, in the middle of an investigation, I couldn't blame him. I was sometimes impatient with myself for wallowing in the past or, worse, in a future that existed only in my imagination.

A cement-walled stairwell led upward. Even from the bottom we could see the glow of the bulb shining above. I heard clicking. Someone using a typewriter? But the clicks were too soft, wood on wood, and much too rapid for a typewriter. Then I realized what the sounds were. Ok-hi realized it at the same time.

"*Jupan*," she whispered.

Someone, an expert, manipulating an abacus.

I led, holding the flashlight. Ernie followed, holding his .45. And Ok-hi came last, stepping lightly so her high-heeled leather boots wouldn't make too much noise on the stairs.

The second floor seemed to be deserted. Still, I took a few steps along the corridor to investigate. Small rooms, open, no doors. I shone the flashlight beam into one. Jam-packed with black-market merchandise, cardboard cases of canned fruit cocktail imported from Hawaii. In the next room, cases of crystallized orange drink were piled almost to the ceiling. The next held boxes of bottled maraschino cherries and about a jillion packets of nondairy creamer. Each room was like that, filled with merchandise taken from the American PX. But these items hadn't been purchased one by one by a lone GI doing weekend shopping. These items had been bought in bulk, probably straight off the truck that had transported them from the Port of Inchon. That implied someone in procurement was involved in the scam, making the sale and also covering it up in the inventory chain. Both Koreans, who did the actual clerical work, and Americans, who supervised them, had to be involved. Using my flashlight, I checked the dates stamped onto some of the cases. Months ago. By the pristine condition of the boxes and the volume of the product, there was no doubt that this black-market operation was sophisticated, widespread, and had at least the tacit approval of someone high up. A lot of money was involved. Did this have anything to do with the death of Private Marvin Z. Druwood? Or with the disappearance of Corporal Jill Matthewson?

Maybe.

One thing that struck me as odd was the size of the rooms. Obviously, this building had never been designed to be a warehouse. These rooms were tiny and there were dozens of them spread down the hallway. Just enough room for a small bed. Just enough room for a young girl to lie down and for a young GI to slip off his boots and pull down his trousers.

Ernie and Ok-hi waited for me at the stairwell. Ernie pointed upstairs. I nodded. The three of us started to climb.

At the top of the steps I allowed my eyes to adjust to the ambient light from the single bulb that illuminated the long corridor. More rooms, like the ones on the second floor, were jam-packed with made-in-the-USA black-market items. This time mostly electronics: tape recorders, stereo equipment, cheap cameras. One doorway stood open, light flooding out into the hallway. We walked forward and as we did so whoever was working inside stopped clicking disks on the abacus. I strolled to the door, Ernie right behind me, and by the time we arrived I'd shoved my flashlight deep into my jacket pocket.

Inside, an elderly Korean woman wearing the traditional *chima-chogori* dress with a white blouse and jade-colored skirt stood in front of a cheap wooden desk, staring back at us. Her sandals were made of white rubber and shaped with the toes upturned into a sharp points. Traditional Korean shoes, so made because during the Yi Dyansty the upturned toe was a sign of beauty. Her hands were on her hips. Gray hair stuck out from a round face in blazing disarray. Her nose was flat, her lips were clamped tight, and her black eyes burned fiercely. Defiant. More than just defiant. Her entire posture radiated indignation and outrage at being interrupted in her work.

"*Anyonghaseiyo*," I said. Are you in peace?

Behind the woman, a window overlooked the shrine to General Yu Byol-seing.

Her outrage built but, finally, she found her voice. "*Weikurei nohnun?*" What's the matter with you?

The voice was gruff, gravelly, deep. Like the history of this building itself. And apparently she had no fear of us.

Ernie stepped past me, reached inside his jacket, and whipped out his CID badge. "We're from Eighth Army," he said, "and you're under arrest."

The woman's face registered surprise, the liver spots on her face expanded like an exploding universe, and then she began to laugh. Uproariously. Bending over, holding her stomach. Tears came to her eyes.

Despite myself, I had to smile. So did Ok-hi.

Ernie became more angry. "You think this is funny?" He put away his CID badge and pulled out his .45.

I grabbed his arm. "Wait, Ernie. Let's talk to her before we blow her away."

Ernie balked, his face still red, but slowly he slipped his .45 back into its holster.

The old woman continued to laugh.

Ok-hi started laughing, too, holding her right hand modestly in front of her mouth. Then I smiled and even Ernie smiled and within a few seconds we were all laughing along with the old woman. Suddenly, she stopped. Gradually, we stopped, too.

"You Eighth Army," she said. "CID. You come here arrest *Chilmyon-jok Ajjima.*" She pointed her forefinger at her nose. "Maybe you arrest me you gotta arrest everybody in TDC. All KNP and, how you say, *sichang?*"

"The mayor," I said.

"Yeah. Mayor. And you arrest all honchos on Camp Casey. After that, then you arrest *Chilmyon-jok Ajjima.*"

She began to laugh again.

We laughed along with her but she'd just confirmed what I'd

been thinking ever since we walked into this building. The black-market activities in Tongduchon were not only widespread but sanctioned by the powers that be, both Korean and American. Would this old woman's testimony stand up in a U.S. Army court-martial? Not a chance. No military prosecutor in the world would have the temerity to put her on the stand. Military courts-martial are decorous affairs. A bunch of American officers, lined up, wearing dress green uniforms, each judge trying to look more severe than the other. The honchos don't like riffraff appearing in front of them. Certainly not someone known as the Turkey Lady.

Ernie sobered up first and asked the old woman the question that we'd really come to ask.

"Where was Druwood when he fell?"

The Turkey Lady stared at Ernie blankly for a moment and I was prepared for the usual criminal response that always added up to something like "I know nothing." I was already planning my counter move. But, as it turned out, I didn't need to threaten her.

"Come on," the Turkey Lady responded. "I show you."

We left the little office with its couch and its coffee table and walked back into the hallway. We were halfway down the corridor when I stopped dead in my tracks.

"What the hell is this?"

The Turkey Lady stopped, as did Ernie and Ok-hi.

I shone my flashlight into a room less than half the size of all the others.

"That new girl room," the Turkey Lady said.

"New girl room?"

"Long time ago, when new cherry girl come Turkey Farm, maybe she don't like sleep with smelly GI. She don't like have boom-boom." Sex. "So house mama-san make her sleep in this room."

"It's too small to sleep in," Ernie said. "You can't even sit down."

"Yeah. Pretty soon she tired, pretty soon she tell mama-san she want sleep in her own room. Then GI come, no sweat."

"And if she gutted it out?" I asked. "If she didn't ask for a larger room?"

"Then mama-san knuckle-sandwich with her. Maybe papa-san, too."

The Turkey Lady told us all this in a matter-of-fact tone, the years, and maybe the repetition, having leached away any emotion the story might've once held for her. Had she once been a "cherry girl" banished to this narrow closet? I wanted to know but there were too many things I wanted to know and we had work to do. Besides, the reason I'd stopped everyone here was not because of the small size of the room but because of what it contained. I shined my flashlight on an open, crate-like framework with a matting of straw at the bottom. Inside the cheap packaging stood a vase. Greenish blue. Celadon, the type manufactured most perfectly during the Koryo Dynasty, more than seven centuries ago. Intricately painted white cranes floated skyward on a blue green background. Wispy clouds, like knotted strings of fluff, glided heavenward. The glow of the flashlight made the delicate porcelain seem not like a solid object but like a dreamscape of jade shading off into infinity. For a moment, I thought I heard the wings of the white cranes flapping but actually it was only Ok-hi, and even Ernie, gasping for breath.

*Breathtaking.* That was the word. I don't think I'd ever seen such an exquisite work of art this close up. Sure, when I was a kid in L.A. we'd gone on field trips to the L.A. County Museum but everything had been trapped behind plastic or glass, safe from our grasping little hands. This vase was alive. It was right here. It was as if the ancient artist stood in the room with us. Smiling. Taking a bow.

"*Chon hak byong,*" Ok-hi said, in reverential tones. The Thousand Crane Vase.

The Turkey Lady beamed.

"Who's this for?" Ernie asked.

The Turkey Lady waved her hand. "Some honcho. Come on. I show you roof."

At the far end of the corridor a rickety wooden ladder led up to a trapdoor in the ceiling. The Turkey Lady climbed up the ladder quickly, her jade skirt billowing. Then she reached up and pushed open the trapdoor and, as she climbed through, Ok-hi, Ernie, and I were treated to a full view of her undergarments, white cotton pantaloons. Then Ernie climbed up followed by Ok-hi and me.

We stood on the flat roof, then strolled around, staring over a three-foot-high cement wall. The entire world of Tongduchon spread before us: The blazing lights of the nightclub district; meandering moonglow reflecting off the East Bean River; the empty darkness of the rice fields to the west. And to the east, the sporadic blinking of the scattered bulbs of Camp Casey. I turned and inhaled the fresh winter air. The cold breeze floated in from the north, off snowcapped mountain ranges. Having blown, I imagined, across Manchuria, all the way from the mysterious heart of Siberia.

A lean-to had been set up, with sturdy wooden poles and a canvas top secured by ropes, probably part of an old bivouac tent used in field maneuvers. Beneath, on a wooden platform, comfortable tatami mats were spread, topped by flat silk cushions, the kind of cushions Koreans use when they sit cross-legged on a warm *ondol* floor. *Huatu*, Korean flower cards, lay scattered about, interspersed with a few Bicycle brand U.S. playing cards. A small refrigerator near the elevated platform was plugged into a transformer and humming. I opened it and, using my flashlight, examined the contents within: bottles of soda water, orange juice, about a dozen cans of beer.

Ernie leaned past me and helped himself to one of the cold beers. After popping the top and taking a slug, he handed the half-empty can to Ok-hi. She sipped daintily.

"Nice set up they have here," Ernie said.

I turned to the Turkey Lady. She'd slipped off her plastic sandals, stepped up on the tatami-covered platform, and seated herself, legs crossed, on one of the flat cushions. Reaching into the folds of her skirt, she pulled out a pack of Kent cigarettes and then a Bic lighter and toked up. Exhaling gratefully, she surveyed her little domain, a beatific smile spread across her lips.

"Who comes up here, *Ajjima*?" I asked. "GIs?"

She shook her head vehemently. "Not all GI. Only MP come here. They can't go village." She pointed to the nightclub district to the south. "So MP come here."

Every MP unit in the U.S. Army counsels its soldiers not to spend their off-duty time in the same hangouts as other soldiers. Too often when a GI becomes drunk and remembers being busted by an MP, trouble starts. To set up their own little getaway, their own little club, is not unusual. And it seems that the 2nd Division MPs had a nice one here on top of this dilapidated former brothel in the heart of the Turkey Farm.

I surveyed the patio. During the day, when the sun shone, it would be a nice place to party. I spotted something against the far wall and shined the flashlight on it.

"Hibachi," Ernie said. "They barbecued up here, too."

"Which MPs came up here?" I asked the Turkey Lady.

"Any MP. Any Camp Casey MP. All the time they bring *yobo*." Their Korean girlfriends. "They bring music, they bring beer, they play poker, they have fun. Sometimes laugh, sometimes argue, sometimes fight."

She frowned and blew smoke out of her nose.

"How about Druwood?" I asked. "Where was he standing when he fell?"

"Right there." She pointed to the spot where Ernie and Ok-hi stood, near the edge. "But he no fell."

I walked over and followed Ernie's gaze. Below, straight across the walkway stood the *heitei*. I shined the flashlight at it. Even from here I could see that the *heitei's* ear had been shattered. Maybe it was a trick of the light but his fangs and cruel lips seemed to be twisted up toward me and his eyes stared into mine.

I switched off the beam of light and turned back to the Turkey Lady. "Druwood didn't fall? Are you saying someone pushed him?"

"I no see."

"Then why do you say he didn't fall?"

"Because I hear." She pointed to her left ear. "They *taaksan* argue. Argue a lot. Everybody mad at Druwood. Say he better go back stateside. He no can handle be Division GI."

"What did they mean by that? Why couldn't he handle it?"

"Because MP in Camp Casey, they got special job. Kind job other MP no have."

"What kind of job is that?"

She knew she had our attention now. Slowly, the Turkey Lady drew deeply on her American-made cigarette, held it, then blew out the smoke.

"Division MP, they gotta take care of honcho. Korean honcho.

GI honcho. All kinda honcho. But they don't mind. They get many things. They makey extra money black market, they get plenty kind of special girlfriend. They get free beer, free food, all the time good time. Everybody happy."

"Sounds nice," Ernie said. "But who pays for all this free food and free booze and free women?"

The Turkey Lady waved her right arm in a circle. "Black market pay all. Everybody happy. Nobody sad."

"Except for Druwood," I said.

"Yeah. He sad. That's why all MP mad at him."

"What did they say to him?"

"I don't know. I don't listen. You ask them."

"Ask who?"

"Ask, what name? Tall skinny MP."

"White GI?"

She nodded.

"Bufford?"

"Yeah. That him."

"He was here that day?"

"Yes."

"Was he the one who pushed Druwood off the roof?"

"Nobody push Druwood."

"Then how'd he fall?"

"He no fall. He jump."

"Why'd he jump?"

The Turkey Lady shrugged. "Everybody say he sad. Sad because his *yobo karra chogi*." His *yobo* ran away.

"Who was his *yobo*?" I asked.

"Not Korean," the Turkey Lady told us. "His *yobo* MP woman."

Ernie and I looked at one another. Even Ok-hi paused in sipping her beer.

"How do you know this?" Ernie asked.

"Every MP all the time say," the Turkey Lady replied. "Everybody laugh at him. Say his *yobo* no want him no more."

GIs are relentless when they find a weak spot. They'll peck at it until it bleeds and then festers, until poison starts to flow in the blood. Was it because Druwood couldn't stand the ridicule that he'd jumped? Or had he fought back and in a tussle lost his balance? Or had someone deliberately decided to eliminate him? I asked a few more questions of the Turkey Lady but she didn't know the answers. Which MPs had been on the roof when Druwood went over? She couldn't provide any names nor any descriptions. "MP all same-same," she told us. The only one she remembered specifically was Warrant Officer One Fred Bufford. Why him? Because as the rank-ing man—the honcho—the other MPs deferred to him.

A Confucian trait. Always be aware of who's the boss, for purpos-es of survival. *Nunchi*, the Koreans call it. The ability to read your supe-riors, be aware of which way the wind blows, and react appropriately.

"Check this out," Ernie said.

On the southern wall, behind a line of large earthenware kim-chee jars, Ernie pointed at splintered wood. I shined the flashlight on it. Using a handkerchief, Ernie bent down and picked up a piece. The leg of a wooden stool. Broken. We knelt and examined some more of the pieces. Brown stains on the jagged edges.

"Blood," Ernie said.

"Maybe."

Evidence of a fight? We left the broken shards the way we'd found them.

Ernie and I stared at one another, unsure of what to do. In Seoul, we'd notify the CID Detachment, which would notify the Korean National Police Liaison Office and in minutes a team of KNP forensic technicians would be up here trying to determine if a crime had been committed. Trying to determine if Druwood had been murdered. But this was Tongduchon. This was Division. To notify the provost marshal and the local KNPs would be to notify the same people who'd not only hauled Druwood's body off to the obstacle course and dumped it there but also the same people who tolerated this huge black-market operation.

"We have to report all this to Eighth Army," I said.

Ernie frowned. "They'll just notify Division of what we suspect, Division will take pains to eliminate evidence, and we'll be back where we started."

Ernie was probably right. Our reputation at 8th Army was that of two troublemakers. And if there's one thing high-ranking military officers hate, it's troublemakers. Although they'd never admit it, they'd much prefer to have all this evidence we'd gathered pulverized by explosives. Besides, Ernie and I had not yet accomplished what we'd come up here for. We had not yet found Corporal Jill Matthewson. And tonight, after curfew, we were going to make our most daring stab yet at finding a lead as to her whereabouts.

Ok-hi hissed for our attention. Her shapely butt was propped on the back ledge of the wall surrounding the roof. Ernie and I trotted over to look. Below, a bunch of guys were entering the back of the warehouse. Not MPs. They weren't big enough. Koreans. There were about a half dozen of them, all thin young men about the same size, moving stealthily. Like cats

"*Kampei*," Ernie said.

Gangsters.

The Turkey Lady stood up, flicked her cigarette away, and said, "*Ganmani issoba*." Wait here. Then she ran back toward the ladder and climbed down quickly.

I stared at the moon, at the evidence surrounding me, and then down at the stone *heitei* snarling upwards, glaring into my eyes. Daring me to act.

# 7

Ernie wanted to confront the *kampei*. I didn't see why. We were here to gather information about the death of Private Marvin Z. Druwood. We definitely weren't here to start a hassle with a local gang of hoodlums. Whatever was going on downstairs, I was sure the Turkey Lady could handle it. At least I was sure until voices were raised in anger and then something smashed against a wall. Pellets pinged off hard surfaces, reminding me of only one thing: a broken abacus.

Ernie rushed downstairs. I followed, Ok-hi right behind me.

It took us a few seconds to lift the trapdoor and then clamber down the old wooden ladder. Then we ran down the hallway toward the open door of the office. As we did so, I spotted the cherry-girl room looking larger now because it was completely empty. Is that what the *kampei* had come for? The Thousand Crane Vase? Maybe it wasn't a reproduction but the real thing, a genuine antique from the Koryo Dynasty. Of course it had looked real to me all along but when it comes to art, what do I know? When Ok-hi and I rushed inside the office, Ernie was already kneeling over the Turkey Lady.

She was alive but the top of her skull had been partially pulped by a blunt instrument. The drawers of her desk and her file cabinets had been ripped open and the contents dumped on the floor. Not as if someone was looking for something, but as if they just wanted to destroy.

Ok-hi squealed when she entered the office but ran forward and shoved Ernie out of the way. She bent over the Turkey Lady and examined her for injuries. "*Ahn chugo*," she told us. Not dead. Still breathing.

Ernie and I rushed toward the stairwell. At the top we stopped. There was a smell that we both recognized: mogas. The cheap, poorly refined gasoline that the U.S. Army uses to power most of its motor vehicles. A cloud filled the stairwell. Not like the wispy cotton clouds that led the white, painted cranes heavenward but a solid, pungent cloud, like a mechanic's fist punching its way into the hallway.

I suppose Ernie and I both expected what was coming next but still it filled me with irrational terror. As we stood there breathing in the odor of cheap gas, a ball of reddish light burst upward from downstairs, along with the whooshing sound of oxygen being sucked into the mouth of a monster. And then a blinding rush of black smoke. We both stepped back.

Panic overwhelmed me. In a flash, I calculated how fast this old wooden building would burn as gasoline-fueled flames gnawed hungrily at dry lumber. Fire grows not gradually but exponentially. Even if Ernie and I ran straight for the exit, we still might not make it out of this old brothel alive. If we went back for Ok-hi and the Turkey Lady, our chances of survival were virtually nil. There was no time to think about it, no time to confer. No time to weigh our options.

We ran back into the office.

Ernie grabbed Ok-hi, jerked her upright, and shoved her toward the door. Then we each grabbed one of the Turkey Lady's sandal-covered feet and dragged her into the hallway. Her body and then her head hit the molding in the corridor, but we didn't even slow down. We ran toward the stairwell. Ok-hi understood our panic now. We took two steps at a time, not caring if the back of the Turkey Lady's skull struck the cement steps. She probably wouldn't live through this but neither would we.

At the second floor, the smoke had already coagulated into a thick wall. That's usually what kills people. The poisonous fumes from plastics and asbestos and rubberized wiring and all the other exotic building materials that are used in modern high-rises. But this old building was made of the same materials that had been used in Asia since time immemorial: wood, iron, brick, and mortar. And now that we were below the floor that held the fancy electronics, we were faced with smoke that came only from those simple materials—and from the gasoline and the hemp sacks full of grain.

Still, the black cloud would choke us to death if we gave it half a chance. I hesitated. Maybe we should flee to the end of the second-floor corridor and take our chances jumping out the far window. Ernie understood my hesitancy but he had none. He plowed forward, into the smoke.

I went with him, the body of the Turkey Lady bouncing behind us, Ok-hi following.

We reached the ground floor beneath a cloud-covering of smoke. Sacks of barley stacked on pallets roared red with flame. The wooden flooring burned in erratic circles, indicating the places where the *kampei* had splashed gasoline. We moved toward the front door but the smoke was thickening now. Ernie stumbled. I wanted to help him up but my eyes and my nose and my throat screamed for me to keep moving, to flee. I had no idea what Ok-hi was doing. In seconds I'd pass out. I let go of the Turkey Lady's foot. Ernie was crawling forward now but I left him and ran blindly toward where I hoped I'd find the exit. I wasn't running so much as stumbling, head forward, trying to keep my feet beneath me so I wouldn't fall. And I didn't fall because I plowed headfirst into a wall.

For a second, I blacked out. When I came to I found myself face-down on the floor and this was good because there was less smoke and more oxygen down here. I slithered to my left, praying as I tried to find the door. I did.

I shoved at it. It rattled and held.

Locked.

Holding my breath, I rose to my knees and twisted the handle. It was hot but I held on anyway. I twisted and twisted again. No dice. It wouldn't budge.

I knew what I had to do. I had to stand up and kick the door open. But knowing and doing are two different things. What I really wanted to do was to lie down and enjoy the last of the breathable air, but if I did that I'd be finished. What about Ernie? What about Ok-hi? What about the Turkey Lady? They were far from my calculations now.

I stood somehow, backed up a step, and with every molecule of strength I possessed, I flung myself at the door. It shuddered, held, and then sprang free.

I fell facedown onto the wooden platform outside, then crawled toward the far edge of the loading dock, still unable to breath. Billowing black smoke followed me outside like a dragon emerging from its den. I continued to crawl until gravity took over and I crashed to the ground below. I lay still for a few seconds. Breathing. Grateful. Enjoying the unbelievable bracing, clear air that filled my lungs.

Ernie! He was still back there.

I rose unsteadily to my feet and through the smoke saw something black moving toward me. I reached out, grabbed a handful of shirt and pulled. The dark thing fell, crashing into me, and we both tumbled onto the ground.

Ernie. I shoved him off me. His face was covered with soot and he gasped for air like a beached fish. But he was alive. I left him there and climbed back onto the platform. Holding my breath, keeping my eyes turned away from the smoke, I reached the doorway once again and crawled through, groping blindly with my hands.

Nothing. Ok-hi hadn't made it this far.

I was running out of breath and about to turn back when my fingers slid across a slick surface. Hard. Leathery. The heel of a boot. Ok-hi. But I required air. No choice. I scurried back through the door and lowered my head over the edge of the loading platform to allow myself a few quick gulps of oxygen.

Ernie came to. He started to rise.

"Take a deep breath," I croaked. "Come on."

I took a deep breath myself, turned, and crawled back into the burning warehouse. This time I found Ok-hi's boot easily. I pulled myself up her body and realized that she lay atop the Turkey Lady.

Grabbing handfuls of material, I tugged them both toward the door. Ernie bumped into me, groped past, and soon he was helping me to drag the two women across the threshold. We slid them along the platform and, with a heave, shoved them off the edge of the loading dock to the ground. We flopped down after them and lay there for a while regaining our strength. Then we started pulling them away from the burning building.

I realized that people were shouting and running every which way. They'd organized a bucket brigade and men were running past us, splashing water ineffectually on the growing flames. A few women started to minister to Ernie and me but we directed them to Ok-hi and the Turkey Lady.

We backed off toward the edge of a hill, about thirty yards away from the warehouse and watched the flames.

They grew higher.

The women cleaned Ok-hi's face with a washcloth and a pan of water. When she was recovered she thanked them and joined us on the side of the hill. On the far side of the warehouse, in front of the shrine to General Yu Byol-seing, jeeploads of Korean National Police had arrived. Someone spoke to them and pointed to the Turkey Lady. She was sitting up now. A KNP marched toward her.

Ernie and I didn't have to talk about it. We had too much to do tonight; we didn't have time to make a lengthy report to the TDC cops. Instead, Ok-hi and Ernie and I slipped away into the darkness.

The midnight to four a.m. curfew had been imposed on the entire country of South Korea when the Korean War ended in June 1953, over twenty years ago. The reason, ostensibly, was to deny the cover of darkness to North Korean communist infiltrators. Since 1953 there'd been hundreds, maybe thousands, of North Korean incursions into South Korea and the midnight to four curfew hadn't seemed to slow them down. What the curfew *did* do was provide a sense of order for the people who live in South Korea. More than one GI told me that he felt the midnight curfew saved his health and his sanity. Otherwise, like a lot of GIs, he'd have ended up partying all night and been unable to roll out of the rack in time to make his "oh-dark-thirty" physical fitness formation. For the general populace, the midnight curfew meant that everybody knew when to close up shop. They didn't have to worry about their competitor next door stealing late-night business. The government itself, maybe unwittingly, was promoting a variation on the old Ben Franklin dictum: "Early to bed, early to rise, makes an entire *country* healthy, wealthy, and wise."

Still, the curfew was a pain in the butt if you were caught away from home after midnight, because then you were forced to stay put wherever you happened to be. No one was allowed on the street from midnight to four and this was enforced by the white clad "curfew police" and by the South Korean armed forces. If you were sneaking around dark alleys and you ignored an order to halt, you risked being shot. This had happened more than once to otherwise innocent civilians, although the newspapers didn't make a fuss about it. They weren't allowed to.

Like a couple of wary moles, Ernie and I worked our way through the narrow back alleys of Tongduchon. Only the three-quarter moon lighted our way.

"What's the time?" I asked.

Ernie checked his radium dial watch. "Twelve-oh-seven."

After leaving the Turkey Farm we'd returned to the Silver Dragon Nightclub. Ok-hi took us upstairs to her hooch and with Jeannie's help brought pans of hot water and towels. As the ladies administered bandages and antiseptic ointment to our cuts and bruises, I thought about the timing of what had happened. How much of a coincidence was it that the *kampei* had arrived only a few minutes after we'd entered the Turkey Farm? Had they known Ernie and I were on the roof? I doubted it. There was no indication that they'd paid any attention to us at all. If they'd wanted to kill us, they had us cornered and couldn't have asked for a better opportunity. My guess was that they weren't after us. But why burn down a money-making operation like that warehouse in the Turkey Farm? And why now?

Those were questions I decided to file away for the moment. Tonight, we were after information that I hoped would lead to Jill Matthewson.

Ernie and I changed into the outfits we'd stashed earlier that evening: sneakers, blue jeans, dark shirts, and knit watch caps. Then we pulled on our army-issue leather gloves, bid good-bye to the ladies, and slipped out the back door of the Silver Dragon.

The doors and windows near the building that housed Kimchee Entertainment were closed and shuttered. Midnight curfew had taken full effect. No one walked down the pedestrian lanes, no vehicles rolled down the narrow road. Neon lights were shut off. No sound from television sets or radios seeped out onto the street because all broadcasting stopped, by order of the government, when the midnight curfew began.

Ernie'd already appropriated a trash cart he'd found at a dead-end dump. He rolled it beneath the second-story window that belonged to the offices of Kimchee Entertainment, tilted the cart on its end, and leaned it against the wall.

I scurried to the narrow asphalt road that ran in front of Kimchee Entertainment and peeked around the corner. Empty. No one moved. I studied the roadway right and left. No delivery trucks, no white jeeps belonging to the curfew police, no vehicles of any kind. And no pedestrians. All windows and doors lining the street were closed and dark.

I took a deep breath. The night air was already beginning to cleanse itself. Less odor of burnt diesel. More of the sharp, clean aroma of rich earth and vegetation, the smell that had originally lured mankind to this lush peninsula.

Ernie hissed. "Come steady the cart."

I ran back and held the sides of the six-foot-long cart while Ernie climbed atop it, stretched to his full height, and grabbed the sill of the window leading into Kimchee Entertainment. I placed my palms beneath the soles of his sneakers and on the count of three, shoved upwards with all my might. Ernie's body rose and simultaneously his fist broke glass. One of the small window panes. The noise was jarring but brief. We'd already decided that it would be too dangerous to linger in the alley outside of Kimchee Entertainment. No time for jimmying the window. I was still shoving upwards on the bottoms of his feet as Ernie reached in and finally found the latch that unlocked the window. He pried it open and wriggled inside. Now he leaned out the window, stretching his open right hand out to me.

As we'd planned, I lowered the cart to its normal traveling position. Then I climbed into the bed of the cart, reached up and tried to grab Ernie's hand, but I couldn't quite reach.

"Jump," he said.

There were still no signs of life up and down the walkway. The minimal noise we'd made hadn't disturbed anyone. I took a deep breath, reached out my hand, and jumped. Ernie grabbed my right wrist and then, with his free hand, my forearm. As I kicked my sneakers against the wall and tried to climb, he leaned back with all his might, pulling, until I had a handhold on the sill. I scrambled up the wall as Ernie tugged. Within seconds, I was inside the offices of Kimchee Entertainment.

Ernie stepped past me and closed the window. I searched for something to cover the broken pane of glass. I found a magazine with a beautiful Korean actress on the cover and managed to stuff that into the opening.

Now, anyone walking below would see a trash cart left in an alley and above that a broken window that had been temporarily repaired. Ernie located a low lamp on a desk. I closed the curtain over the window and Ernie switched on the lamp. A soft green glow suffused the room.

"We're in," I said.

Ernie motioned for me to keep my voice down. We already knew that at least one nosy old woman lived in this building. If she'd heard us climbing in the window, she would've already called the Korean National Police and since they had police boxes all over the city of Tongduchon, someone would be here in minutes. Ernie and I stood stock-still. Listening. If we heard someone banging on the front door, or the heavy tread of boots on cement, we'd have to un-ass the area. Quick. Exactly how that would work, I didn't know. Hopping out the window wouldn't be good because the KNPs would station someone at the sides and rear of the building. One thing the KNPs never lack is manpower.

Ernie and I made a plan of sorts. The best thing to do if the KNPs were alerted would be to go deeper into the building, find the stairs or the ladder that led to the roof and from there hop onto the roof of the neighboring building and try to make good our escape.

We waited. Listening. Barely breathing.

The room looked lived-in. Used. The office of an actively functioning business. Three gray metal file cabinets stood against the wall. Probably army-issue, bought on the black market. The desk was made of unimpressive lumber, thinly varnished, and pocked with cigarette burns. In front of the desk stood a low coffee table and hard-cushioned sofa with two matching wooden chairs. In the center of the coffee table sat an enormous glass ashtray filled with butts and next to that an octagonal cardboard box stuffed with wooden matches.

I checked the butts. Korean-made. Not a single *Miguk* or imported cigarette in the bunch. Mr. Pak Tong-i was a thrifty man. So, apparently, were his clients.

On the wall hung numerous framed snapshots, some of them expensive publicity photos of Korean stars I vaguely recognized. Not his clients, I didn't think. These were faces that belonged on grand stages in Seoul or in front of television cameras. You could bet that none of them had ever performed up here in the hinterlands of TDC. And then there were the lower-quality photos. Photos of bands performing on rickety wooden stages, the backs of short GI haircuts in the audience. Clearly taken in some dive either in TDC or in one of the dozens of other GI villages blemishing the land just south of the Demilitarized Zone. Photos of sequin-spangled strippers stretching insincere smiles, striking awkward poses. Was one of them Miss Kim Yong-ai? I had no way of knowing. More photos of groups of GIs in civvies standing in front of bars or outdoors in picnic areas, always with Pak Tong-i standing in the middle, beaming, his arms around his friends. And a photo of Pak indoors, in front of the flags of the U.S. and South Korea, receiving an engraved plaque from a United States Army colonel in full uniform. The name and the face of the colonel meant nothing to me and it figured they wouldn't because the Pak Tong-i in the picture looked years younger.

So Mr. Pak Tong-i did more than just book entertainment for the nightclubs that stuck like barnacles to the outside of U.S. Army compounds. He also maintained contact with army officers on base. "Community relations," 8th Army calls it. Exactly what services Pak Tong-i performed, I didn't know but whatever it was, he'd received awards for it.

Ernie wandered into a side room. When he returned he thrust his thumb over his shoulder. "Nice setup," he said. *"Byonso."* Bathroom. "And a little bedroom with a cot and next to that a stand with a hot plate and a brass teapot."

So far, no alarm had sounded. We were starting to breath easier. Finally, I noticed the odor in the room. Thick. As if somebody'd left food out.

"Any refrigerator in there?" I asked.

"No. No sign of food."

Maybe Pak Tong-i ordered out. Hot food delivery—both Chinese and Korean—is cheap in Korea and always readily available. But I didn't see any sign of empty bowls or used chopsticks.

"You check the desk," I told Ernie. "I'll take the files."

Both of us carried small, army-issue flashlights and Ernie kneeled down under the desk, determined to be meticulous and start his search from the ground up. I opened the top drawer of the first file cabinet.

It was a mess. There didn't seem to be any particular order to the files, either in the English alphabet—a, b, c—or the Korean *hangul* alphabet—*ka, na, da*. Papers were shoved in willy-nilly. Contracts, payment vouchers, receipts—all of it in a huge hodgepodge stuffed into random folders. The Korean names on the folders, apparently the names of entertainers, did not correspond to the paperwork they contained. I worked quickly through the drawers, from file cabinet to file cabinet, trying to grasp the method of organization, quickly coming to the realization that there was none.

What I did notice was that there was no folder with the name Kim Yong-ai, the stripper who'd become Jill Matthewson's friend. I went back and checked more carefully, even peeking beneath the rows of folders in case the file had slipped down. Finally, I was sure. There was no folder for Kim Yong-ai despite the fact that Pak Tong-i himself had told us that she had been one of his most productive clients. There was no sense delaying my conclusion any longer. Someone—almost certainly not Pak Tong-i—had gone through these files. The mystery person had searched everything, taken everything out, and then thrown the documents back into any old folder and stuffed the entire mess back into the cabinets, totally unconcerned about keeping the records straight for future use or, for that matter, hiding the fact that he'd been here.

Also, whoever had been here before us had stolen Kim Yong-ai's file. Had they stolen anything else? Only Pak Tong-i would know.

Ernie stood up from behind Pak Tong-i's desk. He had reached the same conclusion. "Somebody's been here before us," he said.

Shining both our flashlights in the open drawers, we found the usual accumulation of pencils, paperclips, pens. In the top drawer an accounting ledger. I pulled it out and set it on the blotter. Then we checked the side drawers. An address book. Since all the entries were written in *hangul*, Ernie handed it to me. I thumbed through it. Pages torn out. All Korean names, no American names that I could see. But the *kiyok* section—the Korean *k* sound—was missing. Therefore, no entry for Miss Kim Yong-ai. The accounting ledger held the names of what were probably nightclubs and other entertainment companies. Figures listed in Korean *won*, none in dollars. Again, no American names. The ledger was neat. Like something prepared for display—or for the tax collector.

The rest of the drawers held nothing of interest. A pair of rubber pullover boots, an expensive Korean straight razor with shaving gear, and a half-used bottle of American-made mouthwash.

Who had preceded us? The Korean National Police? The 2nd Division MPI? Some gangster trying to collect money? Or could it have been Corporal Jill Matthewson herself? She'd been a cop after all. Maybe she'd come to retrieve Kim Yong-ai's files for some reason.

I didn't have enough information. The logical thing to do—the only thing to do—was to keep gathering facts.

Ernie held the beam of his flashlight pointing upward beneath his chin. His eyes were dark hollows. "One place we haven't searched," he said.

"Where?"

The office was tiny. Only two rooms and a *byonso*. I thought we'd already covered everything. But Ernie shined his flashlight on the wall directly behind Pak Tong-i's desk. In the darkness, I hadn't noticed. A door made of some sort of gray synthetic material, not wood, was set flush into the wall.

"What is it?"

"A soundproof room," Ernie answered. "For listening to music without bothering the neighbors."

I stared at the door, at the almost invisible hinges.

Ernie placed his flashlight in my free hand and I aimed both beams at the door. Then he grabbed the metal handle.

"On the count of three," Ernie said. "One, two, three."

He pulled. It wouldn't budge. Then Ernie placed both hands on the handle, propped the bottom of his right shoe against the wall, leaned back, and tugged with all his might. The door groaned, held, and then popped open.

It was dark inside, a space not much bigger than a closet. Something moved and at the same time the odor of rotted meat hit my nostrils. As I recoiled, something heavy and flesh-filled plopped sickeningly, with a massive thud, onto the floor. I jumped back, wanting to scream, and gazed down at the thing that lay at my feet.

When I was growing up in East L.A., I knew all kinds of kids—Anglo, black, Mexican—but one thing I realized early on was that Mexican kids are brave. Ridiculously brave. Accepting any sort of ill-considered dare—either to fight someone bigger than them or climb the highest tree or swing by a rope from a power line—was a point of honor. Backing down in front of the other kids was unthinkable. They'd either complete their mission or die trying.

Only two things frightened the tough little *vatos* of East L.A.: *la migra y las brujas*. Immigration and witches. Immigration because, for the most part, their parents were in the United States illegally and they'd been taught to shy away from anyone wearing a uniform. And *las brujas*, the witches, because they represented the power of the ancient world. The world from which their families had fled.

The word witches is misleading. Actually, *las brujas* are female shamans, like the Korean *mudang*. Their power arose from the ancient religions of the Aztecs and the other tribes that populated the Valley of Mexico and its environs since before the beginning of time. *Las brujas* were experts at healing and herbal remedies and mystic spells, and they were rumored to be able to transport themselves into realms denied to normal mortals. And denied for good reason. For one glimpse of these parallel universes—and at the faces of the entities that live there—would drive most men mad.

Did the Mexican *brujas* and the Korean *mudang* evolve from the same traditions, hoary with age? From somewhere in Siberia or along the Bering Strait? No one knew. Probably no one would ever know. But I was aware that both groups of women held positions that were similar. Positions within society of awe and respect, positions of power.

So when Madame Chon told me that her daughter's spirit was hungry and wandering and needed a ritual performed to help it find its way home, that made sense to me. I'd heard such things before. The Catholic Church performs exorcisms to cast out demons but the rites performed by *las brujas* are designed to communicate with the dead, to find out what they want, to share jokes with them, even to make deals with them. I knew how profoundly people believed in such things. So I had no doubt that Madame Chon would never rest until—as the *mudang* ordered—Jill Matthewson was brought to her to participate in a ceremony to communicate with the dead.

Even if I didn't believe that Chon Un-suk's spirit was hungry—and I didn't—I knew that her mother's spirit was. Hungry for rest. Hungry for reassurance that her daughter was well taken care of. And I understood that hunger. Since the day my mother died and left me alone, I'd been hungry myself. Hungry for someone who would love me without reservation. Hungry for someone I could love in the same way.

I saw her from the back bedroom, down the hallway, sitting on the couch in the front room, dressed in a beautiful black silk dress, her hair covered with a black lace mantilla. At that moment, as always, I was hungry for her embrace. Hungry for her kiss. Of course, she'd already been dead for five years. I was growing up, tall for my age, about to start middle school. My foster parents told me it was a dream, that I'd been taking a nap and I'd been disoriented. Others said it must've been someone else, not my mother. Maybe one of the older girls who was staying with the same foster parents. But none of those orphan girls owned black silk dresses or anything as old-fashioned as a lace mantilla.

A priest was summoned to the house. He started to perform an exorcism but I screamed so loudly that he had to stop. The neighborhood women tried to calm me, to explain to me that this ceremony was for the best and that I should listen to the wise words of the priest. I would have none of it. Every time the priest sprinkled holy water around the room, I started to scream again. Finally, he lost patience, picked up his vestments and his chalice, and left. I didn't want him to chase my mother away. She'd come back, for the first time since she'd died, and I didn't want anyone to force her to leave.

Later, the *bruja* arrived. She burnt some bones of a crow and added smelly herbs to the small fire but this time I didn't complain. She promised not to chase my mother away but just to talk to her. The trance lasted hours and I fell asleep. But when the old crone shook me awake, she grabbed my hand in her cold fist and told me that my mother would always be with me.

Ever since then, she has.

As the corpse rolled toward his feet, Ernie leaped backwards.

"What the—" After the body stopped rolling and Ernie managed to gather his courage, I handed his flashlight back to him and he kneeled and studied the pile of clothing beneath us. I held the beam of my flashlight on a face mostly covered by a broad-brimmed hat. Then I leaned forward and touched my fingers to a fleshy neck. No pulse. I pushed deeper. Was I sensing warmth? No. None. How long had this man been dead? Hours, I thought. Involuntarily, my hand recoiled. Ernie slipped the hat back to reveal a face.

Pak Tong-i. Fat tongue hanging lewdly to the side of purple lips. Face flushed red. Not red like a beet but a red so bright that it looked like a clot of blood held together by a transparent membrane of flesh.

We stood silent, trying to gather our wits. Trying to be professional. But in the middle of the night in this cold, cement office building with only the soft green glow of a lamp to comfort us, it wasn't easy. Death never is.

Taking a deep breath, I checked for wounds. I took my time

about it, loosening his clothes, making sure I didn't miss anything. No physical trauma, not even bruises, except for chafing around his wrists. He'd been bound. And there were burns around his neck. Rope burns. The lines ran up his pudgy neck in a steady progression.

"They interrogated him," Ernie said finally. "Tightening the rope each time he refused to answer."

I checked the bone beneath the flesh of the neck. It didn't seem to be damaged and his air passage seemed clear. The rope burns on his neck were superficial. Strangulation was not the cause of death. The vermilion hue of his face told its own story.

"Heart attack," I said. "While he was being questioned and systematically strangled, he popped a valve."

"Heart attack, strangulation, either way it's murder," Ernie said.

We searched Pak's pockets and his wallet. Keys, coins, a few wrinkled *won* notes. Ernie was the one who noticed it first. A bracelet tied above his elbow, hidden by the long sleeves of his shirt and jacket.

"Look at this," Ernie said, holding it up in the dim light.

I took the item from his hand and shined my flashlight on shimmering silver. An amulet. Silver chain, silver heart-shaped setting. Inside, a tiny color photograph of a woman. Overly made-up, bright smile, cheekbones carved from granite, dark curly hair. Korean. On the back of the amulet an engraving in *hanmun*, Chinese characters: JINAIJOK YONG-AI. My darling Yong-ai.

"At least we know what she looks like," I said.

"Who?"

"Kim Yong-ai. This is her."

"So Pak Tong-i," Ernie said, "was getting it on with Kim Yong-ai who was the stripper who was the friend of Corporal Jill Matthewson."

"That's what it looks like."

"And Pak didn't tell us anything because he was covering up for his girlfriend and Corporal Jill."

"Sounds likely."

"But covering up what?"

"I'm not sure. Maybe they never owed two thousand dollars. Maybe they still owe two thousand dollars. Maybe Pak paid it for them. Maybe not."

"What you're saying," Ernie said, "is we still don't know squat."

"That's about it. Except we do know that they ran away and someone is still after them. Someone who is willing to kill."

"And that someone has Kim Yong-ai's file and a big head start on us."

Downstairs a door slammed.

We froze. Then Ernie tiptoed to the office door, opened it slightly, and listened. Footsteps tromped up cement stairs. A pack of them. KNPs? Most likely.

If we stayed we could tell them the truth: We are two 8th Army Criminal Investigation Division agents investigating a case. Except we'd have to explain to the KNPs why we'd broken into Pak Tong-i's office illegally. And we'd have to explain that we had nothing to do with his death. Korean forensic techniques are not the best. Neither are the 2nd Division MPI's. Still, once the time of death was established, they'd see that Pak must've died before we arrived on the scene. That is presupposing that we'd be able to prove that we arrived on the scene only a few minutes ago. The assumption of both the Korean National Police and the 2nd Infantry Division would be that we were guilty until proven innocent. Ernie and I would be stuck in a jail cell for days, hoping to prove our innocence, while whoever actually committed the crime stalked Kim Yong-ai and Jill Matthewson at leisure.

All this ran through my mind in less than a second.

Ernie, apparently, had already made his decision. "Come on!"

I slipped the silver amulet in my pocket, stepped away from the body of Pak Tong-i, and followed Ernie into the hallway. We climbed the staircase swiftly and silently.

Footsteps pounded after us, then someone shouted.

The muscles on my back knotted, anticipating the searing impact of a bullet. We kept climbing. Then we ran, flat out. Panicked.

Kimchee jars were arrayed along a short cement wall that lined the edge of the building's roof. Ernie didn't slow down. He charged the precipice and when he hit the short cement wall he leaped into the air. I expected him to plummet to the dark depths below but he cleared the ten-foot span and landed safely on the roof of the opposite building.

I hesitated and looked down.

KNPs. Swarms of them. Shouting and pointing but no one looking up.

"Move it!" Ernie hollered.

Footsteps clattered behind me and two KNPs emerged from the door at the top of the stairwell. I turned back to Ernie. Across the divide, he was motioning for me to jump. I looked back at the cops. One of them reached for his pistol. That made up my mind for me. From a standing start, I jumped. It seemed as if I hovered over the dark void forever. Finally, my front foot hit cement. Ernie grabbed my waist and pulled me over the ledge onto the roof.

The two KNPs charged straight at us. When they reached the low cement wall, they hesitated. I can't blame them. Ernie had made the leap look easy but he was over a half a foot taller than either one of these policemen, his legs were longer and, more importantly, Ernie was crazy. I could almost hear the question in their minds: "Are we paid enough to do this?"

The answer, apparently, was no.

Instead the two men pulled their pistols, aimed them at us, and shouted, "*Chongji!*" Halt!

Ernie and I crouched and low-crawled until we found cover behind metal vents.

"What now?" I asked.

"Easy," Ernie replied. "We hop to the next building."

"They'll shoot us."

"From that distance? Come on."

Without further discussion, Ernie was on his feet and charging toward the far edge of the roof. When he leaped, a couple of rounds were fired but they missed him by a mile. I knelt like a runner at the starting blocks, taking deep breaths, trying to encourage myself, when from deep in the bowels of the building, boots pounded on cement. A herd of them. That was all the encouragement I needed.

I dashed toward the wall and this time I cleared the gap easily, landed on my feet, rolled, and kept moving. Ernie had already reached the next roof but from the light of the half moon I could tell there was no building after that. Not one, anyway, that was three stories tall.

When I arrived on the roof of the fourth building, Ernie was kicking at a door. He looked at me, his face lathered in sweat, exasperated.

"Can you kick this thing in?"

"Stand back," I said.

I stood with my side facing the wooden door, flexing my knees and half squatting, feeling the spring in my thighs. Since arriving in Korea I'd been training in the Korean art of Taekwondo, which literally means "the path of kicking and punching." At six foot four, with long legs, I believed that my side kick was one of the best in the business. I inhaled and let the air out slowly. From below, the shouts of Korean National Policemen wafted on the cold night air.

"Would you kick the goddamn thing in, for chrissakes!" Ernie shouted.

I ignored him, fully in a trance now. The air drifted effortlessly from my lungs and, without thinking, I hopped forward and my foot slammed into lumber.

The door burst inward.

Ernie ran past me and his footsteps pounded on squeaking wood. I followed him down a dark staircase. It was narrow and wound back on itself. Finally, when I figured we had descended to the second floor, Ernie turned off the stairwell and down a narrow hallway. Moonlight shined through a far window. Shoes and slippers and an occasional metal pee pot sat in front of closed wooden doors. The ceiling was so low that I had to duck. Ernie reached the end of the hallway and zipped to his right. When I rounded the corner he had opened a window and was climbing out.

Ernie lowered himself and then he let go. I heard a thud, looked out, and saw Ernie dusting himself off in a brick alleyway just wide enough for one person. I climbed through the window. Ernie braced me when I hit so I didn't fall backward. Then he pulled me toward the alley that ran behind the building. He squatted, peeked around the corner, and abruptly jerked his head back.

"KNPs," he whispered. "Off to the left about twenty meters. But there's an alley to our right less than ten meters away. We'll be exposed for a few yards but once we jog behind the brick wall, we'll be out of their line of sight. If we move quickly, they might not spot us. Even if they do, we'll have a head start and a clear run into down-town TDC."

"How do you know?"

"I know."

"That alley could be a dead end."

"You're too negative, Sueño."

Maybe I was. But Ernie didn't give me time to think about it. He peeked around the corner again, waved for me to follow, and trotted out onto the dark path. The KNPs didn't seem to notice. They were probably watching the roofs or checking the narrow walkways in front of them. But as soon as I emerged, someone shouted and then a whistle blew and it was as if the entire police force of TDC had zeroed in on my back. We ran. Ernie jogged to his left at the next alley and I followed. It was narrow, maybe six feet wide, lined by brick and wood and cement block walls on either side, protecting small courtyards and homes. The only illumination was from moon-light. The homes on either side were dark and there were no street lamps. I couldn't tell where I was stepping.

Korean sewers run underground, covered by stone blocks with fist-sized vents, lowered into place, not cemented. These blocks are sometimes lifted out for one reason or another or, more often, crushed by something heavy rolling over them. So you never know when a gaping hole may appear in an otherwise level flagstone walk-way. These thoughts surged through my mind as I peered into the darkness, moving cautiously, hoping not to crash into a hole and break my leg.

No similar doubts plagued Ernie. He ran flat-out down the mid-dle of the alley as if he were sprinting on a groomed track at the U.S. Olympic trials.

Ernie twisted and turned like a jackrabbit evading hounds. The warren of homes we passed stretched from the western edge of Tongduchon toward the east. Where we were exactly, I didn't know. Neither, apparently, did the KNPs. At intersections I slowed, glanced backward, and saw nothing coming at us through the darkness.

Finally, after a sharp turn, I almost plowed into Ernie.

Breathing heavily, he gazed down a slope at the shuttered envi-rons of the TDC bar district. The lanes were a little wider here, with shops and bars and coffeehouses, their neon signs switched off.

"Anybody following?" he asked.

"I think we lost 'em."

I bent forward and placed my hands on my knees, trying to regain my breath.

Ernie pointed. "There's an alley off to the left, behind that line of bars. It leads to the railroad tracks and beyond that the main gate."

"We can't go there," I said.

GIs passing through the main gate of Camp Casey this late would be arrested by the MPs for curfew violation and turned over to their unit commanders in the morning. With our 8th Army CID badges, Ernie and I were amongst the elite few in Korea who were exempt from the midnight to four curfew. The MPs wouldn't arrest us but they would note the time of our arrival in the duty log. Under the circumstances not an entry we wanted made.

And the KNPs would almost certainly be waiting for us in front of the main gate. Even though they hadn't been able to identify us specifically, the Korean cops knew—by our height and by our clothing—that we were foreigners. And only one type of foreigner lived in Tongduchon: American GIs.

"So where to?" Ernie asked.

In the Seoul bar district of Itaewon, our home turf, there were plenty of business girls and nightclub owners who would take us in. At least until curfew was over. But up here we were strangers. Mostly. Ok-hi and Jeannie knew us. But the Silver Dragon was on the far side of the bar district.

I was about to respond to Ernie's question when he shoved me against the wall.

"White mice," he whispered.

A few yards in front of us an American-made jeep, painted white, cruised by slowly. We stepped back farther into the shadows of a recessed gateway. Crossed beams from the jeep's headlights caressed the brick in front of us. We held our breath. The lights never faltered. They continued illuminating the brick wall, skipped over us in our dark enclave, and moved on.

When the sound of the jeep's engine faded, we started to

breathe again. It figured that the curfew police would patrol the bar district more diligently than they patrolled other parts of town. Trying to make it all the way to the Silver Dragon was too risky. So where could we go? There was only one other person in town that we knew.

"The Black Cat Club," I said. "It's closer. And some of the girls have hooches out back."

"Maybe they're busy."

"Maybe. But maybe Brandy lives there."

Brandy, the buxom bartender at the Black Cat Club.

"You asked for her address earlier," Ernie said. "They wouldn't give it to you."

"Maybe it's because she lives right there. On the premises."

Ernie snorted, unconvinced. "Well, the Black Cat Club is safer than standing out here all night," he said. "Which way?"

I pointed right. Together we slouched through the shadows.

The back of the Black Cat Club was as dark and as silent as a Yi Dynasty tomb. The double-doored wooden gate was barred from within and the stone wall protecting the back courtyard was topped with shards of broken glass embedded in cement.

"Looks like they don't welcome visitors," Ernie said.

"At least Koreans don't keep a big dog behind the wall," I said. "Our choice is to pound on the gate and make a racket until someone wakes up and comes out to talk to us, or else climb the fence."

"Raising a racket doesn't sound like a good idea."

The curfew police could pass by at any time. And if we made too much noise, a neighbor with a phone—although phones were rare in Tongduchon—might call and turn us in. Better to climb the fence. I cupped my hands in front of me. Ernie didn't hesitate. He stepped into my cupped hands and I hoisted him over the wall. Once inside, Ernie opened the small door in the large metal gate. I ducked through and he shut the door behind me.

It was your typical Korean courtyard lined with maybe eight hooches, sliding oil-papered doors facing inward, earthenware kimchee jars against the walls, and a rusty water spigot in the center of the courtyard with a plastic pail hanging from the valve. More hooches on the other side and then, I supposed, the back door of the Black Cat Club. We were about to slip past the hooches when the sound of human voices—harsh whispers—floated across tile roofs. Ernie waved his hand to signal danger and we crouched.

"Somebody's awake."

That didn't seem too surprising to me what with the noise we'd made climbing the wall and opening the front gate.

"I have to convince them not to call the police," I said.

Ernie nodded. I edged through a passageway between the line of hooches and the stone wall, then emerged into another open area that led to a door with a brightly painted wooden sign bearing a picture of a black cat. I was about to reach for the handle when the back door of the Black Cat Club burst open. Ten men emerged, all of them in various stages of undress, some with silver picks wedged in their hair, others with silk stockings knotted tightly over their skulls. Moonlight glistened off black flesh. Lips twisted into scowls. Cudgels were raised: a baseball bat, a pump handle, an army-issue entrenching tool.

"Hold it!" Ernie shouted.

He stood behind me, his .45 out, pointing at the group of men.

"What you doing here?" one of the men asked. "T-shirts ain't allowed."

A few of the men guffawed. None of them seemed concerned about Ernie's .45.

"Looking for Brandy," I said. "We need to talk to her."

"People need a lot of shit," the same man said. "Don't mean they get it."

He was one of the tallest of the men and, clearly, their leader. I was trying to think of a way to talk my way out of this confrontation but there were a lot of hard feelings between black GIs and white GIs. In the early seventies, the good fellowship of the civil rights movement had long been forgotten. Black GIs no longer waited patiently for the white power structure of the U.S. Army to reform. They were fighting back. Demanding equal promotions, an equal shot at choice assignments. Actually, I agreed with them. But there was a whole other element of the black experience—aside from the legitimate aspirations—that I, as a cop, had to deal with. The draft had been stopped a couple of years ago. To fill the ranks the army had lowered enlistment standards and young men with juvenile records a mile long—and even adult felony convictions—were being allowed to join up. The thinking was that the strict discipline of military life would straighten them out. Any MP could have told the geniuses at the Pentagon that they were wrong. Instead of going straight, career criminals continued their nefarious ways inside the ranks of the U.S. Army. That didn't mean that all the GIs standing in front of me were criminals. But you could bet that some of them were. And those few were the ones who would urge on their fellow soldiers to do things they wouldn't normally do. Like, for instance, beat the crap out of two 8th Army CID agents.

More black GIs appeared in the courtyard behind us. Ernie swiveled, arms extended, his .45 rotating as if on a gun turret.

"Look," I said, "we just want to talk to Brandy for a few minutes. That's all. Then we'll be on our way."

A few of the doors of the hooches slid open. Women appeared, Korean women. Some with Afro hairdos, most wearing silk see-through robes. All of them skinny. None voluptuous enough to be Brandy.

A propeller twirled through the air. I tried to dodge it but it clipped my shoulder and clattered to the flagstone steps below. A *mongdungi*, a wooden stick used to beat dirt out of wet clothing.

The women jeered.

The guy in front of me raised his baseball bat. Ernie swiveled, fired the .45, and the bat splintered into a thousand shards. Women screamed. Ernie shouted, "Get down!"

The men standing in the doorway of the Black Cat Club cursed and took cover in the courtyard.

"Come on!" Ernie said. "Enough of this bullshit!"

We ran past the splintered baseball bat, through the back door of the Black Cat Club, past the *byonso*, until we reached the main ballroom. A fluorescent bulb beneath the bar provided the only light. Keeping the .45 rotating, Ernie made his way to the door. He grabbed the iron handle and pulled. Locked. Barred from the inside.

"Hurry," he said.

I stepped past him, fiddled with the latches, and finally lifted a long metal rod. The door creaked open. A cold breeze drifted through the open crack.

Black men stood at the back exit, glaring.

"Tell Brandy," Ernie said, "that we're sorry we missed her."

With that, he fired the .45 into the rafters above the men's heads. They scattered. We pushed through the front door of the Black Cat Club and scampered out into the deserted streets of the Tongduchon bar district.

The gunfire had alerted the Korean National Police. Whistles shrilled and jeep engines roared, all zeroing in on the Black Cat Club. Ernie and I raced through back alleys.

"Why'd you have to shoot?" I asked.

Ernie answered as if I were nuts. "We have to maintain respect."

"I was talking to them," I said. "We could've worked something out."

"Bull. We'd broken into their hooch. The law was on the brothers' side for once. They were going to do what they do best. Kick the crap out of a couple of T-shirts."

Ernie had a dim view of human nature. Maybe he was right. There was a reason that 8th Army CID issued us .45s and it wasn't because people were reasonable. We rounded a corner and off to our left, from another alley, came the sound of a herd of footsteps stampeding toward the Black Cat Club. We hid in the shadows and watched.

On the main drag of the bar district, Korean cops, holding billy clubs at port arms, trotted in military formation.

"Dozens of 'em," Ernie whispered.

Going to the Black Cat Club hadn't done us any good. Instead of finding either Brandy or refuge, we'd called down the fury of Korean officialdom. We crouched in the dark alley, sweating, breathing hard, trying to calm down.

When the footsteps passed, Ernie said, "Where to now?"

"There are some brothels next to the bars. Maybe we can sneak into one and find some business girl who'll take us in."

Ernie didn't have a better idea.

We reached the main street of the Tongduchon bar district, about a long block east of where we'd seen the platoon of cops. A joint called the Seven Star Club loomed across the street from us. If the back doors were open, we might be able to gain access to the building and climb the stairs to the hooches above. No lights shined in any of the windows but it was the only plan I had. If we could hide until morning, we'd be able to reenter the compound amid the mass of GIs returning to Camp Casey. No one would be able to connect us with either the break-in at Kimchee Entertainment or the disturbance at the Black Cat Club.

I stared at the empty street, calculating our odds of avoiding the KNPs until dawn.

"Maybe we should stay here," I said.

"The patrols will be by eventually," Ernie replied, "as soon as they figure out what happened at the Black Cat Club. Besides, there're warm hooches in the Seven Star Club and pee pots and business girls. All the comforts of civilization."

Ernie was right. We had to chance it. I looked both ways. All quiet. I waved for Ernie and together we slouched across the road.

Looking back, I should've realized that the Korean National Police would figure out where we'd go next. The bar district. Where else would American GIs be welcomed in the middle of the night? Where else would a couple of miscreants like Ernie and me seek refuge? So when we stood behind the Seven Star Club, pleased with ourselves for having sneaked across the main drag, trying to decide whether to open the back door or climb through a window, suddenly, as if materializing out of the dark mist, KNPs converged on us from both ends of the alley.

Ernie elbowed me. "Don't look now."

I looked anyway. They wore riot-gear helmets and held three-foot-long wooden batons. About a dozen of them plugged each end of the alley.

Ernie reached for his .45.

I grabbed him, wrapped him in a bear hug, and held on. He realized the wisdom of what I was doing and didn't struggle. Without further incident, the Korean National Police took us into custody.

# 8

Torture is a relative term.

A person can consider himself to be undergoing torture simply by being denied something he craves. Cigarettes for a smoker. Caffeine for a coffee drinker. Take me for instance. I started drinking coffee during my first tour in Korea in the middle of the frigid winter. Now it's a habit. Every day on the way to work I stop at the 8th Army snack bar and guzzle two mugs of steaming hot coffee that's brewed in huge stainless steel urns. Then and only then do I feel ready to face the day.

Korean cops don't drink coffee. Too expensive. Usually, they have a pot of barley tea brewing somewhere in the station. The lieutenants and other higher-ups might brew a pot of green tea on hot plates behind their desks. But no java. And even if there had been coffee available, the KNPs wouldn't have offered me any. Nor Ernie, who kept raising hell and cussing them out.

I tried to reason with my interrogator. He wasn't a bad guy, actually. Captain Ma was his name and he was a friendly cop with a skinny, chain-smoking body and a wrinkled, smiling face that, since it was always grinning, was totally unreadable. I couldn't tell if he was about to honor me with an award for lifetime achievement or slice out my spleen. I sat on a wooden chair, barefoot, wearing only a T-shirt and pants. The rest of my clothing had been taken from me. Also, in case I forgot to mention it, my wrists were handcuffed behind my back. Tightly. Part of the torture.

No bamboo beneath the fingernails. Not yet.

Without having talked it over, Ernie and I arrived at the same alibi. Of course we were separated immediately after our arrest and were not allowed to communicate in any way—a basic tenet of Interrogation 101. But the fact that our stories dovetailed wasn't miraculous. It made sense if you understood the first rule of lying: Stick with the truth, until it becomes inconvenient. Then say as little as possible.

So we each told the KNPs the same story. We were in Tongduchon searching for leads on the disappearance of Corporal Jill Matthewson and, in particular, we were searching for a woman known as Brandy, a bartender at the Black Cat Club. Why had we been out after curfew? Because we weren't able to find her before curfew.

Why had we fired a weapon at the Black Cat Club? Simply to convince a few local citizens not to interfere with an ongoing police investigation.

Then the big question: Had we been in the western district of Tongduchon earlier this evening, at the office of a man known as Pak Tong-i? This is where the truth became inconvenient. We both answered no.

Had we ever talked to Mr. Pak? I didn't know. The name didn't ring a bell.

Had we ever visited the office of Kimchee Entertainment? I couldn't be sure. I'd have to review my notes. And on it went like this. No violence. Only the threat of it. While Captain Ma grinned, another cop paced the room, cussing in vulgar Korean and slamming his black leather-gloved fist into his open palm.

Of course the Korean cops weren't stupid. They'd spotted two foreigners at the scene of the Pak Tong-i murder and they knew those two foreigners were most likely me and my partner, Ernie

Bascom. But they also knew that the body of Pak Tong-i was as cold as a KNP's heart. He'd been dead for hours and it wasn't likely that we'd have hung around that long if we were the ones who had murdered him. That's why Ernie and I could afford to stonewall. Eventually, they'd realize they had no evidence against us and they'd let us go. Discharging a firearm within city limits and being out after curfew were crimes for normal citizens but not for law enforcement officers. Still, the KNPs wanted whatever information we had and they wanted it badly.

But I'd developed a certain level of skepticism since I'd arrived in Tongduchon. I wasn't sure who was responsible for the disappearance of Corporal Jill Matthewson or the stripper, Kim Yong-ai, nor for Pak Tong-i's death, for that matter. Until I knew more, I didn't feel like trusting anyone.

Captain Ma, under the Status of Forces Agreement between the United States and the Republic of Korea, was required to notify the 2nd Division MP duty officer concerning our arrest. That much he promised. Nothing more.

Through the entire interrogation a third man sat in a chair behind me, off to my left, observing. The foul odor of his cigarette smoke permeated my nostrils. Kobukson, I figured. Turtle Boat brand. I couldn't see him clearly; he was careful to avoid my line of sight, but using peripheral vision, I formed a picture of him. Korean. Older, maybe mid to late forties. Wearing civvies. Jacket and tie, overcoat, even a cloth porkpie hat that he kept on the table next to him. He smoked occasionally, only half as much as Captain Ma, and he held his cigarettes in some sort of holder. Plastic? Ivory? I couldn't tell. He wore gloves that he slipped on and off. He gave the impression of a man who performed every movement, even the tiniest act, with precision.

Captain Ma and the other cop in the interrogation room ignored him. For them, he wasn't there. And for his part, the mystery man didn't say a word.

Just after dawn, representatives from the 2nd Infantry Division arrived. August personages both: Lieutenant Colonel Stanley X. Alcott, the 2nd ID Provost Marshal and Military Police Investigator, Warrant Officer One Fred Bufford. Colonel Alcott shook hands all the way around—but not with me—and grinned a lot. Warrant

Officer Bufford stood awkwardly in a corner, shaking hands with no one, studying me.

I sat up as straight as possible in my chair—as straight as the handcuffs would allow—and thrust my shoulders back as far as they would go. As I did so I checked my peripheral vision. The mystery man had disappeared.

Colonel Alcott peered at me. "What the hell did you *do*, Sueño?"

I didn't feel like answering. Colonel Alcott should've demanded that I be released from my handcuffs immediately. I was a U.S. military investigator, innocent until proven guilty—under American jurisprudence anyway—and the benefit of the doubt should've been automatic. Instead, Alcott was busy glad-handing with the KNPs, ignoring me, showing them by inference that they could do with me whatever the hell they pleased.

Although I was tempted to show my disdain for Colonel Alcott by refusing to answer him, finally, I piped up.

"I didn't *do* anything," I replied. "My partner and I were out after curfew trying to track down a lead."

"But you fired your weapon."

"Only when someone attempted to interfere with our investigation."

Bufford, leaning against the wall, could no longer contain himself. He pointed a bony finger at me.

"You were in west Tongduchon," he said. "A man was murdered out there."

I stared directly at him. "Your ass," I growled.

That shut him up. Colonel Alcott shook his round head. "Sueño, your attitude is not good."

"Take these handcuffs off me," I said. "My attitude will make a miraculous recovery."

Colonel Alcott continued to shake his head. "Unfortunately," he said, "that's not my decision to make."

"The hell," I said. "If you vouch for me, these Korean cops would release me in a heartbeat. And my partner, too."

Colonel Alcott responded with a tone of exaggerated reasonableness. "But how well do I know you? You and Agent Bascom are sent up here to the Division area of operations, supposedly to search for Corporal Matthewson, but you end up investigating god knows what. What am I supposed to tell the KNPs? You're up here doing something but I don't know what it is, and you're out after curfew and weapons are fired and a man turns up murdered and I'm supposed to risk the prestige of the Second Infantry Division to have you released? Based on what?"

"Based on you could call the Eighth Army provost marshal. He'd order it."

"Ah, yes. The Eighth Army provost marshal. That will be done. As soon as the Division chief of staff is fully briefed."

"When will that be?"

"Don't be impertinent." For the first time since I'd known him, the round, pleasant face of Colonel Stanley X. Alcott flushed red. "You don't hurry the Second Infantry Division. We have procedures. We observe protocol. Maybe something you and that Agent What's-His-Name . . ."

"Bascom," Bufford said.

"Yes. Agent Bascom. Maybe you two don't know what it is to follow procedures but up here in Division we have procedures, and we're damn sure going to adhere to them."

Through the entire conversation, Captain Ma kept puffing on his cigarette, smiling, amused that people who appeared to him so foreign could hold such a long conversation. He reminded me of a zoologist observing baboons.

The 2nd Infantry Division chief of staff would be briefed in an hour or two at the daily staff meeting. Then the decision would be made to inform 8th Army about our arrest and then the 8th Army provost marshal would discuss the situation with the 8th Army commander and finally—hopefully—word would be sent down to request transfer of custody from the KNPs to the 2nd Infantry Division.

That gave the smiling Captain Ma, puffing serenely on a cigarette, many hours to mess with me.

It was midafternoon by the time the doors of my jail cell clanged open.

Two KNP recruits, their khaki uniforms pressed to glistening creases, entered the cell, handcuffed me again, and walked me down a long, wood-floored corridor and upstairs into another interrogation room.

This time Captain Ma wasn't there. Instead, the mystery man entered, a middle-aged man in jacket and tie and overcoat and porkpie hat and, what I could see now, were goatskin gloves on either hand. He sat down on the chair opposite mine.

"*Mian-hamnida*," he said. "I'm sorry. The KNPs have treated you very badly."

His face was full, not fat, with fleshy cheeks that bobbed when he shook his head. He lit up a cigarette. I was right. The brand was Kobukson and the holder was made of ivory. Or faux ivory.

"Are you a cop?" I asked.

"Not exactly."

His English—what I'd heard of it so far—was perfect. No hesitation in answering me, each word pronounced crisply, precisely. This wasn't your usual KNP.

"Then what exactly are you?"

"First, let's have those handcuffs removed."

He barked a command and the two young KNPs who'd escorted me into the interrogation room burst through the door. He barked more commands and my hands were freed.

"The rest of my clothes?" I asked. "And my identification?"

"Soon. Someone's arrived from Eighth Army to fetch you."

*Fetch?* This guy's English was becoming more impressive by the minute.

"Who?" I asked.

"In time." He blew smoke in the air from his Turtle boat cigarette. "Now is my time."

His first grammatical failing.

"What do you want to talk to me about?" I asked.

"About Corporal Matthewson."

I tried to hide the surprise on my face.

"We believe she's become a deserter," he said.

*Deserter.* A loaded word. Technically, Corporal Jill Matthewson would begin to be carried on the 2nd Division books as a deserter as soon as she had been absent without leave for thirty days. One week from today. This is standard procedure. But this mystery man was calling her a deserter right now. To classify Corporal Matthewson as a deserter before the thirty days were up, you needed knowledge of her intent, her intent to desert. But I ignored the word *deserter* for a moment.

"Who," I asked, "is 'we'?"

He waved his cigarette in the air. "Unimportant. What's important is that we have reason to believe that you will be opposed, and opposed quite forcefully, if you continue your search for Corporal Matthewson."

"Are you warning me to stop?"

"Not at all. This is just one cop to another. There are dangerous people involved and I feel it is only fair to warn you that this is not your usual—how you say?—fender bender."

"Not your usual missing person's case."

"Exactly."

His big Asian face beamed, satisfied that I was beginning to understand. I felt like a disciple of Confucius who'd just realized the importance of filial piety.

"But you don't want me to stop looking for her," I said.

He shrugged. "That's up to you. And your superiors."

"Are you looking for her?"

He shrugged again.

"Will you try to stop me?"

This time he didn't move. Instead, he puffed on his cigarette and studied me through the smoke. A long silence passed between us.

"We've heard of you," he said. "We Koreans are always impressed when a foreigner takes the time to learn our language, to understand our culture. You're respected. Maybe not your partner, but you. That's why I'm warning you."

He allowed his cigarette to drop to the wood-slat floor. He hoisted himself from his chair and stomped on the burning butt.

"Go back to Seoul," he said. "You'll live longer."


"You guys look like shit."

The man who stood in the reception area of the Tongduchon Police Station was Staff Sergeant Riley, the Administrative NCO of the 8th Army Criminal Investigation Division. He was even thinner than most of the Korean cops and his frail body seemed lost in the starched material of his fatigue uniform. His teeth were crooked and he wore his black hair just a little longer than regulation. During the duty day he greased it down and combed it straight back but at night, when the work day was done, he wore it in a rakish pompadour, like some has-been fifties rock star.

Ernie and I ignored his insult. Maybe we did look like shit. But after being locked in a Korean dungeon for the better part of a twelve-hour period, we were delighted to see him. Outside, a green four-door army-issue sedan stood ready to whisk us to freedom.

"What about my jeep?" Ernie asked.

"Division's bringing it," Riley answered.

"Tell them to keep their paws off it."

Riley ignored him. There was paperwork to complete. On behalf of the 8th United States Army, Staff Sergeant Riley signed receipts for Ernie and me, as if we were items of property. At the time he took us into custody, he assumed responsibility for our future conduct.

I felt like a toaster he'd won at a raffle.

After the paperwork was done, we retrieved our clothing and our identification. The final things the KNPs turned over to Riley were our .45's, wrapped in plain brown paper and tied tightly with twine. He tucked the two weapons under his arm. None of the KNPs came to see us off. Outside, Ernie and I stood for a moment, breathing the late afternoon air, laced with the aroma of burnt diesel and fermenting kimchee. The breeze from the north was bitingly cold but we didn't mind. To us it was the bite of freedom. Down the road, in the TDC bar district, neon began to twinkle to life, as if to fight back against the gray overcast that darkened the sky.

As we sauntered down the sidewalk, Staff Sergeant Riley assured us that we hadn't been charged with a crime. However, Division had lodged a formal complaint with the 8th Army provost marshal about our firing rounds at their soldiers. In response, the 8th Army PMO agreed that we would be withdrawn from the 2nd Division area of operations.

"Immediately if not sooner," was the way Riley put it.

Ernie howled. "What? You've got to be shitting me? We were just starting to make progress."

Riley shook his head. "I'm not 'shitting' anybody. If you were making progress, you should've made it faster. Eighth Army says you're history up here."

Racial tensions were high at all fifty-seven U.S. military base camps throughout the Republic of Korea and the 8th Army honchos were well aware of it. A couple of years ago there'd been riots in Itaewon—black GIs fighting white GIs—and the Command had received horrible press coverage. They weren't taking any chances of that happening again.

As soon as we reached Riley's sedan, three jeeps pulled alongside. Two armed Division MPs sat in the first two. Trailing them was another jeep we recognized. Ernie's. An MP was driving that one, too, and they refused to turn the jeep over to us until we reached the border of the Division AO. Argument was futile, so Ernie and I climbed into the sedan.

As Riley slid into the driver's seat, he said, "Watch the merchandise back there."

Ernie grunted. I looked back and saw an old army blanket covering some lumpy objects. Probably Riley was black-marketeering. The less I knew the better.

We pulled away from the police station, cruising south toward the Main Supply Route. Within a mile, we'd left the city limits of Tongduchon. The two Division MP jeeps and Ernie's 8th Army jeep trailed behind us. No one spoke. Ernie and I were too exhausted. I still hadn't had a chance to tell Ernie about the mystery man. Time for that later.

About five miles on, we reached the southernmost Division checkpoint. The MP guards and the Korean honbyong had been notified by field radio to expect our little convoy. Holding their automatic rifles pointed at the sky, they blew their whistles shrilly, and waved us on. About twenty yards past the checkpoint, we reached the last row of dragon's teeth. Four-foot-high cement monoliths stretched away from the MSR for miles on either side, like a poor man's version of the Great Wall of China.

Riley pulled over and so did the Division MPs. The guy driving

Ernie's jeep hopped out, tossed the keys to Riley, and climbed into the back of one of the Division MP jeeps. Without so much as a fare-thee-well, the Division MPs performed a U-turn and roared off back north, gunning their engines all the while. Irritated, apparently, at having to venture so close to the realms of REMF territory.

Riley tossed the keys to Ernie. "Can you drive?" he asked.

"Can I drive?" Ernie growled out the question, leaving no doubt that he believed he was capable of driving under any conditions.

As Ernie walked toward the jeep, Riley turned in his seat and said, "Okay. You can come out now."

The bundles beneath the army blanket wiggled. Then the old blanket was tossed back and a huge Afro hairdo emerged. With a big smile spread across round cheeks, a voluptuous woman rose from the back seat of Riley's sedan like Athena springing from the brow of Zeus.

"Ain't no bag, man," she said.

Brandy, the bartender from the Black Cat Club, the woman we'd been searching for last night. She stared directly into my eyes, smiling. Amused by the completeness of my surprise.

About five miles farther south—while we were still fifteen miles north of Seoul—Riley pulled off the Main Supply Route and onto a road that led to the main gate of Camp Red Cloud, the I Corps head-quarters. After we were cleared by the MPs at the gate, he drove to a large wooden building with a huge sign out front: The Papa-san Club. I'd heard about it. An NCO club that was rumored to be one of the best in the country.

Riley, Brandy, and I climbed out of the sedan. Ernie climbed out of the jeep, screaming at the top of his lungs.

"Did you see what those bastards did?"

He motioned toward the back seat of his jeep. We all walked over. Our traveling bags sat in the front passenger seat, chock full of our clothing and belongings that had been stuffed into them. Apparently, the Division MPs had checked us out of billeting. But the back seat was what Ernie was upset about. It was in tatters. Black leather tuck-and-roll upholstery, had been shredded systematically with what must've been a very sharp knife. White cotton puffed out of the wounds like popcorn.

"I paid good money for that tuck-and-roll," Ernie said, "and now look at it."

This jeep was exclusively assigned to Ernie. But not officially. Officially, vehicles were rotated based on the priority established by local commanders. However, Ernie made sure a bottle of imported Scotch landed on the desk of the head dispatcher at the 21 T Car motor pool in Seoul every month. Therefore, the jeep was his. And he paid to have it maintained and painted and cleaned regularly. The tuck-and-roll had been an additional touch. If he thought he could've gotten away with it, Ernie would've equipped his jeep with reverse chrome rims and had it painted cherry red.

"Just spite," Ernie told us. "Petty jealousy and spite."

And then he realized that Brandy had joined us and he leaned over and hugged her, a little too long I thought. After Ernie'd calmed down somewhat, the four of us walked up cement stairs into the warm environs of Western civilization. Or Western civilization as its practiced in the military compounds of the 8th United States Army.

After chow, Riley was anxious to get back on the road and return to Seoul.

"You have a day off tomorrow," he said. "It's Sunday. But first thing Monday morning the First Shirt wants you two back on the black-market detail."

"Bullshit," Ernie said.

He expressed my feelings exactly. More chasing GIs—or their Korean spouses—through the back alleys of Itaewon to bust them for selling duty-free PX goods on the Korean black market. A waste of time. Especially when real crime swirled all around us.

The cannon went off outside at I Corps Headquarters and the flag was lowered; a few NCOs drifted into the bar. A Korean go-go girl climbed up onto a round stage and after a few coins were dropped into the jukebox, she started dancing. Brandy watched her intently, perhaps imagining that she'd look even better in the sequined outfit. Then Brandy told us what she was doing here. After the fiasco at the Black Cat Club last night, when she'd heard that we were looking for her, she'd waited until curfew was over and come looking for us. Earlier today, she'd hooked up with Riley. Now, most significantly, she felt guilty that she'd previously held out on us concerning the whereabouts of Jill Matthewson.

"Jill made me promise. Don't tell nobody where she go."

"So where'd she go?" Ernie asked.

Brandy didn't know. But she claimed that she could put us in touch with somebody who did know. Somebody who was desperate to talk to us about the disappearance of Corporal Jill Matthewson.

I pressed Brandy on why she hadn't told us this before. She said at first she couldn't be sure if we were working for 2nd Division. Jill was afraid of the Division, although Brandy wasn't sure why. Once we were arrested by the KNPs, and kicked out of Tongduchon by the 2nd ID honchos, Brandy decided that she'd better fess up.

"Maybe Jill need help," she said. "I don't know. But I trust you guys now."

The new lead Brandy provided made up my mind. We had to return to TDC and follow it up. Ernie agreed with me immediately. Staff Sergeant Riley, however, went into shock.

"You can't go back up to Division," he said. "You'll be refusing to comply with the provost marshal's direct order to return to Seoul."

"Tomorrow's Sunday," Ernie said. "During our off-duty time we can go anywhere we want."

"But Eighth Army specifically told you to stay out of the Division area of operations."

"What they don't know, won't hurt them," Ernie said. "Besides, Jill Matthewson is still missing."

"The Division MPs will find her," Riley replied.

"They haven't yet," I responded. "And after what Brandy just told us, they may not want to find her. Not alive anyway."

"You're full of it," Riley said. "So maybe she can embarrass the Division. It's happened before. They'll survive. But they have no reason to murder her."

"Maybe she's already been murdered," Ernie said.

"Maybe its more than just embarrassment," I added. "Careers could be involved. Did you ever find those ration control plate records I asked for?"

"I checked with Smitty at Data Processing. He says those records are classified. Locked in the OIC's safe." The safe of the officer-in-charge.

"Can he get to them?"

"Maybe. But it's going to cost me."

"We need to know what's on them," Ernie said. "That could bring this whole thing together. Once we lay it on the 8th Army PMO's desk, he'll order that the records be declassified."

Riley sipped on his double bourbon. His thin lips curled as if he were sucking a persimmon. "Do you guys have any idea what you're messing with?"

"Honchos," I said. "They step on little people and don't expect anyone to fight back."

Ernie set his drink down, rose from the cocktail table, and said, "I'm heading back up to Division, Sueño, with or without you. And, this time, instead of being slapped around like a red-headed stepchild, I plan to kick some serious ass."


The new evidence Brandy spilled to us centered around something she referred to as "mafia meetings." She hadn't told the KNPs about them, nor had she mentioned them to anyone else, including us, because Jill Matthewson made her promise not to.

"Jill pissed off," Brandy told us. "She MP, same-same like man, but in jeep she have to carry *meikju*." Beer. "She takey, go from black-market honcho place over to . . . what you call that place? WV something."

Brandy pronounced the letter *v* as something similar to "boo-we." Koreans have a lot of trouble with *v*'s and *z*'s since neither letter appears in their alphabet.

"WVOW," I said. The Wounded Veterans of Overseas Wars. They ran the small casino on the outskirts of Tongduchon.

"Yeah," Brandy said. "That place. Then she have to go pick up from Pak Tong-i, Miss Kim. Takey back WVOW."

It wasn't a pretty picture but not unheard of in the U.S. Army. Some lower-level officer or NCO—in this case probably Warrant Officer Fred Bufford—is given the responsibility of setting up the meeting. The honcho—probably Colonel Alcott—says something like, "I don't care how you do it, just do it." Bufford's not given any money so he uses the resources he has. That is, MPs, MP jeeps, and whatever influence he might have over the businessmen in Tongduchon. Jill Matthewson picks up beer contributed by a local TDC black marketeer and she also picks up a stripper contributed by Kimchee Entertainment. Why would these men contribute such valuable commodities to a mafia meeting? Because the colonels who run the 2nd Infantry Division exercise huge influence in Tongduchon. They can decide, for instance, if GIs are to be given overnight passes on payday or if an entire battalion of 1,200 men should be restricted to compound. Or which contractor will be awarded a bid to build a new officers' club annex on Camp Casey. Also, they can decide how to utilize the provost marshal's finite resources. For instance, should they have MP investigators chase violent criminals or should they assign them to spend their time trying to interrupt the smooth operations of the TDC black market? Faced with this kind of power, Korean businessmen—especially the ones involved in corruption—would contribute to the mafia meeting and contribute gladly.

So Corporal Jill Matthewson transports the entire load over to the WVOW Club. When everything's set up, the honchos arrive: staff colonels from the 2nd Infantry Division, every one a full bird. Then, according to Brandy, Jill was forced to stand outside the front of the club, in uniform, and make sure no uninvited guests entered.

She didn't like the duty. She didn't like what was going on inside the WVOW. She didn't like the additional business girls who were brought over by Pak Tong-i and other local businessmen. And she didn't like the photographs that were shown to her later, photos taken secretly by Miss Kim Yong-ai. Photos of most of the honchos of the 2nd Infantry Division engaged in various compromising positions with the Korean business girls who tended to be less than half their ages.

Actually, I'd heard of mafia meetings before. They're a tradition in the U.S. Army. Staff officers get together during off-duty hours in an informal setting and exchange ideas concerning the best ways to improve operations in the division and the best ways to effectively implement the policies of the commanding general. Nothing wrong with that. But apparently the participants at the 2nd Infantry Division had lost sight of the original intent of the meetings.

Maybe a male MP assigned to the same job as Jill Matthewson would've laughed the whole thing off. Maybe he would've slugged down a few bottles of the free beer and grabbed one of the business girls for himself and pulled her into a back room when none of the honchos were watching. Instead of joining the frivolities, Jill had been forced to listen to the complaints of her friend, Kim Yong-ai. And witness her tears.

"She stripper," Brandy told us indignantly. "Not supposed to be business girl. But honchos grab her while she dance. She say stop but they no stop. Pretty soon her clothes off, she on floor, and they do her same-same business girl."

Ernie didn't laugh although for a moment his eyes twinkled as if he wanted to. But quickly he realized that the distinction between a dancer and a prostitute was an important one, at least to the women involved. In a Confucian society, status and position in society is everything. And when it's violated, especially when it's violated by foreigners, the loss of face hurts almost as much, and sometimes more, than any physical abuse suffered.

You could bet that the young Korean business girls at the mafia meetings didn't really want to be there either. Poverty and neglect had forced them into their world of shame. But at least when they walked into the WVOW, they knew what to expect. Kim Yong-ai, according to Brandy, was outraged by her treatment. But who could she complain to? Not Pak Tong-i; he was beholden for his living to the powers that be. Not the Korean National Police; they worked hand in hand with the honchos at the 2nd Infantry Division and certainly knew about, and maybe even participated in, the mafia meetings. And she couldn't complain to the 2nd Infantry Division Military Police, they were the ones who had set up the party. Miss Kim Yong-ai had no one in the world to complain to. No one, that is, except Corporal Jill Matthewson.

I thought of the two thousand dollars Jill and Miss Kim had paid Pak Tong-i and I asked Brandy about it. "Did Jill ever mention money to you?"

"Money? No. I just know she pissed off. So was Kim Yong-ai."

"So what were they going to do about it?" Ernie asked.

"I don't know," Brandy answered. "Next thing, they *karra chogi*." They ran away.

What Brandy told us was something I should've figured for myself. It was a missing link that stitched a lot of disparate elements together, that showed us how Corporal Jill Matthewson and the stripper, Kim Yong-ai, and the booking agent, Pak Tong-i, and the honchos of the 2nd Infantry Division were tied together.

It had all the elements that so often lead to crime. Money: two thousand dollars that suddenly appeared to pay off Kim Yong-ai's debts. Sex: the daily sexual harassment of an American female MP and the forced sexual degradation of a Korean stripper. Power: the wrath of the 2nd Infantry Division power structure that someone would have the temerity to disappear and cause them embarrassment. An embarrassment that rose not only as high as 8th Army headquarters but all the way to the United States Congress.

# 9

It was too dangerous to drive Ernie's jeep back into the Division AO. The MPs would've taken note of the unit designation and jeep number stenciled on the bumper. Instead, Ernie left it in the care of a buck sergeant with grease-stained fingers at the Camp Red Cloud motor pool, promising him a free pizza dinner at the Papa-san Club upon our return.

Staff Sergeant Riley made us promise once more that we'd be back at 8th Army headquarters for duty Monday morning. "Tonight and Sunday," he said. "That's all the time you've got. If you don't find Matthewson by then, you're back in Seoul where you belong."

We agreed. Then he nodded goodbye to Brandy and drove his sedan back to Seoul.

In front of the Camp Red Cloud main gate, Ernie, Brandy, and I waved down a kimchee cab. Brandy gave directions to a village east of here known as Koyang. We traveled on back roads, avoiding the MSR. Our goal was to dodge all 2nd Infantry Division checkpoints, to sneak back into the 2nd Infantry Division area of operations without being noticed.

Koyang was a small cluster of buildings, one of which featured the Chinese characters for *sokyu*—"rock oil"—overhead: a gas station. The little town also had a noodle shop and a transshipment point for produce. We climbed out of the cab, shivered in the cold February wind, and after we paid the driver, we watched him make a U-turn and speed back toward Uijongbu.

The shadows of quivering poplar trees began to grow long; evening would soon be upon us. Ernie and I checked our pockets. We each had about forty bucks on us, plenty to last us until we returned to Seoul Monday morning.

Brandy entered the noodle shop, chatted with the owner, and within five minutes another local cab pulled up, ready to transport us north to Bopwon-ni. Legal Hall Village. We climbed in and the little sedan sped north. The two-lane road followed a meandering valley. Fallow rice paddies spread on one side and elm-covered hills rose on the other. Swaths of snow clung to the hills although, since we'd arrived, there'd been no new snowfalls. Unusual for February. Atop many of the hills were burial mounds and atop one of them was an elaborate stone-carved statute of an ancient king of the Yi Dynasty.

"It's like another world back here," Ernie said.

I knew what he meant. Even though we were only some twenty miles north of Seoul as the crow flies, there was a mountain range between us and Seoul and smaller ranges of hills on either side of this valley. Few modern amenities existed back here. Telephone and electrical lines paralleled the road and that was about it. Gazing in any direction, one could imagine that he'd been transported back in time to the ancient kingdom known as the Land of the Morning Calm. The sun sank behind the hills to the west, darkening straw-thatched roofs.

There were few military installations in this valley. No U.S. bases and only one or two small ROK Army compounds specializing in communications. Although we were only fifteen or so miles south of the DMZ, we were tucked snugly between the two main invasion routes known as the Western Corridor and the Eastern Corridor. We were slipping into 2nd Infantry Division territory stealthily. And if the KNPs interviewed either one of our cab drivers, neither would be able to give them our entire route.

I still didn't know how Brandy had hooked up with Staff Sergeant Riley. I asked and she told us.

"When you come look for me last night, *taaksan* trouble." A lot of trouble. "All kimchee business girl, all GI soul brother, *taaksan kullaso*." Very angry. "Why I bring MP T-shirt Black Cat Club? they ask me. I say you not MP, you CID."

I'm sure that calmed them down.

"So I go checky-checky KNP police station. Nobody outside. I wait. Pretty soon, GI car come. Not jeep. Not tank. Not big truck."

"It was a sedan," Ernie said.

"Right. So must be Eight Army. Skinny GI get out, crooked teeth, I go talk to him. He like me. He buy me drink before go in KNP station, pretty soon he tell me everything about you two guys, so I tell him I need to talk to you so he let me hide in back of GI car."

"That's Riley," Ernie said. "Spills anything to a pretty face."

"After a drink or two," I added.

As we sped along the narrow country lane, we spoke freely, assuming that the driver couldn't understand English. A safe assumption. The dark shadows of night continued to roll in and by the time we reached Bopwon-ni, the small town was bejeweled with shining light bulbs. No neon. But at the main intersection there was a tea-house and two-story beer hall. SSANG-YONG, the sign said, A Pair of Dragons. It portrayed two enormous reptiles entwined in battle. We ordered the driver to pull over, paid him, and climbed out of the cab.

Inside the beer hall, the odor of salted octopus assaulted our nostrils. It was a nice fishy smell, interlaced with the sharp tang of red pepper powder and raw *nakji*, squid, another specialty of the house. The three of us each ordered a mug of draft OB. We turned down the raw squid, which most of the other customers were pecking away at with their chopsticks. In order to save face, I instead ordered a plate of *anju*, dried cuttlefish with a pepper sauce dip and a couple dozen unhusked peanuts on the side. Koreans believe that it's unhealthy to drink alcohol on an empty stomach and bar owners capitalize on this belief by overcharging for plates of sliced fruit and dried cuttlefish and other snacks. Not to mention the raw squid.

While we nibbled, I studied the crowd. Most of the heavy drinking was being done by Korean businessmen in suits. They had bottles of Scotch in the center of tables and were busy toasting one another, round glasses raised to red faces. At other tables there were young Koreans, college-age, sipping slowly on beer. And a few women in groups, none alone. At the pool tables, at least a dozen men in ROK Army fatigue uniforms. The patches on their left arms showed a globe with a lightning bolt running through it, which led me to believe that they were probably assigned to one of those communication compounds we'd passed.

Not a GI in sight. Nor a Korean business girl. The influence of foreigners had yet to defile the Pair of Dragons beer hall. Therefore, Ernie and I caught a lot of stares. But most of the gawking was reserved for Brandy. Not for her pulchritude. Here, in a Confucian society, she was stared at for her brazenness. For her huge Afro hairdo, for nonchalantly sitting with two foreign men, for guzzling draft beer rather than sipping something more ladylike, like a glass of pineapple juice or a cup of ginseng tea. She created quite a stir. After we finished our beers, I suggested we leave before one of the drunken Korean businessmen said something to her, she snapped back, and Ernie became involved.

To avoid trouble we had to keep moving.

Outside, we flagged down another cab. This one drove us east from Bopwon-ni, down dark country roads, through quiet straw-thatched farming villages. The three-quarter moon still loitered in a dark sky. Then, just as we all were about to become drowsy, we reached our first ROK Army checkpoint.

The driver slowed, turned off his headlights, and we stopped while armed Korean soldiers peered into the cab. Both of the young men did a double take when they saw Brandy but then they regained their stern expressions and demanded everyone's ID. The cab driver fished out his license first and then Ernie and I showed our regular military ID cards—not our CID badges. Finally, Brandy handed over her Korean national identity card. I figured it would be unlikely that these two Korean soldiers, out here standing alone in the frigid night, would go to the trouble of notifying the 2nd Infantry Division of our presence. The ROK Army and the 2nd Infantry Division coordinated major troop movements at the Division level but they didn't cooperate on day-to-day routine. As I suspected, the Korean soldiers barely glanced at our IDs before waving us on. What they were concerned with were North Korean commandos. Not a couple of GIs with a Korean woman who was marked both by her hairdo and by the company she kept, as a business girl.

After we drove on, I mentally started to list the people who might have a reason to murder Pak Tong-i. I started with Jill Matthewson. Would she have a motive? To retrieve her two thousand bucks? Maybe. To make sure that—if he knew where she was hiding—he wouldn't reveal her secret? Maybe. How about the stripper, Kim Yong-ai? Maybe the same two motives. And maybe another one: Pak Tong-i had been instrumental in her degradation. He'd taken her to the mafia meeting and then done nothing to protect her from what Brandy described as gang rape. And the amulet that sat in my pocket indicated that Mr. Pak and Miss Kim had had a thing going. How could he allow his own girlfriend to be abused like that? Certainly Miss Kim had a motive.

How about someone in the 2nd Division Provost Marshal's Office or the provost marshal himself? Pak Tong-i knew about the free black-market goods and the free women, and maybe someone had heard that one of Pak's strippers had taken some photographs. Where were the photos now? With Kim Yong-ai, according to Brandy. But someone had searched Pak's office. Were they looking for those photos? Were they willing to kill to obtain them? Or were they looking for the whereabouts of Corporal Jill Matthewson and Kim Yong-ai?

Maybe the Korean National Police had murdered Pak Tong-i. Maybe they'd been questioning him, asking him about the whereabouts of Kim Yong-ai or Corporal Jill Matthewson. Maybe he'd refused to tell them. Maybe.

I was using the term *murder* in its legal sense. I'm no doctor but it appeared to me that Pak Tong-i had died of a heart attack. Still, if an intruder broke into his office, frightened him, questioned him, maybe tortured him, and this had caused a weak heart to burst, then he would be responsible for his death. According to the Uniform Code of Military Justice, it would be murder.

Maybe gangsters had murdered Pak Tong-i. Maybe he hadn't turned the two thousand dollars over as promised. Maybe they came to collect and Pak no longer had the money or refused to pay.

Maybe the mystery man who'd witnessed my interrogation at the Tongduchon Police Station had murdered Pak Tong-i. Why? All he had told me was that powerful people were somehow involved in this case. Who they were or why they were involved? That, he failed to mention.

Finally, I admitted to myself that I had no idea who had murdered Pak Tong-i. I didn't have enough information. Maybe I'd never have enough information. Our goal up here was still to find Corporal Jill Matthewson, not to solve a Korean civilian's murder. But something told me that before we found her we'd have to solve not only the murder of Pak Tong-i but also resolve the mysterious death of Private Marvin Z. Druwood. And, incidentally, we'd have to put to rest the wanderings of Miss Chon Un-suk's hungry ghost.

The little cab bounced over a hill and then, spread out before us like a sudden gift from the gods, lay the neon-spangled city known as Tongduchon.

The main reason Ernie and I had decided to risk coming back was to find Corporal Jill Matthewson. The second reason was because of what Brandy had promised us: a rendezvous. With a man who knew Pak Tong-i and claimed to have information on the whereabouts of Jill Matthewson and Miss Kim Yong-ai. He'd contacted her early last night, while she was tending bar at the Black Cat Club. Of course he hadn't come in himself, no self-respecting Korean man would enter a GI nightclub. Instead, a boy came in, a raggedy street urchin, and he'd asked for her by name, *Bu-ran-dee*. When Brandy acknowledged who she was, the boy handed her a note and waited hopefully for a gift of food or money. When Brandy had read the note she asked him who had sent it but, frightened, he scurried back into the street.

While we'd sat at that cocktail table in the Papa-san Club in Uijongbu, Brandy showed us the note. Scribbled *hangul* script. I had to read it two or three times to make it out. The writer wanted to meet with the two American cops from Seoul. Tomorrow night— which would be tonight—at eleven p.m. in the Tongduchon City Market at *mulkogi chonkuk*. Fish heaven. They must come alone, the note emphasized, they must bring money, and they would be provided with information on the whereabouts of Kim Yong-ai and— then the script switched to English—MP WOMAN.

I'd kept the note and now, sitting in the front seat of the cab entering Tongduchon, I pulled it out of my shirt pocket and read it again by the dim glow of the instrument panel. It didn't say how much money to bring. Apparently, the guy was willing to bargain. Was the information worth anything? It could be a hoax set up by someone trying to make a quick buck. How many people in TDC knew that we were looking for the MP woman? In the bar district, at least half the population.

We had three hours until eleven p.m. Brandy knew of a *yoguan*, a Korean inn, where we could wait—and hide from the 2nd Division MPs. As we entered the environs of Tongduchon proper, she instructed the cab driver as to what road to take. After a few minutes, she had him pull over and we climbed out. The weather was cold and it threatened to rain. I paid the driver the agreed-upon fare.

We stood in a narrow road on the southern edge of Tongduchon, not too far from the open-air Tongduchon City Market. But what the hell was *mulkogi chonguk*? Fish heaven? A few splats of drizzle hit my face.

"Where's the *yoguan*?" Ernie asked.

"I don't want driver to see," Brandy said. She waited until his red brake lights disappeared around a corner and then said, "Come on." She led us down a block and turned right until we found the *yoguan* in a narrow alley. Brandy was catching on to this fugitive stuff real quick.

Maybe too quick.


It's not like I wasn't used to Ernie chasing skirts. He never tried to hide his nocturnal activities and he certainly wasn't bashful. But what bothered me was the lack of consideration Ernie and Brandy showed me.

The *yoguan* was a wooden-floored, traditional place, with sliding oil-papered doors and warm *ondol* floors. Small rooms featured cotton-filled mats to roll out on the floor as mattresses and thick silk-covered comforters instead of blankets. Immaculately clean and quite comfortable. But after the three of us settled in and ordered Chinese chop from a restaurant in the neighborhood, Brandy and Ernie immediately started playing grab-ass. It was as if they'd been denied one another for so long—about three hours—that they could no longer restrain the heat of their mutual passion.

Luckily, the food arrived before they'd ripped one another's clothes off and since we were all famished, we ate heartily. But then, once Brandy set the tray and the bowls and the chopsticks out in the hall, instead of becoming sleepy and catching some shut-eye before our eleven o'clock rendezvous, Brandy and Ernie started necking. They didn't even bother to turn the light off. Of course, I could've sat there and watched. Neither one of them would've minded. Brandy was proud of her voluptuous body and her smooth golden flesh. I couldn't blame her for that, but I didn't feel comfortable in the presence of all that heavy breathing.

I slid open the door and stepped into the hallway. Neither one of them acknowledged my good-bye.

When I reached the front landing, a soft rain had started to fall. In Korea there are many names for rain, probably because rain is important to Koreans. Without rain, rice doesn't grow and without rice, people starve. Some of the names for rain actually sound like rain. For example, *bosulbi* means a light drizzle. *Busulbi*, with a soft *bu* as the first syllable, means a slightly lighter drizzle. But the name I always remember, the one that seems most poetic to me, is *danbi*. Sweet rain. The *ajjima* who owned the *yoguan* loaned me an umbrella.

I staggered into the narrow flagstone lane. Not from drunkenness but from exhaustion. Last night, I'd spent the evening in a Korean National Police interrogation room. Not the best place to sleep. Now, I had to stay up until eleven to meet someone who might or might not have useful information. A light shined from within a noodle shop. The glass windows were painted over with red lettering advertising *neingmyon*, cold noodles, and *solnong-tang*, beef soup. The small panes were heavily fogged and squeals of laughter erupted from the crowd inside. I thought of entering. It would be a cozy place to sit, indoors, out of the rain. But I knew that as soon as I slid back the wooden door and ducked inside, every pair of eyes in the joint would be on me. And then, after the few seconds of shock at seeing a GI in a place where he doesn't belong, the crowd would turn back to their own business, studiously ignoring me. I wouldn't be able to find a seat. I'd stand there awkwardly until finally the female owner would acknowledge me and maybe ask someone to share a table with me. And then things would start to relax. I'd order food, maybe a glass of *soju*, and eventually someone would speak to me in English. But the awkward period from first walking in the door until first making friends was too much to endure.

I walked past the noodle shop, through the sweet rain, through the cold night air of the city of Tongduchon.


When I was a youngster, East L.A had been a wonderland to me. Full of vitality, I rode my first bike through town, running errands for the foster family I was currently living with. Picking up milk at an Anglo market—and speaking English. Buying *pan dulce*, sweet bread, at a *tortillería*—and speaking Spanish. Sometimes I was tasked with stopping at the local Japanese market to buy fruit or vegetables, although the owner spoke to me in gruff English, never Japanese. I enjoyed running errands. I enjoyed the freedom of speeding around town on my bicycle. And mostly I enjoyed evading, for at least a while, the hard stares of the foster father who seemed constantly surprised that I wanted to eat meals at the same time as his natural kids.

I was an errand boy par excellence. That is until the *cholos* caught me. It was bad enough that they stole my bike—and the few dollars in my pocket my foster mother had provided for shopping—but then they stole, or attempted to steal, what they really wanted. My dignity.

They shoved me to the ground and spit on me. And when I tried to rise, one of them kicked me and then another joined in. I lay still. They laughed. When they started to argue about how to divide the money they had stolen, I leaped up and punched the leader in the left kidney.

It was a good punch. Even then—at the tender age of ten—I was strong. His right knee buckled and the other punks laughed and this enraged him. Although I fought back for the first few seconds, he was five or six years older than me and in the end he pulverized me good. When he was through, he kneeled over me to see if I was breathing; I was. He punched me one more time, on the side of the head, hard, and then rose to his feet, dusting off his loose khaki trousers, turned and strutted away. He could've killed me but he didn't.

Kids were decent back then.


The Tongduchon City Market, partially lit by overhead fluorescent bulbs, was deserted. Wooden stands stood empty, some of them folded and laying on the ground. Canvas roofing vibrated from the steady susurration of sweet rain. The air smelled of green onions and fish, overlaid with a hint of rust. I wandered through the stalls, meandering, heading for a blue light that glowed at the far end.

Brandy's note said that whoever wanted to talk to us would meet us here at eleven this evening. I had come early because I had nowhere else to go. Besides, I wanted to survey the meeting place. Make sure it was safe. Make sure there were no boulders waiting to fall on us or trapdoors ready to open and swallow us whole.

Within the blue glow, shadows shuffled. When I stepped closer, I could see that the blue and now greenish glow came from enormous tanks of live fish. Various-sized creatures wriggled and squirmed through the murky blue waters. More tanks were propped on tables, arranged at odd angles. Was this fish heaven? It looked more like fish hell to me.

The shadows I'd seen in front of the tanks were a Korean woman and her three children. I greeted the woman. "*Anyonghaseiyo*," I said.

She stared at me, wide-eyed. I explained that I was here sheltering from the rain and that later I would meet a friend. Korea is a trusting society. She nodded and proceeded to fuss with her children.

The toddler waddled toward me, holding a red rubber ball that was almost as big as his head. He smiled and let go of the ball, thinking he was throwing it to me. Instead, the ball fell to the ground, bounced once, and rolled listlessly in my direction. I stooped, picked up the ball, and bounced it gently back to him. The toddler squealed with glee and chased the ball, which had somehow managed to slip past him.

The little family's living quarters consisted of sleeping cots and a small hot plate that held a brass bowl of steaming rice. They lived here.

For economic reasons, undoubtedly. Probably also to protect their fish. Where was her husband? I asked. She told me. He was a fisherman and once she had sold their share of the fish, she would return to her village on the shores of the Yellow Sea. Why come all this way? To avoid the middlemen. To pull down a larger share of the profit.

I would've liked to have asked her more questions, to pry into her personal affairs. Because I'm curious about things. And I'm especially curious about people who are different. Ernie tells me I'm nuts. Still, I would've liked to have talked to this woman, to find out more about her life. But there was no excuse. I wasn't a reporter and she wasn't under criminal investigation, so I continued my stroll through the market.

After a few yards, I reached the noodle stands, the same spot where Ernie and I'd eaten lunch just the day before yesterday. The stands were deserted now. No loose pots and pans sitting on the stoves, all bowls and chopsticks and bottles of soy sauce and vinegar locked up in wooden cabinets. Not so much as a napkin left unguarded.

Toward the back of the dining area, shadows ruled. The only illumination to reach this area came from the blue glow of the fish tanks. I found an unvarnished wooden table with folding legs, unlatched the legs, folded them, and lay the table flat on the ground. No sense returning to the *yoguan*. Who knew how long Brandy and Ernie would be at it. Ernie knew we had to rendezvous here at the Tongduchon City Market at eleven p.m. He'd show up. Probably, so would Brandy.

I lay atop the table. The surface was splintered and unyielding, yet it felt wonderfully comfortable. Better even than the cement floor of a KNP interrogation room. With the soft blue glow of fish heaven in my face, I closed my eyes and, almost instantly, I was asleep.

The first thing I heard was a scream. A woman's scream.

And after the scream, a crash. Then the even higher pitched shrieks of children. Terrified children. And water. Water crashing like a wave. In less than a second, I was on my feet, reaching for the .45 in my shoulder holster.

Gunshots rang out. My military training took over and I leaped to the ground. Face first. When I looked up I realized that the blue glow of fish heaven was much weaker than I remembered. Across the vast cement floor, a sea of liquid spread toward me, an expanding tsunami less than two inches high. By a trick of light the liquid appeared violet and for a moment I thought it was blood. But then I stood and the light changed and the liquid became blue again; at least one of the huge fish tanks had been smashed to smithereens.

Another gunshot rang out. Closer this time. Children screamed and a mother's voice tried to hush them. A bare bulb hanging from the rafters above was still intact and by its glow, I saw a man crouching in water amidst flopping mackerel and crustaceans and squid. He held an automatic pistol pointed straight out in front of him and seemed to be aiming and then, squeezing with his entire fist, he popped off a round.

"*Ernie*," I hissed. "It's me."

He swiveled, pointing the gun at me, and I stood perfectly still for a moment. He lowered the gun.

"Where the hell you been?"

"Here." I jerked my free thumb over my shoulder.

"Get down. Some sort of high-power weapon out there. Probably a rifle."

I low-crawled through wriggling sardines until I crouched next to Ernie, behind a short pyramid of cement blocks that had recently supported a fish tank.

"Where's Brandy?" I asked.

"Back at the *yoguan*," Ernie replied. "Said she was too tired. When I entered the market there didn't seem to be anybody behind me. I found this woman and her kids and I tried to talk to her, but she doesn't understand English. One of her kids bounced his rubber ball at me and when I stooped to pick it up the entire goddamned fish tank exploded."

"Could've been your head," I told him.

"Thanks. You see anything out there?"

We both peered over the edge of the cement-block foundation down the long corridor that led past the empty produce market and, after about twenty meters, onto the streets of Tongduchon.

I cursed myself for not anticipating this. A guy sends us a note and sets up the rendezvous for an isolated area with plenty of space like fish heaven, with darkness on the outside and light on the inside so he can see us but we can't see him. When Ernie walks into the market, the guy takes up a position behind the shrubbery outside and doesn't fire right away because he's wondering where Ernie's partner is. When he figures I'm not coming, he decides to take Ernie out. And he would have, too, if Ernie hadn't leaned down to pick up that little rubber ball.

Did Brandy have anything to do with this? She'd gone to extraordinary efforts to contact Staff Sergeant Riley and then us. And she'd been particularly nice to Ernie. But when the moment of truth came, she had decided not to accompany him to fish heaven. Something told me that if we returned to the *yoguan*, Brandy would be long gone.

How much had she been paid to set this up? Or had she been coerced? Either way, I would love to have a chat with her.

A whistle shrilled.

"The KNPs," Ernie said.

"No way," I said. "If they take us into custody for questioning again, we won't be getting out anytime soon."

Ernie backed away from the cement blocks. "Come on."

I followed.

On the way I nodded good-bye to the female fishmonger and her children huddled protectively beneath her arms. *"Mianhamnida,"* I said. I'm sorry. She stared after me, eyes wide with fright.

Ernie'd already reached the noodle stand and was trotting across the dining area with his .45 held in his right hand, zigzagging through the scattered tables and chairs. In back of the market, a large blacktopped delivery area stood deserted. The entire expanse was empty except for a couple of three-wheeled flatbed trucks.

No cops. Another whistle shrilled behind us. The KNP foot patrols seemed to be converging on the front entrance of the Tonduchon City Market. My guess was that the shooter was long gone.

Beyond the truck park, we reached a low wooden fence. Ernie

clambered over it and I followed and then we were in the backyard of some sort of factory for pipe fittings. At the front, we climbed over another locked fence and we were on another street, and then a narrow pedestrian walkway, and then an alley. Ernie slowed to a walk. I caught up with him.

"Where the hell are we?" he asked.

"Somewhere in the south end of Tongduchon."

In the hubbub, I'd forgotten the umbrella the *yoguan* owner had loaned me. Dollops of sweet rain splattered atop my head.

Behind us, more whistles shrilled. The KNPs must be in the market now, interviewing the female fishmonger. How long would it take for them to realize that the two GIs with .45s were Ernie and me? They wouldn't know for sure, but they'd suspect. And they would certainly notify the provost marshal of the 2nd Infantry Division.

"We can't wander the streets during curfew," Ernie said. "Too risky."

"So where do we hide?"

"They'll check the *yoguans*. All of them. And the brothels in the bar district, too. They'll find us and this time they won't be so bashful about charging us with the murder of Pak Tong-i."

Maybe. Maybe not. But at the very least, they'd turn us over to the 2nd ID and we'd be charged with violation of a direct order, the order to return to Seoul. Ernie's claim that on the weekend we were off-duty and could go anywhere we wanted was really only meant to assuage Staff Sergeant Riley's sense of responsibility. Once a commander orders you out of an area, you're required to get out. Of course, we'd originally planned to keep a low profile and continue our search for Jill. We hadn't expected to be shot at.

"You're the smart one," Ernie said. "Where do we hide?"

I thought of the rice paddies outside of town or one of the cemeteries I'd seen on a hill but neither of those options seemed inviting. After a few hours of standing in cold mud, sweet rain wouldn't seem so sweet. And then it hit me.

"There's one place," I said. "The KNPs won't look there and maybe—just maybe—we'll be welcome."

"Where?"

"Come on."

I turned right into another dark alley, heading west. Above us, the sweet rain had stopped. The dark sky seemed to be holding its breath, trying to decide what torment to throw at us next.

Who had shot at us?

That wasn't such an easy question to answer. By the sound and accuracy of the rounds, the weapon must've been a rifle.

Who had access to rifles?

The U.S. Army, the ROK Army, and the Korean National Police. Other than that, gun control is total in Korea. Special permission is required to own a rifle and, even if permission is granted, one has to keep the weapon under lock and key—not at home—but in a secure storage area of a licensed establishment, such as an approved shooting gallery or hunting club. Could gangsters obtain an unregistered rifle? If they really wanted to. But why bother? It would be risky and bring unwanted attention on themselves; they have other ways of killing people.

So who would try to kill us with a rifle?

Someone who had easy access to a rifle. Like a GI or a Korean National Policeman or a soldier from the ROK Army. Or a government official like the Korean mystery man who'd monitored my interrogation at the Tongduchon Police Station.

Whoever shot at us had set the event up. Using Brandy. Could Ernie and I storm into the Black Cat Club right now and find her and question her? Not likely. Not only were there still plenty of irate soul brothers there to hamper our operation but, even more dangerous, the KNPs—thinking we might've returned to town—would probably be watching the place. Questioning Brandy would have to wait.

For now.

As to why anyone would want to kill us, that seemed simple. Someone didn't want us to find Corporal Jill Matthewson.

The upturned tile roofs of the Chon residence sat in darkness and the big wooden gate in the stone fence stood barred from within. In the recessed stone archway, I switched on my penlight and studied the brass name-plate. Etched onto the polished surface was the Chinese character for "Chon." Next to that, a white button on a metal grille. The buzzer and the intercom system. I hesitated before pushing the button. How would I explain myself? I mentally rehearsed my lines in Korean and then pressed the button. A buzzer sounded deep inside the recesses of the residence. I waited. After a minute, I pushed again. It took three tries until a sleepy voice buzzed back through the intercom.

"*Nugu ya?*" Who is it?

A woman's voice. Not Madame Chon. At least I didn't think so. I phrased my Korean as precisely as I was able.

"I wish to speak to Chon Un-suk's mother. It's about the American woman MP. I'm still looking for her and I need help."

I emphasized the words "*Miguk yoja honbyong.*" American woman MP.

There was no answer. But the woman hadn't switched off. The intercom buzzed steadily like a broken transmission from the nether realms.

"What'd she say?" Ernie asked.

"She didn't say anything. I think that's the maid. She's probably gone to fetch Madame Chon."

"I hope the hell she hurries." Ernie wrapped his nylon jacket more tightly around his chest. "It's cold out here." Our blue jeans, our sneakers, our T-shirts, and our nylon jackets were soaked from rolling in spilled water at fish heaven. Our overnight bags were back at the *yoguan.* They were history now because it would be too risky to go back for them. As we'd wandered through the back alleys of Tongduchon, searching for the Chon residence, our clothing had been further dampened by sporadic rain. As I'd suspected, the "sweetness" had long since gone out of the precipitation. Now the rain spurted from low-moving clouds, punching us when we least expected it, like a boxer softening us up with a left jab.

Finally, the intercom buzzed back to life.

"*Nugu seiyo?*" A softer voice. Sweeter. With the polite verb endings of a woman of culture.

"*Nanun Mipalkun,*" I said. I'm from 8th Army.

I went on to remind her that we had talked to her before about our search for Corporal Jill Matthewson and we'd run into some problems and we needed to talk to her and, quite frankly, we needed shelter from the rain and maybe something to eat.

"You haven't found Jill yet?" she asked.

The reproach of the rich. Everything should be convenient. Simple.

"Not yet," I replied.

There was another long silence. Then, like a jolt of lightning, a different buzzer sounded and the small wooden door in the main gate popped open. Without hesitation, Ernie and I ducked through.


The refuge provided by Madame Chon was sweeter than I had hoped. Hot baths were drawn for us by the old housemaid, a nourishing meal of turnip soup and steamed rice was served, and then a good night's sleep on cotton mats with thick silk comforters in a private room. In fact, Ernie and I wallowed in comfort too long and it was almost ten a.m. when we left the warm confines of the Chon residence.

The maid had dried and pressed our clothes. I felt as fresh as a newly minted ten thousand *won* note.

Outside in a narrow alley, a young woman walked in front of us. She had already warned us sternly not to follow too closely and not to indicate in any way that we knew her. Of course, we *didn't* know her. We didn't even know her name. This morning she had appeared in the Chon family courtyard, bowing to Madame Chon. She was a slender young woman, probably in her early twenties, wearing blue jeans and sandals and a red-and-blue patterned blouse; her brown hair was just a little shaggier than a school girl's pageboy cut. We weren't given her name but Madame Chon told us to follow her.

Last night, in talking to Madame Chon, it became apparent to me that one area of Jill Matthewson's activities that we hadn't investigated was Jill's participation in the demonstrations outside the main gate of Camp Casey. Jill had come to apologize to the Chon family for the actions of her compatriots and to say how saddened she was at the untimely death of their daughter. It took a lot of guts for an American MP to do that. And you can bet that the 2nd Division provost marshal didn't approve of any such apology. The U.S. military is always loathe to take responsibility for mistakes. Jill had done it on her own. When she arrived, some of the demonstration organizers had been there, too. Jill was introduced to them and they began to talk.

"Later," Madame Chon told me, "Jill left with them."

I asked how Ernie and I could contact these demonstrators. She took care of everything and this morning our contact, the young woman we were now following through the twisting byways of Tongduchon, had miraculously appeared.

"Maybe," Madame Chon told me, "she can help you find Jill."

She also made me promise that, if I found Jill, I would bring her immediately to the Chon family home. "Any time, day or night," she said. "When you arrive, you are welcome here." A *kut*, a séance presided over by the *mudang*, a female shaman, would be arranged at once.

I just hoped we wouldn't need a séance to contact Jill.

The young female student turned down one narrow pathway and then another.

"Student activists," Ernie said.

I nodded in assent. *Radicals,* most people would call them. But it didn't seem too radical a thing to want crimes committed in your own country to be tried in your own courts. Yet in Korea, under the current authoritarian regime, such an opinion was enough to get you thrown in the "monkey house." Jail.

Occasionally, the girl leading us stopped and peered back along the road. When she was sure we weren't being followed, she turned again and continued. She stayed carefully away from the Tongduchon City Market and far away from the GI bar district. We were in northern Tongduchon now, in alleyways neither Ernie nor I had ever seen before.

"Is she gonna take us all the way to North Korea?" Ernie asked.

Finally, after two quick turns down alleys running perpendicular to one another, the girl stopped in front of a splintered doorway in a brick wall smeared with soot. Ernie and I halted a few yards away and waited. She rang a buzzer. A man's voice answered and she whispered into the speaker. The door in front of her opened. She waved for us to follow.

We stepped into a weed-infested courtyard strewn with broken bicycle parts and rusted charcoal stoves and metal detritus of all types. Bricks formed a walkway and we stepped up onto an unvarnished porch and then into a dark, wood-floored hallway with sliding oil-papered doors on either side, two of them open. The entire house reeked of mold and tobacco smoke. In the largest room, young people with shaggy black hair stared up at us warily, most of them puffing on cigarettes.

The majority were boys. It was difficult to determine sex since the boys had smooth faces unblemished by whiskers and the girls were rail thin and wore the same type of blue jeans and baggy shirts that the boys wore. No one greeted us, but a few students slid backwards on the floor until a space opened. I sat. Ernie did the same.

The girl who'd led us here disappeared into a back room.

A young man sitting directly across from us started speaking in English. No preamble. He immediately threw questions at us. It was an interrogation. I did most of the talking. Ernie was busy still sorting the students by gender.

The purpose of the interrogation was transparent. They wanted to know if they could trust us. A reasonable question since Ernie and I were criminal investigators working for the very institution they opposed: the United States 8th Army. I fired a few questions back at the young man. Some of the other students answered too, happy for a chance to practice their English.

They assured me that they didn't hate Americans. In fact, they admired the American political system and they wanted to emulate it in Korea. But first the Status of Forces Agreement had to be abolished so Korean courts could have full jurisdiction in Korea. So GIs who drove recklessly and murdered innocent people wouldn't be allowed to return to their home country without punishment. They spoke passionately. Whether or not the two GIs in the truck were guilty of negligent manslaughter was beside the point, they told me. The two GIs should've been tried in a Korean court. This was a fundamental demand of their movement: sovereignty of the Korean judicial system. And, incidentally, they wanted all American troops out of South Korea.

As an afterthought.

"Our army is strong," one of the girls told me. "We can defend ourselves."

From what I'd seen of the ROK Army, I had to agree. Their soldiers were dedicated and fierce, and a lot less beholden to the fleshly pleasures of life than American GIs. I told them that my main goal was to find Corporal Jill Matthewson. Suddenly they grew quiet. After a long pause, the most talkative young man said, "If we help you, we need something in return."

Did they actually have information that could help us find Jill? Or were they bluffing?

"What?" I asked.

"Jill," he said, "participated in one of our demonstrations."

I nodded. I knew that. I didn't say that if Ernie and I did manage to find Jill Matthewson alive, she could face court-martial proceedings for having participated in that demonstration. We'd worry about that later.

"Tonight," he said, "after people get off work and before the sun goes down, we are planning another demonstration. A bigger one this time. In front of the Camp Casey main gate."

I nodded. Understanding. Wondering what he wanted from me.

"You and your friend," he said, pointing at me and Ernie, "must accompany us this afternoon. You must join our demonstration."

Ernie stopped making eyes at the cutest of the female students and said, "Are you nuts?"

The students whispered amongst themselves. Not sure of what exactly Ernie meant by "nuts."

"No," the leader said finally. "We are not 'nuts.' You must join the demonstration and you must speak. You say you agree that Korean courts should try all people accused of crimes on Korean soil. Even GIs. If you say that at the demonstration, we will lead you to Jill Matthewson."


There must've been over five hundred people in front of the Camp Casey main gate. Most of them were students who'd been bussed in just this afternoon from Seoul. But a surprising number were locals. Working people. Cab drivers, young women still wearing bandannas and aprons from their work in kitchens, an occasional vegetable vendor with a cart, even one or two shop owners who, much to my surprise, had closed up their tailor shops or brassware emporiums and walked down the street to join in the protest.

"Chon Un-suk *mansei!*" one of the protestors shouted through a bullhorn. Chon Un-suk ten thousand years! Which didn't make much sense since she was already dead.

Some of the students held four-foot-high photographs of the young middle-school student, framed in black.

What must've been the entire contingent of Camp Casey MPs stood in front of the main gate, wearing fatigue uniforms and riot helmets, holding their batons at port arms. More MPs stood behind them with short-barreled grenade launchers cradled in their arms, for launching tear gas into the crowd. Finally, as if he was Camp Casey's last line of defense, the twenty-foot-tall MP stood with his pink-faced grin, staring idiotically at the entire proceedings.

So far, everything was peaceful.

A KNP contingent stood along the railroad tracks, opposite the main gate, behind the protestors. They also wore riot helmets and thick chest padding and wielded long batons that they held in their hands impatiently. All in all, there were almost as many MPs and KNPs as there were protestors, although the cops were much better armed.

Ernie and I crouched in the center of the student protestors.

"If the MPs spot us out here," Ernie said, "we're toast."

"What choice do we have?" I answered. "We were sent up here to find Jill Matthewson. That's what we're doing."

"We'll lose our CID badges."

"We'll tell them we were working undercover."

"Eighth Army will never buy it."

"Screw Eighth Army."

Ernie shook his head. "You're changing, Sueño."

Maybe he was right. I thought about it. One of the protestors screamed through a megaphone at the top of his lungs in rapid Korean.

Finally, I replied. "I'm changing," I told Ernie, "because finding Corporal Jill Matthewson should've been an easy assignment. Instead, at every step of the way someone's tried to stop us. They stopped Private Marvin Druwood and then they stopped the booking agent, Pak Tong-i. Permanently. And last night, they tried to kill us. Why?"

Ernie shrugged.

"We have to find out," I said.

"We could go talk to Brandy."

"We're too hot to enter the Black Cat Club. Or even the bar district. The KNPs are probably watching."

"They're watching us here."

"They're watching the crowd. Not us. This is the last place they'd expect to find us."

"This is the last place *I'd* expect to find us."

"It'll only take a few minutes. Then they promised to lead us to her."

"They might be lying."

"Chon Un-suk's mother believes them."

Ernie shrugged again.

The leader of the protest shouted into his megaphone, speaking in Korean. Occasionally, he paused and the crowd shouted back their assent. Finally, he switched to English, turned, and directed his words at the main gate of Camp Casey.

"Now," he said. "One of your own will speak to you."

He motioned for me to stand. Ernie stared at me, wide-eyed. I rose to my feet. Like Adam accepting the apple from Eve, I grabbed the megaphone.

# 10

I've often wondered what it's like to jump out of an airplane.

To take that final step into the abyss, with the wind rushing by and birds gliding below, and then to fall and twist and float free, away from all restraint, gliding through clouds. Airborne troopers do just that at least once a month to keep their parachute status active and thereby collect an additional fifty-four dollars per month in jump pay.

When I stood in the middle of that crowd and the young Korean man handed me the megaphone and I held it up to my mouth and I started talking, I suddenly knew what it was like to leap out into eternity.

I'm not sure exactly what I said. Ernie recounted it to me later. Something about every country being able to control its own destiny and every courtroom being accountable to the people of that country. It wasn't much and it was garbled, but the overriding point of my little speech—as far as the U.S. Army's concerned—was that I'd participated in a prohibited demonstration. It didn't matter how minor, or how dumb, my participation might've been. Such participation, in and of itself, was a court-martial offense. Of course, so was returning to the 2nd Division area of operations after we'd been ordered not to. So I was just adding one sin onto another.

But what riveted my attention while I held the microphone was not the line of helmeted KNPs lining the railroad tracks, nor the adoring attention of the demonstrators who gazed up at me, nor even the helmeted American MPs barricading the main gate of Camp Casey. What riveted my attention was Lieutenant Colonel Stanley X. Alcott and Warrant Officer One Fred Bufford, both of whom were standing in fatigues before the main gate behind their protective line of MPs; both men perched atop the hood of a U.S. Army jeep. Colonel Alcott, realizing who was speaking, stared at me with his mouth hanging open. Fred Bufford, meanwhile, smirked. A broad twisted smile. Satisfied. As if to say that everything he suspected about me had finally been proven true.

The huge MP statue looming behind the main gate seemed to have changed its expression from bland idiocy to disbelief. Disbelief, apparently, that I could do something so stupid. Stupid, maybe. But it was my only chance of obtaining a lead on the whereabouts of Corporal Jill Matthewson. As a cop assigned to a mission, I do what is required. Regardless of what Stanley Alcott or Fred Bufford thought.

When I finished talking, the crowd of demonstrators roared in approval and then a Korean speaker took over the megaphone and the students holding the photographs of Chon Un-suk started chanting and parading through the crowd. The chanting grew louder and I ducked down next to Ernie. Everyone ignored us. The crowd swirled around us, picking up speed, picking up the volume of its outraged roar. Finally, some of the demonstrators stooped and grabbed rocks from the side of the road and, with wild abandon, launched them at the main gate of Camp Casey. A few of the stronger young men managed to reach not only the main gate but behind it all the way to the MP statue, where the rocks bounced off the big dumb MP's chest and tumbled uselessly to the ground.

One of the vegetable vendors was surrounded by students and I soon realized why. She had smuggled in a pile of rocks in her cart.

Plenty of ammunition. And then the students became organized. When every one had a rock, they began chanting, "Chon Un-suk. Chon Un-suk." And then, timing it by counting down from ten, the students in unison launched all their missiles, like a battalion of ancient Carthaginians armed with slings assaulting the glory that was Rome.

The MPs roared in rage. The students grabbed more rocks and once again began their chant. KNPs along the tracks conferred. Another volley of rocks sailed through the air toward Camp Casey. Again the MPs roared in anger but this time the KNPs along the railroad tracks formed up in a V shape and, on the count of three, charged.

Pandemonium.

Some of the students were overcome with a senseless heroism and counterattacked, running pell-mell into the riot police. Others crouched to the ground in panic. None of them ran. Only Ernie and me. We ran away from the crowd, away from the charging KNPs, away from the main gate of Camp Casey. But in our case, the damage had been done. I'd been witnessed by a field-grade officer participating in an unauthorized political demonstration. The word would be out. We were here, even though we weren't supposed to be, and every MP—and KNP—in Division would be searching for us.

Once inside the bar district, we stopped in an alley and tried to catch our breath. I noticed that there didn't appear to be any people on the street—no GIs, no business girls—but no KNPs or MPs either.

"The place is deserted," Ernie said. "Now's our chance."

"Our chance for what?"

"The Black Cat Club," he said. "Brandy."

He was right. Using the back lanes, we wound our way toward the back door of the Black Cat Club.

The old crone who ran the Black Cat Club was there along with a few of her business girls but no GIs. The GIs had been restricted to the compound in anticipation of today's demonstration. I asked for Brandy and of course they denied that she was here. They had no idea where she was. Since torture was out of the question, Ernie and I performed a quick check of the hooches out back and then searched the Black Cat Club itself.

No Brandy.

We stepped behind the bar. Ernie poured himself a shot of bourbon. I found a ledger. Drink chits is what it recorded. Most bars kept a similar accounting. When a GI buys a girl a drink, she earns credit: a few additional *won* that turn up in her end-of-month paycheck. Who records the chits? At the Black Cat Club, apparently, the bartender does. I studied the handwriting. Quirky, leaning to left, blocklike. Exactly like the handwriting on the note Brandy had shown us.

I stuck the ledger under the fluorescent bulb beneath the bar and spread the note next to it. Ernie peered down.

"Aah," he said. Even though he couldn't read Korean *hangul* script, Ernie could see the resemblance to Brandy's distinctive style. She'd been the one who had written the note that drew us to fish heaven. She'd set us up to be killed.


We could've continued our search for Brandy and when we found her we could've beaten the truth out of her. But our main mission was still to find Corporal Jill Matthewson. Ernie and I talked about it. Whoever had broken into Pak Tong-i's office before us might've found a lead to Jill's whereabouts and that meant, if they hadn't already found her, they might do so at any moment. The whole purpose of my speaking at the demonstration was to obtain the cooperation of the students who had promised to lead me to Corporal Jill Matthewson. So we loitered in the northern end of Tongduchon near the little hooch they used as their hideout. But by late afternoon we realized that waiting any longer was useless. The KNPs had located the student leaders' hideout. Ernie and I spotted them coming and made ourselves scarce. Within an hour, dozens of Korean cops would be swarming over the dilapidated little hooch, searching for clues that would allow them to prosecute the students under Korea's voluminous antisedition laws.

Ernie and I retreated to the only other place where we might be able to make contact with the students. The residence of Madame Chon. No dice. The KNPs weren't searching her home—out of respect for her wealth and connections—but they had stationed armed guards at her front gate.

"We're up kimchee creek," Ernie said. "Trapped in the Division area, no leads to Jill, no way to contact the student demonstrators. We're right back where we started. Except worse."

I didn't have an answer for him. Not yet.

We sat in a Korean teahouse on the western edge of town, a half block from the MSR, the route that led from TDC to the Western Corridor. Not far from where Chon Un-suk had been run over.

"They have us both nailed for disobeying a direct order," Ernie said. "To wit, returning to the Division area after being ordered to leave. And they've got you nailed for participating in a prohibited demonstration. It's over. The best thing for us to do is police up my jeep and return to Seoul. Tomorrow morning we report to work and take our lumps."

Ernie was saying it, and saying it forcefully, but I knew he didn't believe it. Private Marvin Druwood was still dead. Corporal Jill Matthewson was still missing. We couldn't leave now. We couldn't let the bastards win.

A frail young Korean waiter in black pants, white shirt, and black bow tie offered another cup of overpriced instant coffee. We both declined. Bowing, he removed the porcelain cups from in front of us. After he walked away, I said, "He can't wait for us to leave."

"Him and everybody else in TDC."

"Understandable," I said. "We're rocking their boat."

"To hell with their boat."

"Yeah. That's what I say. If we find Jill, we find out why she left and how she managed to come up with two thousand dollars and, given what we've uncovered already, we might be able to put a case together."

"Against who?"

"Against the Division honchos. The guys who run the mafia

meetings. The guys who are black-marketing their butts off in TDC. The guys who covered up Marvin Druwood's death."

"How can we prove they're black-marketing?" Ernie said. "All the evidence was destroyed in that fire out at the Turkey Farm."

"Destroying evidence. That's what's gone on since we arrived. Destroying the evidence of how Private Druwood actually died, destroying the evidence of what those two young MPs were actually doing when they ran over Chon Un-suk, destroying the evidence of black-market activities that had been supporting the mafia meetings. It's all about destroying evidence. You're right, Ernie. And if we return to Seoul now and 'take our lumps' like you said, they'll win. And Jill Matthewson better stay in hiding."

"You don't know that she has evidence that'll help us. For all we know, she might be black-marketing herself. In it all the way up to her freckled nose."

"Could be."

He studied me, with that cagey look in his eye that he gets when he thinks he's reading me like a book. "But you want to ask her, don't you?"

I nodded. "Yes. I want to ask her."

"So do I." He inhaled the pungent, coffee-laced air and then let his breath out slowly. "Okay," he said. "It's still Sunday. We still have a few more hours. How do we find her?"

I called the waiter over and borrowed a stubby pencil and a sheet of brown pulpy paper. After spreading it on the tabletop, I drew a map. As I penciled in the names of towns and villages and rivers and mountain ranges, I realized that I knew more about this part of the country than I thought I did. It was a beautiful part of the world. With lush river valleys and craggy peaks and Buddhist temples and shrines to ancient patriarchs. And then I filled in the DMZ and the military base camps and then the brothels. Suddenly, my map looked as if it were breaking out in an adolescent rash.

Ernie and I barely fit into the seats.

The bus was designed for Koreans so each seat was narrow and legroom was nonexistent. We twisted and turned and, as best we could, folded our legs under the seats in front of us. The middle-aged men in suits and the young people in blue jeans and fancy jackets ignored us. But the old ladies who climbed aboard the bus with massive bundles balanced atop their heads couldn't take their eyes off of us. Foreigners on a Korean bus! We might as well have been space aliens.

Within a few stops after Tongduchon, all seats were filled and the aisles were jammed full of countryfolk ferrying themselves and their children and their belongings—including a crate of chickens and even a small goat—from one village to another. We passed ROK Army compounds and a few military convoys, but along the way no one stopped us.

At one particularly bumpy stretch of road, Ernie felt compelled to rise and offer his seat to one of the country women who was having trouble keeping her balance in the aisle. I did the same and so we were stuck in the aisle on the swaying bus, our heads bowed because of the low ceiling. It was a long ride to Bopwon-ni, Legal Hall Village. Over an hour because of all the stops and all the loading and unloading of passengers and gear.

When we finally arrived, night had fallen. Ernie and I hopped off the bus and strode directly toward neon, into the Pair of Dragons beer hall, the same place we'd stopped last night on our way to TDC with Brandy. We marched to the bar and ordered two draft beers.

In Tongduchon, when Ernie said that we were right back where we started from, he was wrong. We had information. Quite a bit of it. All we had to do was collate it and make sense of it and then use it to formulate a plan of action.

What we knew for sure was that Corporal Jill Matthewson had left Tongduchon twenty-four days ago and, as far as we could tell, she'd never returned. That meant that wherever she was, her needs were being met. If she was dead, of course, those needs would be zero. If she was alive but being held captive, it would be up to her captors to meet her needs. Or not, as they saw fit. But if she was on her own and free—as I certainly hoped she was—she was meeting her own needs. That is, paying for a roof over her head and food and drink and a place to launder her clothes and bathe her body. To do that, she needed a job.

"So what kind of work can she do?" I asked Ernie.

"Law enforcement's out."

"You got that right."

"And all the menial jobs," he continued, "like being a waitress at a teahouse or washing dishes in a restaurant are out because Koreans take those jobs."

"So what else is open to her?" I asked.

"You know the answer to that."

I did. Prostitution. But from everything I'd learned about Jill Matthewson, I didn't believe she'd stoop to that.

"Besides that," I asked Ernie, "what else could she do?"

"She could strip. Like Pak Tong-i said, she has big *geegees*."

"And she has a girlfriend who already knows the business," I added. "So we have to put that down as one of the possibilities. Still, I don't think she'd become a stripper."

"Why not?" Ernie asked. "It pays well."

"For an American woman it would pay great," I agreed. "But it would also attract attention. A lot of attention. There'd be advertising. Posters announcing when she was going to perform, that sort of thing."

Ernie nodded his head. "I see what you mean. So something more low-profile." Then he thought of it. "Hostess."

"Exactly."

Ernie meant a bar hostess in a fancy drinking establishments. A tradition in Korea. No self-respecting Korean businessman wants to sit alone, or even with his pals, and drink the night away without a "beautiful flower" to laugh at his jokes and pour his drinks and light his cigarettes. The fanciest of these drinking establishments were called *kisaeng* houses. *Kisaeng* in ancient Korea were highly trained female performers who were responsible for entertaining royalty. Somewhat like Japanese geisha. Since the Yi Dynasty, however, their job has degenerated to merely acting as the beautiful and charming hostesses to rich businessmen in private clubs. The pay can be fabulous. In the higher-class clubs some of the sought-after *kisaeng* are remunerated out of corporate expense accounts and pull down hundreds of dollars per night. But that's for the most high-class girls. In most of the dives in and around Seoul, bar hostesses are lucky to pull down the equivalent of ten or twenty dollars a night. As an American, however, and a blonde verging on beautiful, Jill Matthewson could demand top dollar right from the start.

"But there's jillions of *kisaeng* houses," Ernie protested.

"Right. But maybe we can narrow down our search geographically."

"How?"

The bartender checked our half-empty mugs. Much to my surprise, Ernie declined a refill.

"Jill had taken the time to put two thousand dollars together before she left Tongduchon. So she probably took the time to plan her escape. That meant that she had both a low-profile job and a low-profile place to live waiting for her," I said.

"She'd already been hired?"

"Yes. I think so. That's one of the reasons she has been able to hide so successfully. An American woman traveling from bar to bar searching for a job would've been spotted."

"So Pak Tong-i set her up with a job."

"I think so. Both her and his girlfriend, Kim Yong-ai."

"But the job could be anywhere. And there are a lot of bars in Seoul."

We both knew that if Jill Matthewson had gone to Seoul and taken work at some obscure nightspot, living in a hooch on the premises, it could take months to find her.

"Maybe not Seoul," I said. "First, when I searched Pak's files they were all for work in and around the 2nd Division area, both Eastern and Western Corridors. Nothing in Seoul."

"Seoul's not his territory."

"Right. And with a good-looking girlfriend like Kim Yong-ai, it also makes sense that he'd want to keep her nearby. He wouldn't want to send her down to Seoul, into the hands of those sharks. Not voluntarily."

"So not in Seoul. But he wouldn't want to land them a job in Tongduchon either."

"No way. Too risky."

"So he'd find them work in the Western Corridor."

"Exactly."

That's why I'd drawn my map. I pulled it out now.

The newly built highway, Tongil-lo, Reunification Road, runs down the center of the Western Corridor, a fertile valley filled with rice paddies that has been an ancient invasion route for the Chinese, the Mongols, and the Manchurians. It runs from Seoul Station up through Bongil-chon to the city of Munsan. From there, it continues north until it hits Freedom Bridge crossing the Imjin River. Beyond that, civilians are not allowed, not without special permission. But the road continues north into the Demilitarized Zone, until it finally hits the Military Demarcation Line that separates South Korea from communist North Korea in the truce village of Panmunjom. All the way from Seoul to *Jayu Tari*, Freedom Bridge, there are *kisaeng* houses and other bars that cater strictly to rich Korean businessmen. It isn't unusual to see a small convoy of black sedans cruising north out of Seoul to reach a *kisaeng* house in the countryside. Out of town they can forget the hustle and bustle of the big city and enjoy a relaxing business meeting, the overworked businessman catered to by a bevy of beautiful women. These places are busy during the lunch hour and busy again at night. And more than one wealthy businessman has promoted his favorite hostess to be his well-compensated mistress.

Jill Matthewson would fit into this world like a goddess dropped from the sky.

"So we search every *kisaeng* house and high-class Korean bar," Ernie said. "From Munsan down to the outskirts of Seoul."

"Not exactly," I said.

"What do you mean?

"I think we can narrow the search further."

"How?"

"If you were on the lam from the honchos of the 2nd Infantry Division, what would you be worried about?"

"Them finding me."

"And if you were as smart as Jill Matthewson . . ."

"What do you mean 'if'?"

"I mean *since* you are as smart as Jill Matthewson, you'd want a backup plan in case they found you."

"Right."

"You'd want to still have a chance of getting away if they stumbled onto your location."

"Right."

"So you'd have to plan a second escape."

Ernie studied the map I'd drawn. Then he saw it. "You'd want to be close to Seoul. If you had to run, you'd have a better chance of disappearing if you could get lost in the crowd in a city of eight million people."

"Right. You wouldn't want to be stuck up north in Munsan, near the DMZ. There'd be nowhere to go."

That was an exaggeration. There'd be some places to go but the options for escape into the teeming metropolis of Seoul would be better if you could locate yourself at the southern edge of the Western Corridor.

Ernie glanced again at the map, at the southernmost city within the 2nd Division area of operations.

"Byokjie," he said.

Because of its nearness to Seoul, it had a plethora of *kisaeng* houses. In the two years since Tongil-lo had been completed, making the drive from Seoul to the countryside more convenient, they'd sprung up like sunflowers after a summer rain.

"Byokjie," Ernie said, almost reverentially. Then he brightened. "We ain't there yet?"


Byokjie was nothing more than a good-sized intersection. Reunification Road, all four lanes of it, ran north and south along the edge of miles of fallow rice paddies. Bright headlights zoomed by in the darkness. Another road, this one two lanes, stretched from Uijongbu in the east and ran west until it smacked right up against Tongil-lo, forming a T-shaped intersection. The little village of Byokjie, sitting along the stem of the T, was lit up by floodlights. The small collection of buildings was what you'd expect: a *sokyu* sign for the gas station, a tire warehouse, a mechanic's workshop, and then a few noodle stands. All of the establishments were still open, hoping for late-night business. A well-lit sign next to a large bus stop listed the connecting runs between here and numerous farming villages, all of them home to some people, adults or students, who commuted into Seoul every day.

The cab driver who'd driven us from Bopwon-ni asked us where to stop.

"*Kisaeng*," Ernie said.

The driver laughed and waved his hand. "*I kuncho manundei*," he said. In this area there are a lot of them.

And there were. We had him cruise slowly east from Byokjie, along the road that headed toward Uijongbu. Every few meters, hand-carved wooden signs and even a few signposts made of marble were engraved with the names of exclusive entertainment establishments. Each had its own gravel-topped driveway that led off the main road and up into the tree-covered hills. Occasionally, a dark sedan drove up one of the gravel roads.

"Take your pick," Ernie said.

After I spotted more than two dozen signs I said, "We need your jeep."

"That we do."

I ordered the driver to continue eastward toward Uijongbu, promising once again that because he had to leave his authorized area of operations in Bopwon-ni, we'd pay him double meter.

An hour and a half before midnight we returned to Byokjie, this time in Ernie's jeep. Methodical as usual, we cruised down the road, Ernie pulling over each time he saw a signpost. In this manner I jotted down the names of the various *kisaeng* houses and located the turnoffs on our map. After a few of these stops, Ernie said, "This is going to take forever."

"You're right. But one of those *kisaeng* houses back there, the Koryo Forest Inn, seemed to have more business than anybody else."

"And?"

"So we reconnoiter."

"How? They'll spot our jeep as soon as we drive up."

"So we park in Byokjie, at the gas station, and hoof it back there."

Ernie sighed. "You really are nuts, you know that Sueño?"

I didn't answer.

Ernie pulled the jeep into the enormous gas station and parked at the edge of the gravel lot. I talked to the attendant, flashed my CID badge, and told him we would be back for the vehicle in an hour. He didn't argue and I purposely didn't give him a tip. As long as he thought I was here on official business, he wouldn't dare complain. A nice thing about living in a police state is that people support local law enforcement. Whether they want to or not.

"It's cold up here," Ernie said.

"Hush."

We huddled in the tree line on the edge of the forest, gazing across a parking lot filled with compact black sedans. Most of them were Hyundais, made in Korea, but a few were imported Volvos and BMWs. Rich crowd. White-gloved chauffeurs, slim young Korean men all, stood in clumps, bundled up against the cold, smoking and joking.

The front of the Koryo Forest Inn looked like an ancient palace. A gate painted in red lacquer and carved with the faces of fierce, green-eyed dragons. Beyond the gate, water trickled over rocks in a lush garden and beyond that loomed the raised, varnished floor of the inner sanctum of the Koryo Forest Inn.

"Nice place they got here," Ernie said. "But expensive."

We were used to paying a hundred and fifty *won*, about thirty cents, for a bottle of OB beer in the dives we frequented. Here, in the Koryo Forest Inn, they probably wouldn't stoop so low as to tell you how much they were charging for booze. And no self-respecting businessman would lower himself to ask. The bill was presented, it was paid out of the company expense account, and that was it. Guys like me and Ernie, who wanted to see a price list before ordering, were not welcome.

"So what's your plan?" Ernie asked.

"The usual," I answered. "We go in. We ask questions."

For once, Ernie Bascom was intimidated. "What if they charge us?"

"For what?"

"For talking to a hostess. I heard they slap a ten thousand *won* charge on you the minute she sits down."

"So we won't sit down. Come on."

I pushed through the underbrush and walked between two parked cars. By the time the chauffeurs noticed me, I was already underneath the hand-carved wooden portal of the Koryo Forest Inn, Ernie right behind me.

Stunted trees, raked gravel, koi luxuriating in ponds, all lit by hanging Chinese lanterns. We followed the flagstone steps to the elevated porch and as I was about to slip off my shoes, two beautiful young Korean women, decked out in full regalia—jade hairpins, silk-embroidered *chima-chogori*—stepped forward and bowed.

In unison, they said in lilting, singsong voices, "*Oso-oseiyo.*" Please come in.

When they rose from their bows their heavily made-up eyes widened.

"*Ohmaya,*" one of them said, raising her cupped fingers to her mouth. Dear mother. An expression of shock.

The other hostess had more presence of mind and scurried off into a side hallway. I stood on the lacquered wooden floor in my stocking feet, speaking to the remaining hostess.

"*Yogi ei Miguk yoja ilheissoyo?*" I asked. Has an American woman been working here?

She stared at me without comprehension, still in shock at seeing a long-nosed foreigner plopped down right here in the midst of the opulent Koryo Forest Inn.

Ernie had reached the landing now.

"So they haven't seen a big nose before," he said. "Who gives a damn."

He stepped forward into the main hallway.

The surprised woman found her courage. She scooted in front of Ernie, blocking his path, and bowed. "*Andeiyo,*" she said. Not permissible.

Ernie kept moving. She stood her ground.

"*Andei,*" she said again. "*Sonnim issoyo.*" Not permissible. There are guests.

Ernie understood that part. He pushed past her saying, "Screw your high-class *sonnim*. I'm a guest, too."

Ernie had recovered from his initial reticence. And the way the two young women reacted to our presence had made him determined to make sure that everybody on the premises was aware that their cozy little pleasure dome had been defiled by the presence to two *Miguks*.

The entrance hallway ran through the building to another garden out back. But to the right, the sound of laughter and low male voices floated down a long varnished corridor. The odor of fried shrimp followed the voices like an oily cloud. Ernie pointed his nose toward the sound and pounded his way down the hallway. Light filtered through the first oil-papered door. He slid it open and stepped into the private room.

The hostess who had scurried away returned, this time with two burly young Korean men in suits. One glance told me that they were weightlifters. By the light of the overhead bulb, I could also see that the one standing closest to me had noticeable calluses on the knuckles of his right hand. Martial arts. No doubt.

I nodded toward the two men who stared at me impassively. Without showing fear—or at least hoping I wasn't showing fear—I stepped forward and pulled out my credentials. I told them in Korean that I was from 8th Army CID, here as part of a criminal investigation.

Down the hallway, someone shouted.

I turned and ran, the two weightlifters right behind me.

Ernie stood inside the private room. It was about twelve tatami mats square. A low rectangular table occupied the middle of the room with eight or nine businessmen seated around it. *Bulkogi* and bottles of Scotch and boiled quail eggs overflowed the table. The businessmen had taken off their coats, which were hung on the wall behind them. *Kisaeng* sat next to them. Beautiful Korean women, most of them dressed fashionably, in Western skirts and blouses, as opposed to the traditional clothing of the two girls who had greeted us at the front door.

The faces of the Korean businessmen were flushed with booze. And maybe something else. Shock at the fact that some big *yangnom*, foreign lout, had barged his way into their private party. The oldest of the businessmen, the only one with streaks of gray in his hair, stood toe-to-toe with Ernie, shouting at him, waggling a short finger at Ernie's pointed nose. For his part, Ernie yelled at the man in English while the man shouted back in Korean.

"*Yoja,*" Ernie was saying. "Woman. You know, *Miguk* woman." He made wavy motions with his hands. "You *arra?*" You understand? "American MP woman."

What the red-faced businessman shouted back was too rapid for me to decipher, but I do know that it was filled with invective. I grabbed Ernie by the elbow. "Come on." When he seemed reluctant to leave, I said, "There are more rooms down the hallway."

He shot a withering look of contempt at the enraged business-man and backed out of the room. Ernie proceeded down the long corridor, sliding open every oil-papered door, revealing groups of businessmen and other wealthy gentlemen drinking and enjoying themselves. Some of the *kisaeng* were dressed smartly in Western clothes, others wore the full traditional silk *chima-chogori*. But what we didn't find, and what everyone denied knowledge of, was a *Miguk yoja.* An American woman.

The weightlifters had stayed close to us but so far they hadn't made a move. I'm sure they were held back out of their respect—and fear—of my badge. But by now the entire Koryo Forest Inn was in an uproar and *kisaeng* and customers stood in the halls shouting. Ernie ignored them. He paraded up and down the corridor as if he owned the Koryo Forest Inn, the city of Byokjie, and the entire province in which it sat.

Finally, when he started to check the rooms out back, the weightlifters became fed up. One of them started to speak to Ernie in Korean, as if he wanted to reason with him, convince him to stop this disconcerting search through their little establishment. When the weightlifter reached out to touch Ernie's arm, Ernie swiveled and shot a straight punch at the man's nose. Within seconds, Ernie was flat on his back. Instead of jumping in to wrestle with the guy, I backed off a few steps, pulled my .45, and aimed it at the two burly martial arts experts. They froze.

Down the corridor, the hubbub of outrage ceased, changing to a stunned silence. Ernie rose to his feet, dusted off his pants, and shot a long hard stare at the man who'd dropped him on his butt. For a moment, I was afraid he was going to repeat his stupidity. Instead, he regained his self-control. Before he lost it again, I motioned to him and he and I walked toward the front entrance. In Korean, I told everyone to stay put. Quickly, Ernie inspected the upstairs area and the empty side rooms that we hadn't looked into yet and finally the gazebo out back that was used during the spring.

"Nothing," he said when he returned.

"I guess that does it then."

Speaking in Korean, I thanked everyone for their cooperation. Ernie and I backed out of the Koryo Forest Inn. The chauffeurs stopped smoking when we passed by. Together, we hustled down the gravel road.

"They'll call the KNPs," Ernie said.

"Yeah. Thanks to you."

"Well, what did you want me to do? They weren't answering your questions."

"I hadn't started asking questions."

"Same difference."

We returned to the jeep, Ernie started it up and we drove toward Reunification Road.

The time was ten minutes until midnight. Ten minutes until the midnight to four curfew. Ernie and I sat in the jeep in a cleared area next to Reunification Road that was normally used as a bus turn-around. For the last twenty minutes we'd been observing a steady stream of expensive sedans—Hyundais, Volvos, BMWs—streaming south, back toward Seoul.

Nobody was driving north.

"There must be a million of them," Ernie said.

"Yeah. Which means a big demand for *kisaeng.*"

"Some of those gals back at the Koryo Forest Inn were good-looking hammers."

"You noticed."

"I did."

The traffic in front of us started to thin. The vehicles that continued south were routinely breaking the speed limit, in a hurry to make it back to Seoul and get off the street before curfew.

"Here we are," Ernie said. "Cold as shit, we haven't uncovered anything new, and curfew's about to descend on the entire world."

"What's your point?"

"My point is that I don't want to sit here in this freaking jeep all night long."

I thought about that for a minute. "Good point."

"Glad you concur." He waited for the silence to lengthen and then he raised his voice and said, "So what in the hell are we going to do about it?"

"Oh, yeah. Sorry. I was thinking about the case."

"The case? But we didn't learn anything new tonight."

"Sure we did."

"Like what?"

"Like Jill Matthewson has never worked at the Koryo Forest Inn."

"Great. That narrows down our search."

"And during the hubbub you created, one of the *kisaeng* was holding on to another *kisaeng*'s arm, whispering to her."

"Sweet. Whispering what?"

"Whispering '*Chil Un Lim.*'"

"What does that mean?"

"Forest of Seven Clouds, I think. But I'd have to see the Chinese characters to be sure."

"You and your Chinese characters. So what do you make of it?

"The girl knew we were looking for an American woman, she whispered the name of a *kisaeng* house to her girlfriend. What do *you* think that means?"

"It means that she heard that a *Miguk* woman was working at that *kisaeng* house."

"Exactly."

"She might be right; she might be wrong."

"That's true."

"So where is this place?"

"I haven't the slightest idea."

"That helps."

"At least you're becoming more optimistic."

"Yeah. Now if I don't freeze my spleen tonight, my attitude will perk up even more."

"Wouldn't want to dampen your attitude."

We drove off toward the nearest village, searching for a place to flop. We found it. In a *yoinsuk*, a Korean flophouse with an outdoor toilet and communal sleeping rooms. A half-dozen Korean trucks drivers were snoring so loudly that I thought the tile roof would fall off. That part didn't bother Ernie. He can sleep through anything. What did bother him was their kimchee breath.

"If I had a knife," he told me, "I could cut the stink up into bricks and package it."

As soon as he said that, one of the truck drivers farted. Ernie groaned and rolled over on his sleeping mat.

An hour before dawn, the proprietress provided—for a small fee—towels and pans of hot water and black-market shaving equipment. After we washed up, she provided us with a complimentary bowl of rice gruel and *muu maleingi*, slices of dried turnip. Thus refreshed, Ernie and I started our search for the Forest of Seven Clouds.

Or at least I thought we were going to start our search for the Forest of Seven Clouds.

# 11

Ernie balked. He'd been more than willing to come up here during our time off and take the risk of playing cat-and-mouse with the Division MPs, but he wasn't willing to directly defy 8th Army.

"In two hours," he said, "we're going to be AWOL."

We sat in the jeep, parked next to the wood-slat wall of the *yoinsuk*. In front of us, at the end of a gravel access road, the paved Tongil-lo highway, Reunification Road, sat on its earthen foundation elevated above the rice paddies that spread through the valley. A blanket of fog lay on the land. Our breath formed clouds on the windshield of the jeep.

"You're wrong, Ernie," I replied. "Failure to repair. That's the most they can slap us with."Missing mandatory formations is punishable, but it's not AWOL.

Ernie looked at me as if I were out of my gourd. "Failure to repair, AWOL, either way we're in line for an Article Fifteen. It's now zero-six-hundred on Monday morning, Sueño, in case you forgot. We have two hours to show up for work—clean shaven, shoes shined, smiles on our chops—at the Criminal Investigation Detachment on Yongsan Compound. That's by direct order of the Eighth United

States Army provost marshal. If we leave now, and the Seoul traffic's not too bad, we just might make it."

"Your shoes aren't shined."

"Don't change the subject."

"I'm not changing the subject. We go back now, they'll never let us return to Division. The honchos will stick together and not one of them will be willing to take responsibility for making a decision that directly contradicts the 2nd Division request to have us recalled."

Ernie kept his arms crossed. "Not my lookout," he said. "When we get back we tell them what we know. If the provost marshal sees it our way, he'll send us back up here to finish the job."

"By then," I said, "it might be too late."

Ernie studied me, his eyes squinted. I explained.

Whoever had snuffed Pak Tong-i at the office of Kimchee Entertainment in Tongduchon most likely had obtained an excellent lead on the whereabouts of Corporal Jill Matthewson by stealing Pak's file on the stripper Kim Yong-ai. Chances were good that the file contained either her new address or the location of her new job or some other information that could lead to Kim Yong-ai and, from there, to Jill Matthewson. Maybe they'd already found her. Maybe they were still looking. But after a fitful night's sleep, an idea had come to me. I explained it to Ernie.

"Camp Howze," I told Ernie. "We check there. They'll know if someone's been looking for Jill. It'll only take a few minutes."

Ernie cursed but in the end he started up the jeep and, when we hit Tong-il Lo, he turned north.


Camp Howze clung to the edge of a steep hill, overlooking the squalor of Bongil-chon. The morning fog had started to lift but the entire GI village looked raunchy and raw. Unlit neon signs advertised nightclubs: the SEXY LADY and the SOUL BROTHER and the PINK PUSSYCAT. Above the village, rows of Quonset huts perched on a craggy ridge looking down on the fertile invasion route of the Western Corridor. Other than the fur-capped guards at the gate, there seemed to be no life on Camp Howze. And no life in the ville. And no *kisaeng* houses.

Two MPs manned the guard shack at the front gate. Ernie drove up to them and, as I'd instructed, turned the jeep around and kept the engine running, prepared for a quick getaway. I hopped out of the front seat.

I flashed my CID badge to the MP but within milliseconds I'd folded it and stuck it back inside my jacket.

"Bufford," I told the MP. "MPI Warrant Officer from Camp Casey. He been around?"

The MP look surprised, almost as if I'd woken him up. There wasn't much traffic here at the main gate of Camp Howze. Only an occasional jeep or army deuce-and-a-half and no civilian traffic at all. It wasn't allowed.

The MP glanced back at another MP sitting at a wooden field table reading a comic book. There were a stack of alert notifications next to his elbow but they looked untouched. One of them, I figured, mentioned me and Ernie. Out here, at this sleepy little outpost, who really paid attention to such things?

"Jonesy?" the MP asked. "You ever heard of some investigator from Casey named Bufford?"

Jonesy looked up from the dog-eared comic. "The one with the big nose? Skinny?"

"That's the one," I said.

"He's been *living* out here," Jonesy replied, disgust filling his voice. "Him and that sidekick of his. What's the name? Earwax?"

"Weatherwax," I said.

"Yeah. He's an arrogant asshole, too."

"Why do you say that?"

"They always want Camp Howze MPs to do their legwork for them. They're hunting some big important fugitive, according to them."

"They say who?"

"How would I know? They don't tell me nothing. I work the gate."

"Is Bufford still here?"

The MP shrugged. "Ain't my day to watch him."

I thanked the two MPs, told them to take it easy, and ran back to the jeep. Before either MP had a chance to give us much thought, Ernie and I were zooming toward Tongil-lo. After I briefed him,

Ernie started honking his horn, forcing kimchee cabs to swerve out of our way. We understood now that speed was everything. And compared with the fact that Corporal Jill Matthewson was being hunted—now—by Mr. Fred Bufford and Staff Sergeant Weatherwax, our bureaucratic troubles with 8th Army really didn't mean much.

I only hoped we weren't too late.

We started our search by heading toward Seoul. I wanted to locate on my map every *kisaeng* house between Seoul and the DMZ and since we were closest to Seoul, it was easier to start on the southern end. However, after five minutes of driving, Ernie and I reached the dragon's teeth, the rows of concrete monoliths that were designed to stop the North Korean communist armored divisions from invading Seoul. This marked the southernmost edge of the 2nd Division area of operations. Ahead, about a hundred yards away, stood the concrete bunker that was the Division checkpoint in the Western Corridor, manned by American MPs and Korean *honbyong*.

Ernie pulled over to the side of the road. "We don't want to go there," he said.

"No, we don't."

He waited until the traffic cleared and performed a U-turn on Reunification Road. We were heading back north and now I knew for sure that the first *kisaeng* houses north of Seoul were in Byokjie. When we reached the Byokjie intersection, we turned east on the road heading toward Uijongbu. It took us about a half hour to finish mapping the few remaining *kisaeng* houses in the area. All of them were shuttered and closed but I was able to read their names on the signposts. None of them were called the Forest of Seven Clouds, or anything close to it.

We returned to Tongil-lo, turned right, and continued north toward the Demilitarized Zone. After passing Bong-il Chon again, we were able to mark the positions of about a half-dozen more *kisaeng* houses along the road, none of which was named the Forest of Seven Clouds. We came to the turnoff for Kumchon. Kumchon is the largest town between Seoul and Munsan, and the county seat of

Paju, the agricultural county through which we were now traveling. We'd reached about halfway along our planned route.

"There must be plenty of *kisaeng* houses over there," Ernie said.

"Must be. Let's try it."

To be fair, Ernie and I were using the term *kisaeng* very loosely. During the Yi Dynasty, girls of intelligence and beauty were taken from their families and taught the gentle arts: calligraphy, the playing of musical instruments, dancing, drumming, even how to write a form of short lyric poetry called *sijo*. Once trained, they were sent off to the royal or provincial courts to entertain aristocracy. Sometimes they were even transported to remote military outposts. The advantage they received over normal women was education. The disadvantage was that they were forced to leave their families and never marry; their lives were unbearably lonely. Some of the greatest Korean poetry has come from *kisaeng*, usually dealing with longing and loss.

The women we were seeing in the modern, so-called *kisaeng* houses were, for the most part, poorly educated country girls. And their work was only one step above that of common prostitutes. Still, they were called *kisaeng*, women of skill, and that gave them status. A rock upon which to rebuild their pride.

The town of Kumchon sat two kilometers west of Tongil-lo. Already we'd seen two or three signs pointing up gravel roads that led into the hills, advertising establishments with elaborate Chinese characters in their names. Characters like "dream" and "cloud" and "flower" and "palace" and "peony." *Kisaeng* houses all. But not the one we were looking for.

When we reached the outskirts of Kumchon, Ernie slowed the jeep to about five miles an hour. A two-lane road passed through the center of town. Shops framed of weathered wood lined either side of the road and farmers pushed carts laden with sacks of grain or piled high with glimmering winter cabbage. Old men in jade-colored vests and billowing white pantaloons, holding canes and wearing the traditional Korean horsehair stovepipe hat, strolled unconcerned across the road, expecting vehicular traffic to make way for their venerable personages. It did. Even impatient young truck drivers refused to honk their horns at the elderly. The entire city of Kumchon reeked of fresh produce and raw earth.

"Like going back in time," Ernie said.

On the shops, handwritten signs advertised their wares: hot noodle eateries, fishmongers, silk merchants, porcelain vendors, even a little shop with a glowing acetylene torch advertising ironworks. One of the names of the shops was slashed with red Chinese characters: *Kongju Miyongsil*. Princess Beauty Shop. It caught my eye:

We reached the end of town which tapered off into smaller buildings and then empty lots and finally we were cruising, once again, through endless fields of fallow rice paddies. No signs for *kisaeng* houses out here. After about a half mile, we turned around.

It was almost ten in the morning and I realized that Ernie and I were two hours AWOL, although I didn't mention this to him. In fact, I tried to banish the thought from my own mind, but without much success.

As we were driving back through Kumchon, I noticed that someone had switched on a light inside the Princess Beauty Shop.

"Pull over," I told Ernie.

"Why? No *kisaeng* houses around here."

"No. But that beauty shop's open. I want to ask some questions."

"What beauty shop?"

"Never mind. Just find a place to park."

He did. At the edge of town near an eatery that catered to cab drivers. We chained and padlocked the jeep's steering wheel and hoofed our way into downtown Kumchon.

I rapped twice on the door of the Princess Beauty Shop and entered, poking my nose in first.

"*Anyonghaseiyo?*" I asked. Are you at peace?

One young woman sat in a chair with a pink cloth draped over her body, her hair in curlers, gaping at this strange creature—me—who'd just entered her world. A middle-aged woman wearing a white beautician's smock stood behind her. In Korean, I said, "Sorry to bother you. Do you think it would be too much trouble if I use your telephone?"

Involuntarily, both women glanced at a counter in the waiting area. On a knitted pad sat a clunky black telephone. Telephones are status symbols in Korea. Not everyone has them, not by a long shot. The phone company, which is a government monopoly, demands a costly security deposit—often well over a thousand dollars—before it will entrust anyone with phone equipment. But it figured that a going concern like the Princess Beauty Shop would have a telephone because they had to be able to make appointments with the wealthy ladies who were their clients.

The two women sat in stunned silence. Another two women in the back room had apparently heard my voice. Both wore beautician's smocks and peered out through a beaded curtain. Ernie entered the beauty shop and this gave the women even more to gawk at.

I strode over to the phone saying, "I'm sorry but I have to make a call to Seoul."

The eldest beautician started to say something in protest, but I pulled out a five hundred *won* note, a little more than a buck, and laid it on the counter next to the phone. That shut her up. Pretending to ignore her, I dialed the number for the 8th Army exchange.

Ernie strolled around the shop, smiling, studying the color photographs of beautiful women with beautiful hairdos. I stared at the photos, too. Korean women of unearthly beauty. I listened to clicking sounds and various pitches of dial tone.

Phone systems in Korea in the seventies are primitive. Lines are easily overloaded, and it isn't unusual to wait twenty minutes just to be able to get through to the 8th Army operator. As I waited, I watched the beauticians. The two young ones had emerged from the back room and pretended to be busy preparing their work areas. Ernie smiled at them. They smiled back. Amongst themselves they whispered.

I held the phone slightly away from my ear, listening.

"*Muol hei?*" What are they doing?"

"The big one wants to use the phone."

"I can see that. What are they doing here in Kumchon?"

"Who knows?"

And then the clicking grew louder and suddenly, above the static, a Korean-accented woman's voice said in English, "Eighth Army Operator Number Thirty-seven. How may I help you?"

I gave her the number to the CID administrative office and waited. In Korean, I said to the beauticians, "*Miguk kisaeng dei dei ro yogi ei wassoyo?*" Does the American *kisaeng* sometimes come in here?

The women's eyes widened and they stared at one another.

Staff Sergeant Riley's voice came over the line.

"Sueño?" he asked, after I'd identified myself. "Where in the hell are you?"

"On our way to Seoul," I said. "But first we have to pick up Corporal Matthewson."

"You found her?"

"Just about."

"'Just about'? What is that supposed to mean?"

"We have a solid lead." About as solid as a whiff of perfume in a windstorm.

"The first sergeant has a case of the big ass," Riley said. "So does the Eighth Army PMO."

"Stall 'em for us, Riley. We almost have her."

"I don't know if I can do that. The Second ID honchos have been teletyping messages down here like mad. Apparently, you—or somebody who looks like you—was spotted at a student demonstration in Tongduchon."

"Do you believe everything you hear?"

"That's not an answer," Riley growled.

"How about the ration control records? The ones that were classified?"

"Smitty says he should have them by tonight. But what do I tell the First Shirt?"

"No time now. Got to run. Tell them we'll be back as soon as we can."

He started to say something more but, quickly, I hung up.

I noticed that the Division hadn't messaged 8th Army about the shooting incident at the Tongduchon Market. Nor had they mentioned the fire at the Turkey Farm. Division was being, as usual, selective in their outrage.

I turned back to the beauticians, flashed my best smile, and bowed. "Thank you for the use of your phone."

The eldest woman nodded.

One of the younger beauticians blurted out, "Ku yoja arrassoyo?" You knew that woman?

I didn't like the use of the past tense but I kept my face as impassive as I could. Ernie stood still, sensing that I'd just been stunned by something the young beautician had said.

"Of course, I knew her," I replied.

"Then you know what happened?"

All the women waited for my response. They were testing me. I decided to take a chance.

"You mean at the Forest of the Seven Clouds?"

They all exhaled together.

"Yes."

"I heard something about it. Can you explain?"

"No. We don't know either. All we know is that many powerful people were angry and the women who work at the Forest of the Seven Clouds haven't been in here to have their hair done since then."

How long ago, I thought, but I didn't want to show my ignorance. They might stop talking. So I said, "Can they go that long without a hairdo?"

One of the youngest of the beauticians giggled, modestly covering her mouth with cupped fingers. "It's only been three days," she said.

I grinned. "Yes. Only three days. So no one from the Forest of the Seven Clouds has been in since that time. Not even the American woman?"

They shook their heads sadly. The youngest one piped up again. "Her hair was lovely. Gold with just a little red. And each strand so thin." She rubbed her thumb and forefinger together as if caressing silk.

"Where is the Forest of the Seven Clouds from here?" I asked.

"Not far. Usually they take a taxi."

The youngest one piped up again. "*Kisaeng* are rich." Another beautician elbowed her to be quiet. The young one pouted.

I bowed once again to the women. "Thank you so much for your help."

On our way out, Ernie grinned and saluted them. They waved back, the youngest beautician saying, "Bye-bye."

We were halfway back to the jeep when Ernie asked, "What'd they say?"

"I'll tell you in a minute."

An empty kimchee cab was cruising down the road toward us. I waved him down. When I opened the door and started asking him questions, his face drooped in disappointment. Obviously, he thought that Ernie and I were two GIs stranded far from our compound and a fat fare was in the offering. When I asked him for the location of the Forest of the Seven Clouds the disappointment on his face became more profound. He wasn't working us for a tip. Most Koreans, especially those who live in the countryside, don't think that way. They're not born to hustle. They're born to be polite. I reached in my pocket and pulled out a one thousand *won* note. Two bucks. He shook his head. Not necessary, he told me.

Then he explained that the Forest of the Seven Clouds was one of the highest-class *kisaeng* houses in the entire Paju County region. It was situated by itself on the side of a hill overlooking the valley. He pulled out a pad of brown pulp paper and a pen and sketched a quick map for me. I took the map and thanked him and tried once again to offer the thousand *won* note. Again, he refused. I told him that his time was valuable and so was his information and asked him not to embarrass me by not accepting my gift.

Reluctantly, the young man pocketed the money.

The narrow road was bordered by rice paddies. The fog had lifted but no sun came out, only a cold gray overcast that shrouded the world. We were traveling east. A few farm families pushing wooden carts were traveling west, pushing their wares toward the markets of Kumchon.

I studied the cab driver's map. The roads were clear enough but his handwriting was difficult for a foreigner like me to make out. We came to an intersection. Ernie slowed. The signpost pointed off to the right toward the village of Chuk-hyon. The map, although indecipherable by itself, clearly showed the same name, now that I knew what I was looking for. We turned right. After a hundred yards, the road curved left, up towards hills, and then we were rising rapidly.

As we rounded a bend in the road, off in the valley below, three white cranes rose from the muck and winged their way gently into the dark sky.

Just the fact that the Forest of the Seven Clouds was so far from

Seoul made it more high class. In order to have the time to drive all the way out here, you had to be a powerful boss who didn't worry about punching the clock.

The remoteness also had another advantage, at least from Jill Matthewson's point of view. There were no American military compounds within miles. And I'd be willing to bet that they'd never seen a GI up here in the entire history of their establishment, with—I was hoping—the possible exception of Corporal Matthewson.

The time was just after eleven but already fancy sedans covered about half the parking lot. Must be nice to take that much time off work, to drive out in the country and be catered to by beautiful women. Maybe Ernie and I were in the wrong line of work. Ernie's thoughts must've been similar to mine.

"Assholes ought to be shot," he said. "Making all that money, having all that fun, and not having to do any freaking work."

The "assholes" he was referring to were a group of suit-clad Korean businessmen piling out of three sedans that had just pulled up, in a small convoy, to the front of the Forest of the Seven Clouds. We huddled once again as outcasts at the edge of the tree line, our jeep parked out of sight some fifty yards beyond the entrance road. As the men strode through the lacquered wooden gate a bevy of beautiful young women clad in traditional silk gowns bowed and cooed. The businessmen nodded to the women and strutted like peacocks through the carefully raked garden and into the inner confines of the Forest of the Seven Clouds.

The parking lot grew quiet again. Three uniformed chauffeurs lit up *tambei*, cigarettes, and stood leaning against one of the cars, smoking, and chatting with one another.

"Jill Matthewson worked here?" Ernie asked me.

"The women at the Princess Beauty Shop didn't say so exactly but they said there was an American *kisaeng* who worked here, and she'd take a taxi into Kumchon to have her hair done."

"Living the high life," Ernie said.

"Maybe. But they also implied that something had gone wrong and she wasn't here anymore. And none of the women who work here had been seen in three days."

"What could go wrong out here?"

Ernie indicated the pine-covered forest and the fresh air and the snow-covered peaks above us.

"Let's find out," I said.

We strode out of the trees, across the parking lot. The chauffeurs stopped talking and stared at us. I nodded and said, "*Anyonghaseiyo?*" Are you at peace?

Dumbfounded, they nodded back.

Inside the main gate, Ernie and I made our way through the garden and at the entrance, I started to take off my shoes. The varnished floor was elevated, in the traditional Korean manner, about two feet off the ground. At least a dozen pairs of elegant men's shoes sat neatly arranged beneath the platform. Ernie grabbed my elbow.

"Let's keep 'em on," he said.

Horrors! In Korean culture about the grossest thing a person can do is step onto an immaculately clean *ondol* floor wearing shoes that have picked up filth from the street.

When I hesitated, Ernie said, "We might have to leave in a hurry." To further make his point, he pulled his .45 out of his shoulder holster.

I didn't like it but I couldn't argue. If there'd already been trouble here, there could be a lot more trouble when Ernie and I barged in and started asking questions. Reluctantly, I stepped onto the immaculately varnished wooden floor still wearing my highly-polished, army-issue low quarters.

The clunk of our shoes down the long hallway sounded to me like the tolling of the bell of death.

The Korean businessmen thought we were mad; they were just as outraged as the group we'd encountered last night at the Koryo Forest Inn. How could we possibly have the temerity to defile their expensive sanctuary? But through all the shoving and shouting and red faces blasting whiskey-soaked breath, Ernie and I held our ground. Even during the outraged shouts about our shoes and how we'd spread dirt throughout the palatial grounds and how we had no business upsetting honest customers and hard-working *kisaeng*, nobody threw any punches. But finally, the elderly woman who managed the place pulled us aside.

She wore the most elaborate *chima-chogori* I'd ever seen. The silk of her vest and skirt was hand-embroidered with tortoises, phoenixes, and dragons—lucky creatures all. She stood on her tiptoes and hissed in my ear. *"Tone,"* she said. Money. She'd give us money if we'd just leave.

I told her that we didn't want money. We only wanted information. Then, I showed her the locket containing the photo of Kim Yong-ai. I also showed her the military personnel jacket photo of Corporal Jill Matthewson. She stared at both photos long and hard, and then nodded her head in surrender and said she'd tell me the entire story. But the quid pro quo was that Ernie and I had to return to the entranceway and take off our shoes.

We did so.

Immediately, silk-clad *kisaeng*, heavily made-up and reeking of expensive perfume, grabbed moist towels and, folding them neatly, began to scrub the floor. From the spot where Ernie and I had entered these hallowed precincts all the way to where we'd encountered the irate businessman, they cleaned as if their lives depended on it. As if this was their last chance to eradicate the influence of filthy foreigners. Somehow, I think they knew that the floor would never again be as clean as it once had been.

We sat with the aging *kisaeng* on a wooden bench in an inner garden. She told me that her name was Blue Orchid and she'd been sold by her parents to a *kisaeng* house near the outskirts of Pyongyang when she was twelve years old. Her training had been rigorous and traditional. When the Korean War broke out and General MacArthur's United Nations Command bulled its way through Pyongyang, heading north toward the Yalu River, she and some of her fellow *kisaeng* had become refugees. After months of hardship, they made their way to Seoul. Since then, she'd held many positions but she'd been at the Forest of Seven Clouds for almost twelve years now.

"Never before," she told me in Korean, "did we have as much trouble as we did this week."

A young woman, just a girl really, brought a tray with folding legs and set it on the bench next to us. Ceremoniously, she poured handle-less cups full of green tea. Ernie and I sipped the warm fluid. Blue Orchid watched and cooed in approval as the young girl left.

Blue Orchid straightened her skirt before she started to talk.

"Jill was very popular here," she said. "We called her *Beik-jo*." White Swan. "She was so gracious. Friendly with all the women and charming to the customers. You should be proud of your compatriot," she told me. "We've never had a woman before—not even Jade Beauty—who's been so popular with the powerful men from Seoul."

I wanted to ask who Jade Beauty was but we didn't have time. Jill Matthewson was in danger. Not to mention the time pressure on us to return to 8th Army as soon as we could. Reluctantly, I prodded Blue Orchid to return to the main story. She did.

Jill Matthewson started working at the Forest of Seven Clouds a little more than three weeks ago. That jibed with when she'd gone AWOL. The position was procured for her, and for her friend, Kim Yong-ai, by a friend of a friend of the owner who happened to be a business associate of the entertainment agent, Pak Tong-i.

I didn't tell Blue Orchid that Pak Tong-i was dead.

Jill had to be taught many things, Blue Orchid told us. She had to be taught how to kneel on a hardwood floor, how to offer everything to a guest—whether it was a warm hand towel, or a plate of quail eggs, or a shot glass full of imported Scotch—with two hands. Never use one hand; that would be insulting. She had to be taught when to bow, when to giggle politely, when to light a man's cigarette, and when to open her eyes wide in astonishment when he explained his business triumphs—even when she didn't understand a word he was saying. And she had to be taught how to never turn her back on a guest, to back out of the room bowing and facing the guest in a respectful manner. And she had to be taught how to dress and how to wear her hair and even how to apply her makeup. And after all these lessons were learned, she still made mistakes. But the Korean men were indulgent. They were impressed that an American was getting even a few of their customs right. And they were flattered when she turned her full radiant attention on them, what with her big, round blue eyes and her intent way of staring at a man, a boldness that a Korean woman would never be allowed.

"Everybody like," Blue Orchid said, switching to English. "Many men come from Seoul. Want to see *Miguk kisaeng*."

The *Miguk kisaeng*. The American woman of skill.

Ernie was becoming antsy. Still, I didn't rush Blue Orchid. She'd stopped using Korean now and had switched almost exclusively to English. This told me that during those years of hardship during and after the Korean War, before she'd landed this gig at the Forest of Seven Clouds, she'd made her living not as a *kisaeng* but as a business girl—for GIs. As I hoped, Blue Orchid finally reached the point in her narrative where something went wrong.

"Two days ago, man come." Blue Orchid's face crinkled in disgust. "American man. GI. He drive up in jeep, have another GI with him. They both wear uniform. Everything dirty. Clothes dirty, boots dirty, even GI teeth dirty."

"What did he look like?" I asked.

"Tall. Almost like you. But skinny, like him." She pointed at Ernie. "But more skinny than him."

"An MP?" Ernie asked.

"Yes. He wear black helmet with "MP" on front."

Warrant Officer Fred Bufford. Had to be.

"And the driver?"

"Black man. Small guy. Skinny, too. He don't say much."

Maybe Staff Sergeant Weatherwax.

"So what happened?" I asked.

"He walk in wearing boots. Same like you." The cardinal sin. "Then he find *Beik-jo*."

"She sit in room with customers. Important customers. They drink much whiskey. Buy *taaksan anju*."

*Anju* means "snacks." *Taaksan* is Japanese for "much." English, Japanese, and Korean all in one sentence: Buy *taaksan anju*. Blue Orchid was slipping back into GI slang.

"Tall GI find Jill, he pull his gun." Blue Orchid mimicked a man pointing a .45 automatic pistol. "He tell Jill she gotta go back compound. She say, hell no! He try to grab her. Then Jill knuckle-sandwich with him." Blue Orchid waved a small fist through the air. "Tall, skinny GI go down, drop gun, Jill pick it up. Point it at GI, take him back outside, make him and black GI *karra chogi*." Go away.

"And she kept the pistol?" Ernie asked.

Blue Orchid nodded vigorously.

"Bold," Ernie said, once again impressed with the exploits of Corporal Jill Matthewson.

"What'd she do next?" I asked.

"She . . . how you say?"

Blue Orchid mimicked grabbing things and placing them in a container.

"She packed her bags?" I said.

"Right. Pack bags. She and Kim Yong-ai. Right away, they go."

"Kim Yong-ai was working here, too?"

Blue Orchid nodded. "Not *taaksan* popular like Jill. But she good woman."

"Where'd they go?"

Blue Orchid shrugged her narrow shoulders. "*Moolah* me." I don't know. "They cry, they thank everybody for helping them, they so sorry they gotta go but, anyway, they gotta go."

"They left that same night?"

"Yes. They leave same night. After they go, maybe one hour, GI come back. This time he have many jeeps and many MPs. They search every room, make our customer *taaksan* angry. They ask anybody where Jill go but nobody tell them nothing because nobody know."

"Were there any KNPs with them?"

Blue Orchid shook her head. "None."

"But they searched your premises. Did you report them to the KNPs?"

"No. We no call. Later, when KNP honcho come drinkey, I tell him. He *taaksan kullasso*." Very angry. Blue Orchid was using English, Japanese, and Korean again.

"Did he do anything about it?"

Blue Orchid shrugged again. "I don't know."

Probably not. For the local boss of the Korean National Police to admit that 2nd Infantry Division MPs had taken it upon themselves to search a legitimate business enterprise without a warrant, an enterprise over which they had no jurisdiction, would be a tremendous loss of face. The KNP boss would never report the breach of legal procedure officially but, you can bet, he'd be waiting for his chance to take revenge.

We asked if we could see Jill Matthewson's room. Blue Orchid not only agreed but escorted us there herself. I was disappointed. It was just a little cubbyhole with a vinyl-covered *ondol* floor and cherry tree wall paper furnished with a down-filled sleeping mat and a plastic armoire. It had been totally cleaned out. Nothing was left to indicate Jill Matthewson's brief residence. Kim Yong-ai's room was the same.

I grabbed Blue Orchid by her silk-covered shoulders and swore to her that Ernie and I weren't here to harm Jill Matthewson. I told her of the letter from Jill's mother and I even showed it to her. After she'd read it—or pretended to read it—I asked her to tell me anything she knew that could help me find Jill, and find her before she was located by her enemies.

Blue Orchid shook her head. "Jill Matthewson smart woman. She know that if she tell us anything, someday we tell somebody else. So she no tell us nothing. I swear." Blue Orchid raised her right hand. "*Beik-jo* didn't tell us where she go."

I believed her.

As a group, the *kisaeng* of the Forest of the Seven Clouds followed us out to the exit. I thanked them for their cooperation. As one body, they bowed as we left.

"Zippo," Ernie said. "*Nada*. Not a goddamn thing. That's what we have to show for all these days of work. She's gone. She's in the wind and we don't have a clue as to where she might've gone."

Ernie was right. I didn't want to admit it, but he was right.

We were in the jeep, driving back toward Kumchon.

"And furthermore," he continued, "we now have one day of AWOL on our record. One day of bad time."

By "bad time" Ernie meant that any days of absence without leave do not count toward earning a twenty-year military retirement.

He was right again. Our gamble hadn't paid off. Bufford had reached Jill Matthewson before us. But how? Then I remembered the body of Pak Tong-i; I remembered how he'd been tortured, systematically strangled. He'd probably revealed information before he'd been stricken down by a heart attack. The timing was right. Bufford had learned the whereabouts of Jill Matthewson and Kim Yong-ai and then he and Staff Sergeant Weatherwax had hot-footed it over to the Forest of Seven Clouds.

What had he planned to do with Jill? Was he just going to arrest her and return her to 2nd Division custody? Somehow, I thought not. Pak Tong-i was dead; Druwood was dead. If Warrant Officer Fred Bufford was in any way responsible for their deaths, bringing Jill Matthewson back to Camp Casey would be too dangerous. My guess was—and judging by Jill's reaction it was probably her guess, too—that Bufford intended to kill her. That's why she'd threatened his life with his own .45. And that's why she'd left no word with the women of the Forest of the Seven Clouds as to where she was going.

"For all we know," Ernie said, "she went to Seoul and we'll never find her."

He was becoming gloomier by the minute. I was fighting the feeling but gloom was overwhelming me, too. No matter how I turned it over, all the things we'd learned since arriving in Division gave us no clue as to where Jill might've gone.

Additionally, it now looked as if our work concerning the black-market activities of the 2nd Division honchos and the suspicious circumstances of Private Marvin Druwood's death might come to naught. Once we were back in Seoul, even if Staff Sergeant Riley managed to come up with those classified ration control records, any anomaly they showed would be handled through regular channels. That is, the Division provost marshal himself, Colonel Alcott, would be notified immediately. Any covering up he had to do he could handle at his leisure. The same with the death of Private Marvin Druwood. Alcott would be asked to investigate his own MPs. The worst that could happen is that there would be some embarrassment on the 2nd Division commander's part and Alcott would be relieved and transferred back to the States.

One thing you could be sure of is that Ernie and I would be kept strictly away from the investigation. When the integrity of honchos in positions of power is threatened, investigations are handled with the utmost delicacy. And delicacy isn't what Ernie and I are known for.

Would Jill Matthewson eventually be hunted down and murdered? Possibly. Along with her friend, Kim Yong-ai. If their bodies were dumped in a ditch, or tossed into the fast-flowing Imjin River, they'd never be heard from again. And Ernie and I would still be working the black-market detail down in Seoul, busting the Korean wives of enlisted men for selling maraschino cherries and dehydrated orange drink. Standing around with our thumbs up our butts while a good soldier was stalked and murdered.

Ernie's thoughts must've been running parallel to mine. His face was twisted in anger and his knuckles on the steering wheel were white. He raced faster than he should have through the city of Kumchon, passed the Princess Beauty Shop without slowing down, and when we reached Reunification Road, without a word to me, he turned south toward Seoul.

I sat with my arms crossed, brooding. It was late afternoon now; the sun was lowering, cold and damp, behind enormous banks of gray clouds.

At Bongil-chon Ernie threw the jeep into low gear. He turned off the main road and drove under the overpass toward the compound that sat on the craggy peaks. Before reaching the road that led up to the compound, he turned into the narrow lanes of the village and gunned the engine, letting it whine. Like a crazed road-race driver, he roared through the narrow lanes, splashing mud everywhere. People jumped out of his way. He zigzagged back and forth, up and down, until he located the central road of the village. It was lined with nightclubs.

Along the main drag, he found a place to park the jeep. He chained and padlocked the steering wheel, turned to me, and said, "Let's go get drunk."

As if to help me with my decision, one of the neon signs blinked to brilliant life. YOBO CLUB, it said. I pondered my decision for about three seconds, finding no flaw in Ernie's plan.

"We ain't there yet?" I asked.


The time was about an hour and a half before midnight. Ernie and I were so drunk that we were starting to hold on to the edge of the bar to steady ourselves. We must've hit every dive in Bongil-chon and of all of them, this one was probably the worst. The Bunny Club, they called it. It was full of half-dressed business girls and half-crazed GIs with pockets full of spending money and access to more cheap booze and rock and roll and women than they'd ever seen in their lives.

Ernie and I loved it.

We'd spotted the local ville patrol a couple of times; it was composed of an MP from Camp Howze and a Korean MP from a nearby ROK Army compound and, of course, a surly Korean National Policeman. They hadn't bothered us or seemed to notice us in any way. Ernie and I were just two more drunken GIs wasting their money as far as the ville patrol was concerned. Even though the Division was looking for us—and these MPs had probably been notified—it's not the type of thing that a busy MP spends a lot of time worrying about. Two 8th Army CID agents, how dangerous could they be? Besides, even if Division managed to distribute photos that quickly, nobody pays any attention to that stuff. A cop on patrol has other things to worry about.

Tomorrow, Ernie and I would return to Seoul to face the music. Tonight, we were partying. At least we were trying to. Actually, though, we were just drowning our sorrows. For whatever drunken reason, Ernie and I decided to leave the Bunny Club and stagger to another bar. It was a good thing we did because just as we pushed our way through the swinging doors of the Bunny Club, an MP jeep rounded the corner. Ernie and I kept walking at our normal pace. I grabbed Ernie by the elbow.

"What?" Ernie asked.

"MPs."

"So?"

"So look." I pointed a shaky finger. MPs climbed out of either side of the jeep, one of them tall and skinny, the other not quite as thin but shorter.

"Bufford," Ernie said. His fists knotted.

Before I could stop him, he was staggering back toward the Bunny Club, leaning forward at the waist, his entire posture one of determination. Ernie Bascom had decided to kick some ass.

By now, Bufford and the other MP were approaching the front door of the Bunny Club. In the overhead light, I could see that the other MP was indeed the man we'd surmised had accompanied Bufford to the Forest of the Seven Clouds: Staff Sergeant Rufus Q. Weatherwax. The left side of his nose was still a dark purple from that night in TDC when Ernie had punched him. Both MPs drew their .45s, all their attention riveted on the entranceway of the Bunny Club, and together they pulled back their slides.

Under normal MP procedure, a weapon is drawn only when you know that your life is in danger. These guys looked not as if they were worried about being hurt, but as if they'd already decided to go in firing.

I ran after Ernie, trying to pull him away.

Startled by our footsteps, Bufford and Weatherwax turned. They were about ten yards away. I grabbed Ernie's shoulders and yanked him backwards. Just as I did so, a round was fired. I felt hot air pass above Ernie's arm, and then we were both tumbling backward, somehow keeping our feet. Another round blasted into the night, but by now we'd slid into one of the narrow alleys running alongside of the Bunny Club. Ernie'd forgotten about kicking Bufford's ass and he'd regained his balance—and regained his sobriety. The two of us were running shoulder to shoulder, bumping into one another, down the narrow alley. Ernie dodged to his left at the next alley, me with him, and as we did so another round blasted out, this one exploding into a brick wall behind us where we'd just been standing.

Our feet turned into flying machines. Bufford and Weatherwax stayed close. I could hear the pounding of their boots and their occasional shouted commands to one another. Ernie and I twisted and turned and dodged and since Bufford and Weatherwax had to slow occasionally to see which way we had gone, we were starting to lengthen our lead.

I wanted to keep running. Even though Ernie and I were both armed, I didn't want to turn and fight. If, and when, Ernie and I returned to 8th Army headquarters in Seoul, we'd have enough explaining to do. I didn't want to add two dead MPs to our list of indiscretions. Not if I could help it.

There were no streetlights back here. When I looked back I could see the beam of an MP flashlight bouncing against brick.

Ernie turned and turned again and then found a small inlet into which to dodge. We stopped, breathing heavily, listening to our pounding heartbeats. A streetlamp about twenty yards away cast a dim glow but we were hidden in shadow. Ernie pulled his .45. If they closed in now, it would be an all out firefight. Their footsteps pounded a couple of alleys away. The steps retreated and then returned and then paced farther away in the opposite direction. Finally, after a long wait, all was quiet.

Ernie whispered, "Where are we?"

"Somewhere on the western edge of Bongil-chon, I think."

"Can we make it back to the jeep?"

"They probably already have it spotted. Best if we catch a cab to take us to Seoul."

We still had about another hour until curfew. Enough time to take a kimchee cab to the northern edge of Seoul. Once there we could switch cabs and head back to 8th Army's Yongsan compound on the southern edge of the capital city.

"Okay. I'll go first," Ernie said.

We started to return to the land of the living when suddenly, out of the shadows, something moved. At first I thought it was simply the play of light, but then I heard the tread of shoe leather on gravel. Before I could react, cold steel pressed into the hot flesh of my neck.

"Freeze."

The voice was low, forceful. A woman's voice. An American woman's voice.

Ernie raised his hands; I raised mine also. Then, I stepped away slowly and turned. She switched on a flashlight and aimed it at her highly polished jump boots. From its glow I saw the outlines of a shapely woman, a woman wearing a full uniform of pressed green fatigues, a web belt with a brightly polished brass buckle, and a black leather holster hanging at her hip. The rank insignia of corporal was pinned to her collar along with the crossed-pistols brass of the United States Army Military Police Corps. Even though the light was dim, her black helmet glistened and the big white letters MP shined like neon. But mostly I saw the unholy pit of the barrel of the .45.

"You've been following me," the voice said from behind the pistol.

I didn't deny what she said. Neither did Ernie.

"My name is Jill Matthewson." the voice said again. "You will keep your hands in full view at all times." She motioned with her .45. "Do you understand?"

Ernie and I both nodded. We understood.

# 12

Jill relieved Ernie of his .45.

She didn't touch mine but told me to keep it holstered and continue to keep my hands in plain sight.

"You have a vehicle," she said.

"Yes."

"Let's go there."

Up on the ridge on Camp Howze, roving headlights indicated that emergency units were starting to roll. I could imagine the notification over the MP radio: *Shots fired. Bongil-chon*.

We turned and walked, Jill Matthewson right behind us.

After all this time, I couldn't believe we'd found her. Or, more accurately, she'd found us. But how had she known we were looking for her? How had she found us in Bongil-chon? How had she known to be waiting in that alleyway at that particular time?

These were all questions I wanted answered but all questions that would have to wait. In the distance, jeep engines roared. Probably more Camp Howze MPs pouring into the ville. I didn't have a beef with the Camp Howze MPs but I knew that if they caught us we'd be transported back to Division headquarters at Camp Casey. That's what I didn't want. Warrant Officer Bufford and Staff Sergeant Weatherwax had already shown a willingness to shoot to kill. They were desperate now. They knew we were close to blowing apart their entire operation. Private Marvin Druwood and Mr. Pak Tong-i were already dead. I didn't want Ernie and me added to the list.

Dirty streetlamps illuminated our way. I glanced back as we walked. The .45 in Jill Matthewson's hand continued to be pointed at our backs. It never wavered.

"How'd you find us?" I asked.

She shrugged. "I keep in contact with my friends."

"But the women at the Forest of Seven Clouds swore to us that they didn't know where you were."

"They didn't. I call them. Once or twice a day."

I filed that one away. I hadn't asked the right questions. Maybe, if I'd received some inkling that Jill occasionally called the women at the Forest of Seven Clouds, I could've convinced Blue Orchid to relay a message.

"But we stopped in Bongil-chon instead of driving straight to Seoul. How'd you know to look for us here?"

She smiled. It was a great smile, wry and wise and full of laughter.

"I hate to break it to you guys but you're predictable. Anybody who knows you would know where you'd stop. The first GI bar district you came to."

"But you don't know us," I countered.

She laughed. It was like a brass bell ringing. "I know you well enough."

Ernie straightened his jacket, uncomfortable at not having his .45.

"So you've been shadowing us," Ernie said. "So you must've seen Bufford and Weatherwax. Are they alone or are there more MPs backing them up?"

"Alone. Come on," she said, motioning with Ernie's .45. "No more talk."

At the mouth of the alley, she motioned for us to wait and then stepped past us. She looked both ways and then entered the narrow pedestrian walkway. She trotted down the path, past brick-walled residences, until she reached a muddy thoroughfare. She waved for us to follow. When Ernie and I approached, she tossed Ernie's .45 back to him. He caught it in midair.

"Be careful with that thing," she told him. "Are you sober enough to drive?"

"Always."

She turned and we followed her through the alleys until we reached neon. Ernie's jeep sat thirty yards away. Still padlocked. Still untouched. Between us and the jeep, rows of bars were still open, rock and roll blaring out of open doors. Korean women stood in front. Business girls. Now, less than an hour until the midnight curfew, they could no longer wait demurely for some GI to wander into their club and sit down next to them and start spending money on them. They had to parade along the street and hustle. The few GIs who were still out were being accosted by the girls. Some of the GIs stopped and chatted. Some allowed themselves to be pulled into a nightclub, maybe for a last drink, maybe to negotiate a night with a beauteous lady.

At a distant intersection, a Camp Howze MP jeep roared past. We took that as our cue to emerge from the shadows and jog toward the parked jeep.

The business girls backed up as we ran past. A few of them glanced at Ernie and me, but most of them kept their eyes riveted on Corporal Jill Matthewson. They'd seen uniformed MPs before, plenty of them, but they'd never seen one shaped like this. Jill seemed slighter than she had appeared in her official photo. Even beneath her bulky fatigues one could see that her waist was small and her ample bosom had to be firmly held in place. Most of the business girls would never have seen a female American soldier before because the few American women assigned to Division were all stationed at the headquarters at Camp Casey.

As soon as the Korean business girls realized what they were seeing, a murmur arose amongst them. They elbowed one another, pointed, and stared in awe as Jill Matthewson waded through them. Jill didn't acknowledge their attention. Her focus was on the jeep. But it was clear to me that these young, put-upon, Korean business girls, had just seen something akin to a miracle. A woman in a position of power. A woman leading men. A woman wearing a pistol and a uniform, set on her own self-determined goal, not letting anything stand in her way.

Ernie noticed the reaction and said to a couple of the business girls, "Hey, what about me?"

They ignored him.

As we climbed in the jeep, I folded myself into the tattered back seat; Jill sat up front next to Ernie. The business girls approached the jeep, as if mesmerized. Still, Jill Matthewson acted as if she hadn't noticed their reaction.

For a moment, sitting in the back seat, I thought of pulling my .45, disarming Corporal Jill Matthewson, and placing her under arrest. But then what would I do? Take her back to Seoul? Charge her with being AWOL? Eventually, I'd be forced to turn her over to the Division provost marshal. No way. First, I was going to encourage her cooperation and hear what she had to say. Then we'd make a decision as to what our next move would be.

Ernie started the jeep, jammed it into gear. He rolled forward slowly because of the awestruck business girls surrounding us. Finally, when he was clear of them, he gunned the engine to the next intersection and started to turn right, toward the main paved street that led to Reunification Road.

"Not right," Jill told him. "Left. Back to the Bunny Club."

"Why?" Ernie asked.

"You'll see. Just do as I tell you."

Ernie shrugged and turned the wheel to the left. As we approached the Bunny Club, the glow from the neon out front illuminated the jeep that Bufford and Weatherwax had driven up in. Still sitting there, untouched.

"Pull over!" Jill shouted.

Ernie did. Before the jeep had come to a full stop, she leaped out, running, and for a moment I thought she was escaping. She ran toward the front of the Bunny Club. The designation stenciled in white lettering on the jeep's bumper said: HQ CO, 2ND ID PMO. Translation: Headquarters Company of the 2nd Infantry Division Provost Marshal's Office. I pulled my .45, fearing that Bufford and Weatherwax might appear at any moment.

Jill Matthewson approached the jeep, drew her .45, and took aim. She fired six rounds; two into the radiator, one each into the four tires. Satisfied, she reholstered her pistol, trotted back, and jumped into the passenger seat next to Ernie.

"We ain't left yet?" she asked.

Ernie stared at her for a moment, immobile. Then he seemed to come to his senses, nodded grimly, let out the clutch, and jammed the little jeep into gear. We lurched forward. He gunned the engine, twisted the steering wheel, and after a few hairpin turns, the three of us sped off toward Reunification Road.

When we told her that Private Marvin Druwood was dead, Jill Matthewson slammed her fist into the wall of the hooch. The entire building shook.

"Damn!" she shouted.

She wouldn't look at us. She stared at the floor, shaking her head, and then she gazed out the open sliding double doors of the little hooch.

"Damn, damn, damn," she said. "Private Marvin Druwood, United States Army Military Police Corps. Innocent little Marv Druwood."

I thought of asking something like, You knew him well? But every sentence I composed mentally sounded lame, so I kept my mouth shut.

After leaving Bongil-chon, Jill had instructed Ernie to turn north on Reunification Road, guiding us farther away from Seoul. A mile later, she had us turn left onto a two-lane highway running east. For twenty minutes, we drove through rice paddies and wooded hills barely illuminated by a rising moon. Finally, we reached the town of Wondang. There were no U.S. military compounds anywhere near here and, as far as I could tell, no ROK Army compounds either.

We'd parked the jeep near the city center in front of a Buddhist temple. According to Jill, the temple held an ancient bronze bell that was sounded by bald monks every morning at dawn. Two blocks farther on, we reached a walled compound into which were crammed about a dozen hooches, including Jill's.

Inside the hooch, we sat on an *ondol* floor. It was a comfortable little hooch, old but well maintained; Jill Matthewson seemed to have mastered all the intricacies of Korean housekeeping. As soon as we arrived, she'd unlaced her combat boots and slipped on a pair of rubber sandals. She used metal tongs to reach into a subterranean stone furnace at the base of the outer wall of the hooch. She pulled out one flaming charcoal briquette and replaced it with a new one. Next, she carried the spent briquette over to a cement storage space tucked away from the other hooches so as to prevent fire.

Then she observed as Ernie and I slipped off our shoes and stepped up onto the wooden porch. After we had entered the hooch, she used a moist rag to wipe down the porch's immaculate varnished surface. In the cement-floored kitchen—adjacent to the one-room living space— she had used a wooden match to light a single butane burner. Then she'd gone outside to fill a brass teapot with water from an outdoor spigot. Fifteen minutes later she'd unfolded the legs of a one-foot-high, mother-of-pearl serving table and Ernie and I were sipping Folgers instant coffee ladled from a short bottle with a Korean customs duty stamp emblazoned on it. We sat on flat, square cushions covered with silk.

"Where's Kim Yong-ai?" I asked, once Jill had settled down.

"At work," Jill replied.

"Where does she work?"

Jill eyed me suspiciously. "Why do you want to know?"

I raised two open palms in mock surrender. "Just curious."

"I know you're curious," she replied. "That's why you spent so much time looking for me. You want to find out what's really going on in Division."

I did. But first I thought I'd show her something. I pulled out the photocopy of the letter that her mother had sent to her congressman. I handed it to her. While Jill read, Ernie stirred more sugar into his coffee, content for the moment to let me handle the interview. Anything touchy-feely, Ernie held no truck with.

Jill read the letter, then read it again. She began to cry. Angry at herself, she wiped the tears from her eyes.

"It's understandable why you didn't write your mom. Don't be so hard on yourself," I said.

"It's not that," Jill replied. "It's just that she pulled it off so well."

"'Pulled it off'?" I asked. "What do you mean?"

"Mom's not real good at writing letters. But I called her from a pay telephone on Camp Casey. Told her what I was planning to do."

Now it was Ernie's turn to be amazed. "You told your mom that you were planning to go AWOL?"

"Right," Jill said calmly, stirring more sugar into her coffee. "And I told her why."

Ernie and I glanced at one another. Waiting. Both of us afraid to interrupt Jill Matthewson.

"I told my mom to write the letter to her congressman," Jill said. "And I told her what to say, and I told her when to send the letter."

"Why?" I ventured to ask.

Jill stopped stirring her coffee and stared at each of us in turn.

"To get you guys up here," she said. "I need help. From Eighth Army or the Marines or the FBI or somebody." She waved her arms in a broad circle. "I can't do all this on my own. And somebody has to put a stop to what's happening in Division."

Neither Ernie nor I responded. Maybe we were both too dumb-founded by this turn of events. Or maybe it was because once a principal in an investigation starts answering questions you didn't ask, the best thing to do is keep your trap shut. Jill examined the cover letter from the office of the congressman from the district that encompasses Terre Haute, Indiana. She snorted a laugh.

"Finally, somebody up top is interested in what goes on in Division."

"What do you mean 'finally'?" I asked.

"'Finally,' because first I went to the IG." The Inspector General. "The Division IG?"

"Yes. I told him about the black marketing, the whole thing, from A to Z. Then he called the provost marshal."

"They called the very guy you were complaining about?"

"Right. Told him I needed some 'extra training' as they put it."

"What about the IG report?"

"There was no report. Not that I ever saw anyway."

Any 2nd Division IG report would've made its way to 8th Army. Ernie and I'd checked before we left Seoul. No reports concerning Jill Matthewson existed. In addition, a copy of any IG complaint should've been attached to the Division serious incident report. It wasn't.

"So they buried your complaint?" Ernie asked.

"What else?" Jill replied. "The Division IG is one of the colonels who attends their mafia meetings."

The inspector general is, theoretically, an independent ombudsman who examines all aspects of the operational capability of military units. This includes reports of wrongdoing that can't be handled through the normal chain of command. This independence is theoretical. In fact, he lives cheek by jowl with the rest of the officer corps and you can bet the Division commander watches his every move. It takes a lot of nerve to be a truly independent IG. Most of them don't have enough of what it takes.

Someone knocked on the gate outside. Jill jumped up, slid open the oil-papered door, stepped outside the hooch, and, wearing big plastic slippers, clomped across the small courtyard to the outer wall. There, she unlatched a small door in the larger gate.

A woman ducked through. A Korean woman. Her hair was long and curly and she kept a thick cloth coat wrapped around her slender body to ward off the chill of the cold Korean night. She started to walk across the courtyard but stopped when she saw Ernie and me sitting in the well-lighted room. Jill held a whispered conversation with the woman. As she did so, I studied her features. Kim Yong-ai. The stripper pictured on the locket we'd found on a chain around the forearm of the booking agent, Pak Tong-i.

When the two women stopped whispering, they approached the hooch. Jill entered first. Sullenly, Kim Yong-ai followed but rather than speaking to us, she kept her eyes averted, ducked through the small entrance to the cement-floored kitchen, and shut the door behind her.

Jill sat and picked up her tea. "She's not comfortable with men. Not yet."

"You want us to leave?"

"Where would you go? Curfew hits in five minutes. You're stuck here tonight."

And so we were. Jill continued to talk and heated more water for coffee; Kim Yong-ai stayed in the kitchen. Pots and pans rattled, so apparently she ate some kimchee and rice. Eventually, Jill took a couple of silk comforters into the kitchen for her.

Jill and Kim Yong-ai were two terrifically good-looking women. Ernie and I had been known, from time to time, to be attractive to the opposite sex. But there was no orgy in that small hooch that night. After talking until she was exhausted and answering all my questions as best she could, Jill lay down against the far wall of the hooch, bundled herself in blankets, and slept with her back toward us. Ernie and I lay on the warm *ondol* floor, our necks propped on cylindrical cloth pillows filled with beads.

We'd found her at last.

When I dozed off, Ernie was already snoring.


It wasn't a sound so much as a vibration. A vibration that traveled through the air and the stone wall outside and the wood of the hooch and through the soil of the earth beneath us. I felt it before I heard it and when I sat up it was still vibrating. A deep, profound, low wail of a sound. Soft but rich. Powerful. Unstoppable. The gong of the bronze bell of the Buddhist temple.

I was fully alert. But calm. Reassured, somehow, by the deep low sound that had awakened me. Ernie still snored. Jill Matthewson had already folded up her blankets and piled them in the far corner of the hooch. Inside the small kitchen, brass pots and earthenware jars bumped against one another, making the gentle sound of early morning activity.

I rose and made my way to the outdoor *byonso* and, after squatting there for a while, I used the water spigot and a metal pan in the center of the courtyard to wash up. Jill provided soap and small towels and even a razor blade so I could shave. Ernie was up shortly thereafter and performed the same ablutions, what the Koreans call *seisu*, the washing of the hands and face.

Kim Yong-ai prepared a breakfast of rice gruel and dried turnip and while we ate, I became less surprised that Jill Matthewson had lost so much weight. On this diet, anybody would. She looked great, by the way.

Ernie noticed, too. Jill wore blue jeans and a T-shirt with a tight-fitting sweater. Her hair was tied up in the Korean style with a pair of wooden chopsticks holding the topknot in place. Kim Yong-ai looked terrific also but we barely saw her. She refused to come out of the kitchen.

What was their relationship, these two? Ernie and I were wondering the same thing, occasionally casting one another knowing looks. Kim and Jill were constantly whispering to one another and seemed as close as twin sisters.

I was still collating all the information Jill had given me last night, trying to see it from the perspective of a trained investigator. What should I go after first? How could I make a case that would stand up not only before a panel of judges in a court-martial, ultimately, but also to the honchos at 8th Army who would have to give the green light to go ahead with such a prosecution?

It wasn't going to be easy. Both Ernie and I were keenly aware that this was the start of our second day of being absent without leave. And we also both knew that if we returned to Seoul, 8th Army would take over our investigation and although some people might be prosecuted and some things might be changed, for the most part the nefarious activities Jill Matthewson had reported to us would be corrected bureaucratically, not by criminal proceedings. 8th Army would never tolerate the bad publicity that would come from admitting that the leadership at the 2nd Infantry Division was rotten to the core.

While Ernie and I sipped more coffee and pondered our next move, Jill Matthewson made up our minds for us.

"First," she said, "we kick some serious butt."

Ernie looked up from his coffee.

"Starting," she continued, "with the asshole who offed Marv Druwood."

"Maybe Druwood's death was an accident," I said, "like Division claims. Or suicide."

"No way. I go AWOL, Marv Druwood goes nuts and becomes dangerous to them, a few days later they find a way to kill him, making it look like an accident. That's what happened."

She reached inside the plastic armoire, the only piece of furniture in the room, and pulled out what GIs call an "AWOL bag." A traveling bag, smaller than a suitcase. Carefully, Jill packed her combat boots and her web belt and her MP helmet, along with a few more civilian "health and welfare" items. Finally, she packed her most prized possession, her army-issue .45 automatic pistol.

She stood and said, "Time to move out."

"You could go back to Seoul," I told her. "You'd be safe there."

"So would you," she said. "But you won't. You want these assholes as bad as I do."

"Once we start arresting people," Ernie said, "it could get hairy."

For the first time since I'd known her, Jill Matthewson's face flushed with anger. "I'm an MP! Don't tell me about danger."

I glanced at Ernie. He stared at her with a look of goony admiration. Not insulted in the least. I wondered if we were doing the right thing. As Ernie had said, once we started arresting people, the stuff would really hit the fan. And as dangerous as that would be— up here alone in the Division area with no backup—it would be even more dangerous if 8th Army decided not to sanction our investigation. If they decided to actually carry us as AWOL and therefore pull our jurisdictional authority. Then we'd be wallowing in deep kimchee up to our nostrils. Ernie knew all this. Still, he looked at me and nodded his approval.

Now it was up to me. Should we actually go through with this? Start arresting men of higher rank than us while standing on jurisdictional ground that could turn into quicksand? Take the risk of accruing another day of AWOL? Another day of time that would never count toward our twenty? Or should we just handcuff Jill Matthewson and transport her back to Seoul?

I thought of Marv Druwood's lifeless body, the pale coldness of his flesh. I thought of Madame Chon, bowing her forehead to the ground before a row of flickering candles. I thought of the open mouth of Pak Tong-i, gasping for a last gulp of air that would forever be out of reach. I thought of the haunted, hunted look that festered even now in the exotic, dark eyes of Kim Yong-ai.

"Okay," I said finally. "Let's do it."

For the first time since last night, Kim Yong-ai emerged from the kitchen. She and Jill embraced. As we crossed the courtyard Kim Yong-ai followed us and then stood at the gate, holding the door open, watching as we ducked through and made our way down the narrow pathway. At the end of the pathway, Jill stopped and turned and waved to Kim Yong-ai. The frightened Korean woman bowed, lowering her head all the way to her waist.


What Jill had told me last night, during our long conversation in her little hooch, matched what Ernie and I had picked up since arriving in Division. The honchos were black-marketing; they were using the money to have mafia meetings; women were being abused; but it was in the details, as they say, that the devil lurked.

When she first arrived in Division, Jill Matthewson was familiar with the catcalls and lewd remarks and gestures that GIs make whenever they see a female soldier. She'd suffered it innumerable times in the two years she'd already spent in the army. But what she wasn't used to was the intensity. Up here in Division, GIs are far away from home, far away from their families, far away from their churches, and so far away from their normal way of conducting their lives that they might as well be stationed on another planet. And like men adrift anywhere, they'd lost all sense of proportion. In Korea—especially in Division—anything goes. GIs could hoot and howl and rub themselves to their heart's content when Jill Matthewson was around and nobody did anything about it. The Division honchos wanted American GIs to be on time for military formations, on time for alerts, and on time when they reported to work every day. Other than that, GIs in Tongduchon could do whatever in the hell they wanted to do. Why not? The honchos were doing the same damn things.

As one of the first females in Division, and the very first to be assigned to the military police, Jill didn't have to be a genius to figure that she wasn't wanted. Camp Casey—and especially Tongduchon— had been an all-male American enclave for decades. A GI playground. Nobody needed a stuck-up American female around to ruin things. No matter how Jill tried to conduct herself, whether in a professional manner or as one of the "boys," she was never accepted. She was always the odd woman out.

Jill told me, while we sat sipping coffee in the middle of the night in her cozy hooch in Wondang, that she could have lived with all that. It was to be expected. If she wanted to succeed in her military career, if she wanted to make her mother proud of her, she'd known from the day she enlisted that it wouldn't be easy. She'd deal with it. She was determined to do so.

It was corruption that pushed her over the edge.

At first it seemed innocent enough. Go over to the main PX and purchase a new wristwatch using the provost marshal's open ration control plate. Every GI in Korea is issued an RCP and he is severely limited as to what he can or cannot buy in the PX. For example, a male GI is not allowed to purchase perfume or nylon stockings. Because the worry is that he'd give them—illegally—to an unauthorized Korean *yobo* down in the ville. He could, however, buy a wristwatch, but only one per year. And, upon leaving the country, he had to produce the wristwatch, to prove that he hadn't sold it on the black market.

Colonel Alcott, however, was buying a wristwatch every week. That is, Jill Matthewson was taking his RCP to the PX and purchasing it on his behalf. Before the purchase, she was handed cash by Warrant Officer Fred Bufford and a handwritten note with the exact model and brand of wristwatch to buy. This one's for Colonel So-and-so, Bufford would tell her, a ROK Army officer, the Commander of the Such-and-such Infantry Battalion, and Colonel Alcott is providing the watch to the Division chief of staff so he can present it as a gift to the Korean colonel in return for the support his battalion has provided to the Division during Operation Freedom's Shield. At first, Jill told me, it seemed innocent enough. It was for contingencies such as these that the open ration control plate was provided to high-ranking officers in the first place. But week after week, Jill purchased more wristwatches, for one Korean colonel after another, until she thought the entire ROK Army would soon be outfitted with the latest in timekeeping instruments.

Eventually, Alcott and Bufford had her buying other things: radios, expensive clocks, stereo equipment, toaster ovens, even television sets. And other MPs were performing the same services, including Private Marv Druwood. The amount of marketable goods and the amount of cash needed to purchase them was enormous. Jill started wondering where the cash was coming from. And she wondered why some of the male MPs weren't wondering the same thing. She asked Marv Druwood about it. He was the one who told her about the Turkey Farm.

"They even had live rock bands up there on the roof," Jill told me, "especially on Saturdays and holiday weekends. And the beer and liquor were provided free along with food. All of it procured by that old woman who ran the place, the one they called the Turkey Lady."

Even the *yobos*, the Korean girlfriends, were provided with gifts. The largesse of the military police corps, according to Jill, was common knowledge amongst the business girls in Tongduchon. And it went a long way in making a young MP appear a lot more attractive than he might normally be.

In addition to buying black-market goods in the PX, MPs were also tasked with transporting the merchandise, in MP vehicles, to the Turkey Farm. There it would be logged in and sold and the money, supposedly, returned to Colonel Alcott.

"He was pocketing the money himself?" I asked.

"No," Jill said. "He was only the front man. The group of colonels controlling the Division, the ones who attended the mafia meetings were behind it. Alcott presented formal reports to them during those meetings, accounting for every penny made and spent. All such business was conducted before they brought out the strippers and the business girls."

"You'll testify to this?"

"I was there, supposedly providing security for them. Actually, just running errands. They liked the way I kept the business girls calm."

"How'd you do that?"

"I didn't, actually. I just talked to them, treated them like human beings. At first I had no idea why they were there."

I didn't press Jill further on this because I knew from other sources that it was at one of these mafia meetings that her friend, Kim Yong-ai, had been raped. Not only raped, but apparently gang raped.

"You were seeing bits and pieces of what was going on," I said, "but how did you know for sure how the operation was run?"

"Fred Otis told me about it one night."

"Sergeant Otis?" I asked. "The guy who works desk sergeant?"

"Yeah. Him. He told me that all the black-marketing had started innocently enough. Years ago, when he was first stationed at Division, the ROK Army colonels were constantly inviting the American honchos over to their compounds for meetings and shows of traditional Korean dancing and Taekwondo demonstrations and stuff like that. The American officers could hardly refuse and while they were there they were treated to food and drink and even, once they were away from the compound, offered girls at *kisaeng* houses. Of course, the American officers were flattered and enjoyed the attention, but after a while they started to feel guilty that they never gave anything back to the ROK officers."

Korean hospitality can be prodigious. And when an honored guest is invited to your home, it is expected that you will do your best to entertain him. Even if that means going into debt. However, I doubted that these ROK Army officers were going into debt, personally, while entertaining the American officers. The U.S. government provides millions of dollars every year to the Korean defense establishment. Most of the money is earmarked for spending on contracts with the U.S. arms industry, but some of it is for discretionary spending. My guess is that some of those U.S. dollars filtered down to a level as low as battalion commander, especially when he needed an entertainment budget to provide good face for his country. Ironically, the American officers were probably being entertained with American tax dollars. However, they'd still felt obligated to reciprocate.

"So they started black-marketing," I said.

Jill nodded.

In order to reciprocate, the American officers didn't want to pull that much money out of their own pockets. Even though an American colonel is well paid—especially from the point of view of a corporal who clears 140 dollars a month—they often don't have a lot of spending money while stationed in Korea. Their family is back in the States. They have a house payment, a car payment, a household budget, maybe one or two kids attending college or getting ready to start college. After all that, even a full-bird colonel might only have a hundred dollars a month to spend on himself, if he was lucky.

The Division brass had to come up with an alternative source of

income. Back in the sixties, local commanders controlled the nonap-
propriated fund budget, the profits of the NCO clubs and the officers' club on base. Although prices were purposely kept low and little was made from club operations themselves, the shortfall was
more than made up for by slot machines. The one-armed bandits
produced plenty of money for everyone. But in the late sixties,
Congress got wind of widespread corruption and banned slot
machines from military bases. After that, the 2nd Infantry Division
brass was desperate for a source of off-the-books revenue. That is,
money not available for inspection by government auditors.

Open ration control plates, and the Korean black market, was
the answer.

Human nature being what it is, soon the operation expanded far
beyond what was necessary to host a few Korean officers four or five
times a year. The mafia meeting came up with new projects to fund.
Some of them were good, according to Jill. Equipment like electrical
generators and imported refrigerators were donated to Korean
orphanages. A Christmas party, complete with an NCO dressed up
like Santa Claus, was thrown every year for the few American depen-
dents who lived outside Camp Casey. Medical supplies were provided to farming villages in the Division area of operations that had
been hit by fire or flood or other disasters.

But once those things were taken care of, there was the free
booze and food and entertainment for the MPs at the Turkey Farm,
and the fee to rent a hall and provide refreshments and entertainment at the mafia meeting. Then, when a ranking American officer
completed his tour of duty in Korea and was on his way back to the
States, a going-away party had to be thrown in his honor. And a gift
had to be provided. Not something routine out of the PX, but something that would be a true memento of his time in Frozen Chosun,
like a valuable Korean antique. The fact that it could be shipped
back to the States in the officer's hold baggage, and was not likely to
be checked by U.S. Customs, and the fact that he could legally resell
the item once it was in the States for ninety days, was only inciden-
tal, supposedly, to the sentimental value of the gift. An overworked
and underpaid American colonel could clear a few thousand dollars
by reselling that antique back in the States. And who said he didn't

deserve it? After protecting his country selflessly as he'd done? And the money would go for a good cause. To remodel his retirement home or pay for junior's college tuition or allow a harried military wife to have that plastic surgery that she'd always dreamed of. So what's wrong with feeling good about yourself?

Jill became so passionate about this subject that I had to slow her down. Ernie still snored. Kim Yong-ai still hid silently behind the door leading to the kitchen.

"Okay, Jill," I said. "They broke you in buying wristwatches and then larger items and having you transport them from the PX out to Tongduchon. You were working nights on the ville patrol. Then one morning, as you were getting off duty, something bad happened. Something involving a deuce-and-a-half."

Her face soured. She sipped her lukewarm coffee, composed herself, and then resumed. The outline of what she told me, I already knew, having been briefed by Sergeant Bernewright, the Division Safety NCO. Two GIs were coming back from the Western Corridor, hungover and driving too fast and the road was slick with intermittent rain. As they approached a group of middle-school girls waiting for a bus, the driver lost control of the truck on a slippery curve and slid into the crowd, injuring two and mortally wounding young Chon Un-suk.

"I wanted to shoot the bastards," Jill told me. "I even pulled my .45 and held it to the driver's head. He believed I was gonna do it, too, and I almost did." She barked a short, mirthless laugh. "The silly bastard wet himself."

"And then you gave the girl first aid?"

"I tried. But someone had informed her father and he showed up, absolutely in a panic, and he started to lift her up and people were helping him and I told them to stop, that the medics would be here any minute and if she had a spine injury that they could cripple her for life. But they weren't listening and when I tried to stop them, her father shoved me. I kept trying to reason with him but other men in the crowd helped him carry the little girl and I could see her head lolling backward and her tongue hanging out, pink, and I was afraid they might snap her neck. I tried again to interfere and this time some-one smacked me and I smacked him back and then we were fighting, and a jeep full of MPs arrived firing their weapons into the air and everyone backed off. Except me. I ran after the father, followed him to his home and, without anyone asking me to, I went through the gate. Her mother was hysterical. Tearing her hair out. Moaning over her daughter. I pushed my way through and felt the carotid artery and there was nothing left and I knew that Chon Un-suk was dead. She'd died on the way over, while being carried by her father."

A long silence ensued. I sat cross-legged on the *ondol* floor, trying to picture the scene, trying to feel what Jill Matthewson must've felt. Finally, she spoke again.

"What pissed me off," she said softly, "was why those two doofus MPs were sent to the Western Corridor in the first place. And why they were driving back so early in the morning."

"Why?"

"Fred Otis told me the story," Jill said.

Him again? Why was I surprised? He was a veteran NCO, well aware of what was going on around him, experienced, and it figured that a young MP as bright as Jill Matthewson would gravitate toward him for advice.

Otis told Jill that the two MPs had been sent to a notorious GI village in the Western Corridor known as Yangjukol. Spending the night there had been their reward for driving the deuce-and-a-half after regular duty hours and picking up an ancient vase from some Korean antiques dealer and transporting it back the next morning to Camp Casey.

"The Division honchos are busy black-marketing their butts off," Jill said, "and little Chon Un-suk gets herself killed because of them." Jill shook her head and whispered softly. "Bastards. And to cover it up, they let the two guys in the truck off easy. Sent them back to the States, out of harm's way."

"What type of antique were they transporting?" I asked.

"I caught a glimpse of it when I first approached the truck. Tied in the center of the bed of the truck, all by itself, partially encased in wood. Beautiful."

"A celadon vase," I said, "covered with white cranes."

"How'd you know?" Jill asked.

"Just a guess."

We talked about Pak Tong-i. Yes, he'd had a soft spot for Kim Yong-ai but the feeling was not mutual. She'd played along with him mainly because he was the only man who could provide her with steady work. "She's been poor all her life," Jill told me. "Born to a farming family down in South Cholla Province. Her father died when she was twelve. She had to quit middle school and go to work to help support her mom and her younger sisters."

"Doing what?" I asked.

Jill frowned. "You don't need to know."

I dropped the subject.

What I needed was evidence of black-marketing. If the operation was as widespread as Jill Matthewson claimed it was, I should be able to get it. That, coupled with her testimony, which I had to admit was extremely believable, would nail them.

Just before dawn, we talked about Marv Druwood.

"He was sweet," Jill told me. "A couple of years younger than me and still a kid, you know. I liked him but I didn't like him *that* way. He had a crush on me so I tried to be nice to him. He was no happier about the black-market situation than I was and he told me that everything that went on at the Turkey Farm made him sick, but I noticed that he didn't stop going there."

"Did he have enemies?"

"No. He took a lot of ribbing because he was so mild mannered. He's from some country town in Iowa. What must've happened is that after I left he stopped cooperating with Bufford about the black-marketing. If that happened, they'd immediately become suspicious. Probably afraid that because of his friendship with me, he might decide to turn them in, go above the Division IG, report the operation to somebody."

"Reason enough to kill him?"

"Maybe. Maybe not. But it's reason enough to start in on him. Start needling him. Start making him angry. He had a temper, you know."

"Tell me about it."

"It only flared up occasionally. It was kind of cute in a way, like a little boy throwing a tantrum. Nothing dangerous. But it might've been enough so that he said things or threatened things that maybe got him killed."

"They're that desperate that they'd kill a fellow GI?"

"They shot at you, didn't they?"

More than once.

"These guys," Jill told me, "are out of control."

I thought of Marv Druwood's corpse. I believed she was right.

Everything Jill Matthewson told me made sense. It all tied together. She wanted to put a stop to the corruption in high places within the 2nd Infantry Division and therefore she'd put her mom up to writing to her congressman. But why not just come to us directly? I asked her.

"Because then everybody at Eighth Army would know," Jill told me. "They'd notify Division. The cover-up would start and be completed before you even got here. I had to lure you up here for another reason."

"Like finding a missing female MP."

"Exactly."

One more thing was bothering me. Jill Matthewson had good reason for everything she was doing. Still, people don't face charges of desertion and possible time in a federal penitentiary just to mollify their sense of right and wrong. Usually there's a personal reason. A deep-seated personal reason. We were both tired. Both yawning. Both ready to go to sleep. I popped the question.

"I know you're angry at these SOBs, Jill. And I know they deserve all the punishment we're going to try to lay on them. But what about you? What made you go AWOL? What made you chuck your entire military career? What, exactly, did Colonel Alcott and Mr. Bufford and the honchos at Division do to *you*?"

She set down her coffee cup and stared at me long and hard. Finally, she spoke. "Never," she said, "and I mean never, ask me that question again."

With that she rose from her cross-legged position, opened the sliding door, and stepped out into the dark courtyard. She stood alone in the cold night air, arms crossed, head bowed.

# 13

---

**O**ur first problem was trying to figure out how to return to Tongduchon. My guess was that after the gunplay last night in Bongil-chon, the Division MPs would set up roadblocks throughout the Division area.

That meant we couldn't use the jeep.

"Where will we leave it?" Jill asked.

The three of us stood next to the jeep, in the raked gravel lot in front of the Wondang Buddhist temple.

"Back to I Corps," Ernie said.

Camp Red Cloud, where we'd left it before, was the logical place to stash the jeep. I Corps was a higher headquarters than Division and the 2nd ID MPs had no jurisdiction there. But to get to Red Cloud we'd have to return to Reunification Road, drive south past Camp Howze in Bongil-chon, and then turn east at Byokjie. Anywhere along that route, the 2nd Division MPs might be waiting for us.

"I have a better idea," I told Ernie.

While Jill and Ernie waited, I entered the temple, taking my shoes off at the elevated wooden floor. I pushed my way through a heavy wooden door and entered a room filled with carved effigies of devils and demons and gods. Candles were lined up on an altar, along with bouquets of pungent incense. No people. I knelt in front of the central figure of the Hinayana Buddha and waited.

Soon a bare-headed monk appeared. He kneeled beside me and bowed three times to Buddha. In Korean, I asked for a favor. Could we leave our jeep in his parking lot for a couple of days.

"You're here to help the American woman?" he asked.

"You know about her?"

"Wondang is a small community."

"Yes," I said. "I'm here to help her."

"Then, by all means, leave your jeep."

"It will only be two days."

"Two days. Two years. It will be here when you return."

I asked if I could make a contribution to the temple. He told me it was up to me. Then he guided me to a bronze urn near the entranceway. I shoved a few military payment certificates into it, bowed to the monk, and exited.

Outside, Ernie said, "We can leave it here?"

I nodded.

"For how long?"

"Until you attain enlightenment."

"I thought I had already.


The bus that ran most often out of Wondang Station was the bus to Seoul. Second to that was the express to Uijongbu, the one we bought three tickets for. After waiting twenty minutes, we hopped aboard. The seating, as usual, was tightly packed. There were two seats on either side of the aisle. I had hoped to sit next to Jill but Ernie aced me out. I was across from them, listening to their conversation, but unable to participate over the whine of the big diesel engine. The little old Korean lady who sat next to me smiled and nodded repeatedly but didn't attempt to engage me in conversation. Instead of moping about not being able to talk to Jill, I decided to use the time to think. I leaned back in my tiny seat, inhaled the aroma of stale kimchee and cigarette smoke, and closed my eyes.

So far, the only hard evidence I had of the 2nd ID black-marketing were the ration control records of Colonel Stanley Alcott's open RCP. And, actually, I didn't have them yet. Staff Sergeant Riley down in Seoul was still trying to obtain a copy of the records from his buddy, Smitty, who worked at 8th Army Data Processing. But as Riley'd told me before, the records were classified and therefore Smitty was having trouble getting a copy. Even if we obtained the records, all they would prove is that Alcott had bought truckloads of merchandise from the Camp Casey PX. They wouldn't prove that he'd broken army regulations and Korean law by actually selling those goods in Tongduchon. For that, we'd need the testimony of the MPs who'd made the purchases on Colonel Alcott's behalf and then transported them in military vehicles to the Turkey Farm. Incidentally, that would result in another charge: misappropriation of a military vehicle. However, there was a big flaw in all this.

Jill had told me that it was Bufford who handled the day-to-day use of the open ration control plate. Colonel Alcott was the man responsible for the plate, the RCP's "owner" in effect. Alcott could always testify that he didn't know what Warrant Officer Bufford nor Corporal Matthewson nor Private Druwood nor any of the other MPs involved in the black-marketing were doing with his open RCP. He could claim they'd used it without his knowledge. Of course, no one would believe that such a huge operation could be operated using his RCP without his knowledge. He'd be reprimanded for not supervising his subordinates more closely, he'd almost certainly be relieved of his position as Division provost marshal, and probably he'd be shipped back to the States fast enough to make a brass Buddha's head spin. But he wouldn't be found guilty of any crime.

Somehow, I had to nail Alcott with evidence that would tie him to the black market. Jill told me about the money he kept in his safe. I'd seen for myself, albeit briefly, the meticulous records that the Turkey Lady had kept of the incoming and outgoing black market merchandise at the Turkey Farm. Those records had been destroyed by fire. But what good are records on one end of a transaction, if the seller doesn't have comparable records on the other end of the transaction? That would be the only way to insure that the men ultimately in charge of this black-market operation—the colonels of the mafia meetings—weren't being ripped off by the Turkey Lady. Alcott must have kept records of his own. Could they be in the same safe in his living quarters where, according to Jill Matthewson, he kept piles of cash?

Most likely. Alcott would want to keep the records close, so he could destroy them if the heat was ever turned on. Well, the heat would be turned on soon. I decided to call Riley, check on our duty status at 8th Army, and see about getting the 8th Army JAG to provide us with a search warrant for Lieutenant Colonel Alcott's living quarters. I was still hopeful that 8th Army would see the light and allow us to do what needed to be done.

Something woke me. I checked my surroundings. Jill and Ernie seemed to be sleeping. So was the elderly Korean lady sitting next to me. The bus had been zooming eastward toward Uijongbu, but the driver was now downshifting and pumping the brakes. That was what had roused me. Why was he stopping? We weren't in Uijongbu yet. I tapped Ernie on the shoulder. He opened his eyes.

"Trouble," I said.

From his aisle seat, Ernie leaned across Jill and poked his head out the window. He turned back to me.

"Roadblock," he said. "They'll check everybody."

"Let's get out of here," I said.

"How?" Jill asked. She was awake now.

"The back door."

We all rose, the only three *Miguks* on the bus, and hurried down the aisle to the rear. Most of the old-model Korean buses, the ones that ran country routes, had large doors in the back for accepting oversize loads. When they weren't transporting passengers, some of the seats could be taken out and something large and boxlike could be slipped onto the bus through that rear door. Usually, it was a coffin. Buses were often chartered to carry entire families out to the countryside, with the dearly departed in his or her elaborately painted Korean coffin in the back, and professional mourners in hemp cloth robes riding up front.

Politely, I asked the young man in the back seat to move.

Groggily, he looked up at me and said, "*Weikurei?*" What's the matter with you?

The bus had stopped now, behind a line of vehicles being inspected at the checkpoint.

I asked the young man again to move. He pouted and stared up at me as if I were mad. Ernie grabbed him my his jacket, tugged, and pulled him roughly to his feet. Other men sitting nearby stood and started to shout and wag their fingers at Ernie. Jill tried to mollify them but it wasn't working. Koreans are usually unfailingly polite. But if they believe that one of their own is being mistreated by a foreigner, hostility can take the place of propriety. Quickly.

Ernie growled at the men, shouted back, and wagged his own finger.

I kneeled in front of the door. The long handle had been painted over with gray paint. I tried to move it but it wouldn't budge. I needed more leverage. It had to be pulled up. I stood, grabbed the handle with both hands, and hoisted upwards with all my strength. ROK Army soldiers were at the front of the bus now, shouting instructions at the driver, motioning for him to pull closer to the side of the road.

You could bet that 2nd Division MPs were up ahead as the last line of defense.

My fingers were red and indented from pulling but so far the handle hadn't budged. I took off my jacket, folded it, and slipped it beneath the door handle. This time I flexed my knees and took a better grip. Two-handed again. Using the strength of my thigh muscles along with my shoulders and my arms, I heaved with every ounce of strength I possessed. Jill knelt and examined the handle, seeing if there was anything she could do to help. There wasn't.

Korean men were now shoving Ernie. As soon as he started shoving back the fists would begin to fly and we'd never get out of here.

I was about to give up, wondering if we could climb out a window, knowing that the ROK Army MPs would spot us if we did. I gave the handle one more pull, it moved this time, just slightly, groaned, and then popped upwards. I fell sideways onto two young women huddling next to the window.

Jill kicked the door open and, still clutching her AWOL bag, hopped out. I regained my balance, grabbed Ernie, and dragged him toward the back door. He was punched in the back a couple of times as I pulled him out onto the road. He tried to go back to finish the fight but I told him we had to get out of there. Finally, he followed.

Jill led the way down the waiting line of vehicles. Kimchee cabs mostly. A few three-wheeled trucks loaded with winter cabbage or mounds of fresh garlic. As we zigged and zagged between the vehicles, we heard a shout behind us. An American voice.

"Round eye," he shouted. A Western woman. Up here, that could only be an American. Boots pounded on cement.

There was a small farming village just off the road. A few of the hooches were roofed with tile but most were thatched with straw. The three of us sprinted for the hooches. Off to the left were rice paddies. Above the hooches, on a hill, were terraced cabbage patches and, beyond that, woods. But between the road and the village was an open space of about twenty yards. As we sprinted across it I expected to hear the sound of rifle shots. But there were none. Only shouted commands for us to halt.

These MPs, unlike Bufford and Weatherwax, weren't willing to shoot fellow Americans in the back just because they'd been ordered to take us into custody.

Lucky for us.

In the village, we dodged pigs and chickens and a couple of toddlers wearing only T-shirts, staring up at us with mucous-encrusted lips. Cute kids, but we didn't have time to tickle them and watch them giggle. Jill and Ernie stayed right behind me, trusting me to guide them. At the rear of the village, I ran uphill, crossed a cabbage patch, and with a last burst of speed, plowed into the woods.

Breathing heavily, I held branches aside, making way for Jill and then Ernie, to take cover behind the tree line.

"Come on!" I said, continuing to climb uphill.

We blazed our way through the small forest until we reached the top of the hill which was covered by grave mounds. I crouched behind a row of tombstones and studied the village below. The MPs had stopped to inspect some of the hooches. They were attempting to interrogate the villagers—in English.

"Big nose, like me," one of the MPs said, pointing at his nose. "*Odi ka?*" Where'd they go?

The village woman he was questioning stared at him blankly. We had been in and out of the village so fast that few, if any, of the villagers had seen us. Except for the toddlers. The MPs milled around for a while, inspecting the tiny barnlike structures that were just big enough to house one animal. Usually an ox. The MP who seemed to be in charge gazed up past the cabbage patches into the woods but didn't show any enthusiasm for continuing further. He gathered his men and marched them back to the road.

On the field radio back at the checkpoint, he'd report our sighting to the Division PMO. In minutes, Bufford and Weatherwax and whatever reinforcements they could muster would be on their way south. We had a blonde American female with us. There'd be no doubt it was us.

"Let's move out," Ernie said.

Jill nodded, so did I. No discussion necessary.

The rest of the day consisted of a long afternoon and a longer night. We stayed away from the Main Supply Route and military patrols and military checkpoints. We cadged rides on three-wheeled tractors, on the backs of trucks, and even, for a while, on an ox-drawn cart. Steadily but surely we made our way north. After night fell, we walked; afraid to take one of the country kimchee cabs because the Division MP checkpoints would be moving from spot to spot and their mobile patrols would be prowling the back roads. Best to stay on foot, on ancient pathways leading from village to village. As far as I knew, the Division MPs didn't even know these pathways existed.

Convoys of headlights prowled the paved roads.

Finally, about an hour before the midnight curfew, we stopped at a *yoinsuk*, a traditional Korean inn. It was situated atop a gently sloping hill that had three pedestrian pathways leading to it, but no parking lot. The building's lumber was ancient; it had probably been constructed long before the Korean War. When I asked the proprietress about it, she told me that the inn had been built before the Japanese Occupation in 1910, back in those halcyon days when the king of Korea still sat on his throne in Seoul. The name of the inn was the *Chowol-tang*, Temple of the Autumn Moon.

It was a dump.

The soup they brought had no meat in it, only bean curd, and I had to pluck a couple of tiny pebbles out of the rice that accompanied the soup. Still, after a day of hiking through the hills of Kyongki Province, the chow tasted delicious. Once again, we three slept in the same room, on the warm *ondol* floor, but this time a family of strangers stayed with us, huddled together on the other side of the room. After eating, I was too exhausted to even attempt to speak Korean to them, so I spread out my gray cotton sleeping mat, pulled a tattered silk comforter over my sore shoulders, and was asleep before my head hit the bean-filled pillow.

At dawn, the three of us were up and ready to go. I sorely wished that I could take a shower and change into clean clothes, but there were no shower facilities here at the Temple of the Autumn Moon and the bag containing my change of clothes had been left behind after Ernie and I were ambushed at fish heaven. I was stuck with the same old sports shirt, the same old blue jeans, and the same old nylon jacket. After using the outdoor *byonso*, we declined breakfast, hoping we could find something better down the road. We did. Pears plucked fresh from an orchard.

Before noon, we stood on a hill looking down on the fog-shrouded city of Tongduchon. To the east, Camp Casey spread like a slothful potentate reclining across acres of arable land. Behind the heavily fortified main gate, the statue of the twenty-foot-tall MP, his pink face still smiling, seemed to be staring right at us.


First, I found a phone.

In a run-down teahouse a couple of blocks west of the Tongduchon City Market, the place where Ernie and I'd been shot at. The sleepy proprietress barely found the energy to shove my two hundred *won* into the pocket of her sleeping robe. Then she shoved the red phone across the counter, turned, and slid back a door that led to her sleeping quarters. She wasn't open for business yet but Ernie and I had insisted she open.

I dialed the number for the 8th Army operator and waited. And waited. And waited. I hung up and tried again.

Still the same sound of static and clicking, but no human voice.

"The lines are down," Ernie said.

Happens all the time, but why now?

"We'll try again later," Jill said.

"Right."

I tried not to let it bother me. Still, it seemed an omen. Ernie and I were in over our heads, 8th Army wasn't backing us up, the 2nd Division provost marshal had apparently unleashed his men on a murderous rampage. How often do GIs knowingly shoot at other GIs?

Not often. GIs steal from one another, they seduce one another's wives, they lie about one another in order to cop a quick promotion, they do all those things but they seldom shoot at one another. Still, that's exactly what'd been happening routinely ever since Brandy brought Ernie and me back to Division.

"Brandy," I said. "At the Black Cat Club."

"Too dangerous," Ernie replied.

He meant that the ville would probably be crawling with MPs.

Jill started to tell us about Brandy.

"She was nice to me," Jill told us. "She helped me find my hooch and she introduced me to Kim Yong-ai and then she even came to my hooch to show me how to change charcoal and where the trash goes and things like that."

Since we had a minute, I asked Jill what exactly had happened at the Forest of the Seven Clouds. How had she and Kim Yong-ai managed to escape when Bufford and Weatherwax had come looking for her?

"Colonel Han," she said. "A ROK Army colonel. He'd been in there before with important businessmen and Kimmie and I served him. He speaks English really well and he was curious about my situation, but I didn't tell him that I was AWOL. The day Bufford and Weatherwax came looking for me, Colonel Han put me and Kim in the back of his canvas-covered jeep, threw a tarp over us, and drove us right past the checkpoints the MPs had set up."

It figured. In Korea, what with 700,000 bloodthirsty communist soldiers across the DMZ just itching to invade, the ROK Army is untouchable. Even the president of the country is a former ROK

Army general. Nobody can inspect ROK Army jeeps. Not even 2nd Infantry Division MPs.

The idea hit me suddenly. It seemed so obvious, once I thought about it, that I must've been awfully tired not to have thought of it earlier.

"I know where we can find a phone."

"We have a phone," Ernie said.

"But also a place to hide out, while we wait for the lines to be reconnected."

Ernie saw it, too. "The Chon family residence," he said.

Then I told Jill about what Madame Chon had said about a wandering ghost. And about the *kut*. Without hesitation, Jill agreed to help.

Ten minutes later, we were standing at the front gate of the Chon family residence.

Jill pressed the button of the intercom and told the person who answered who she was. Immediately, the gate buzzed open. The elderly maid stepped off the lacquered front porch and into her slippers, and following her came Madame Chon. She rushed toward Jill, her arms thrown open, and the two women embraced. Both of them were crying.

I turned to Ernie. He turned away from the two women. Then he said, "Enough of this bullshit. Let's go shoot somebody."

"We will," I told him. "But first we have to talk to a ghost."


The only light in the large back room of the Chon family residence came from the flickering glow of thirty-six candles. Above the candles sat a gleaming bronze effigy of Kumbokju, the chubby god of plenty of Korean myth. The sharp tang of incense permeated the room, and about thirty guests sat on the floor on plump, silk-covered cushions. The guest list included myself, Ernie, Corporal Jill Mathewson, and what seemed like every middle-aged matron in the city of Tongduchon. Since his daughter's death, Chon Un-suk's father had been working long hours at his business in Seoul and seldom showed his face in Tongduchon. Maybe because of grief. Maybe he had a mistress. Who knows? But one thing I knew for sure is that no self-respecting Korean male wants to attend a *kut*.

The name of the *mudang* was the Widow Po.

She was a tall woman, buxom, with a regal, oval-shaped face that might've been beautiful except that her skin had been ravaged by smallpox. Her black hair was long and tangled and now streaked with sweat. She had begun her ceremony by banging on a handheld drum and dancing, then shaking rattles and shrieking at the top of her lungs, all designed, Madame Chon told us, to frighten away evil spirits. It had worked pretty well. The 2nd Division MPs hadn't come anywhere near.

The time now was midnight. Madame Chon, in her usual gracious style, had allowed us to eat and bathe and rest; Ernie and Jill Matthewson and I felt a lot more human. While we'd rested, I had managed to put a call through to the 8th Army CID Detachment.

"Smitty came up with the records," Riley told me. "Beaucoup purchases out of the Camp Casey PX. Then I did what you told me. I laid it all on the desk of the 8th Army provost marshal. I told him what you said about the mafia meetings and the rape of the stripper and the systematic black-marketing at the Turkey Farm. I even told him about your suspicions concerning the death of this Private Marvin Druwood."

"How'd he react?"

"How do you think he reacted? He went ballistic. First, you and Ernie go AWOL, you don't leave the Division area of operations as ordered, and now you're casting aspersions on the integrity of every ranking field-grade officer on the Division staff."

I waited.

"They want your ass back here," Riley said. "They want your report in person and they want it now."

"If we do that," I told him, "Division will have time to cover up all the evidence, threaten their MPs so they won't testify, and nobody will be busted for anything."

"How's that your lookout? You're supposed to report to the PMO. That's it!"

"That's not it," I said. "As part of the Division attempt to cover up, they've shot at Ernie and me, trying to kill us, and they might've murdered Private Druwood. And maybe a ROK civilian by the name of Pak Tong-i."

"You have no proof."

I did what I seldom do. Instead of reasoning with the man I was having a disagreement with, I started screaming.

"How in the hell am I going to get proof if I have to return to Seoul?"

Riley waited for the sound of my voice to fade. Then he said calmly, "They didn't buy it, Sueño. You have to come back."

I waited, allowing the pause to grow.

He said, "Sueño? Sueño? You don't want to do this."

I listened to his breathing for a while. Then I hung up the phone.


A row of candles flickered in the darkness of the main worship hall. Food had already been served. Food for the *kut*. The séance. Rice dumplings, for the spirits supposedly, but Ernie grabbed a couple and popped them in his mouth. When glasses were poured full of *soju* for the pleasure of spirits from the great beyond, the neighbor women helping Madame Chon realized that Ernie wasn't able to resist. Instead of making him suffer, they poured an extra glassful for him. He offered me some but I refused, as did Jill. His behavior, as is the case so often, was irreverent. Ernie has no time for proprieties, for ancient customs, even for respect for the dead. But I noticed that neither the local women, nor Madame Chon, nor even the smiling bronze face of Kumbokju, seemed offended. Only Jill and I were embarrassed. But when Jill leaned toward me and started to complain about Ernie, I placed my hand on her forearm and told her to be patient. I was right. As time went by, the women fed Ernie more and more dumplings and poured him more and more *soju*. Apparently, what Jill and I considered bad manners, they recognized as signs of possession.

Suddenly, from within the crowd, one of the women started chanting. Her voice was strained, singsong, as if she were warbling some sort of discordant tune. Madame Chon translated for me. "Her son is speaking," she said. "He was killed in a car accident."

"Killed?" I asked.

"Yes. Twenty years ago. She all the time come *kut*."

Madame Chon's answer was completely matter-of-fact. She and all the women in this room believed that communion with the dead was routinely achieved by *mudang* such as the Widow Po.

Jill Matthewson, listening to our conversation, rubbed her upper arms and bowed her head and murmured a prayer.

The Widow Po beat her drum and danced closer to the wailing woman.

"*Mal hei*," the Widow Po said. Speak. "*Mal hei, Wan-sok-i.*"

Apparently, Wan-sok was the spirit's name.

Wan-sok's mother, still using a tightly pitched voice, started to speak.

"I'm cold, mother," the voice said. "I'm cold because I've lost your warmth. Why, when I was alive, did you treat me so badly? Why, when I was alive, did you give me everything for which I asked? Why, when I was alive, did you purchase me a car? Why, when I was alive, did you let me go out at night? Why, when I was alive, did you let me drive so fast? Why, when I was alive, did you not keep me closer to your heart? Why, when I was alive, did you turn your back on me?"

Then the woman shrieked and collapsed into the arms of the women around her.

Ernie sipped on his *soju*. "Phony," he said. Jill elbowed him.

The Widow Po banged rapidly on her drum. "Hear me, oh spirit," she shouted. "Hear me, spirit of Wan-sok. What kind of son are you to punish your mother? What kind of son are you to blame her for your greed? What kind of son are you to torment the woman who gave you birth? Desist spirit!" She banged on the drum. "Desist in your lies!" She banged again. "Desist in your torment of your good mother!" This time she banged repeatedly, deafeningly, and the woman who had fainted groaned and started to come to.

Ernie offered his bottle of *soju*. It was passed to Won-sok's mother and liquid was poured across her lips. She coughed and choked and wiped away the *soju*. Her eyes shot open and she sat up and placed her flattened palms in front of her nose and started to pray.

"This *mudang*," Ernie said, "knows how to work the crowd."

Like a whirlwind, the Widow Po banged rapidly on her drum and twirled through the women seated cross-legged on the floor, heading straight for Ernie. When she stopped banging, she stood directly over him, red eyes blazing, candlelight flaming behind her, voice wailing.

"*Chumul-cho!*" she screamed. Then she banged on her drum again. Ernie looked at me, confused. "*Chumul-cho!*" the Widow Po screamed, more loudly this time. Her drum became an incessant roar.

"Dance!" I told Ernie. "She wants you to stand up and dance."

"Bull! I don't know how to dance."

"Its not that kind of dancing," I said.

"*Chumul-cho!*" the Widow Po screamed again and this time Ernie bounced to his feet as if he were being pulled up by strings. The Widow Po let go of her drum with one hand and slapped him. Hard. The splat of flesh on flesh resounded throughout the room. "*Chumul-cho!*" she shouted.

Ernie began to dance.

His legs shook at the knees and his arms flailed akimbo and the Widow Po seemed pleased and grabbed Ernie's hand and dragged him out in front of the glowing bronze Kumbokju. She wailed and drummed and swirled around him and Ernie kept up his flailing, looking for all the world like Elvis Presley gone spastic.

Jill started to laugh. So did I. And then all the women in the room were roaring and this seemed to encourage Ernie. The Widow Po drummed madly and Ernie flailed more wildly and finally, his face slathered in sweat, the Widow Po flung Ernie like a rag doll back into the arms of the women in the crowd.

Exhausted, he collapsed onto his pillow. One of the women took pity on him and, grabbing another bottle of *soju*, poured fiery rice liquor across his lips like a mother feeding a baby.

The drumming stopped. The Widow Po stood stock-still, her back to all of us. Perspiration on her black hair glistening in the candle glow. Her body started to quiver. Not move. Just quiver. As if something hideous was passing through her, entering through a cavity in her body and filling every pore of her being with a power that could only be expressed by the quaking of her statuesque torso.

Then she screamed.

The collapse to the floor was total. She slammed into wood. Rib cage, skull, everything crashed against the solid surface as if she'd fallen from a thirty-foot precipice. I thought she'd killed herself. I started to rise, but Madame Chon grabbed my arm with surprising strength and forced me to sit back down.

Like a butterfly, effortlessly, now the Widow Po started to rise.

She floated. Or it seemed that she floated. Probably she was standing on her tiptoes like a ballerina. But in the dark room in the flickering candlelight it seemed for a moment that she was actually levitating. And then she twirled. Her face was hideous. Contorted, angry, frightened. Aggressive and frightened at the same moment, which I knew from real life was the most dangerous state a person could be in.

She growled.

"*Ohma!*" Mother.

The voice came from somewhere deep in the Widow Po's throat.

Madame Chon sat up as if someone had jabbed her in the butt with an electric prod. "Un-suk-i?" she asked.

"*Na pei kopa!*" I'm hungry. "Why didn't you come look for me? Why was your door locked to me? I've been searching for you. Where are you, Mother? Where have you been?"

I hadn't noticed earlier, but now I realized that off to my right for the last few seconds I'd been hearing an incessant humming. Like a bumblebee but louder. Jill Matthewson was praying. Her eyes were closed and she was humming through moist lips and then, without being called, she rose to her feet and walked forward, stepping deftly between the cushions and the seated women, with her eyes still closed, heading straight for the Widow Po.

"*Nugu syo?*" the Widow Po asked. Who is it? But she asked it in the voice that Madame Chon recognized as her daughter's.

"Jill," Corporal Jill Matthewson said. "It's me. I'm here for you."

She spoke in English, but the Widow Po—or Chon Un-suk or whoever it was—seemed to understand. Once more, the Widow Po collapsed to the floor. This time she lay on her back, writhing and moaning like a child. A pitiful sound emerged from her full-grown body. A sound any human being would react to. The sound of a child in pain. The sound of a child dying.

Jill knelt next to her. I scooted to my left to see better. Jill's eyes were still closed but her hands performed the movements they'd been trained to perform. First, she cleared the air passage. Then she checked for bleeding. Then she took off her own blouse and covered the Widow Po and grabbed the drum that lay on the floor and used it to elevate the Widow Po's feet. Then she leaned forward and said in English, "You're going to be all right, honey. You'll be all right. Someone's coming to help you. They'll be here soon."

The Widow Po said, "*Ohma*," and then she took a huge breath, held it, and as she let it out her entire body shuddered. She lay still.

I thought the Widow Po was dead; I was sure she was dead. So did Jill Matthewson. Or the person who once called herself Jill Matthewson. In a trance, Jill leaned down, touched the body's chest over the heart, pinched the carotid artery, and lowered her cheek in front of the Widow Po's open mouth. When she was sure that the body below was dead, Jill began to cry. I tried to rise to my feet. No one, not even a *mudang* as skilled as the Widow Po, could hold her breath for that long. I tried to rise to my feet but Madame Chon grabbed my elbow with two hands and, with the strength of a man, held me where I was.

Nervously, Ernie slugged down another shot of *soju*.

Then, Jill Matthewson leaned further over the body, slid her forearms beneath the body's back, and raised the body of the Widow Po into the air. The Widow Po, tall and as heavy as she was, hung lifelessly in Jill Matthewson's arms. Jill, still on her knees, turned and finally her eyes opened. She seemed to be searching for someone, and then she found her. The woman sitting next to me, Madame Chon, the mother of Chon Un-suk. Jill rose to her feet— almost effortlessly considering all the weight she was carrying— and walked toward Madame Chon. Everyone rose to their feet, sighing, crying, hugging one another. When Jill stood in front of Madame Chon, she bowed and as if she were offering a bouquet of roses, she placed the lifeless body in Madame Chon's arms. Tears streamed from Madame Chon's eyes but she grabbed the body, enfolded it, clasped it against her breast, and kneeled. Jill helped her lower the body until the Widow Po lay, lifeless, across the lap of Madame Chon.

No more sound came from the Widow Po. Only whimpering from the crowd.

Jill left the room. Ernie and I found her out in the courtyard, leaning next to the stone well.

Vomiting.

The next morning, Madame Chon assured us that the Widow Po was all right.

"She do all the time," she told us.

"She dies all the time?" Ernie asked.

"Yes. Then come back. No problem."

Jill punched Ernie in the shoulder.

They were starting to like each other. I'd noticed that, and I can't say that I was happy about it. Brandy, I didn't mind, but now Ernie was after Jill Matthewson. It wasn't any of my business, I knew that rationally, but it bothered me nevertheless. I liked the way she smiled and the freckles across her nose and the way she was determined to do the right thing.

After a breakfast of steamed rice, roasted mackerel, and pickled bean sprouts, we were ready to start our day. As we sipped barley tea, I made Jill go over it again, the story of how she and the stripper, Kim Yong-ai, overnight, raised two thousand dollars U.S.

"She helped me all the time," Jill said. "How to change the charcoal, how to cook on the butane stove, how to wash my laundry and where to hang it up to dry. With everything."

"So you became friends?" Ernie asked.

"Yeah. She lived right next door. We drank tea. We talked."

"Her English was pretty good?" I asked.

"Okay. I taught her some. She taught me Korean. Out of her dictionary."

"So the Division honchos did a number on her at the mafia meeting," Ernie said. "She had a case of the ass."

"Wouldn't you?" Jill asked.

"I suppose I would," Ernie replied.

"She wanted out of the life," Jill continued, "but she was two thousand dollars in debt to gangsters for key money for her hooch, and for costumes, and for transportation to gigs, and for money just to live."

"So she asked you to help?" Ernie said.

"Why do you make it sound that way? Like she was trying to con me or something? I knew about it, she told me, but she never asked me for money."

"Until after she was raped by the Division honchos."

"Even then," Jill said, becoming angry now, "she didn't ask me for money. She asked me to help her get even."

"And the best way to do that . . ." Ernie let the question hang.

Jill frowned.

Their romance was deteriorating quickly but I knew Ernie was just doing his job. *Skeptical* and *cop* are the same word.

"She showed me photographs another girl had taken," Jill said. "Of old farts with pot bellies on top of her. And on top of the other girls. Even Colonel Alcott."

"Why do you say 'even' Colonel Alcott?" Ernie asked.

"Because he always made a big deal about being a deacon in his church back home and made speeches about trusting in God and all that stuff but as soon as he had a chance, he hopped on a helpless Korean business girl just like every other GI in the ville."

She glared at Ernie. The statement was more like an accusation. Ernie crossed his arms and stared back at her. She continued.

"So we decided to use the photographs to get money. Not money out of their pockets, all of them were too cheap for that, but money out of the slush fund. The mafia meeting slush fund."

"Where was this slush fund located?" Ernie asked.

"On compound. In Colonel Alcott's room. It's more than a room really, it's almost like a little house. Bigger than the trailer me and my mom lived in. He has a safe in there."

"So you just waltzed up one day," Ernie said, "showed Colonel Alcott the photographs and demanded two thousand dollars?"

"That's pretty much it. He wanted to bargain but I told him he could replace the money with one black-market run out to the ville and I told him that I didn't care about my military career and I would write my congressman in a heartbeat if he didn't come across. So he did. Two thousand big ones."

"And then Miss Kim thanked you," Ernie said, "tears in her eyes."

"You're laughing at me." Jill said.

"Not laughing," Ernie said. "It's the oldest con in the ville. But usually it's worked on GIs who are only thinking with their dicks. With you, she had to rely on your sympathy for a woman set upon by the male power structure."

"Screw you, Ernie."

"Any time. But you were taken, Jill. Miss Kim Yong-ai used you to get at that mafia meeting slush fund."

She thought about it for a while. "No," she said finally. "Miss Kim didn't use me. I'm glad she's free."

"Free to work in a teahouse?" I said.

"How did you know?"

"If she's not stripping, and not selling herself, the only place in Wondang that would stay open until curfew would be a teahouse."

"She's a hostess to wealthy men," Jill said, "but it's better now." Then she stared at me and Ernie, defiant. "So how do we get the proof to bust these assholes?"

They both looked at me.

I sipped my barley tea. Madame Chon had left us but the old maid was rustling around the cement-floored kitchen. I found her and asked for a paper and pen. In a few minutes, she'd cleared the eating table, wiped it down, and laid out a ballpoint pen and a fresh pad of writing paper. I drew a map.

Camp Casey has four gates. The main gate, the supply/motor pool gate, and the gate leading to Camp Hovey are all guarded by Division MPs. They are heavily armed with automatic pistols, M-16 rifles, and .50-caliber machine guns. The chain link fence surrounding the massive compound is topped with rolled concertina wire and is patrolled twenty-four hours a day by guards hired by a security contractor approved by the Korean government. All the Korean security guards are well trained, motivated to keep one of the few jobs in country with good pay and benefits, and almost all of them are Korean War veterans since they receive priority in hiring. Each guard is armed with an M-1 rifle and knows how to use it.

The fourth and final gate is the gate leading to the Camp Casey firing ranges where GIs practice their marksmanship. These gates are chained at night but not guarded by MPs, merely patrolled by the subcontracted security guards.

None of it seemed too promising as far as surreptitious entry went and Jill Matthewson, who'd actually visited all of these gates, didn't like the idea of trying to sneak our way in.

"Those security guards are sharp," she said. "They're not asleep at the switch. They've had North Korean commandoes try to slip in before, and they know they'll be fired if someone breaks in on their watch."

"I don't like it either," Ernie said. "Too risky."

"So how do we get to Colonel Alcott's safe?" I asked.

"There's a way," Jill said.

We listened. She took a deep breath, as if revealing something very important to us. "Tomorrow is March first."

I knew what it was. *Samil jol*, it's called. The March First Movement. A Korean national holiday to honor the student-led civil uprising against the Japanese colonial occupation that took place March 1, 1919.

"All the students are off," Jill said. "The GIs aren't."

"So they're coming up here," Ernie guessed, "for another demonstration?"

Jill nodded. "This is going to be the big one."

"How do you know?"

Then she told us about the Colonel Han she'd mentioned, the man who'd helped her and Kim Yong-ai escape from the Forest of the Seven Clouds when Bufford and Weatherwax had come to arrest her. Colonel Han Kuk-chei was the Commander of the 1611 Communications Brigade. What made him unusual for a ROK Army officer was not that he frequented *kisaeng* houses. That was routine. Rather, it was that he was involved with student demonstrators and he was opposed to the current regime. He belonged to an old *yang-ban* family, Confucian scholars and landholders, and he considered the current occupant of the Blue House—the Korean version of the White House—to be an usurper of an office that rightfully belonged to him and his kind. That's why he was cooperating with radical students.

His goal, however, according to Jill, was more radical than even the most radical student. His goal was to reunify the Korean

Peninsula—both North and South Korea—into one country. A country to be ruled under traditional Confucian principles.

I took Jill's hand. It wasn't soft. It was a hand used to work, used to holding the butt of an automatic pistol, but it was a woman's hand nevertheless.

"We can bust these black-market honchos at Division," I said. "It won't be easy but we can do it. But if you're caught in the middle of some political game with the Koreans, there's no telling what could go wrong. You could be hurt."

"Thank you," she said. "But I promised him."

"'Him?'"

"Colonel Han."

"You promised him what?"

"I promised that I'd help, at the critical moment. The plan is beautiful really. And when you listen to him talk about why it's necessary, you'll be as convinced as I am."

"We're Americans, Jill. This is Korea. It's their country."

"But we're involved," she answered. "We're the reason why their country is divided."

Ernie rolled his eyes. I felt the same way. That's all we needed. A political radical along with all our other problems. I still didn't know what all this had to do with us gaining access to Camp Casey and the black-market records held in Colonel Alcott's safe.

The front buzzer rang. We sprang to our feet. Madame Chon appeared and whispered something to the elderly maid. She nodded and they both walked to the front of the house. The maid returned with our shoes and Madame Chon walked across the courtyard to the front gate.

"*Nugu seiyo?*" she asked. Who is it?

"Sohn *Tamjong,*" a man's voice said. Agent Sohn. Then he asked if he might speak to her, using honorific verb endings and sounding very polite. I remembered the voice. I grabbed my shoes from the maid and asked her where to find the back exit. She led the way.

Ernie whispered, "What's up?"

"That voice," I told him. "I've heard it before. Come on. We've got to get out of here."

Ernie and I headed for the rear of the house. Jill grabbed her bag and followed. We reached the back door and went outside, past the *byonso* reeking of bleach, to a brick wall with a short metal door in it.

"Who was it?" Ernie asked.

"At the KNP station, here in Tongduchon, when we were interrogated, he sat in back of me. Observing. Only speaking at the end."

"KCIA," Ernie said. The Korean Central Intelligence Agency. The agency responsible for quelling internal political dissent.

"What makes you say that?"

"Who the hell else would it be?"

He was right. Only the KCIA had the power to butt in on KNP operations.

A padlocked, rusty iron rod barred the small back gate. The maid reached into the pocket of her skirt, pulled out a key, and popped open the padlock. Then she backed up and pointed. Ernie stepped forward, grabbed the rusty rod and, twisting it, managed to pull it free. With a squeak, the little door swung open. Ernie pulled his .45 and peeked through.

Immediately, he ducked back inside. I stepped past him and looked outside. A narrow passageway between brick walls, barely wide enough for a man to pass through, ran off in both directions. To the right was a T-shaped intersection, but to the left stood two bored-looking Korean men wearing coats and ties. Their attention was on the front of the house.

"KCIA," Ernie whispered.

I asked the maid if there was another way out. Some sort of subterranean drainage ditch or a passage over the rooftops, although I could see that the neighbor's roof was too far for us to reach.

She shook her head.

At the front door voices were raised. Madame Chon was denying entrance to Agent Sohn. He was insisting on searching the grounds. Whether or not he had a search warrant, in a society where national security takes precedence over everything, Sohn would have his way.

Ernie and I had participated in a student demonstration. So had Jill. Technically, we could be arrested just for that.

"We could run for it," Ernie said.

"They'd spot us."

"We're armed."

Now it was Jill's turn to roll her eyes. I spoke for both of us when I said, "We can't shoot KCIA agents, Ernie."

"We can if they shoot at us," he said.

Just what we needed. A running gun battle through TDC. That'd bring the MPs down on us.

Meanwhile, the maid hustled over to a far corner of the courtyard and rolled back a small wooden cart. Frantically, she motioned to me and then pointed at a row of earthenware kimchee jars shoved up against the brick wall.

"*Bali*," she said. Hurry.

I understood. Ernie and I and Jill hoisted one of the large earthenware jars onto the bed of the cart. It must've weighed fifty pounds. The voices at the front gate grew louder. The maid's brow crinkled and she said, "*Andei.*" Not good. She told us to put another jar on the cart. We did.

"What's she going to do with those?" Ernie asked.

I didn't answer because I was busy making way for the maid. She shoved the heavily laden cart forward. I opened the small gate for her and helped her lift the two rubber tires of the cart over the threshold. Then she ducked outside and propelled the cart which, picking up speed, headed directly at the two men standing at the end of the alley.

# 14

The side of the cart scraped against brick then bounced over the cobbled lane, the lids of the earthenware jars rattling, and then another bump—presumably on the opposite side of the passageway—and then a groaning of wood and metal and finally, a crash. Earthenware smashing, vegetable matter and brine reeking of garlic and anchovies splashing onto the dirty stone roadway. The maid screeching, Korean men cursing. I imagined them hopping about, trying to keep their highly polished shoes away from the puddle reeking of fermented kimchee.

"Now," Ernie said.

Ernie, then Jill and then I ducked through the small door. We turned right and the three of us barreled down the narrow alleyway.

One of the Korean men behind us shouted, "*Yah!*"

But we had a good lead on them and, I imagined, the maid was doing her best to block their passage with the cart. All the passageways were narrow, sometimes walled with brick, sometimes stone, occasionally thick wooden planks. Finally, we reached a wider alleyway and we knew we must be nearing a regular street. Koreans are used to living like this, with houses all jammed together. That's why their interpersonal customs are so elaborate. If everybody follows the rules, it lessens the chance of someone getting on someone else's nerves.

Usually.

Ernie was getting on my nerves now. He ran down one alley with plenty of space to maneuver—at least six feet on either side— with recessed doorways spaced every ten yards or so, reached the end of it, and then stopped. He stared at us, arms akimbo, palms open. Jill and I almost ran into him.

"What?" I said.

Ernie gazed around. "Dead end," he said.

Around the corner, shoe leather pounded on stone.

Ernie reached for his .45.


If the man who identified himself at Madame Chon's front door as Agent Sohn was indeed an agent of the Korean CIA, that explained a lot. First, it explained why he had been monitoring my interrogation at the KNP station in TDC. He wasn't interested in me or Pak Tong-i, the person I was suspected of murdering. But, he must've had information that the person I was after—Jill Matthewson—had somehow made contact with student protesters and, of greater significance, with people in power who might back them up. Insurrection, or a military coup, was never completely out of the question in South Korea. In the early sixties, the Syngman Rhee government had been overthrown because of rioting in the streets. Not just demonstrations by leftist students, but massive movements of the people—shopkeepers, laborers, educators, the works—and the pressure had been more than the corrupt regime could withstand. Later, the current President of Korea, Pak Chung-hee, had taken power via a military coup. No wonder his government was paranoid. To Americans, the Korean student protestors seemed harmless. But the Korean government took them seriously.

The KCIA used bribery and intimidation. If they offered you a stipend and you were poor, you'd accept it gladly. If you refused their money, they might explain that unless you played ball with them, your younger brother would never be accepted to university. People cooperated.

I knew now that the highest echelons of the Korean government were taking recent events in Tongduchon seriously. Very seriously indeed.

We were trapped, in a dead-end street lined with ten-foot-high walls made of stone. Then I heard shouts and the footsteps of the KCIA started toward us.

"Each of you take a door," I shouted. "Push the button. Pound on it."

At the end of the pedestrian walkway and on either side were thick wooden doors recessed in the stone walls. Koreans design their homes for security and don't mess around. I pounded on the door nearest me, pushing the door buzzer next to the intercom speaker at the same time. Ernie pounded on another door and Jill still another.

No answer.

I couldn't shout. The KCIA agents were only yards away from us, somewhere in the maze of little alleys. I didn't want to make their job any easier. I was about to give up and try climbing the wall when Ernie hissed. His door had opened. He'd already stuck his foot inside so the frightened woman who peeked out around the wooden gate couldn't slam it shut. Jill and I raced toward him. As we pushed through the gate I spoke in rapid Korean.

"*Mianhamnida*," I told the woman. "We just want to pass through your yard and go out the back. Please show us the way."

She was a petite Korean woman, maybe in her early thirties; her mouth hung open and her lower lip quivered. She'd opened her front gate to three giant, big-nosed, sweating foreigners. We entered a neat courtyard with a few shrubs, mostly paved with cement. As Jill closed the gate, I heard footsteps and shouts. They'd spotted us but the locked front gate would slow them down. I grabbed the frightened woman by the arm and steered her around the edge of her house, through the narrow passageway between the wall of the home and the side fence. The area in back was even smaller than the courtyard out front: the strong biting smell of an outdoor *byonso*; a discarded stove starting to rust; no back exit.

Ernie didn't hesitate. He hopped on top of the stove and climbed atop the fence. Then holding out his hand he helped Jill up, then me. I waved goodbye to the frightened woman and we hopped down into another alleyway.

We ran. This time I heard no footsteps. We'd lost them. But what would they do to Madame Chon and her maid? No time to think about that now. We had to hide. Jill had told us that the *Samil* demonstration was scheduled to start at noon tomorrow in front of Camp Casey's main gate. It had become clear to me that the reason Colonel Han Kuk-chei had helped Jill Matthewson to escape from the Forest of Seven Clouds was because he wanted her in Tongduchon for this demonstration. He had some function for her. Would she speak again? Jill only had two more days until her thirty days of AWOL was up and she officially became a deserter. If she let that happen, she'd receive a general court-martial. For twenty-nine days of AWOL she'd only get a summary court-martial. As a returned AWOL, she'd face forfeiture of pay, restriction to compound, reduction in rank. Not good. But as a deserter, she'd face time in the federal penitentiary at Leavenworth, Kansas.

Ernie and I made our way to the bar district. We were like homing pigeons. We felt comfortable near business girls and booze. We passed the Black Cat Club and kept going. In an alley behind the Silver Dragon Nightclub, we paused to catch our breath. I looked back, thinking this would be a good time to talk to Jill about turning herself in somewhere safe before she became a deserter. I opened my mouth to speak.

She wasn't there.

I went back and searched the alleyways. No dice. Ernie helped me and together we retraced our steps. No sign of Corporal Jill Matthewson.

"Why'd you let her go?" Ernie asked.

"I didn't *let* her go. She just went."

"Why?"

Ernie couldn't figure it out. Neither could I. But maybe Corporal Jill Matthewson was on a mission.

\* \* \*

Ernie and I found shelter in Ok-hi's hooch. That night, after the ville patrol passed through the Silver Dragon Nightclub on their regular rounds, Ok-hi trotted up and told us that the coast was clear. About two minutes later, Ernie and I were sitting at the bar of the Silver Dragon, sipping on cold draft OB, exchanging theories as to where Jill Matthewson might have gone.

"She used us," Ernie said. "Let us escort her back to Tongduchon so she could attend Mrs. Chon's *kut*, and when she had no more use for us, she dumped us."

The band on the Silver Dragon's elevated stage hammered out a rock song. On the small dance floor, a battalion of voluptuous Korean business girls jitterbugged with one another. A handful of GIs lurked amongst cocktail tables, leering at the girls on the floor, nursing cheap drinks, generally acting like the Cheap Charlies they were.

If Ernie was right, and Jill had dumped us, we were up kimchee creek without a paddle. We were absent without leave, didn't have enough evidence of 2nd ID's black-marketing to force a prosecution, and the entire local military police corps was searching for us.

"I don't think she used us," I said finally.

Ernie stared at me as if I were dumb enough to play catch with mortar rounds.

"Then what?"

"She's investigating."

"Investigating what?"

"Investigating the murder of Private Marv Druwood."

"On her own?"

"Yes. She can be more effective on her own. A couple of big ugly Eighth Army CID agents tagging along would make people nervous. Both Koreans and GIs."

Ernie scoffed. "She's probably back in Wondang by now. Her and Miss Kim Yong-ai, packing up and moving on. Probably on their way to Seoul where we'll never find them. I'm telling you, Sueño, we've been had."

"Maybe."

We drank a couple more beers in silence. I knew what we had to do. Bust into Lieutenant Colonel Alcott's office and grab his black-market records. But what if they weren't there? What if he'd moved them? Even if we found them, without Jill Matthewson's corroborating testimony our case would be weak. So weak that 8th Army might decide not to prosecute. Especially when we'd been granted no legal authority to bust into his office. But what was the alternative? We were toast here in Division. And if we caught the first train back to Seoul tomorrow, what would we have to show for our efforts? Nothing except four days of bad time on our records. And an Article 15 in our future for being AWOL. And fond memories of the murdered Marv Druwood and the murdered Pak Tong-i and the rape victim, Miss Kim Yong-ai. Maybe Ernie could write off Jill Matthewson, but I couldn't. I simply could not believe that she'd cut out on us. There had to be a reason.

I peered into the bottom of my empty beer mug and searched for it. It wasn't there. I switched to bourbon. Maybe that would help. It did. What had we been talking about just before the Korean men in suits barged into Madame Chon's home? How to gain access to Camp Casey. As fugitives, we couldn't waltz through the main gate anymore. Something told me that Jill had left us in order to tackle that problem.

Had she gone by herself onto the compound? Unlikely. She'd gone to seek help. Help that would assist us in gaining access to Camp Casey. I told this to Ernie. He admitted that it was possible, but he wasn't optimistic that it was true.

The rock band had just stopped clanging when a hubbub broke out toward the back of the Silver Dragon, beyond the pool tables. People, both Korean business girls and American GIs, were crowding around someone, like fans begging for autographs. Some of the women squealed. GIs laughed.

I elbowed Ernie. "At zero-three-hundred. Altercation brewing."

Ernie sat up and stared greedily toward the back door, ready to invest all his frustrations in a fight.

The crowd parted and someone walked through. A shiny black helmet bobbed and, for a second, Ernie and I prepared to run. MPs. And then I realized that there was only one. The helmet bobbed through the crowd until I could see strands of blonde hair peeking from beneath its edge, and suddenly a face that I recognized appeared: Corporal Jill Matthewson. Still surrounded by admirers, she strode out of the crowd onto the center of the dance floor. All of the Korean business girls gasped and cooed and "aahed." Jill was outfitted in full MP regalia: spit-shined jump boots, pressed combat fatigues, embroidered leather armband, polished black helmet, canvas web belt cinched tightly around her trim waist, and finally a holstered .45 caliber automatic pistol, her palm resting lightly on the hilt.

The business girls squealed and some began to applaud. And then, like an avalanche of flowers, they surrounded Jill. All of them giggling, laughing, patting her on the back and shaking hands, holding out two of theirs to clasp one of hers. Many of the business girls stepped back and bowed as she approached and then embraced her.

Ernie gazed at me, eyebrows raised.

What were these young Korean prostitutes so happy about?

I thought I knew. Finally, after all the decades of foreign men parading in and out of these bars and brothels and clubs, parading in and out of their lives, men who had no respect for women in general and Korean business girls in particular, finally, after all these years of suffering during and after the Korean War, here was a woman, a GI woman, and, better yet, an MP woman. Someone who would listen to them. Someone who could understand them. The business girls called her by name, "Jill! Jill!" warbling like a flock of doves.

Jill smiled and waved and embraced and shook hands and returned fond greetings with the good grace of a woman to royalty born. I had to remind myself that she was a fatherless Hoosier teenager who'd grown up in a trailer park. But tonight, at this moment, in the village of Tongduchon in the nightclub known as the Silver Dragon, she conducted herself like a queen.

When she approached the bar, I stood. She hugged me. I hugged her back.

Ernie slouched on his barstool. Jill stared down at him.

"You're late," Ernie said.

Jill grinned. "Had some work to do."

"Like ironing your fatigues?"

"And other things."

"Like what?"

Jill glanced around the Silver Dragon. "Not here. The ville patrol's liable to double back. Outside. We'll talk."

It took her almost as long to walk out of the Silver Dragon as it had taken her to enter. And this time even the band members roused themselves and lined up to shake her hand, as if it were their last chance to meet face-to-face with someone famous.

Outside in the cold February wind, some of the luster faded from Jill's face. The alley was lit by the yellowish glow of a street-lamp and a smattering of fluorescent rays that leaked out the back door of the Silver Dragon.

"Where you been all day?" Ernie asked.

"Making arrangements."

"Arrangements for what?"

"For getting at Colonel Alcott's records."

I knew it. Ernie didn't stop to congratulate me for my insight. He continued to question Jill. "What kind of arrangements?"

"You don't have a need to know." She thrust back her shoulders. "Tomorrow, you'll find out. Until then, I need your help."

"Hey," Ernie said, "who do you think's running this show?"

After all, Jill was merely an MP Corporal still on her first tour in the Army. And an AWOL corporal at that. Ernie and I were 8th Army CID agents. Seasoned veterans. At least that's the way we thought of ourselves.

Jill hooked her thumbs over the rim of her web belt, took a step closer to Ernie, and stared up at him. "In Division," she said, thrusting a thumb at her chest, "I'm in charge. And if you want to find out who did a number on Private Marv Druwood, you'll listen to me and do as I say."

Ernie glared at her, dumbfounded, not sure what to do. If she'd been a man, he might've punched her. Jill swiveled away from Ernie and turned to me. "Ville patrol," she said. "Weatherwax is on duty tonight. You two divert the attention of the KNP and the Korean MP so I can corner Weatherwax and get the info I need. Got it?"

"Got it," I said.

"Let's go."

Jill turned and started trotting down the dark alley. We followed. She twisted through the narrow lanes as if she'd been through them many times before, occasionally pointing at a broken "turtle trap" and hollering at us to avoid stepping into the gaping hole. Ernie stayed a few feet behind, just close enough for me to hear him swearing under his breath, cursing all females. The narrow alley emerged onto a broader lane. Above us neon glared: a startled feline with red eyes. The Black Cat Club.

Ernie groaned. "Not again."

Down the road, the ville patrol emerged from another night club. We crouched and Jill led us out of their line of sight and then around the back. The gate leading to the hooches behind the Black Cat was open. Ernie and I followed Jill past darkened rooms until we stood at the open back door of the club. The voice of James Brown wailed from the jukebox. Conversation and laughter floated out, on a roiling cloud of cigarette smoke.

Jill peeked into the back door then ducked back out.

"The ville patrol's in," she said. "When they come back here to search the men's and women's latrines, create a diversion." She pulled her .45. "While you keep them occupied, I'm going to have a little talk with my old friend, Staff Sergeant Weatherwax."

Weatherwax was the man who'd shot at Ernie and me in the alleyways of Bongil-chon. Ernie and I wanted to interrogate him, too, but Jill knew all the MPs up here. She'd be able to spot lies easier than we could. Still, I was worried about her state of mind. Was she out to gather information or was she after revenge?

"Take it easy, Jill," I told her. "All we want is information."

"Right," she said. "Right."

Ernie interrupted. "Here they come."

Two uniformed Korean men marched down the narrow hallway. The ROK Army MP shouted a warning and then pushed his way into the female latrine. The KNP followed. A black American MP I recognized as Staff Sergeant Weatherwax entered the men's latrine. Ernie charged forward, plowing his way into the women's latrine. I followed, standing just inside the door, ready to help if needed.

Behind me, Jill elbowed her way through the swinging door of the men's latrine.

"*Weikurei?*" Ernie shouted. What's the matter?

He was acting drunk. Staggering. The Korean cops stared at him, wide-eyed. Inside the open door of a stall, a young woman squatted over a porcelain-lined hole, her skirt up, terror filling her eyes.

"What's the matter you?" Ernie said. "Why you come GI club?"

The KNP started to shove Ernie toward the hallway. Ernie spun away from him, staggering against the cement wall. Both of the Korean men turned on him.

I stepped forward. Smiling. Nodding. "My *chingu*," I said, pointing at Ernie. My friend. "*Taaksan stinko*." He's very drunk.

The two cops let me step past them and grab Ernie. I started to pull him out of the latrine and into the hall but he resisted. I motioned for the Korean cops to help me. They did, pushing Ernie out the door and down the hallway toward the main ballroom of the Black Cat Club.

I could've maneuvered them into shoving Ernie out the back door but I wanted to take advantage of this opportunity to search for Brandy again.

The reception we received wasn't friendly. Two white GIs—drunk white GIs—wrestling with two Korean cops. Not exactly what the soul brothers of the Black Cat Club wanted to see while they were trying to relax and socialize. They reacted with hostility.

Ernie bumped into a group of GIs standing with their arms around Korean business girls. Drinks splashed out of cups. Men cursed. They shoved Ernie and he reeled toward me.

As I held him, I whispered in his ear. "Brandy's here."

Ernie sobered. The show was over. Jill had yet to emerge from the men's latrine. Apparently, she was still having her heart-to-heart talk with Staff Sergeant Weatherwax.

Brandy stood wide-eyed behind the bar, glancing this way and that, searching for a means of escape. The last time we'd seen her she'd spent the early evening in a *yoguan* with Ernie, and then he'd almost been killed at fish heaven by a rifle round aimed his way.

Ernie lunged toward her, ramming into two GIs sitting on stools at the bar. They shouted. Ernie leaned across the bar, stretching out his hand, but Brandy ducked, barely escaping his grasp. She broke for the end of the bar, but I was already moving. I would've cut her off easily but by now all eyes in the club were on us. Curtis Mayfield was moaning sweetly from the jukebox. Two men blocked me. I plowed into them; they reeled backward. I'd reached the end of the bar but Brandy kept moving, heading for the front door. In two steps I would've had her but a punch to my ribcage threw me off stride and then three more bodies plowed into me. I punched back. As I did so, I heard the big double front doors open and then slam shut. I tried to move forward but more screaming bodies were in my way. Ernie was behind me now, cursing and punching and kicking, and for the first time I stopped worrying about Brandy escaping and started worrying about surviving.

I was just about to grab a chair and hit somebody when the blast of a pistol shot filled the room, followed immediately by an explosion of glass and metal accompanied by electrical sparks and the screeching halt of Curtis Mayfield's smooth falsetto. Corporal Jill Matthewson stood at the back of the room, holding her .45 in front of her with both hands gripped firmly around the hilt.

"Make a hole!" she shouted.

She moved forward through the crowd until she reached Ernie and me and together the three of us backed toward the front door. The mumbling started again. Cursing now about the jukebox and screaming invective from the old woman behind the bar. But before anyone could retaliate, we were out the door, down the steps, and running.

"What'd Weatherwax tell you?"

We were running through dark alleys, heading northwest, away from the TDC bar district.

"Never mind about that now," Jill told me. "You saw Brandy? Right?"

"Yes. She hightailed it out the door before we could stop her."

"Have you ever been to her hooch? Either of you?"

I glanced at Ernie. He shook his head negatively.

"No," I said.

"Then she'll think she's safe there. She didn't see me."

"You know where Brandy lives?"

"I sure do."

After a couple more blocks we slowed to a walk, all three of us breathing heavily. Since Ernie and I were wearing civilian clothes, we scouted out front, watching for KNP patrols. Jill led us to a district of TDC very close to the area Ernie and I had recently become familiar with.

"The Turkey Farm," Ernie said.

Jill nodded. "Convenient for black-marketing."

"Brandy was into black-marketing?" I asked.

Jill nodded again. "Up to her pretty little neck." She held out her hand. "Quiet now. We're getting close."

It was a nice hooch. Old but well kept up, with bright blue tile on the roof that must've been recently replaced. Moonlight shone down into an immaculately clean courtyard with a metal-handled water pump in the center and neatly tended bushes and a row of earthen kimchee jars.

Ernie and I balanced on top of the ten-foot-high cement-block wall, gingerly placing our hands so as to avoid shards of jagged glass sticking out of plaster. With her .45 pointing at the moon, Jill Matthewson stood in front of the main gate, waiting for us to jump down and open it for her.

"You see any movement?" Ernie asked.

"No."

All the hooches were dark.

"She's in there," Ernie said.

"How do you know?"

"I smell her. Brandy's close and she's overwhelming."

Actually, I thought Ernie might be right. Not about how he sensed her but about the fact that Brandy must be home. There were shoes lined up in front of the hooch, women's shoes spangled with sequins. But they weren't neatly aligned. One pair lay on its side, as if it had been rapidly kicked off. And earlier, as we had approached the main gate down a dark alley, I thought I'd glimpsed a dimming of light. As if someone was listening and when they'd heard the tromp of combat boots, they'd clicked off the electric light. A lace curtain breathed in and out inside the hooch, pulsating through the narrow opening left by the partially closed sliding door.

"She's watching us," I whispered.

"Yeah. And we make good targets perched up here."

With that, Ernie hopped down into the courtyard, hitting the ground and rolling as he did so. I kept my eyes riveted on the door. Movement? Or was it my imagination? As Ernie hurried to unbolt the front gate, I leaped down into the courtyard, jarring my knees and ankles, rolling, and quickly coming to a squatting position. The sliding door that a second ago had been partially open was now completely shut.

I ran forward, keeping my head down.

When I reached the low wooden porch in front of the hooch, I leaned forward, grabbed the sliding door, and pulled. It trembled but didn't open. Inside, a metal lock rattled.

Ernie and Jill ran up behind me.

"Someone's in there," I said. "They just locked the door."

Ernie stepped past me and kicked the door in. Oil paper and fragile wooden latticework shattered. He reached in, unlatched the door, and ripped it off its hinges.

Jill Matthewson shone her flashlight inside.

Ernie and I entered, he found the overhead bulb and switched it on. The entire room was bathed in light. No Brandy. An expensive armoire with mother-of-pearl inlay, silk-encased comforters folded in a corner, a hand-painted porcelain pee pot, a dressing table with a mirror and various lotions and cosmetics. No sign of anything masculine. This, I guessed, was Brandy's refuge from the world of GIs.

But these observations were made primarily to avoid focusing on the first thing I'd seen. It sat in a corner by itself, still partially encased in wood framing, cradled atop straw, glowing like an endless sky of blue and green. *Chon Hak Byong*. The Thousand Crane Vase.

I kneeled and examined it. The flock of white cranes floated into the celadon sky, their black eyes pointed toward heaven. Except for one, on the upper bulge of the vase. His eyes stared straight out. Straight into the eyes of the observer. And this crane's feet were deformed. Deformed into a shape that appeared to be a Chinese character: *bok*. Good luck. Very probably the name of the artist. I was sure this magnificent piece of art was the same vase that had been stolen by gangsters from the burning inferno of the grain warehouse just yards from here in the heart of the Turkey Farm.

Wood bumped against stone.

"Out back," Ernie shouted.

He ran out the front door and zipped around the edge of the hooch. I continued deeper into the dwelling, into the cement-floored kitchen and exited a side door. The three of us—Jill, Ernie, and myself—met at the narrow opening between the back of the hooch and the cement-block wall. Brandy stood atop a short ladder, trying to get a handhold on the top of the glass-covered wall. Jill shone her flashlight on Brandy's cute round butt.

Brandy turned, her shoulders slumped, and she gingerly retreated down the ladder. Staring at the three of us she said, "Ain't no bag, man."

A few minutes later, the four of us sat in a circle on the floor of her comfortable hooch, under the glow of a bright electric bulb, facing one another. The story Brandy told us was interesting and, I had to assume, laced with lies.

She claimed to be holding the Thousand Crane Vase for a friend. Who was this friend? She wasn't at liberty to say. She knew nothing about the fire at the grain warehouse in the center of the Turkey Farm other than that she'd heard about it and it was a great tragedy, but she had no idea how such a thing had happened. And also, she was unaware that the Thousand Crane Vase had been stolen by gangsters. She thought that it might've been a different vase. When I pointed out to her that it was the same vase and I explained why, she thought that her friend must've been very careless in paying good money for a vase that had been stolen.

"How much did he pay?" Jill asked.

Brandy shrugged. "I know nothing about these things."

Ernie asked her about *mulkogi chonguk*, fish heaven.

Brandy seemed shocked that we'd been shot at. "Who would do such a thing?" she asked.

I pointed out to her that she probably knew exactly who, since her handwriting matched the writing on the phony note that had set up the appointment. Now she seemed offended. It couldn't be her handwriting, she claimed, since she hardly knew how to write.

Finally, Jill questioned her about Marv Druwood.

Brandy had no idea about who was at the grain warehouse that night or what had happened to Private Marvin Druwood.

Without warning, Jill leaned forward and slapped Brandy.

Her full cheeks quivered and then turned red; she held the side of her face. I expected tears to well up but instead Brandy's eyes spit venom.

"You know who was there," Jill said. "Otis told you."

Otis. Sergeant First Class Otis. The desk sergeant who'd confided in me about the Turkey Farm and hinted at irregularities in both the disposal of Marv Druwood's body and in the 2nd ID provost marshal's ration control procedures.

"Otis, he no want you," Brandy said. "He want me." She jabbed her thumb between pendulous breasts.

Jill's face turned crimson. "You little bitch. You know who killed Marv. You know!"

Jill flung herself on Brandy and the two of them rolled on the floor for a moment, scratching and butting heads, until Ernie and I ripped them apart. Ernie held Brandy while I escorted Jill outside the hooch. In the courtyard, Jill straightened her uniform. Inside, Brandy nursed cuts and bruises. We confiscated the Thousand Crane Vase. Brandy cursed as we left and swore revenge. Actually, we should've arrested her. But as fugitives ourselves, what were we going to do with her? We couldn't turn her over to the 2nd ID MPs nor to the Korean cops because they'd arrest us at the same time.

As we stalked through dark alleys, I wanted to ask Jill about Sergeant First Class Otis and his role in all this. Jill knew more than she was telling me. But she was fuming, and I knew this was the wrong time.

When we reached the bar district, we paused. Ernie and I set down the vase. It was heavier than it looked. The time was half past eleven. In thirty minutes, curfew would start. Jill told us to hide the vase at Ok-hi's hooch at the Silver Dragon. Tomorrow, we'd meet up and then enter Camp Casey and take possession of Lieutenant Colonel Alcott's ration control records.

"How?" Ernie asked.

"How what?" Jill replied.

She was still distracted by her confrontation with Brandy.

"How in the hell are we going to bust onto the compound and confiscate the records?"

Jill waved her palm in the air. "Not to worry. I'll take care of that." She started to leave. "See you tomorrow."

"Where are you going?" I asked.

She smiled. "You don't have a need to know."

"Where will we meet you?" Ernie asked.

"At the same place everyone's going to be tomorrow," Jill said, walking away into the darkness.

"Where's that?" Ernie hollered.

"At the demonstration."

After she left, I realized that she still hadn't revealed what she'd learned from Staff Sergeant Weatherwax.

"Looks like we're back where we started."

After sleeping late the next morning, Ernie and I once again sat on the floor of Ok-hi's hooch, a room on the third story above the Silver Dragon Nightclub. The Thousand Crane Vase stood alone in a corner. Ok-hi, as happy to see us as ever, served us tea on a foot-high varnished brown table, then switched the radio to AFKN, the Armed Forces Korean Network. There was nothing on the news about student demonstrations or the KCIA or the murder of Pak Tong-i. Nor about the death of Private Marvin Druwood nor about two 8th Army CID agents gone berserk north of Seoul. Plenty about the latest shenanigans in Washington and, of course, plenty of sports.

"Not back where we started," I told Ernie. "We know what we have to do next. Bust a bunch a black-marketing field grade officers."

"If we find the proof."

"Jill will help us find the proof."

"How?"

"She told us where to find the proof. In Colonel Alcott's safe in his quarters. And she promised us that we'd be able to bust onto the compound."

"Over some MPs' dead bodies."

Ernie and I sat silent for a moment, both pondering the implications of what he'd just said. Was today's demonstration going to be violent? I mean truly violent? Not just a few stones thrown by overexcited students. But arms, Molotov cocktails, explosives? Ok-hi told us that most of the business girls had gone to the bathhouse early today because they'd heard about the student demonstration and they expected it to be bigger than any of those Tongduchon had seen in the past. I asked her why.

Her eyes widened, as if the answer was obvious.

"Chon Un-suk-i die," she said. "GI supposed to go monkey house. Instead, GI go stateside. Everybody *taaksan kullasso*." Everybody very angry.

Ernie seemed to have been listening to my thoughts. "The Division MPs must know there's going to be a demonstration," he said. "They'll be prepared for anything."

Ok-hi tilted her head. At first I thought it was to show off the hoop earrings she was wearing. Then I realized she was listening to something. Something faint and far away.

"You go," she said finally.

"What?"

"You go compound. Alert."

Ernie switched off the radio. The wail of a siren, coming from the direction of Camp Casey. Alert. All GIs were to report back to the compound.

"You're right," I told Ernie. "They are taking this demonstration seriously."


Thirty minutes later, Ernie and I stood on the roof of the Silver Dragon Nightclub watching tanks, two-and-a-half ton trucks, and armored vehicles—by the dozens—roll out of the front gate of Camp Casey.

"Move out," Ernie said. "Division wide."

A Division-wide move-out alert meant everyone goes to the field, even the headquarters staff, as if an actual war had broken out. Still, since an alert is only training and not war, some people would be left behind to guard and maintain the compound. Even though all MPs in the Division area are considered to be combat MPs—that is, they can assume a combat role if actual hostilities break out—you could bet that enough MPs would remain behind to protect the compound from the student demonstrators. Even now, we could see bunches of MPs milling around the towering MP statue in front of the Provost Marshal's Office, slipping on their riot-control helmets, playing grab ass, donning their protective vests.

"Probably glad they don't have to go to the field," Ernie said.

Field duty—days and even weeks in the rain and the mud—grows old fast. Still, it seemed odd to me that a move-out alert had been called only an hour before a well-publicized student demonstration was to begin. Who had called the alert? Eighth Army? The United Nations Command in Seoul? I had no way of knowing. Maybe someone thought that calling an alert at such a time would replicate real-world situations and therefore provide realistic training. After all, war can break out anytime, even when it's inconvenient. Maybe. But I didn't believe it. My mistrust of coincidence made me think that something was up. Maybe something bigger than anyone imagined.

More troop transports full of infantry soldiers rolled out of the main gate of Camp Casey, followed by heavy artillery pieces and jeeps and commo vehicles and mess trucks and vehicles of all shapes and descriptions.

"Look." Ernie pointed down the MSR about a mile at a gas station near the outskirts of town. Buses pulled in. Vans, taxicabs, all sorts of civilian conveyances. Students wearing black armbands and carrying picket signs written in both English and Korean were starting to gather. A steady stream of vehicles snaked down the MSR, heading toward Tongduchon. As we watched, the crowd grew larger. To the west about three blocks, at Tonduchon Station, the local train from Seoul pulled in. When it stopped, like a centipede shedding eggs, a jillion students popped out of the ten or so cars. Leaders with megaphones formed them into groups, shouting instructions, handing out black armbands and signs.

"Christ," Ernie said, "half of Seoul is coming up here."

"And a train is due every thirty minutes."

"They're really serious. Not like that paltry little group last time."

We went back downstairs. Ok-hi fed us: steamed rice, kimchee, bowls of *dubu jigei*, spiced bean curd soup. She also found us two strips of white cloth that she helped us tie around our heads. Then, while we kneeled in front of her, she used red paint—mimicking blood—to write in *hangul* the name Chon Un-suk. Thus outfitted, Ernie and I thanked Ok-hi and, though she tried to refuse, I paid her for her time and the food and the effort she'd expended to help us. She promised to guard the Thousand Crane Vase with her life.

Ernie and I bounced out into the street, keeping a wary eye out for both the MPs and the KNPs. It was easy enough to avoid them. The Korean National Police were preoccupied with protecting the TDC police station and with setting up an assault position near the railroad tracks across from Camp Casey's main gate. The American MPs were on compound, bracing for trouble.

Ernie and I slipped through a narrow alley between the bar district and the Main Supply Route. Once on the MSR, we strolled casually into the stream of protestors shouting and marching toward the main gate of Camp Casey. Picket signs saying YANKEE GO HOME and JUSTICE FOR CHON UN-SUK competed with the dozens of black-edged blowups of the deceased middle-school girl. Soon, the stream we were in joined other streams and, as we approached the line of MPs guarding the main gate, we became part of a mighty river.

# 15

Ernie and I pushed through the crowd, occasionally raising our fists and shouting indecipherable remarks that blended in with the periodic shouts from the crowd. This type of activity had ingratiated us to the protestors at the previous demonstration. Many of them had smiled and said *"komapta"*—thank you—and some of them had patted us on the back. But this group was much larger and much more sure of their power, and, therefore, more surly. For our efforts, Ernie and I received dirty looks and for once I didn't feel safe amidst a crowd of Koreans. We kept moving. Not only because we were nervous, but because we were looking for a way to slip onto Camp Casey.

All that had happened for the first few minutes were a bunch of monotonous speeches shouted through megaphones. Madame Chon hadn't spoken yet and I wasn't sure if she would. Probably not. Maybe the KCIA had arrested her. Jill wasn't visible either. Were Jill's assurances that we'd be able to slip onto the compound during the demonstration a diversion to distract us while she looked for an opportunity to slip away herself? I didn't think so. Something was going to happen soon.

No more vehicles were leaving Camp Casey. The rest of the Division, other than the four or five dozen MPs guarding the main gate, had already moved out.

"This is bull!" Ernie said. "We have to make something happen."

A roar went up from the crowd. Two, maybe three thousand people were jammed into the road in front of Camp Casey, and it seemed that each and every one of them had riveted their attention on the KNPs lined up along the railroad tracks.

But then I saw that it wasn't the railroad tracks the crowd was staring at but rather a soldier, in a U.S. Army uniform, who'd just climbed up on a platform. The soldier's back was to me but I could see the black leather armband and the shining black helmet of an MP. Then one of the students handed the MP a megaphone and the MP turned around to face us. The crowd roared their approval. It was Military Policewoman Corporal Jill Matthewson, in full regalia. Once again, she looked squared away. A real soldier. Then she saluted the crowd, which exploded into applause.

It dawned on me that every action of Jill's to this point had been done with a purpose in mind. Jill raised the megaphone to her mouth and started to speak. As she did so, a young Korean man climbed onto the platform next to her, and using his own megaphone, repeated what she said in Korean.

Her speech was nothing new to me and Ernie. But coming from a soldier in uniform, its impact was overwhelming. The crowd was energized by her words and as she continued to speak, the level of outrage seemed to grow, swelling each heart with indignation.

Jill Matthewson spoke of arrogance. Of the arrogance of the men running Camp Casey who thought of women as objects for their entertainment. Of the arrogance with which they flouted the laws of the Republic of Korea, selling cheap imported PX goods on the black market, thus stifling the growth of indigenous Korean industry. Of the arrogance of men who allowed American soldiers to operate dangerous vehicles under poor driving conditions and didn't hold them accountable for their recklessness. Of the arrogance that caused Korean women to be raped behind closed doors. Of the arrogance that caused the bosses on Camp Casey to sneer at the Korean judicial system. Of the arrogance that allowed two GIs—GIs who had admitted killing Chon Un-suk—to return to the United States without facing Korean justice.

The crowd was in a frenzy now, surging toward Jill, reaching out their hands. The Korean student with her was shouting through his megaphone, *"Chon Un-suk kiokhei!"* Remember Chon Un-suk! *"Jil Ma-tyu-son mansei!"* Long live Jill Matthewson!

As the crowd reached up to her, Jill touched their hands and then grabbed the rim of her MP helmet and whipped it off. With a sweeping motion, she tossed it into the crowd. The crowd screamed and men jumped to grab the helmet. Then she reached behind her head, unhooked a metal clasp and, shaking it loose, allowed her long, reddish blonde hair to swing free. The crowd roared madly.

She lifted her megaphone to her lips and pointed at the giant MP looming some twenty yards behind the Camp Casey Main Gate.

"He must die!" she shouted.

Then she swiveled and pointed at the KNPs lining the railroad tracks across the MSR from Camp Casey. This time she spoke in Korean.

*"Bikyo!"* she shouted. Make way. *"Bali bikyo."* Make way quickly.

Behind the tracks, from amongst the shops that lined the road that led to the Western Corridor, an engine roared. Almost as loud as a train but not running on rails. From between the shops a wooden prow appeared. Dark green. Massive. Growing larger as its engines groaned. And then the huge moving mass crossed the slight ridge behind the tracks and came fully into view.

"What the hell is it?" Ernie asked.

I'd seen one before. When I was in the artillery and we practiced moving trucks and howitzers across fast-flowing rivers.

"A pontoon," I shouted. "Mechanized."

Eighteen wheels below, a boat-shaped body and a folding platform on top. Only just enough space in a carved-out corner for a driver with goggles. The driver stepped on the gas and aimed the enormous river-crossing vehicle directly at the line of Korean policeman.

Jill shouted through her megaphone once again. *"Bikyo. Balli Bikyo."* Get out of the way. Quickly get out of the way.

The KNPs turned, staring in amazement at the great vehicle bearing down on them. Some of them broke ranks. The rolling pontoon bounced as it crossed the ridge and roared directly at them.

The KNPs dropped their weapons and ran.

Before the crowd had time to cheer at this development, Jill and the student next to her were screaming into their megaphones for them to make way, too. The crowd parted like the Red Sea. Ernie and I jumped, but we were only a few feet from the wheeled pontoon as it chugged past us, heading directly for the main gate of Camp Casey.

Jill Matthewson didn't order the American MPs to disperse; she didn't have to. They scattered, clearing a path for the huge vehicle as it headed right at the MP guard shack in front of the gate. At the last second, the pontoon swerved to the right, clipped the guard shack and then plowed into the tall chain link fence that surrounded Camp Casey. The fence buckled, held for a second, and collapsed. The pontoon kept rolling and the wooden arch above the gateway—the one that said 2ND INFANTRY DIVISON, SECOND TO NONE!—folded backwards and then fell onto a growing pile of chain link, concertina wire, and splintered wood.

The crowd roared once again and the student protestors surged through the gate, ripping and tearing as they went.

Ernie and I fought our way through. When we passed the giant MP and neared the front door of the Provost Marshal's Office, we ripped off our white bandannas of protest. MPs had gathered there, preparing to make a last stand. Because we were Americans, the MPs didn't take notice of us—the dragnet for two 8th Army CID agents was forgotten. They allowed us to enter the premises of the 2nd Division Provost Marshal's Office.

The front desk was pandemonium. The on-duty desk sergeant was on the radio, signaling frantically to Division headquarters out in the field and then I Corps headquarters down in Uijongbu. A couple of MP lieutenants ran into one another, shouting orders, but I wasn't sure what they expected to accomplish. The mob was on compound now, moving wherever it wanted to.

Temporarily, the student demonstrators had become fascinated with tearing down the PX hot dog stand, only ten yards inside the main gate. Sodas and buns were being tossed out to the crowd. The white-smocked Korean girl who ran the hot dog stand fled in terror. The pontoon vehicle was blocked by the debris of the main gate but the driver was backing it up, and some of the students were helping to untangle the chain link and wire knotted beneath the front axle. In a matter of minutes, it would be back in operation.

Had the timing of the Division-wide move-out alert been sheer coincidence? I didn't think so. Colonel Han Kuk-chei came from a revered *yangban* family and would have connections throughout the ROK military and the government. Jill might be involved in something bigger than she'd admitted to us. Perhaps Colonel Han's friends in high places were able to maneuver the United Nations Command in Seoul into ordering an alert just when Colonel Han needed it. This melee might be part of a larger coup against the government.

But what I needed desperately was proof that the Division honchos had been illegally black-marketing, which would be a motive for murdering both Private Marvin Druwood and the entertainment agent, Pak Tong-i. And attempting to murder Corporal Jill Matthewson and Agents George Sueño and Ernie Bascom, because we were on the verge of exposing them. Their careers would be over; they'd be stripped of privilege and rank and, not incidentally, their retirement checks. And very likely they'd do hard time in a federal penitentiary.

So far, the Korean National Police and the American MPs had shown admirable restraint. They had not fired on the crowd. Only a few ineffective tear gas canisters had been launched, but they'd been haphazardly placed and had been disposed of quickly by the braver students.

Ernie and I ignored the pandemonium of the PMO front desk and trotted down the hallway toward Colonel Alcott's office.

One of the conceits of field-grade officers and high-ranking NCOs when they're stationed overseas is to have their own customized living quarters. Their wives and children are back stateside so, naturally, a man who's had a long and illustrious military career believes that he deserves his own bachelor pad. One of the status symbols is to move your quarters out of the staid old BOQ, Bachelor

Officers' Quarters, and have private quarters within walking distance of your workplace. The more rank and influence you have, the more likely you are to be granted this amenity. As Provost Marshal of the 2nd Infantry Division, Lieutenant Colonel Stanley X. Alcott rated nothing but the best.

A middle-aged Korean woman sat at a desk in the reception area of Colonel Alcott's office. She wore her raincoat and her galoshes and nervously toyed with her umbrella.

"*Wei ankayo?*" I asked her in Korean. Why haven't you left?

"*Motka,*" she answered without thinking. I can't go. Then she switched to English. "There are too many demonstrators outside. I can't go now."

"Where's the Colonel?"

"Outside," she answered. "Somewhere. I'm worried for him."

"I'm glad," Ernie said. "Where are his quarters?"

"His what?"

"*Chimdei,*" I said. His bed.

The woman's eyes widened at the unintended double entendre. "*Na ottokei allayo?*" she replied. How would I know?

I slammed my fist on her desk.

"*Odi?*" I shouted. Where?

I hate to be rude, but I had no time to tiptoe around this woman's sense of propriety. She stood up as if she'd been given an electric shock.

"I show," she said.

We followed her into Colonel Alcott's office. A mahogany desk, leather chairs, the flags of the Republic of Korea, the United States, and the United Nations hanging from poles behind the desk. The walls were lined with bookshelves packed with bound copies of Army Regulations and volumes concerning the Uniform Code of Military Justice. There was a back door. We walked out into a grassy area behind the PMO complex. The woman followed a cement walk and stopped at a door leading into an unmarked Quonset hut.

"I don't have the key," she told us.

Ernie eased her out of the way, took a step back, and then lunged forward with all his strength. The sole of his low quarters hit the front of the door near the knob and the door groaned but didn't break.

The secretary stepped back farther, holding both hands over her mouth.

I took the next try. A side kick. It landed flush in the center of the door, which crashed open and slammed into the wall behind it. Ernie and I walked in. The secretary scurried back to her office.


When Colonel Alcott stepped through the broken front door of his quarters, he was flanked by two MP escorts. Ernie and I sat in comfortable lounge chairs, our .45s out, both of them aimed at the colonel and his bodyguards.

"Take your weapons out of their holsters, slow and easy, and place them on the floor in front of you," Ernie said.

The MPs did as they were told.

"Now," Ernie said. "Step into that closet over there and close the door behind you."

Outside, we heard shouting, screaming, and the occasional tear-gas canister being popped into the air. Apparently, the KNPs had regrouped and charged the protestors who had broken through the main gate. However, there were fewer than a hundred KNPs and only four or five dozen MPs versus maybe two thousand protestors. The battle raged on.

"Over here," Ernie told Colonel Alcott. He motioned with his .45. Colonel Alcott, his face red with rage, did as he was told. He stepped past his bed into the lounge area, past a color television set and stereo equipment on specially made shelves and past a stand-up bar with two stools. When he reached the safe, Ernie told him to stop.

Ernie slipped Colonel Alcott's .45 from its holster and handed it to me. I took out the magazine, dropped it into my pocket, and placed the weapon atop the safe. I also picked up the weapons of the two MPs and performed the same ritual.

Then Ernie pulled back the slide on his own .45 and stuck the muzzle into Lieutenant Colonel Stanley X. Alcott's ear.

"Open it," Ernie growled.

Colonel Alcott dropped to his knees and started fiddling with the combination.

We weren't worried about a search warrant.

If we'd gone back to 8th Army and asked for one, the provost marshal would've either denied the request immediately or he would've passed it to the 8th Army chief of staff and, if the request wasn't killed there, it would be passed on to the 8th Army JAG, where the entire idea of searching the quarters of a field-grade officer would be endlessly debated. Even if the request was finally approved, there would so much gossip around headquarters that the division commander and members of his staff would hear about it. Forewarned is forearmed, as they say, and Colonel Alcott would have plenty of time to destroy, or hide, any incriminating information he might have in his safe. This is the way the game is played in the military. If you're a peon, you never hear what headquarters is planning. You're squashed before you know what hit you. If you're a field grade officer and a player, someone will spill the information to someone at happy hour at the 8th Army Officers' Club and the word will get back to you. You'll have time to take steps to ensure nothing untoward is revealed. Why does the 8th Army commander put up with this? He doesn't always. Sometime he wants *everything* kept secret, and he makes damn sure that it stays secret. But other times it's much less embarrassing to his command if the alleged evildoers are warned in advance. The bad behavior stops, and the command's reputation remains unsullied.

It was true that anything Ernie and I found in the safe would be unusable in a formal prosecution but we knew there was no way we'd ever be able to obtain anything from that safe that would be so usable. Certainly not by requesting a search warrant.

But we were forcing Colonel Alcott at gunpoint to open his own safe, to protect ourselves, mainly, but also to protect Corporal Jill Matthewson.

If Ernie and I couldn't prove that we had a good reason for everything we'd done, we'd be court-martialed. And Jill's fate hardly beared thinking of. So the suspense was killing me. If there was no evidence of black-marketing in that safe, then there'd have been no motive for murder and attemped murder and Ernie and I could say goodbye to freedom.

When the safe popped open, Ernie grabbed Colonel Alcott roughly by the arm and waltzed him over to the bed against the far wall and told him to sit down and not to move. I reached into the safe.

Letters from home. From his wife back at Fort Bragg, North Carolina. Photos of his kids in high-school graduation garb. Pornography. Magazines of the raunchiest kind. Personnel files of fellow field-grade officers. Apparently, Alcott fancied himself a later-day J. Edgar Hoover: Collect dirt on everyone; use it to protect yourself. And then I found it. A ledger. Dates, dollar signs, a description of the type of property: television sets, tape recorders, stereo amps, wristwatches, cameras. All prime black market material. And then an amount in *won*, usually two or three times the original value. And a section for expenditures: hall rental, catered food, musicians, dancers, occasionally even hired transportation. They'd held mafia meetings not only at the WVOW Hall but also at *kisaeng* houses here in the Eastern Corridor.

There was also money in the safe. Stacks of greenback twenties. Fifties and hundreds were monitored by 8th Army Finance, so twenties were safer. And stacks of ten thousand *won* notes. With the exchange rate at about five hundred *won* per dollar, each note was worth about the same as a U.S. twenty. I counted the bills, even wrote down some of the serial numbers in my notebook. I left everything in the safe as I'd found it, except the ledger, which I kept. For leverage. With the ledger, we could embarrass 2nd Division—and therefore 8th Army—if we had to. Maybe send it to a newspaper reporter, or maybe a congressman. Maybe the same congressman who'd made the original inquiry about Jill Matthewson.

I tucked the black market ledger under my arm.

"Thank you, Colonel," I told Alcott. "We'd appreciate it if you'd remain here a few minutes. My partner and I are going to escort Corporal Matthewson back to Seoul. We don't expect to be harassed. And we don't expect our progress to be impeded in any way. Otherwise this information will be made public rather than being handled through internal channels. Do you understand?"

"I understand," Alcott said. "I understand that Fred Bufford was right. You're up here to smear the Division. To make us look bad."

"You did a pretty good job of that," Ernie replied, "all by yourself."

Alcott's red face seemed to flush even redder.

"You don't understand the pressures I've been under," he told us. "You do your jobs and take your piddly promotions, but you don't know what it is to go for serious rank in this man's army."

Colonel Alcott started to rise from the bed but Ernie shoved him back down.

"You don't understand," Alcott continued, "what it is to have a full-bird colonel or a general officer tell you 'I don't care how you do it, just do it.' And to know that everything you've worked for, everything you've hoped to provide for your family, rides on whether or not you're able to give him what he wants. You can sit back and sneer and pass judgment on me because you're not in competition for the big promotions. You don't know what it is to have some pervert base your efficiency report on whether or not he has four girls or five girls at some *kisaeng* house. About him telling you what some air force colonel bragged about at the Officers' Club in Seoul, and how he works hard and he should rate at least as much as some zoomie. You don't know what it's like to do your job day in and day out without a flaw and still be expected to cater to the whims of every officer appointed above you. You can act superior but you're not serious players. In fact, you two are *nothing*."

"Maybe," Ernie replied. "But we'll be something as long as we have this ledger." He held his .45 pointed at Alcott's forehead. "*Anyonghikeiseiyo*." Stay in peace.

We stalked out the broken front door.

The pontoon vehicle was still being untangled from the concertina wire and chain link barriers that had been created when it knocked down the main gate leading to Camp Casey. Ernie and I retied our white bandannas with Chon Un-suk's name printed in red and were accepted again by the rioters. The hot dog stand had been completely demolished and the mob had turned its attention to a PX bakery that was similarly being systematically torn apart. The KNPs, meanwhile, retreated across the MSR. Two or three hundred protestors had set up a makeshift barrier of overturned military vehicles and lumber from the old MP shack in front of what had been the Camp Casey main gate. I spotted the KCIA man who called himself

Agent Sohn, standing across the street behind the KNP ranks, conferring with KNP brass. They were on the radio, almost certainly requesting reinforcements.

The MPs in front of the Provost Marshal's Office, like the 7th Cavalry at the Little Big Horn, were bracing themselves for an assault. Probably they'd notified the Division headquarters—on the move-out alert somewhere north of here—by field radio. Almost certainly some units had been ordered to return to Camp Casey to protect the base camp. These protestors were having a jolly old time, but both Ernie and I knew that as soon as reinforcements arrived, they'd be hammered.

I climbed atop the cab of a quarter-ton truck, searching for Jill Matthewson, but I couldn't spot her. A large crowd of protestors still held vigil outside the main gate and many of them had cameras. Both film and still shots were being taken of virtually everything that happened. But this incident would only make the evening news if the Korean government allowed it to make the evening news. You could bet they wouldn't.

The pontoon boat rolled right at me.

I jumped off the truck. Ernie and I ran off to the side, to the shade beneath a clump of pine trees. Then we realized where the ponderous vehicle was headed.

Ernie said it. "PMO!"

The whale-like vehicle was rumbling toward the MPs preparing to make their last stand in front of the 2nd Infantry Division Provost Marshall's Office. As it rolled, the pontoon picked up speed. Five, then ten, then fifteen miles per hour. That much weight moving at that much speed represented an enormous force. The amphibious pontoon vehicle rounded a little stand of pine trees and turned right, into the PMO parking lot. From behind their makeshift barricades, the MPs opened fire. Rounds spattered off the wooden sides of the oncoming vehicle; some pinged off the edge of the cabin where the driver crouched. The pontoon veered left and headed straight toward the giant MP.

The big pink face of the MP statue with its wide blue eyes seemed momentarily shocked, even offended. I knew it was my imagination, but I could have sworn that the fatigue-clad statue puffed out its giant chest, as if to say *How dare you?* and then held its outraged stance until the prow of the huge pontoon slammed into its web-belted gut. Then it bent forward at the waist. The pontoon vehicle kept rolling inexorably forward and the giant U.S. Army MP cracked and tumbled backward under the onslaught, its big helmeted skull crashing onto the ground, almost reaching the MPs behind sandbags who ran screaming from the flying splinters. Still, the pontoon vehicle kept rolling. It smashed through the barricade, MPs scattered every which way, and finally it crashed into the front Quonset hut of the Provost Marshal's Office. With dust and debris flying everywhere the big vehicle ground to a halt. Some MPs kept firing. Some of them cried out, trapped beneath the rubble.

The little driver's cab popped open and two people climbed out: One of them was a Korean officer. A colonel. The other was Corporal Jill Matthewson.

They hopped onto the blacktop and ran back toward the front gate. Once there, the ROK colonel tried to rally the rioters. He climbed up on the same quarter-ton truck I'd stood on briefly and shouted at them to listen. The looters stopped and gathered round. Jill stood next to him atop the truck, breathing heavily, her right hand resting on the butt of her .45.

This had to be Colonel Han Kuk-chei, the one she'd met at the Forest of Seven Clouds. The one who'd helped her escape from Bufford and Weatherwax.

Colonel Han continued shouting orders. He wanted the barricades facing the KNPs reinforced and he wanted a new barricade set up between the protestors and the American MPs back at the now half-demolished Provost Marshal's Office. His plan was to claim a section of Camp Casey as sovereign Korean territory, and to set up a court and to retry—in absentia—the two men who'd run down Chon Un-suk. The crowd, both inside and outside the compound, cheered at the proposal and dozens if not hundreds of the peaceful protestors still waiting patiently outside the walls of Camp Casey started to raise their banners and march through the smashed main gate onto the camp proper.

Ernie and I stood amongst the pine trees, partially hidden from the main action by a clump of greenery.

"They're nuts," Ernie said.

"Absolutely. But how are we going to bust through all these people and try to talk some sense to Jill?"

"You can forget it. Whatever's between her and that Colonel Han, she's hooked. She ain't going nowhere."

"It'll be a lot more dangerous here in a few minutes."

"You and I know it," Ernie replied. "Colonel Han knows it, maybe Jill knows it, but I don't think most of these protestors know it."

I was still perspiring, breathing hard, trying to remain calm, trying to think of what to do next. And then I felt it. Cold steel on the back of my neck.

"Freeze, soldier," a voice said. Low, husky, a voice I recognized.

Ernie started to move but the same voice told him if he tried anything funny, his partner's head would be blown off. Both of us raised our hands. Then the man slipped Colonel Alcott's ledger out of my grip, tucked it under his own arm, and told me to turn around.

I did.

Sergeant First Class Otis glared at us, his .45 aimed right at the center of my chest.

"I don't want to kill you," he said, "but I will if I have to."

Then from behind him, the slide of a .45 clanged, metal on metal.

"No, you won't, Otis," someone said. "Not if you want to live through this mess."

Jill Matthewson crouched behind a broken forearm of the giant MP, her .45 pointed directly at the back of Otis's head. Perspiration poured off his forehead.

"You killed him," Jill said, still crouched behind the forearm of the giant MP.

"I didn't," Otis protested. Most of his attention was on her but the barrel of his .45 was still aimed at my chest. I wished he'd turn that thing away. Standing next to me, Ernie's eyes were darting to and fro. He was about to do something. I prayed that he wouldn't. Even a reflexive twitch on Sergeant Otis's part would mean that a .45 slug moving at a jillion miles per hour would crack through my sternum and slam into my heart.

"Weatherwax told me what happened," Jill said. "You were the one who threw Marv Druwood off that building."

"Weatherwax wasn't even there," Otis replied. "He doesn't know shit. Druwood was angry, that was true. He knew why you left. He knew most of it. Because you were pissed about the black-marketing and you were pissed about what the asshole officers did to your friend, that stripper. And so he was mad at the world. And drunk. And taking swings at everyone. Even me. I backed away from him, toward the edge of the roof, but only because I had nowhere else to go. It was either that or let him bust me in the chops. I should've been more careful, I admit that. I should've punched his lights out and then he would've had a headache the next morning, but he'd still be alive. But I felt sorry for him. I didn't want to hurt him."

Jill snorted.

"It's true," Otis continued. "He had a thing for you and he never liked the army much and he didn't like the black-marketing any more than you did. So he was drunk and angry at the world and I kept backing away from him and his punches kept missing. He tossed a big roundhouse windmill punch at my head but by the time it reached where I'd been, I'd already moved. He lost his balance. But he regained it and he would've been all right. Then Warrant Officer One Mr. Fred Bufford showed up."

Sergeant First Class Otis, like a true seasoned NCO, was still using Bufford's proper title.

"Bufford was furious," Otis continued. "He knew that Druwood was going to be a hardhead and snitch on the entire black-market operation. Bufford told him just that, then Druwood swung on *him* and they started to fight. Mr. Bufford did all right at first, with that long straight jab he has, but Druwood wouldn't give up no matter how much punishment he was taking and somehow he got Mr. Bufford into a headlock. Weatherwax showed up and he jumped in and other MPs were helping."

"You being one of them," Jill said.

"No. I tried to stop them. I told them all they were making a big mistake. But there was no stopping Mr. Fred Bufford. He and the other MPs beat on Druwood unmercifully and then they started dragging him to the edge of the building. Druwood realized what was coming and he fought like a madman. Grabbing for handholds, screaming, cursing, his clothes being shredded, until finally four or five of them including Bufford and Weatherwax dragged him to the edge. Bufford managed to break Druwood's grip on the cement and he shoved him off the ledge and tossed him over." Otis paused, breathing heavily, the .45 still aimed at my chest. Then he continued. "A couple of the guys, including me, tried to grab for him but we were too slow. Druwood went over. Head first. And slammed into that Korean statue down below, that lion or monster or whatever it is. And we heard a crunch like you couldn't believe. A crunch that would break your heart."

Jill Mathewson's fist quivered. I thought for sure she was going to pull the trigger. Then she said, "So, according to you, you're innocent."

"Yes."

"But you let them lie about it. You let them take Marv Druwood's body over to the obstacle course and pretend he had fallen there."

"Bufford did that. They wanted to divert attention away from the grain warehouse. Away from the Turkey Farm."

"Because of the black-marketing."

"You know it."

"And what about the Thousand Crane Vase, Otis? You and your girlfriend, Brandy set it aside for yourselves."

Otis didn't deny Jill's accusation. "A man has to make some money in this world. The honchos here are stashing away fortunes. Where are they at oh-dark-thirty when I'm wrestling with a drunken GI or having my eyes scratched out by his pill-crazed business girl *yobo*? I'll tell you where they are. Back in their hooches snoring and dreaming about the money that we make for them. That's where. I've slept out in the rain and the snow and the mud for almost twenty years and I deserve something."

"How many other vases have you moved?" Ernie asked. "How many antiques?"

Otis shrugged.

"And my partner and I," Ernie continued, "were about to bust everything wide open. Even after we returned to Seoul you knew we could cause trouble. Which is why you sent Brandy to bring us back to Division, bring us back to Tongduchon, and send us to *mulkogi chonguk*, to fish heaven, so you could take a bead on us and blow our brains out."

The barrel of Otis's .45 veered toward Ernie.

"I was just trying to scare you off."

"Bull," Ernie said. "If I hadn't bent down to retrieve that rubber ball, the top half of my skull would've been history."

"Drop it, Otis," Jill growled.

Indecision flashed in Otis's eyes. A group of demonstrators, carrying torches and clubs headed toward the Provost Marshal's Office. The MPs in front had fled. Nothing stood between the enraged Koreans and what was left of the 2nd Infantry Division Provost Marshal's Office.

Sergeant Otis must've realized that he couldn't take down all three of us. There was no way out for him. His crimes would be exposed.

"Hold steady, Matthewson," Otis said. "Hold your fire. I'm moving away. I'm moving slow and steady. Hold your fire and I'm no threat to you or your friends here."

He dropped Colonel Alcott's ledger to the ground.

"I'm a noncommissioned officer," Otis continued, "and a good one. As an NCO, whether I been black-marketing or not, I have a job to do. I have my duty to attend to. You understand that? There's a good girl. Slow and easy."

Otis backed away from us, keeping his .45 aimed at my chest. When he was about twenty feet away he turned and stood still for a second, as if expecting a round from Jill Matthewson's .45 to smash into his back. When it didn't, he lowered his .45 to his side and started sprinting toward the Provost Marshal's Office. He arrived before the demonstrators did and ordered them to halt. When they kept coming he raised his .45 and fired over their heads. The demonstrators screamed and dropped to the ground. Some of them fled. But about a dozen of them got up and threw stones at Sergeant Otis. Most of them missed. But a couple hit their mark. Otis flinched and then the demonstrators hurled more stones at him. He tried to fire while covering his eyes with his free arm but the round went high, and then some of them reached him. I heard his .45 clang to the blacktop and skitter away, and now Jill was running toward the demonstrators, firing her pistol into the air, shouting at them to stop. As if smelling blood, dozens more of them emerged around the corner of the clump of pine trees and charged toward the Provost Marshal's Office. Ernie and I ran after Jill, caught up with her, and dragged her back to the safety of the tree line.

As we did so, from where Sergeant Otis lay we heard the heavy thump of wood on bone. A final scream and then silence.

Reinforcements arrived. I climbed up on a low branch of one of the trees. Two-and-a-half ton trucks, maybe a dozen, pulled up behind the railroad tracks to the rear of the frightened KNPs. A ROK Army officer leaped out of the cab of the first truck and saluted Agent Sohn. After a short conference, with Sohn gesturing toward Camp Casey, the ROK Army officer nodded. He shouted orders and men started jumping out of the backs of the trucks. They fell into unit formations. ROK Army infantry, the White Horse Division, the best of the best. Vietnam veterans. Each soldier armed with an M-16 rifle. While standing at attention, they were ordered to don their protective masks. They looked like a hive of lethal insects. Within seconds, they marched past the grateful KNPs and formed themselves into one massive V-shaped formation. They fixed bayonets with a clang of metal on metal. Then the officer shouted an order and, pounding one foot in front of the other, the V-shaped formation started shuffling toward the main gate of Camp Casey.

I jumped down to brief Ernie and Jill on what I'd seen.

"Colonel Han," she said. She ran through the crowd. Ernie and I followed.

As we approached Colonel Han near the quarter-ton truck, a few protestors hassled us. One of them blocked my way. I tried to push past and he shoved me. I shoved back. Just as his buddies were about to jump in, Ernie pulled his .45. He fired into the air. Startled, the men dropped back.

For just a moment, after the gunshot, the advancing hive of ROK soldiers halted. Warily, they searched the crowd. When they realized no gunfire was directed their way, they resumed their advance.

Colonel Han shouted at his followers to let us through.

When we reached him, Jill stood at his side.

I shouted at both of them. "It's over. Those ROK Army soldiers are going to use whatever force is necessary to quell this demonstration. Blood will be shed. People will be hurt. Time to call it off, Colonel."

"No," Jill shouted.

"*No?*" Ernie mimicked. "What are you? Out of your mind? Those ROK soldiers mean business."

"We've worked too hard," Jill said, "and planned too long. The world has to know what's happened here, that innocent children are being killed and women raped, and something has to be done about it."

"Done? Like what?"

"Like what we planned." She turned back to Colonel Han. Smiling beatifically, he patted her on the shoulder.

It was then that it hit me. I'm not sure why. It had nothing to do with what we were facing at the moment but maybe it was the depth of Jill Matthewson's emotion that triggered all the contradictory information I'd gathered in the last few days to suddenly fall into place. Maybe her reaction was the last clue I needed. But I knew now and so I said it.

"You were there," I told Jill. "The night Pak Tong-i died."

She looked at me, so did Colonel Han, so did Ernie, all of them waiting for me to continue. I did.

"You slipped back into Tongduchon and maybe you had a key but somehow you gained entrance to his office." I was staring directly at Jill now, daring her to deny my words. "When you found him there you tried to force a full confession out of him. About how he'd provided women to the Second Division honchos for years, about how he'd set the women up, letting them think they'd be dancing or performing, although Pak knew they'd be raped by whichever officer took a fancy to them. And you wanted his records, to document the years of black-marketing that had gone into paying for all these mafia meetings and other boys-will-be-boys excursions. You were too close to Kim Yong-ai to let it go. You wanted to prove it all to the world. But there wasn't enough there. Pak was cagey. He kept few records. But he was so frightened that he told you about Colonel Alcott being deathly afraid of being cheated by Koreans, or by

Bufford or Weatherwax so that he kept meticulous records of all black market transactions. When you questioned Pak Tong-i, you had to threaten him with your .45. He was a weak man, a man who never exercised and ate too much and smoked too much and drank too much, and suddenly something inside of him went bust. His face flushed red, he couldn't breathe and you knew the symptoms meant heart attack. When he died, you shoved him into the closet, closed it, and exited Kimchee Entertainment without being seen. That's what happened, Jill, isn't it?"

The ROK Army suddenly halted. The commanding officer shouted more orders and repositioned his forces. They broke into smaller groups, then reformed again. Now five V-shaped formations were pointing right at us. Then they started, once again, their slow forward shuffle.

"He deserved it," Jill snarled.

Even Colonel Han flinched at the sound of her voice.

"They all deserve it," she continued. "Paying for sex with girls who are just out of middle school. Girls who still have their hair bobbed, for Christ's sake, because they finished the ninth grade only weeks ago. Now those same girls are made-up like whores and dancing in sequined outfits and these middle aged men with wives and children in quarters back on army bases in the States grab them and paw them and make them giggle and then stick their tired old pricks inside that soft virgin flesh. And the men laugh about it. And boast. And don't even seem to care that I'm a woman and despise every one of them, and then they have the nerve to make comments about me. About my butt. About why a woman would be an MP. And they ask me dumb questions, like if I've ever burned my bra, and there were so many times"—Her fist tightened into knots—"so many times when I came that close to pulling out my .45 and blowing their fucking brains out."

"Jill," Colonel Han said. He placed his hand gently on her shoulder. Her face relaxed and she turned to him and smiled.

"It's time, Jill," he said. "Time for us to do what we planned."

"Yes," she said.

Jill stepped away from Colonel Han and stared at me once again. She pointed at the ledger in my hand. "You have the proof now. I know you two guys. I respect you. You'll make sure that the truth comes out. And one other thing. It's true that I roughed Pak Tong-i up a bit. But when I left him he was still breathing. Maybe later, God forgive me, he died of a heart attack. I'm not proud of that."

Colonel Han shouted something to a group of men who'd been hovering nearby. They stepped between me and Ernie and the quarter-ton truck. Colonel Han climbed back on top and helped Jill up. Then he started to address the crowd.

Exactly what he said, word for word, has been transcribed from tape recordings made by protestors who were there. The transcribed speech has been passed around Korea and has now, in translation, been passed around the world. What he said, in effect, was that Korea must control its own destiny. It was time for Koreans, both in the North and the South, to reject foreign influence, to expel all foreigners, and to reunite. The first step was to take back Korean sovereignty, both on the land and in the courts. Once he'd made these points he said that Koreans were strong enough to defend themselves and, once the Americans were expelled, if the northern communists refused to reunite, then the soldiers of the Republic of Korea should march north and force reunification. Blood would be shed, people would die, but to prove his sincerity he was going to do more than just talk. He was going to act.

Most of the speech was in language too sophisticated for me to follow. But the last part, when he said he was going to act, I understood.

He and Jill Matthewson leaped off the truck, strode past the destroyed Camp Casey main gate, and marched across the open pavement toward the advancing ROK Army troops. The crowd was silent. Jill Matthewson pulled her .45.

"No!" I shouted. Frantically, I lunged forward. Both Ernie and the men assigned to us by Colonel Han held me back.

"No!" I shouted again, because what they were about to do seemed perfectly obvious to me.

Jill held her .45 aloft and then aimed it at the KCIA man standing behind the row of KNPs. She popped off a round. At that range, twenty or thirty yards, the round flew high but the reaction of the

KNP brass was immediate. They fell to the ground. Now Colonel Han stepped in front of Jill. He pulled his pistol and aimed it at the advancing ROK troops. They didn't wait for an order. A fusillade of M-16 rounds slammed into Colonel Han's body. He didn't twirl in the air as he would've done if this had been a movie. His body slammed to the pavement as if he'd been sucker-punched in the chest by a twenty-foot-tall giant.

Jill stepped over Colonel Han's body until she was straddling it, kneeled down in his spreading blood, and kissed him on the forehead. When she stood again, she started to raise the .45 in her hand.

That's when I broke free of Ernie's grip and charged at the ROK soldiers in front of me. "*Sagyok chungji!*" I shouted. Hold your fire!

Jill looked back.

It was just that one or two seconds of hesitation that allowed me to sprint across the road. I slammed into her and executed a tackle that would've made my old coach at Lincoln High proud. Jill fell, Ernie arrived, and soon we three were stumbling away from the line of ROK soldiers. Jill struggled but Ernie punched her and I slipped handcuffs on her.

We were in a Hyundai sedan, heading south, Ernie driving. The vehicle had been loaned to us by Madame Chon. While we were still in Tongduchon, Jill had changed into civilian clothes and since none of us were now in uniform—and we were riding in a civilian vehicle—we hoped that we could slip past the southernmost 2nd Infantry Division checkpoint on the MSR. They had no jurisdiction over civilians. With any luck, we could make our way back to Seoul.

"Back there," Ernie said, "you told us that you all but killed Pak Tong-i."

"He died the same night. So I've felt responsible for his death. His heart must've been weak."

"You weren't the one who killed him, Jill," I said.

"Then who did?

"Bufford. And maybe Weatherwax. They interrogated him after you left. That's how they obtained the information that led them to the Forest of Seven Clouds."

Jill sat in silence, thinking about that.

"Did you use a rope on him?" Ernie asked.

"A rope?"

"To strangle Pak Tong-i. To scare him into talking."

Jill shook her head.

"Then it wasn't you who killed him. It had to be Bufford and Weatherwax."

"I hope you're right," she said finally.

"I'm right," Ernie replied.

Stanchions blocked the road ahead. Ernie slowed.

"Easy now," I told him. "These civilian license plates should ward them off. Of course, they'll see we're *Miguks*, and Ernie and I have short hair and look like GIs, so they might try to talk to us anyway. But what we do is we ignore them and keep rolling slowly through the checkpoint. They have no authority to stop us."

"Seems like up here at Division," Ernie said, "people don't worry much about the legal extent of their authority."

"Maybe," I said. "But these MPs have no reason to stop us."

"Unless they figure that you're those Eighth Army CID agents they've been looking for," Jill said.

"Or that you're an AWOL MP," Ernie shot back.

"Not AWOL any longer."

We'd taken the handcuffs off of Jill and she'd voluntarily submitted to our instructions to return with us to Seoul. So she was once again under military jurisdiction and—technically—no longer absent without leave. And since she'd returned to military jurisdiction prior to thirty days after leaving her unit, she couldn't be charged with desertion.

We passed the reinforced concrete bunker with the M-60 machine gun. Beyond that stood an armed ROK soldier. He peered into the car, saw our civilian license plates, and waved us on. The last obstacle was the American MP. He was tall and skinny and held his M-16 rifle at port arms, his back toward us.

"He isn't even paying attention," Ernie said.

We were about to cruise past him when suddenly he turned, lowered his rifle, and stepped in front of us. Ernie slammed on the brakes. From beneath the MP's helmet, a long skinny nose pointed out.

Jill screamed.

Ernie shouted a curse but it was too late for him to step on the gas. The MP had leveled his weapon and was pointing it right at Ernie's face. Warrant Officer Fred Bufford. In the flesh. I popped open the passenger door and rolled onto the blacktop. Ernie sat frozen behind the wheel. Jill ducked but it was too late, Bufford had spotted her. He started shouting for us to get out of the car, hands up. Shielded by the side of the vehicle, I pulled my .45.

Boots clomped behind me. I turned. The ROK Army soldier's rifle was pointed directly at my face. I lowered my .45, dropped it to the ground, and raised my hands in surrender.

At the point of a gun, Bufford marched Jill Matthewson into the bushes.

Ernie and I stood at the side of the road, our hands up, guarded by the ROK Army MP. Another ROK Army MP had taken over at the checkpoint, glancing into vehicles, waving them through. What had happened to the American MP who normally worked here? Probably, Bufford had sent him back to his unit, with a bullshit story about the move-out alert. Ernie and I were both worried about the same thing. What was he going to do to Jill?

I started speaking Korean to the ROK soldier. His name tag, hand embroidered, revealed that he was Private Yun. I told him that I was an agent for 8th Army Criminal Investigation Division and that my credentials were in my inside coat pocket. At first he ignored me. I kept at him. I told him that Warrant Officer Bufford was a fugitive from justice and Yun was now taking orders from the wrong man. I warned him about how much trouble he would be in if he didn't listen to me. Finally, Private Yun, still holding his rifle on us, reached into my jacket pocket and pulled out my CID badge. I warned him that he now had thirty seconds to lower his rifle and return our weapons.

The young man's face flushed with indecision. He shouted at the other ROK Army MP. They conferred in rapid Korean. Finally, they decided that one of them would cover for the other while they used the radio to call the sergeant of the guard. That wasn't quick enough for us. By the time they ran the information up the chain of command and a decision came back down, Corporal Jill Matthewson might be dead.

From the north, from the 2nd Division area, a car screeched up to the checkpoint. A long sedan. Black. A driver in a dark suit popped out of the front door and another dark-suited man emerged from the passenger's side. The driver opened the back door and a man climbed out. Agent Sohn, the KCIA man. When he held up his badge, the ROK Army MP nearest him shouted a martial greeting. Private Yun, still standing in front of us, glanced back. That's all Ernie needed. He charged low, diving for Yun's ankles. I stepped to my left and then threw myself at the ROK MP. A shot rang out. Apparently, it didn't hit me because I was able to thrust my shoulder full force into Private Yun. He went down. Ernie scrambled for the rifle, seized it, and pointed it at the KCIA men. They backed off. While Ernie held them at bay, I retrieved our .45s.

Ernie shot out the tires of the KCIA sedan. We ran into the woods, following a trail of broken branches and trodden grass left by Bufford as he'd forced Jill at gunpoint into the forest. Through the tree line and beyond, ten-foot-high cement megaliths stretched in a double row. Dragon's teeth. As far as the eye could see.

Ernie and I stopped when we saw them. They lay between two dragon's teeth, near a creek in a grass-covered meadow, perhaps twenty yards away. It was clear what was happening.

He was naked. Bony knees, pale flesh, elbows rubbed raw and red. He held Jill's .45 in his hand, finger on the trigger, the barrel propped beneath her jaw. Her pants were pulled low but her legs were still locked, and she lay back with her butt pressed against mud. Her eyes were clenched tightly and she was crying. Not tears of helplessness but tears of rage.

Ernie pointed the rifle and fired. A round caromed madly off one of the dragon's teeth. Bufford looked at us but he didn't climb off of Jill. He shouted that he'd pull the trigger if we didn't back off.

"You're finished, Bufford," Ernie shouted. "Even if you kill her, there's no way out."

"I'll kill her now!" Bufford said.

As he shouted at Ernie, the barrel of his .45 shifted, just slightly. But it was enough. Enough for Jill Matthewson to know that this was her chance.

She brought a fist up in a looping left cross and at the same time propelled her knee up right between Bufford's legs. He screamed. The gun went off. Ernie and I sprinted forward. Through the smoke and confusion I couldn't tell what had happened to Jill. We stumbled and clawed our way through the mud and as the smoke cleared I realized that she was still alive. I've never seen anyone in such a rage. By the time Ernie and I approached she was on top of Fred Bufford. His pistol lay uselessly in the mud and Jill Matthewson was pulverizing him and had started to gouge out his eyeballs. It took Ernie and me two minutes to pull her off of him. We handcuffed her because it was the only way we could stop her from killing Bufford with her bare hands. Our mistake was that we handcuffed her with her hands in front rather than behind her back.

Bufford lay unconscious next to the creek. Blood trickled from his eyes, nose, and mouth.

I policed up the .45 and found Jill Matthewson's wallet lying next to her torn blue jeans. A couple of photographs had fallen out. I picked them up and held them up to the light. A rape scene. I saw three men: Lieutenant Colonel Alcott; a man I recognized as H.K. Pacquet, the Chief of Staff of the 2nd Division; and Warrant Officer Fred Bufford. All naked. All working on some poor young woman who'd been bound and gagged. The lighting was dim. I studied the woman. I expected her to be the stripper, Jill's friend, Kim Yong-ai. But then I realized that she wasn't Kim. She wasn't even Korean. She was American. And then I realized who she was. The impetus for Jill Matthewson's rage became clear to me.

Ernie was too busy to look at the photos, what with handcuffing Bufford and helping Jill climb out of the mudhole she was lying in. When the KCIA men appeared at the edge of the clearing, Ernie warned them back with the M16 rifle. They stood and observed, as Jill pulled up her pants and adjusted what was left of her torn shirt and blouse.

Before Ernie could notice, I stuffed the photographs into my pocket. I didn't want Ernie, or anyone other than Jill, to see them. I handed her the wallet. Automatically, she searched for the photos. When she didn't find them, she looked up at me. I pulled them out of my pocket and handed them to her. She refused to take them.

"It's over now," she told me.

"Okay," I answered. "What should I do with them?"

"Destroy them."

"We might need them to get you out of this mess."

"I don't care. Destroy them."

I did. I borrowed a lighter from one of the KCIA men and set them on fire.

While Ernie talked to the KCIA men and the photographs burned, Jill dragged the now conscious Fred Bufford near the creek behind one of the dragon's teeth. We weren't paying attention, all of us still in shock. Warrant Officer Fred Bufford didn't shout for help. Maybe he couldn't. Jill, her wrists still handcuffed in front of her, shoved Bufford's head face-first into the mud. She held him there. By the time we realized what she was doing, Warrant Officer Fred Bufford was dead.

# 16

There were more student demonstrations. Tons of them. In Seoul, in Pusan, in Kwangju. There was enormous pressure for the regime of President Pak Chung-hee to reduce the number of American troops stationed in Korea. And it almost happened. Contingency plans were written up in the Pentagon, professors at American universities wrote articles about how Korea was ready to be fully self-reliant. But, at the last moment, a new evaluation of the North Korean threat was released. Suddenly, it was discovered that instead of 700,000 troops in their army the North Koreans now had one million. The South Koreans, meanwhile, could only field an army of a paltry 450,000 soldiers. So plans for a U.S. draw down were rescinded.

The incident at Camp Casey never hit the *Pacific Stars & Stripes*. It was reported by Reuters and the international press and, eventually, even AP and UPI. But they played it as just another student demonstration, one that had proven to be a little more violent than others but just a demonstration nevertheless.

Ernie and I kept Colonel Alcott's ledger in a safe place, at the hooch of Ernie's latest girlfriend in the red-light district of Itaewon.

When we were debriefed, the ledger was never mentioned. *Blackmail* is an ugly word anywhere but particularly in the hallowed halls of the 8th United States Imperial Army. Not only did we not want to have to threaten anyone with blackmail, the 8th Army provost marshal didn't want to admit that he had ever been black-mailed. Therefore, the existence of the ledger, although rumored, was never mentioned in any official file.

Ernie and I were faced with a number of possible charges. The first was being absent without leave and then there was our return-ing to the 2nd Division area when we weren't supposed to. That was fixed easily. The 8th Army PMO just pretended that he'd never ordered us withdrawn.

The problem of Colonel Alcott's black-marketing was fixed by rescinding his ration control plate. Supposedly, there was a reevalu-ation of the entire policy of ration control plates being open and unaccountable for high-ranking officers in sensitive positions. Alcott was transferred back to Fort Bragg, North Carolina, having promised that as soon as he hit stateside he would put in his retirement paper-work. Staff Sergeant Weatherwax pleaded guilty to assisting Warrant Officer Fred Bufford in transferring the body of Private Marvin Druwood from the actual place of his death to the obstacle course on Camp Casey. He received a thirty-day forfeiture of pay and ben-efits and a general discharge from the U.S. Army under honorable conditions. The body of Sergeant First Class Otis was shipped back to his wife and children quartered at Fort Hood, Texas with full mil-itary honors. Our report never mentioned his antique-smuggling operation with Brandy. We didn't want to complicate things. Besides, his family didn't need that kind of grief.

None of this seemed fair, of course. Warrant Officer Fred Bufford, after all, had been guilty of rape. The rape of a fellow soldier. In addi-tion, according to the testimony of the late Sergeant First Class Otis, Mr. Fred Bufford had been guilty of the murder of Private Marvin Druwood. But with Otis dead, we had no proof. And Weatherwax wasn't talking. Colonel Alcott and Brigadier General H.K. Pacquet were also guilty of rape. Jill told me it had begun when she'd physi-cally tried to intervene in the goings-on in one of the mafia meetings. The honchos had objected to her butting into their affairs and decided to teach her a lesson. What started as a plan to humiliate her by stripping her had turned into out-and-out rape. After that, Jill started on her crusade. She swore Ernie and me to secrecy about the rape. She was too humiliated. We argued with her, told her it wasn't her fault and she had no reason to be ashamed, but in the end she won out. We kept mum. As far as the KCIA witnesses who'd been standing nearby at the dragon's teeth, they hadn't seen much and what they had seen, they weren't about to talk about.

The next problem was the death of Warrant Officer Bufford.

Ernie and I simply said that when we arrived at the scene Bufford was already dead. During his attempted assault on Corporal Matthewson, she'd exercised her right of self-defense. Bufford had hit his head against one of the dragon's teeth, and while we were tending to her, he had apparently died of asphyxiation, facedown in the mud. 8th Army had to accept this story because they had no evidence to contradict it.

Why were Ernie and I so concerned with engineering an unwritten deal not to embarrass 8th Army? Because of Corporal Jill Matthewson.

At first, there'd been talk of charging her with treason.

After all, she'd been instrumental in the occupation—however brief—of a U.S. Army installation by foreign nationals. She'd assisted in the knocking down of the Camp Casey main gate and in the obliteration of the statute of the giant MP, not to mention the demolition of the front half of the 2nd Division Provost Marshal's Office. In addition, she'd gone AWOL for twenty-nine days. Some of the honchos at 8th Army wanted to slap Jill Matthewson with a dishonorable discharge.

Ernie and I stood our ground. If we hadn't retained possession of Colonel Alcott's black market ledger, if it hadn't been tucked away safely in a business girl's hooch in Itaewon, we would've had no leverage. As it was, 8th Army knew that if they charged Jill Matthewson with treason, we'd fight back and the entire command structure of the 2nd Infantry Division would go down, all the way up to the level of a brigadier general.

We went so far as to demand that Jill be given an honorable discharge. This was a little more difficult to sell. We claimed Jill had been acting as an undercover agent and that she had to gain the confidence of the protestors. This was all nonsense but we said it anyway. The proof of this assertion was that Jill Matthewson attempted to fire on the ROK Army troops who, she thought, were about to encroach on Camp Casey.

It was crazy but it worked. The overriding desire of the 8th Army bosses was to avoid scandal. They didn't want history to record that the first female MP ever assigned to the 2nd Infantry Division had been driven to armed insurrection.

On the day she left Korea, Ernie and I drove Jill out to the countryside north of Seoul. Madame Chon met us there, amidst hills covered with well-tended lawns and dotted with stone monuments. The two women embraced. Madame Chon led Jill over to one of the tombstones. Chon Un-suk's name, in Chinese characters. had been freshly carved into granite. The sky glowed a greenish blue, and was veiled with wispy gray clouds. Jill and Madame Chon burned incense, breathed in the sharp odor of jasmine, and bowed to the spirit of the departed girl.

Madame Chon was happy. Now her daughter's ghost could reside with her ancestors and would no longer have to wander.

I hoped that was true

On the drive back to Seoul, I told Jill that during her tour in the 2nd Infantry Division, she and Marv Druwood had been the only two real MPs the Division had.

From a muddy rice paddy, a white crane flapped its wings, lifted into the sky, and flew lazily off into an endless eternity of blue.